BY GREG WEISMAN

Rain of the Ghosts
Spirits of Ash and Foam
World of Warcraft: Traveler
World of Warcraft: Traveler—The Spiral Path
Magic: The Gathering—Ravnica: War of the Spark

MAGIC™

WAR OF THE SPARK
RAVNICA

MAGIC™

WAR OF THE SPARK
RAVNICA

GREG WEISMAN

DEL REY
NEW YORK

Copyright © 2019 by Wizards of the Coast LLC.
All Rights Reserved.

Published in the United States by Del Rey,
an imprint of Random House, a division of
Penguin Random House LLC, New York.

DEL REY and the HOUSE colophon are registered trademarks
of Penguin Random House LLC.

WIZARDS OF THE COAST, MAGIC: THE GATHERING, MAGIC, their
respective logos, War of the Spark, the planeswalker symbol,
all guild names and symbols, and characters' names are property
of Wizards of the Coast LLC in the USA and other countries.

Hardback ISBN 978-1-9848-1745-7
Ebook ISBN 978-1-9848-1793-8

Printed in the United States of America on acid-free paper

randomhousebooks.com

4 6 8 9 7 5

Book design by Elizabeth A. D. Eno

To my high school English professors, Joy Diskin, Beverly Wardlaw, John West, Philip Holmes, Elliot McGrew and Beverly Wardlaw (again). You were confident and encouraging guides into worlds of wonder and intellect that made learning and reading and writing into the epic journey of my lifetime. If I'm a Planeswalker today, the five of you helped me find my Spark . . .

DRAMATIS PERSONAE

Jace Beleren—Planeswalker, Human, Gatewatch Mind-mage.

Nicol Bolas—Planeswalker, Elder Dragon, Would-Be God-Emperor.

Dack Fayden—Planeswalker, Human, Self-Proclaimed Greatest Thief in the Multiverse.

Gideon Jura—Planeswalker, Human, Gatewatch Founder, Hieromancer.

Kaya—Planeswalker, Human, Orzhov Guildmaster and Ghost-assassin.

Chandra Nalaar—Planeswalker, Human, Gatewatch Pyromancer.

Teyo Verada—Planeswalker, Human, Shieldmage Acolyte.

Liliana Vess—Planeswalker, Human, former Gatewatch Necromancer.

Vraska—Planeswalker, Gorgon, Golgari Guildmaster and Assassin.

Ral Zarek—Planeswalker, Human, Izzet Guildmaster and Storm Mage.

GUILDS OF RAVNICA

Azorius Senate
Dedicated to bringing order to the chaos of Ravnica's streets, the Azorius Senate strives to educate the compliant—and restrain the rebellious.

Boros Legion
The zealous Boros Legion is united in pursuit of a peaceful and harmonious Ravnica, no matter how many bodies its forces must step over to achieve it.

House Dimir
The agents of House Dimir dwell in the darkest corners of the city, selling their secrets to those who hunger for power, and their steel to those who need enemies silenced.

Golgari Swarm
Death brings new life. All life must die. The guild-members of the Golgari Swarm are guardians of this cycle, feeding the citizens of Ravnica, and preparing them to feed the earth in turn.

Gruul Clans
Once, the Gruul Clans ruled over the untamed wilds of Ravnica, but as the city has grown they've been

forced further and further into exile to escape its crushing weight. They're ready to crush back.

Izzet League

With their endless public works, the genius Izzet League maintains the sprawling splendor of Ravnica . . . when their experiments aren't accidentally blowing it up.

Orzhov Syndicate

The Orzhov Syndicate is ruthlessly ambitious and endlessly acquisitive. If you owe the Orzhov, they will collect, even after death.

Cult of Rakdos

Entertainers and hedonists, the Cultists of the demonic lord Rakdos know that life is short and full of pain. The only thing that matters? Having as much fun as you possibly can, no matter the consequence.

Selesnya Conclave

The Selesnya guild is the voice of Mat'Selesnya, the mysterious manifestation of nature itself. They search constantly for more believers to add to their Conclave—and a larger army to defend it.

Simic Combine

Nowhere is the balance of nature and civilization more important—or more threatened—than in a city that spans the world. And the Simic Combine stands ready to maintain it . . . or *revise* it to their own unique specifications.

PRELUDE

ONE

TWO DRAGONS

The Spirit Dragon and the dragon spirit were having a little chat.

"How long can your device there preserve you?" asked the Spirit Dragon.

"A century or so," replied the dragon spirit. "I stripped the mind of an Orzhov pontiff to confirm it was compatible. They're experts on that sort of thing. On ghosts, that is. The tech's all mine. And it's brilliant."

"Of course." The Spirit Dragon glanced down at the little silver box, with all its delicate filigree, sparking clockwork gears, and shimmering crystals, as it projected the dragon spirit's essence right above it into the crisp gray dawn. "Nice of Sarkhan Vol to deliver it here."

"Nice isn't the word."

"Necessary."

"Yes. Necessary."

There was a long pause.

Eventually, the dragon spirit swallowed hard—or in any case, unconsciously mimicked that biological tic—and stated, "Our plan will work. It must work."

The Spirit Dragon looked around, at the serene waters, at the carefully manicured ruins his brother had created and curated, at the giant horns rising out of the Pools of Becoming, curving inward on themselves and marking this plane as his twin's personal retreat. "It *can* work," he said at last. "But our strategy is like your mechanism here. All the gears must act in concert. All the players must play their assigned roles. We can count on Sarkhan to play his. But the other Planeswalkers, and all those souls on Ravnica . . . ? If my brother remains invulnerable, all other precautions are useless."

"Zarek will do his part. I was tough on him to toughen him up, but I think my lessons will hold."

"Like they held with you, little cousin? It seems to me that if you'd learned your lessons, you wouldn't be half as dead as you currently are. My brother led you around like you had a ring in your snout."

The dragon spirit took some umbrage at this, his semi-transparent shoulders rising, his pale-red wings flaring slightly. "No one speaks to me that way."

The Spirit Dragon took a little umbrage of his own. "Because you're accustomed to spending your time around mortals. I am not that." Then he settled back down, taking on a more conciliatory tone: "But take no offense. I've fared no better. And my point was that defeating Nicol Bolas will take more than a good plan. It will take near-perfect timing and damn good luck."

"I don't believe in luck. I believe in preparation."

"That won't be enough. Nicol is prepared to overcome any

conceivable opposition. If this struggle was only about preparation, we wouldn't stand a chance."

"Then the Multiverse is doomed," said the dragon spirit rather bloodlessly.

"I hope not. We have one advantage. My brother puts too much faith in himself and too little in absolutely anyone else. His well-earned arrogance and unfailing contempt for anybody who isn't Nicol Bolas presents us with this opportunity."

"Which in failure will result in the deaths of thousands."

"Millions, more likely. But even in success, the stakes are high. Hundreds will most certainly die today. It's unfortunate but unavoidable."

"As always," said the dragon spirit. "I've been alive for sixteen thousand seven hundred and sixty-eight years, and you've lived, what, twice that long, three times?"

The Spirit Dragon scoffed.

The dragon spirit rolled his eyes. "My point is we've seen it all before. Mortals rise. Mortals fall. The show begins. The show ends. And another performance follows. If I weren't already dead, I wouldn't lose a wink of sleep over one more cataclysm, no matter how devastating the carnage."

"It's worse than that, and I believe you know it. If my brother wins the day, it won't be just another cataclysm. The show will end, all right, but the next performance will be entitled *The Infinite Reign of Nicol Bolas*. And no other performer will ever take the stage. And after *'a century or so'* when that fancy toy of yours ceases to function, will you really be calling for an encore?"

This silenced the dragon spirit for a few minutes. When he spoke again, his voice was flat, clinical. "So what do we do now?"

"Now? We wait for the curtain to rise, Niv-Mizzet. We wait for the curtain to rise . . ."

ACT ONE

TWO

TEYO VERADA

His pack heavy on his shoulders, Teyo Verada trudged through the sands beneath his world's twin suns, along the edge of the dune, trying to ignore the farting carry-beast in front of him as he daydreamed of the miracle . . . of the lavatory.

Born in a tiny village nineteen years ago, Teyo was now returning from what had been his first visit to a big town like Oasis. Much to Abbot Barrez's chagrin, the keeper of Oasis' only inn had refused to house the acolytes in her stables. Honored to have actual shieldmages in her establishment, she had insisted on lodging them in guest rooms for the same cost as a straw-filled stall. The abbot attempted to explain that acolytes were not yet shieldmages and deserved no such luxury. But for once, the voice of his absolute authority fell on deaf ears.

So it had been two acolytes to a room twice the size of Teyo's cell back at the monastery, which he normally shared with Arturo, Peran and Theo. But that wasn't the real wonder of the place. There were no chamber pots. No latrines. No washbasins that required refilling from a jug, which required refilling from a pump a hundred yards away. Water was piped right into a small lavatory down the hall for drinking, washing, bathing and, well, waste. And said waste was then piped away somehow to somewhere that wasn't just outside your window, causing a stink worse than the carry-beast's gases. It was a kind of miracle to Teyo, and his mind just wouldn't, couldn't let it go.

But Oasis was two leagues back, and now, laden with a year's worth of supplies, the party was headed for home in single file, crossing the sand dunes of Gobakhan, the abbot in the lead, followed by a carry-beast, followed by acolytes, followed by another carry-beast, followed by more acolytes, followed by a last carry-beast, followed by Teyo Verada, lowliest of the low, least talented of all Abbot Barrez's students (as the abbot was so fond of telling him).

He daydreamed of becoming an accomplished monk of the Shieldmage Order, assigned to a big town like Oasis, where one's own worse stink was carried far away as if by magic.

Maybe that's *a magic I could master,* he thought ruefully. *What'd the innkeeper call it? "Plumming"?*

He wasn't sure what the running water had to do with plums, but he had always liked plums. They were sweet and juicy and the acolytes were each given two on Solstice morning. Teyo sighed audibly and trudged on, knowing that his meager skills with a shield wouldn't earn him a place in Oasis or anywhere like it. He'd be lucky to land a village the size of the unnamed place he'd been born, and later orphaned, during his first—

Suddenly someone grabbed him by the shoulders, shaking

him into the moment. "By the Storm," the abbot shouted over the rising wind, "are you deaf as well as blind? Take off your pack and prepare! We're in for it! Now!"

Teyo scrambled to comply, shedding his pack, as sand from the Eastern Cloud sliced past his bare cheeks. Squinting, he raised his hands, tried to focus, and began chanting the geometric lore of the shieldmage.

Barrez moved forward. "Shields up!" he shouted, his voice enhanced by magic to be heard over the now roaring wind.

Teyo concentrated. A triangle of shimmering white light formed across the palm of each hand. Then second triangles formed at offset angles from the first two. Third triangles. And on his strong left hand, a fourth. But three-point shapes wouldn't do, and he knew it. He needed diamonds to thwart diamonds. And Acolyte Verada was not particularly good at four-pointers. Not particularly good, particularly when under pressure. Like when the abbot harangued him during morning exercises. Like when a diamondstorm was imminent.

His shields were off balance. His left hand, his eastern vertex, had always been much stronger than his right. He turned in profile toward the coming storm to compensate while summoning up a perfect glowing white circle beneath his right ear in an attempt to even the mana scales. It worked, more or less.

Teyo knew the drill and willed himself to follow it.

Four points. Four points. Four points. Four points.

Concentric circles formed above, below, and to the left and right of his two sets of triangular shields.

Form the lines.

He joined each set of four circles to the others with bright white lines of sharpened thought.

Fill the shapes.

He expanded his western and eastern vertices to create two overlapping diamond-shaped shields. He'd be protected now. He could take a breath. But the job was only half done.

As the abbot taught, if all a shieldmage could protect was himself, he was a pretty poor shieldmage.

Teyo was at the end of the line, but at minimum he needed to enlarge his shields to safeguard the hunkering, lowing carry-beast and the supplies on its leathery back.

He took a half step forward, leaning into the sand and wind, which was already sparkling. Had he been a second slower, micrograins of diamond would already be shredding his clothes and skin. They *were* already lodging themselves into the thick hide of the beast, which groaned mournfully at the pinpricks of pain. Teyo used the wind as a vertical platform upon which to expand his shields. It wasn't orthodoxy.

The abbot wouldn't approve.

But it worked for him. The shields—the seven triangles and the two four-pointers—merged into one larger rhombus. His geometry was holding, and the now protected carry-beast rewarded him with a relieved sigh and a rather stinky emission.

And just in time. Larger diamonds, the size of small hailstones, began striking his shield and the shields of his fellow acolytes. Teyo glanced to his left and saw Arturo sporting a mighty trapezoid.

Show-off, Teyo groused silently. *Who's he trying to impress?*

Teyo knew the answer to that question, of course. For there was the abbot, moving up and down the lines with only a small personal oval, shouting in his enhanced voice to hold the line, to *be* the geometry. The windblown diamonds got larger, now the size of Solstice plums, thud, thud, thudding against Teyo's rhombus. Seven or eight hit at once, and for a moment Teyo thought the impacts would shatter his concentration and his lore. But he sucked it up, leaned in, renewed his chants and maintained.

And then the lights started.

Lights? How can there be lights? It makes no sense!

The sand and diamonds kicked up by the powerful desert

wind should have completely obscured all sky and all light. Yet there they were, above and before him, lights sparkling in the sky like enormous rubies and emeralds and sapphires and obsidians and, yes, more diamonds. It drew his eye, his mind, his concentration, and ultimately his lore away from the task at hand. A diamond the size of an apple glanced off his shoulder before he realized his shield was faltering. He tried to recover, but the geometry was lost to him. The beast crooned in pain as Teyo struggled to recover his lore. And even then, the lights-that-could-not-be in the sky-he-should-not-see called to him.

Again, Abbot Barrez appeared from nowhere, forming a wide four-pointer that protected both Teyo Verada and the carry-beast. "Seriously, boy, what is wrong with you?"

"The lights . . ." Teyo murmured, pointing weakly upward.

"What light? You're lucky I could see you failing and flailing in this murk. Child, of all my students, *you* teach me despair."

"Yes, Master," Teyo said automatically, his true focus still on high. Briefly he wondered why the abbot couldn't see the lights. But even *that* mystery couldn't hold his attention. The lights spoke to him now, reaching somewhere deep in his soul, creating a foreboding sense of doom and—despite that— a kind of summons that pulled him forward.

Finally, the diamondstorm began to fade. The diamonds themselves had passed on, but sand still blew in fiercely. Teyo hardly noticed. The abbot moved on, saying, "Find your lore, acolyte, or find yourself sand-scoured." Teyo ignored him. Raising no shield, chanting no chants, he stumbled forward toward the lights, deeper into the dying storm.

Arturo called out, "Teyo!"

Abbot Barrez looked back over his shoulder and shouted, "Verada, maintain the line!"

But the abbot's student couldn't seem to help himself.

Sand—and one last stray diamond—indeed scoured his skin. He could feel blood dripping down his cheek. He closed his eyes against the storm—and could *still* see the sparkling, summoning lights behind his eyelids. He stumbled off the dune, tumbled down its side. He vaguely heard his master and his fellows calling out his name. He tried to rise but was already buried up to his shins in rising sand. He thought he would probably die. He thought he should try to raise a shield. He thought only a sphere could save him now, but he'd never managed one bigger than his fist. The sand was up to his waist and seemed to be actively trying to drag him down. He tried to yank himself free, but the sand drift grabbed his arm and did drag him down. A bit of the dune gave way behind him, and he was covered . . .

Buried alive.

He struggled to move, struggled to breathe. Desperate and panicked, he forgot all his training and opened his mouth to suck in air, only to suck in sand instead. He was suffocating. It was completely dark. And yet it wasn't. The lights. The lights. The lights would be the last things Teyo Verada ever saw . . .

Then somewhere in his core, in the center of his heart vertex, an *ember* became a spark. There was a final burst of white geometry, which felt like death, as Teyo disintegrated into grains of sand . . .

THREE

CHANDRA NALAAR

Chandra Nalaar, Planeswalker and pyromancer, sank deeper into the over-soft armchair in her mother's new apartment in the city of Ghirapur on the plane of Kaladesh. She was anxious, frustrated, angry, frightened and more than a little bored.

Pia Nalaar had prepared a tray of dark, rich hot chocolate for her daughter and her daughter's friends and had then departed for a council meeting, saying her goodbyes to Chandra—as she always did—as if she might never see her again.

Only this time, she might be right.

Now Chandra, cup of chocolate untouched on a side table, slouched with her chin practically touching her chest as she glanced around at her companions. Over on the sofa, the mind-mage Jace Beleren, looking weary and haggard, stared into his own cup of brown liquid, as if somehow it might reveal the true secret of defeating the Elder Dragon, Nicol Bolas. Beside him, the time-master, Teferi, leaned back, resting his eyes and breathing deeply. Perched on stools at the kitchen counter, the lion-headed healer, Ajani Goldmane, chatted pleasantly with Chandra's sometimes pyromantic mentor, Jaya Ballard, about bird-watching, of all things. The silver golem Karn stood motionless in the corner, seemingly engrossed in perfecting his already phenomenal resemblance to a statue. Planeswalkers all, they were the Gatewatch, the supposed saviors of the Multiverse. Well, technically, Jaya and Karn hadn't actually joined the 'watch, which is to say they had declined to take the Oath. But they were here to fight beside the rest against the dragon Bolas. To fight and probably to die.

In a hurried motion, Jace put his cup down on the coffee table, as if the hot chocolate suddenly frightened him. "He's taking too long," Jace said.

"*He*" was Gideon Jura, the soul of the Gatewatch—or so Chandra had come to believe. Gids had planeswalked back to Dominaria to find yet another member of the 'watch, the necromancer Liliana Vess, who should have met them here on Kaladesh but had failed to show. Jace had already made it abundantly clear he thought Gideon was on a fool's errand, that Liliana had never had any intention of joining them in their fight against Bolas, that she had exploited the Gatewatch as a tool to slay her own personal demons, *literally*, and that now that those demons were dead and gone, her use for her so-called friends had likewise come to an end.

But Gids had refused to believe that, and Chandra had agreed with him, as had Jaya, Karn and Teferi. All five of them felt strongly that Liliana—despite her own well-manicured façade of selfishness—was indeed their true friend and ally. That she cared about them, even Jace. Maybe *especially* Jace.

They had slept together, right?

But Liliana definitely cared about Gideon, whom she mocked unceasingly but with affection. And Chandra didn't think she was flattering herself believing that Liliana cared about her, too. Chandra thought of Liliana as an older sister.

A way older sister. A centuries-older sister.

But a sister nonetheless. Chandra was confident Gideon would return at any moment with Liliana in tow, ready to join the conflict—*the final conflict*—against the evil dragon mastermind.

But Chandra had to agree Gideon was taking too long. She wasn't exactly worried about him. Gideon's powers made him nigh-on invulnerable. The rest might fall—Chandra might fall—yet Gids would fight on. And on, and on, and on . . .

It's just who he is, she thought.

The indomitable warrior, the unrelenting juggernaut with that unerring sense of justice and those washboard abs. Once upon a time, Chandra had sported a major crush on Gids. She was over that now, but he pretty much remained her best friend in the world. On any world. In the Multiverse.

Whatever.

She sighed. She had been a Planeswalker since she was a preteen, but it was still occasionally difficult to adjust her vocabulary to what that meant. Chandra Nalaar was one of a select group of individuals who could travel—planeswalk—between dimensions, passing from one plane to the next, from one world to another. Every world she had ever 'walked to had its own set of troubles and turmoil. So none of them needed new dangers arriving from planes unknown. That's why the Gatewatch had been formed. So that Planeswalkers who gave a damn would be there to fight, to safeguard worlds from interplanar threats like Nicol Bolas.

Well, not like *Bolas. From Bolas.*

It had become clear over the last few weeks that every single threat they had faced had been generated, initiated, concocted by the dragon himself. And that's not even counting their encounter on the Plane of Amonkhet, where Bolas had flat-out kicked their collective asses. Of course, the Gatewatch hadn't had Jaya or Teferi or Karn with them then. Just Chandra, Jace, Gids, Liliana and . . .

She sank still deeper into her chair. Gideon *was* taking too long. If the seven (or hopefully eight) of them were going to arrive at their destination ahead of Bolas and prepare for the coming battle, they needed to get planeswalking already. Frankly, the suspense was killing her.

Chandra stuck out her lower lip and blew upward, a lazy attempt to move one of her wild red tresses out of the way of her left eye. It had literally no effect. She tried again. And a third time.

And then she shot to her feet, galvanized by a call from across the planes. The others reacted with less motion but no less concern.

"You feel that?" Chandra asked, knowing they had.

All of them nodded silently. She looked upward, toward the sky, and of course saw only the roof of her mother's apartment. But between her and the roof were lights that sparkled like gemstones and called out to her to follow them to . . . to . . . *to Ravnica!*

"Ravnica," Jaya stated.

There was a murmur of agreement from each of the others.

"What does this mean? Are we too late?" Karn asked.

No one answered right away. They all knew that Bolas wanted them on Ravnica. That he had set a trap of some kind for them there. They had hoped to arrive before him and thwart his trap, his invasion and any other nefarious plan. But prior experience with Bolas indicated that *he* was a helluva lot more likely to be the one doing the thwarting.

Jace spoke carefully, slowly, as if trying to convince himself. "It could be a call for help from those who know Bolas is coming to Ravnica."

Teferi shrugged. "It could mean he's already there."

Chandra was still staring at the sparkling lights. Blue, green, red, white and glowing black, they called to her, promising nothing but doom and yet fostering a powerful urge to planeswalk with them to another dimension, another Plane, to the world-city of Ravnica.

"You feel that *pull*?" she asked, knowing they did.

Again there were nods all around.

Just then a burst of golden light heralded the arrival of Gideon Jura as he planeswalked into the room, looking every inch the hero, his hand upon the hilt of Blackblade, the soul-drinking sword that they hoped would kill Bolas since nothing else had.

Okay, yeah, thwarting is all fine and good, but really we just want the damn dragon dead. Gods know he deserves it.

"*Finally!*" Chandra and Jace said in near-perfect unison.

"Sorry," Gids said. "It took all my strength to come to Kaladesh. I felt a powerful call to go straight to Ravnica. Still feel it. You?"

Jace nodded, raising his hood. Chandra thought maybe the action was meant as a slight distraction, because Jace suddenly looked fairly heroic in his own right—which meant he had probably generated an illusion of his better days to compensate for his general exhaustion . . . or to unconsciously compete with the no-need-for-an-illusion Gids.

Gideon said, "Well, that's doubly disturbing. Do we think Bolas' trap is already set?"

Teferi shrugged again: "Better to assume so."

Chandra blurted out, "Where's Liliana?"

Gideon looked away. "There was no sign of her on Dominaria. She had planeswalked away—but she obviously didn't come here."

"Maybe she felt the call to Ravnica and couldn't help herself," Chandra said, ever hopeful.

Gideon shook his head. "She may have gone to Ravnica, but if she did, she went before this summons, or whatever it is. And she knew we were all supposed to come here first."

Jace said, "I don't want to say I told you so."

Gideon scowled. "I think that's *exactly* what you want to say."

Jace actually looked hurt. "I don't take any pleasure in this, Gideon. No one wanted to believe in Liliana more than I did. No one had more *riding* on it than I did."

"Except Liliana," Gideon countered.

Jace inhaled and nodded. "Yes. Except her."

Jaya scooped up her long gray hair and tucked it into her own hood as she raised it over her head. "It's a damn shame. We could have used her experience, her skills, her power."

Ajani stated, "There's nothing we can do about that now."

Gideon said, "There's nothing we can do *for her* now. I know that. We have to get to Ravnica and face whatever Bolas has in store. We know it's a trap, which may help us avoid it. And even if we can't avoid it, we go anyway. We can't let the dragon do to Ravnica what he did to Amonkhet. In a city the size of a planet, there are just too many lives at stake."

No one moved. Chandra felt herself heating up.

Jaya must have sensed it, too, as she shot a glare at her protégée that clearly instructed: *Breathe, child.*

As Chandra had no desire to torch her mother's new apartment, she took the unspoken advice and silently counted to ten. She was angry with Liliana. And she feared for her, as well. But truly, her thoughts weren't with Liliana Vess at all. As much as she missed her "sister," she missed Nissa Revane even more, secretly wishing that the elf woman were there beside them.

Beside me.

Nissa was the last original member of the Gatewatch. But she had abandoned their cause months ago, leaving Chandra and the rest behind. Nissa had been a source of strength for Chandra, for all of them. In some ways, even more so than Gideon.

But there's no helping that now, either.

They had lost Nissa as surely as they had lost Liliana. The seven of them were on their own.

The seven of us will have to be enough.

Chandra glanced around the room at the grim faces.

"Look, it's not all bad," she said, feeling the need to buck them—and herself—up.

"She's right," Ajani said. "I recruited Kiora and Tamiyo to our cause. They haven't sworn any oaths, but they both promised to meet us on Ravnica."

"And Jace is still the Living Guildpact of Ravnica," Chandra added, giving Beleren a friendly punch on the shoulder. "His word there is magical law. *Literally.* Even Bolas can't change that, right?"

"Right," Jace said, rubbing his shoulder while affecting a confidence that perhaps he didn't feel. "So let's get on with it." He disintegrated into a complex crisscross pattern of blue light as he planeswalked to Ravnica.

Gideon and Ajani followed in storms of gold; Jaya, in a conflagration of red flame. Teferi seemed to transform into a blue whirlwind that swept him and itself away, and Karn simply vanished with a sharp metallic *PING.*

Chandra paused, looking around the now empty room. "Bye, Mom," she whispered. "Wish us luck."

Then, with her own burst of fire, she planeswalked away from her home plane of Kaladesh toward whatever awaited them on Ravnica . . .

FOUR

RAL ZAREK

On Ravnica, Ral Zarek, Planeswalker and de facto guild-master of the Izzet League, crossed to his ally, Kaya, Planeswalker and reluctant guildmaster of the Orzhov Syndicate. The ghost-assassin was lying unconscious on the floor of an Azorius Senate bell tower, a few feet from the humming Beacon, which Ral had just activated. The lightning storm he had summoned was dying now, but high winds still howled through the shattered seven-foot-tall arched window.

Ral knelt beside Kaya and shot a glance at Lavinia, also unconscious, a few feet away. Then he allowed himself a quick look at Hekara, lying in a pool of her own blood. In the end, it had come down to the four of them. Well, the four of them plus Vraska.

Kaya stirred, moaning softly. Ral touched the metal side of

the (patented) Accumulator on his back, discharging the last of the static electricity coursing through his body, before gently stroking his pale fingers against Kaya's dark-skinned cheek. He whispered her name like an invocation, summoning her back to consciousness.

Squinching one eye, she looked up at him blurrily. "Ral?"

"Uh-huh."

"Did we win?"

He didn't answer, didn't know quite how to answer, but he helped her to her feet. Instantly, her eyes fell upon Hekara, and her grip tightened on him for support, moral or otherwise.

"Oh, no . . . Hekara . . . Ral, I'm so sorry."

"It couldn't be helped."

Although Hekara and Ral were of different guilds, of different temperaments and had next to nothing in common, the exceedingly quirky and chipper razorwitch had sacrificed her life to save his, simply because she considered Ral Zarek to be her friend. In hindsight, this emissary from the Cult of Rakdos may have been one of the best friends Ral had ever had, which only served to increase his grief and guilt, not only over her sacrifice, but also over the way he had treated her when she was alive: more often than not, as a nuisance he wished to be well rid of.

Tomik should be here, he said to himself, though honestly he was glad Tomik Vrona had missed the fight.

The last thing Ral needed was to see another person he cared deeply about lying dead on the floor.

It had been a costly battle. Just another in what had become a costly war.

And really, it hasn't even begun.

Nicol Bolas was determined to conquer Ravnica, and Ral had been running around like a headless chicken, trying to do everything in his not inconsiderable power to mount a defense. Nearly every effort had been met with dismal failure and death.

Following the orders of his former guildmaster—Niv-Mizzet, the Firemind—Ral had attempted to unite all ten of Ravnica's guilds to grant the dragon Niv the power to go head-to-head against the Elder Dragon Bolas. Ral had gathered—or believed he had gathered—a core group of like-minded individuals to help him, including Kaya, Tomik, Lavinia, Hekara . . . and the gorgon Planeswalker Vraska. Ral had been slow to trust Vraska, who had admitted up front that she had once been an agent of Bolas and had risen to power as guildmaster of the Golgari Swarm thanks to his aid. But Ral had his own dark history with Bolas and had eventually come to think of Vraska as a true friend and ally—right up to the point where she betrayed them all.

The fragile alliances Ral had been building among the ten guilds had shattered like the bell tower's glass window. Niv-Mizzet was forced to face Bolas without the boost in power he had been expecting. Now Niv was dead, Hekara was dead, and Bolas was loose on Ravnica.

"And Vraska?" Kaya asked as she disengaged from Ral.

"I blasted her with enough lightning to fry her to a crisp— but not enough to completely incinerate her. Since her corpse is nowhere to be found, we'll have to assume she planeswalked away."

"Do you think she'll come back?"

"When the smoke from Bolas' fire clears, maybe. I hope so. And I hope I'm still alive when she does. I very much want to kill her for all this."

"Ral."

"She made her choice."

"Or Bolas made it for her. You and I both know what he's

like. How easy it is to fall under his sway. How hard he is to break from."

"And yet somehow we both managed."

She didn't respond.

But another voice said, "Apologies." It was Lavinia. She had regained consciousness and was standing over Hekara's corpse.

Ral swallowed with difficulty and forced himself to speak: "It wasn't your fault. It may have been your hand that slew Hekara, but only because Bolas had possessed you."

"I know that," Lavinia said coldly, like the hard-ass officer of the law she had once been. "I wasn't apologizing for killing Hekara. I was apologizing for giving Bolas' henchman the opportunity to get the drop on me in the first place. For allowing Tezzeret to slap the device on my neck that gave the dragon control of my mind."

Kaya said, "It's just another reason to bring the dragon down."

"We didn't need any more reasons." Lavinia turned away from Hekara and seemed to instantly forget about her. She approached the Beacon. "You managed to get this thing working?"

Ral joined her in front of the large humming device and looked down at its locked and coded keyboard. "Yeah," he said. "The Beacon should summon Planeswalkers to Ravnica from throughout the Multiverse to help us fight Bolas. And neither the dragon nor his minions will be able to shut it off. Hell, *I* can't even shut it off."

"I hope you're right. The ten guilds have never been so divided, and the Living Guildpact is still missing."

Ral found himself shrugging: "Maybe the Beacon'll draw *Mr. Guildpact* back to save us." He heard the bitter sarcasm in his voice and frowned. Ral had decidedly mixed feelings about

Jace Beleren but reluctantly admitted to himself that there was no one he'd rather see at this moment. Beleren's my-word-is-magical-law Guildpact powers might be their last best chance against Bolas.

From behind them, Kaya said, "He can't get here soon enough . . ."

They turned to see a wide-eyed Kaya staring out the broken window in fascinated horror.

"Why?" Ral asked. "What now?"

FIVE

LILIANA VESS

Liliana Vess stared daggers at Nicol Bolas, Elder Dragon, former God-Pharaoh of Amonkhet, former God-Emperor of multiple multiversal planes *and current God-Damned psychopath.*

He took no notice, and she eventually gave up, silently lowering her eyes in bitter frustration.

Bolas and Flunky Supreme Tezzeret were manipulating some rather impressive magics to raise the ground beneath their feet, with Liliana along for the ride. Utilizing no subtlety whatsoever, they sculpted something akin to a stone step pyramid on the far end of Ravnica's Tenth District Plaza—directly across from the Embassy of the Guildpact, where Jace Beleren kept his office, library, living quarters and quaint notions about right and wrong. The new structure was big, bulky and brutalist, an aesthetic nightmare completely out of place amid the elegance of Ravnica's multifaceted architecture.

And the noise. The cacophony filled the air with the cracking of pavement, the toppling of neighboring buildings and the scraping of massive stone block against massive stone block.

Plus the shouting. There'd be plenty of that today, no doubt.

Nor was the dissonance limited to the observable world; Liliana was a necromancer not an elementalist, yet she could practically hear the land screaming in protest over the forced creation of this monstrosity.

As he did his master's bidding, sunlight glinted off Tezzeret's armor and his fully mechanical—and fully monstrous—right arm. The artificer had done his best and cruelest work upon himself. Below his dreadlocked head, he was more machine than man. Liliana thought him appalling. Bolas merely thought him useful.

When the pyramid had reached a sufficient height to be seen from all four horizons, Bolas and Tezzeret ceased their efforts. Liliana glanced up and spotted an armored angel, her crown helmet gleaming in the morning sun, pull up short in midair and then quickly fly off to inform her Boros Legion superiors of what by now they couldn't have helped noticing even from their Sunhome Fortress half a district away.

Towering over his two minions (*because,* she thought, *what am I at this point except another minion of Bolas*), the dragon regarded his work with a devious smile that contorted his features and flattish head into a death's-head grin.

Something's missing, he thought to them, not bothering to speak out loud.

Then from the air itself he conjured up a stone throne, which floated thirty feet above the pyramid's flattop apex. With a single flap of his wings, he rose and sat upon it. Now if Liliana and Tezzeret wanted to look at his ugly face, they would have to crane their necks back as far as they could stretch. It made Liliana feel small and insignificant, which she was quite sure was the point.

We'll call it the Citadel of Bolas, thought the self-satisfied dragon.

"You're giving them a target," said a frowning Tezzeret.

Exactly. In fact, I believe I'll give them two . . .

With one crooked finger, Bolas gestured toward the marble pavement in the middle of the plaza. Instantly a huge obelisk in the style of Amonkhet began to rise up into the sky, towering even higher than the God-Emperor's new Citadel. Bolas smiled again, mouth open this time to show his complete set of razor-sharp teeth. Then he spit a gout of fire, which traveled as a flaming whirlwind toward the top of the obelisk. The blaze engulfed its capital before quickly calcifying into a life-sized statue, patinated copper with accents of gold, of the ever-modest Bolas himself.

Now, that *is a target,* he thought at them smugly.

He laughed telepathically, the simulated sound of his unfiltered mirth entering Liliana's mind, contaminating her psyche with pure unadulterated Nicol Bolas. She thought she might vomit. In fact, she must have thought it clearly enough that for the first time since her arrival on Ravnica, he actually deigned to look at her.

You vomit, he threatened, *and you clean it up. With your tongue.*

She scowled but said nothing.

He telepathically chuckled, probably to test her. She maintained her scowl but otherwise didn't react.

With supreme confidence, he dismissed them with a slight wave of the tip of one wing.

You both know what to do.

Tezzeret nodded as the armor covering his abdomen irised open, revealing a hollow core where his innards should have been. He planeswalked away, his body imploding into his own void.

It was a beautiful morning. It had rained just before dawn, and the air now tasted crisp and clean. The sun had risen just a few minutes ago, and the skies bore the colors of ripe plums and peaches. Knowing what was in store for the day, Liliana felt like crying. And a part of her *wanted* to cry. Wished she could cry. But there were no tears. The woman that could allow herself to cry was a century gone, and she possessed no necromancy powerful enough to bring that woman back to life, nor to raise actual tears from soul-dead eyes.

Lowering her head, Liliana slowly descended the Citadel's steps. She glanced back only once: Bolas wasn't watching her, had all but forgotten her, taking her cooperation—*her servitude*—for granted. Instead he admired his handiwork and smiled.

SIX

TEYO VERADA

Teyo Verada was on his hands and knees, coughing up sand. The first thing he noticed was the stone beneath him. Not shifting sand. Stone.

The next thing he noticed was that he was alive.

He was covered in sand. Covered in it. Not buried in it. He wiped a sandy arm across his eyes in a futile attempt to clear his vision, and looked up, expecting to see the lights. But the lights were gone. Instead he saw the light of a single rising sun shining between two massive buildings of stone and glass, each big enough to hold four monasteries of the Order.

Wait, one sun? Where's the other one?

He thought he must be dreaming, but he didn't believe he had the imagination to dream what he was currently seeing. This wasn't the desert. This wasn't his village or the monastery. This wasn't even Oasis.

By the Storm, where am I?

Still spitting up sand, he lowered his head and saw a bronze-skinned, dark-haired girl sitting on an iron railing, regarding him with curiosity. She appeared to be about sixteen, and her garb was truly bizarre, decorated with patches of fur and tusks, ribbons and bells hanging from her shoulders, her tunic cinched with braided vines of leaves and berries. Studying Teyo intently, she absently picked a small blood-red berry off her belt and popped it in her mouth.

The blood from his still fresh diamond wound trickled into his own mouth, its copper taste mixing with the sand. He spit again, endured a fit of coughing, and—still on his hands and knees—called out to the girl for help.

Surprised, she pointed to herself and said, "Me?"

He nodded desperately and coughed out, "Please . . ."

She grinned broadly, hopped off the railing, and raced to his side, saying, "Hardly anyone notices me. I'm so insignificant." She helped him to his feet and began brushing sand off his tunic.

He murmured a thank-you and struggled to order his mind.

"Where am I?" he asked, finally.

"Transguild Promenade," she said with a shrug.

"What?"

"You're on the Transguild Promenade. And there'll be thrull-carts coming through here any second in both directions. So unless you want to be crushed beneath 'em, we better move."

He let her pull him forward. Rubbing his hand furiously back and forth over his scalp, Teyo tried to get the sand out of his hair as he walked across a stunningly massive bridge beside the petite girl with the dark hair and strange clothes. She began talking nonstop at a mile-a-minute pace.

"We haven't been properly introduced. I'm Rat. I mean Rat's not my real name, of course. It's more of a nickname.

Folks call me that. Well, not a lot of folks. But you get the idea. My real name—or, you know, my *given* name—is Araithia. Araithia Shokta. So Rat is shorter, easier to say. You can call me Rat. I'm not offended by the name at all. Truth is, it's kinda perfect for me. Perfecter than Araithia, I guess. Although I think Araithia is prettier, you know? My mother still calls me Araithia. So does my father. But they're pretty much the only ones. Well, there's this centaur I know, but he's kinda my god-father, so it's the same idea. Parents get stuck on the names *they* pick. But I'm fine with Rat. So you go ahead and call me Rat, okay?"

"I—"

"I'm currently Gateless, in case you were wondering, but I was born into Gruul Clans, so my parents want me to offi-cially join their guild, except I just don't think I'm angry enough, you know? Plus I have good friends in Rakdos and Selesnya—yeah, yeah, they couldn't be more different, but some days I feel like I fit well in the one, and then the next day, the other. Anyway, those are my big three: Gruul, Rakdos, Se-lesnya. I'll definitely join one of those. Probably. Are you in a guild? I don't recognize the outfit."

"I—"

"Oh, and what's your name? That should come first, I guess. I don't talk to a lot of new people, so I may not get the order of things right. I always have so many questions, but I usually have to figure out the answers on my own, you know?"

"I—"

"That was rhetorical. We just met. I don't actually expect you to know how I get through life instantaneously. Besides, we're having a conversation here. There's no rush. We'll get to all the important stuff eventually, right? How's your head? That's a pretty nasty cut. I don't think you'll need stitches, but we should really get it cleaned up—get the sand off it and ban-dage it or maybe find you a healer who can cast a little mending spell. I can take you somewhere they can do that for you, but even a *little* healing magic can get a little pricey. Still, it's *such* a little cut, they might do it gratis, if you ask nice. Or if you're too shy to ask a stranger for help—you seem shy to me, but I don't want to presume too much since we only just met— I can patch you up myself. I mean, I guess I'm a stranger, too. But I feel like we're bonding a little. In any case, I'm a fairly decent medic. I've had to learn to do that for myself over the years. It's not like my mother wouldn't do it for me, but she's a Gruul warrior. She's not always available. Besides, I've never really been hurt all *that* badly, you know? Cuts and scrapes. I'm relatively short and bigger folks are always bumping into me if I'm not too careful. Ravnica's a busy place, you see."

"I—"

"I don't have any healing magic, mind you, and I don't think I have anything I can use as a bandage, but I can steal something easy enough. Or maybe you wouldn't want a stolen bandage. I forget that not everyone's okay with me being a thief. The Azorius Arresters wouldn't approve, that's for sure. Um, you're not Azorius, are you?"

"I—"

"Nah, look at you. You can't be Azorius. I'm guessing you're—"

At his wit's end, Teyo stepped into her path, faced her and roughly grabbed her by her arms, shouting, "Listen!" In fact, he was so rough, he hesitated, worried he might have hurt her.

But she seemed pleased by the contact, smiling up at him with her bright eyes. He noticed she had irises of a deep-violet hue. "I talk too much, don't I?" she said. "I spend a lot of time alone, and I talk to myself too much. I'm always telling myself that. Then I get with other people, and you'd think I'd learn to listen more. I want to learn to listen more. So yeah, I'll listen to you, uh . . . You know, you still haven't told me your name. Start with that, and I promise I'll listen."

Flustered and flummoxed, he said "Teyo," his voice rising at the end, as if *he* was asking *her* whether he had his name right. Truthfully, he was so completely off balance, if she'd told him he had it wrong he wouldn't have been particularly surprised.

"Teyo," she repeated. "That's a nice name. Are you in a guild, Teyo? You're injured and off your game. Is there somewhere I should take you? Someone I should take you to?"

"I'm not in any guild. I'm an acolyte of the Shieldmage Order."

"Huh. Never heard of it."

"You've never heard of the Order? How is that possible? What do you do during a diamondstorm?"

"Never heard of a diamondstorm, either, but it sounds pretty. Sparkly. I like sparkly things. It's kind of immature, but there you have it. If I see something sparkly, I take it. I mentioned I'm a thief, right?"

Teyo let go of her arms and walked to the bridge's stone railing, looking down at the immense river passing beneath. He'd never seen quite that much water in any one place. The single sun was just rising. It was morning, early morning, dawn, basically. But it had been late afternoon when the Eastern Cloud began to blow; he was sure of that. And he was sure he hadn't been buried overnight. He'd have died if he'd been buried for *that* long.

And where is the second sun?

His hands gripped the railing tightly, turning his knuckles white. He muttered, "She's never faced a diamondstorm? Never heard of the Order? That makes no sense. The Monastic Order of the Shieldmage is famous the length and breadth of Gobakhan. The people depend upon it."

Joining him at the railing, she smiled and shrugged, speaking quietly and at a more moderate pace: "I've never heard of 'Gobakhan,' either."

He slammed his hand down on the railing and stomped his

foot on the ground. "This is Gobakhan! Our world is Gobakhan! You're standing on Gobakhan!"

She put her arm through his and propelled him forward. Again she spoke slowly, softly, kindly. "Teyo, *this* . . ." Without slowing her pace, she gave a little hop on the paving stones, her bells jingling softly. ". . . . is Ravnica. This world is Ravnica. Teyo, I've a feeling you're not on Gobakhan anymore. I'm guessing you're a 'walker."

"We're walking. *I'm* walking. Of course I'm a walker." He was angry, though the truth of what she was saying—to the extent he understood—was starting to dawn.

"Not *that* kind of walker. I don't know too much about it. Just stuff I overheard Master Zarek and Mistress Vraska discussing when they didn't know I was hanging around." Her voice began to speed up again. "I mean Hekara asked me to follow Master Zarek, so it was almost a mission, an assignment, right? She wanted to know where they went when they went wheres without her. That's almost a quote, by the way. She talks like that, Hekara. Anyway, I was supposed to follow them, but I also eavesdropped a bit. I probably shouldn't admit this, but I'm a chronic eavesdropper. I really can't help myself."

"I swear by the Storm, I don't know *what* you're talking about."

"Okay. Yeah. I get that. I mean I saw you materialize all covered in sand back there, so I probably should have guessed. But your mind always goes with the simplest explanation first, you know? I figured you knew how to teleport from place to place. Do you know how to teleport from place to place?"

"No!"

"Exactly. So what you *can* do, if I've got this right, is teleport from world to world, Plane to Plane."

"I promise you I don't know how to do that, either!" But

even as he said it, *shouted* it, Teyo Verada began to suspect that just maybe he did.

"I think maybe the first time, it's like an accident or, no, um, I mean not on purpose. Like an involuntary flight thing. Like to save your life maybe? Was your life in danger, maybe?"

She waited. He stared at her wide-eyed. "How—how'd you know that?"

"Oh, yeah, no. I didn't. But I think those might be the rules. Like I said, I overhear things. Plus I'm very intuitive, and you were *really* covered in sand. Buried alive, maybe?"

He nodded dumbly. Or at any rate, he felt dumb. "So I'm not on Gobakhan?"

"Ravnica."

"Ravnica." The word sounded strange in his mouth. The grains of sand he had coughed up had felt more at home on his tongue.

"And you don't—you couldn't—know anyone here, right?"

"Just you, I suppose."

She smiled and gave his arm a squeeze. "Then I'm officially adopting you. Until you're ready to leave, you and I are family. Don't worry; I'll take good care of you. I'm great at that. I've had to learn to take care of myself, you know?"

"Uh-huh." He felt numb.

"So let's think about what you need to know to live on Ravnica." She tapped her chin with her finger. He watched her for a moment with something like awe. He was grateful to this girl and not a little terrified of her. Or maybe not of *her* but of what she might reveal.

He tore his eyes away and began to look around. This world, this Ravnica, was clearly more . . . *more* than anyplace on Gobakhan he'd seen or even heard of. They passed people wearing so many different types of clothing, garments made from polished leather and silks and materials he could not identify. He stared up at buildings of stone and glass—*and magic:* some with archways, foundations and battlements floating in midair. The city was huge and filled with corners and shadows. The smell of rain was heavy in the air. Though the sun was out currently, the streets still shone from a pre-dawn downpour that must have preceded his . . . *arrival* . . . by mere minutes.

"Okay," she said at last. "Here's what you need to know: Ravnica is one big city. And a lot of folks live here. A whole lot. Mostly humans, I guess, like you and me. But plenty of elves and minotaurs and cyclops and centaurs and goblins and angels and vedalken and viashino and giants and dragons and demons and, well, pretty much anything you can think of. Mistress Vraska's a gorgon. I've only ever seen three of those, but I think they're really, really beautiful, you know?"

"I—I don't think I've ever seen a gorgon."

"They're striking. You can trust me on that. Anyway, I don't know who runs things on Gobakhan . . ."

"Abbot Barrez? Or, no. He just runs the monastery."

"So you're like a monk? I thought all monks had to shave their heads."

"I'm not a monk yet. I'm an acolyte. And shaving your head's not a rule. At least I don't think it is." He threw up his hands. "Right now I'm not sure of anything!"

"Calm down. That's why I'm telling you stuff. So the abbot runs Gobakhan. But here on Ravnica, it's the guilds. There are ten guilds and between them they run everything."

"They had guilds in Oasis. That's a big town on Gobakhan." They were coming to the end of the bridge, and he stopped before a courtyard that Oasis could have fit into nicely. "I suppose Oasis isn't *that* big."

"But it's big enough to have guilds?"

"Yes. There's the Carpenters' Guild. And the Stablemen's Guild. But I don't think they run anything. I think they just get together to drink ale and complain. At least, that was my impression. I was only in Oasis for a few days."

"Well, our guilds are kind of a bigger deal. Although I'm sure they drink ale and complain as much as they do anything. I know my father drinks ale and complains a lot, and he's an important warrior in the Gruul Clans."

"So you're in this Gruul guild?"

"I told you already. I'm Gateless. That means I haven't committed to any guild yet. Gruul, Rakdos, Selesnya. They're all kind of wooing me. I'm in high demand." She laughed. He didn't get the joke. "I'm kidding," she said. "I'm *not* in high demand."

"All right. If you say so."

"You're sweet."

"I am?"

"I think so. I like you already. I'm glad I adopted you."

"I—" He laughed, though he wasn't exactly sure what he was laughing at. Maybe it was just a release. "I think I'm glad of that, too."

Suddenly shy, she smiled and looked away. "Stop it," she murmured, more to herself than him.

He took a deep breath and asked, "What else do I need to know?"

"Oh, um . . . let's see. The guilds are always fighting with each other. It seems idiotic to me. It feels like they should all be able to get along, since they're all so different. What they care about barely overlaps. But they think being different means they need to pick at each other and stuff. So if things start to get out of control, the conflict's supposed to be resolved by this guy named Mr. Jace Beleren. He's called the Living Guildpact, which means whatever he says goes. You know, magically. Problem is, he's been missing for months and months. I think he's like you. Traveling from world to world. Only on purpose, maybe. Anyway, with *him* gone—

things have gotten iffy, you know? The guilds all tried to get together to stop some kind of evil dragon, who's supposed to be on his way. But Mistress Vraska—she's the Golgari guildmaster—assassinated Mistress Isperia, the Azorius guildmaster."

"Wait, she killed her?"

"Uh-huh. And now the guilds all hate each other. Or, you know, don't trust each other anymore."

"And the evil dragon?"

"I dunno. I guess he's *still* on his way."

They turned a corner, and she stopped in her tracks. Teyo followed her gaze to see a tall obelisk topped with a statue of a dragon. An evil dragon, if he had to guess.

"Huh," Rat said. "That's new."

SEVEN

JACE BELEREN

With a flurry of crisscrossing blue lines, Jace Beleren walked into his office, his sanctum, the Chamber of the Guildpact inside the Embassy of the same. Immediately he felt a familiar harness wrap around his most basic and primal Spark—the inherent magic within his being that made him a Planeswalker. He was fairly confident he knew the cause, but the premise would have to be tested. And the test would have to wait.

Ravnica is Bolas' trap, he reminded himself as he prepared for an immediate attack, creating an illusion of himself across the dark room and hiding his own form within a spell of invisibility.

Nothing happened—except that Gideon and Ajani appeared in a shower of golden light, followed by Jaya arriving in flame. Teferi's blue whirlwind signaled his arrival, and Karn's was preceded by a clear, silvery tone.

Looking around, a worried Gideon just had time to say, "Where's Chandra?" before she appeared in a blaze of orange and red. Jace heard Gideon breathe an audible sigh of relief. The soldier didn't want to lose another comrade. And Jace couldn't blame him.

Ajani turned to Jace's illusion and said, "Be on the alert. This is your base. He'd count on you coming here."

Jace's illusion nodded and raised a finger to its mouth, while the real Jace linked them all psychically. (Linking Karn was a bit of a struggle, the golem's inorganic mind was so alien, but Jace managed.) He broadcast his thoughts: *Proceed carefully and quietly. There's dust everywhere. Looks like no one's been here for weeks.*

Chandra thought: *Yeah, no way Lavinia would let anything gather dust. It smacks of disorder, and your deputy hates disorder. I wonder where she went?*

I wonder if she's dead, Gideon thought grimly. He frowned. Jace could tell Gideon hadn't meant to think that "out loud." *Sorry. No matter how many times we do this, it still takes some getting used to.*

They heard fast-approaching footsteps and without any thought, each assumed a fighting stance. (Jace, in fact, assumed two.)

The doors opened, revealing Lavinia.

Chandra thought, *Her ears must have been burning.*

"I'm happy to see you, sir," Lavinia said sternly.

Dropping illusion, invisibility and mind-link, Jace said wryly, "I can tell. You nearly cracked a smile."

Ignoring the jibe, the unflappable woman looked around the room until she found and addressed the true Jace: "I was hoping the Beacon would bring the Living Guildpact home. I'm glad it did."

Jace started, "Ravnica is not my—" But he cut himself off. It was beside the point, anyway. He said, "Lavinia, we have reason to believe the dragon Nicol Bolas is coming to conquer Ravnica. In fact, he may already be here."

Lavinia raised an eyebrow. "Oh, really?"

She walked to a window and threw open the shutters. They all approached. Jace had to suppress a gasp. In the center of the plaza stood a large pillar, an obelisk, that hadn't been there before. Atop this column was a massive statue of Bolas himself. Beyond that, at the far end of the plaza, a huge stone pyramid had risen from nowhere. A citadel.

Lavinia, the former arrester, cast a quick telescopic spell over the window's glass. Now they could all see that Bolas himself was sitting on a throne that hovered above the pyramid.

"I don't like him just sitting there," Jaya Ballard said. "It racks my nerves. What's he doing?"

Gideon unsheathed the soul-drinking Blackblade and stated, "He's waiting to die." He turned and marched toward the door.

Ajani and Karn both stepped into his path.

"It cannot be that easy," Karn said.

Ajani's one good eye locked on Gideon as he reminded him, "This is the trap."

Gideon hesitated . . . then nodded and sheathed the sword.

Jace turned back to Lavinia. "Bring us up to speed."

Lavinia's update was concise and coherent. Bolas had been working behind the scenes for months in an attempt to sabotage the guilds—or at any rate the fragile truces among them.

"He tried to get to the Izzet League through Ral Zarek, who seems to have had a prior relationship with the dragon. Fortunately, Zarek defied Bolas and attempted to unite the ten guilds to amend the Guildpact. With you missing," she gestured to Jace, "the plan was to grant the Izzet's own dragon guildmaster, Niv-Mizzet, the requisite power to battle Bolas head-on."

"And?"

"It was a debacle. Bolas had already recruited the assassin Vraska, helping her to become guildmaster—queen—of the Golgari Swarm. She murdered the Azorius guildmaster Isperia during the summit, setting every guild against the others."

Jace's face showed nothing, but he was internally furious with himself.

This is all my fault!

He and Vraska had been allies. More than allies. And they had formed a plan. She had begun doing Bolas' dirty work before knowing who or what he truly was. When she learned the truth, she became just as determined as Jace to stop the dragon. But she'd still have to face Bolas, face his telepathic ability. So at her request, to offer her temporary protection, Jace had erased from her mind all knowledge of their alliance, of their feelings for each other, of Jace Beleren entirely. And he had erased all knowledge of Bolas' true nature. She was to return to Ravnica while Jace gathered up the Gatewatch and formed a plan. Then Jace would have come to Ravnica, located Vraska and triggered her true memories. And together they would have brought the dragon down. But gathering the Gatewatch had taken more time than he had anticipated—mostly due to Liliana, who had dragged most of them off to join her personal quest on Dominaria. But Jace was also late returning. He had planeswalked to Zendikar to track down Nissa Revane, a founding member of the Gatewatch. It had taken weeks to find her and days to realize he could not convince her to rejoin the cause. In the interim, anything Vraska did in service to Bolas was not her fault.

"With the failure of the summit," Lavinia was saying, "Ral moved on to Plan B. Niv-Mizzet had ordered a Beacon to be built. Ral activated it to draw Planeswalkers here from across the Multiverse. It seems to have worked."

"It worked," Gideon said. "But we were coming anyway."

"It's quite effective. It'll lure more than just the seven of us," Jace said darkly.

"'*Lure*'?" Chandra asked, picking up on his tone.

He ignored her and asked Lavinia, "What else do we need to know?"

Lavinia continued, giving the status of each guild, one by one.

The Golgari Swarm.

"Vraska herself has fled the Plane, leaving various Golgari factions fighting for supremacy. We can't expect help from that quarter."

"No sign of Vraska at all?" Jace asked as neutrally as he could manage.

"No," Lavinia stated, with a raised eyebrow that told Jace his attempt at neutrality had been less than successful.

The Simic Combine.

"They departed the failed summit and have barricaded themselves within their territories, unwilling to parlay."

The Selesnya Conclave.

"Bolas had infiltrated Selesnya, but Ral helped the elven healer Emmara Tandris dispatch the collaborators. But like Simic, Selesnya has withdrawn behind its borders. It is rumored that Selesnya's guildmaster, the dryad Trostani, has gone silent. And Tandris doesn't dare make a move without her consent."

Jace flinched again. He had once had feelings for Emmara, feelings she had not reciprocated. But she had been kind to him. And he hadn't protected her, either. Emmara, Liliana, Vraska.

Caring for Jace Beleren is akin to a curse.

The Gruul Clans.

"The cyclops Borborygmos had attended the summit over the objection of many of the other clan leaders. When it failed, he lost face and was deposed as guildmaster, replaced by a young fool named Domri Rade, who isn't quite fool *enough* to repeat his predecessor's 'mistake.'"

The Cult of Rakdos.

"Hekara, the Rakdos emissary, was killed . . . while fighting Vraska. Rakdos himself hasn't taken the loss well and has cut off all contact with us."

Jace noticed Lavinia's pause. She was leaving something out about this Hekara's death. But he knew Lavinia well enough to feel confident she wouldn't leave out anything that would matter in the long run, so he let it pass.

The Azorius Senate.

"After Isperia's death, Dovin Baan was—"

"Dovin Baan?" Chandra exclaimed. "How did that sonnova—He's not even *from* Ravnica; he's from *my* world!"

"Well, he showed up here and made himself very popular very quickly by promoting the construction of thousands of his 'thopters,' small mechanical spy devices that—"

"We know what they are," Ajani said. "They were Baan's favorite tools on Kaladesh."

"They were a good fit for the Azorius, as well," Lavinia said ruefully. Azorius was her guild, and Jace could tell it pained her to speak ill of it. But she was too pragmatic to sugarcoat things. "Baan's thopters were everywhere, watching everything. Providing more intelligence of crime, of our enemies . . . of our friends. More knowledge gave the Senate more control over the city. Isperia was impressed. She respected Baan's abilities, and he rapidly ascended to become her Grand Arbiter—and her replacement as guildmaster upon her death."

"Guildmaster? But Baan can't be trusted!" Chandra's outrage glowed red in her eyes. Flames danced around her hair.

Jaya crossed to Chandra and put a calming hand on her shoulder. "Child," she warned. "Watch your temper. And your temperature."

Chandra nodded curtly, and her flames—if not her outrage—receded. Through gritted teeth, she said, "On Kaladesh, Baan was working with Tezzeret, who was working for Bolas."

"Yes, that would have been helpful to know a few months ago. But we realized Baan's connection to the dragon too late. Having Vraska kill Isperia ended any hope of united guild opposition to Bolas, but it also served to elevate Baan to guildmaster. And he's solidly in Nicol Bolas' pocket."

"But now that you know . . ."

"Now that we know, I myself am leading a rebel faction within Azorius to overthrow Baan. Unfortunately, Azorius guildmembers are not exactly the rebellious type. Baan is their legal guildmaster, and the Senate respects the law above all else. I've won a few to my side, but only a few."

Gideon said, "Is it all bad news? Every guild you've named is either actively working for the dragon or has withdrawn, refusing to join the fight against him."

"We have a few allies," Lavinia said, and continued.

The Orzhov Syndicate.

"Bolas hired the ghost-assassin Kaya to eliminate the Obze-dat Ghost Council, and she was successful down to the last ghost. The unexpected result was that Kaya became the Orzhov's new and unwilling guildmaster."

Karn said, "The new Orzhov guildmaster is dead?"

Lavinia looked taken aback. "What? No."

"You said she was a ghost-assassin."

"I meant she's an assassin who specializes in killing ghosts. She's not a ghost who's also an assassin. She's alive."

Karn frowned. "Then *'ghost-assassin'* is a very imprecise term."

"So this Kaya is beholden to the dragon, too?" Teferi asked, trying to get things back on track.

"No. That was clearly Bolas' intent, but Kaya refused to help him any further, and I believe she's a reliable ally. Though I'm not sure how much support she has within her guild. She's been forgiving debts."

"Oh, *that* must be going over well with the Orzhov bankers," Jace said sarcastically.

"Pretty much as you'd expect."

House Dimir.

"Bolas had infiltrated the spy guild, as well, but its Guild-master Lazav seems to have cleaned house. Not that Lazav is all that trustworthy, either. Still, he seems to regard the dragon as a serious threat and remains a—probable—ally."

The Izzet League.

"Without the amendment to the Guildpact, Niv-Mizzet was forced to fight Bolas under his own power."

"I take it—" Jace began.

"The battle was brief, leaving only Niv's charred bones behind. Zarek is the new acting guildmaster, and one of the few still ready and willing to fight the dragon."

The Boros Legion.

"Guildmaster Aurelia remains solidly on our side."

"Of course she is," Gideon said with a satisfied smile.

"Indeed," Lavinia said. "But you just missed their first attempt to put Bolas down. Minutes after his Citadel and statue appeared, they attacked with two squadrons. The dragon routed them easily, effortlessly. Without budging from his throne. Aurelia has withdrawn the Legion to regroup. They're maintaining a wide perimeter around the plaza, keeping bystanders clear. But there are easily a few thousand civilians still within the boundary, and there's been no organized attempt to evacuate them."

Jace made a quick assessment: "So we have two guilds we can count on. Izzet and Boros. Two more, Dimir and Orzhov, that are likely allies. Four—Simic, Selesnya, Gruul, and Rakdos—who believe they can sit this battle out."

"The fools," Ajani said.

"Well, there's plenty of foolishness to go around. Baan has placed Azorius staunchly on Bolas' side. And . . ." He trailed off.

"The Golgari," Lavinia said, raising that single eyebrow yet again.

Jace cleared his throat. "Yes, the Golgari. In disarray with no leadership. Unless Vraska returns."

"If she does," Lavinia said, "she'll have nine other guilds after her head. Especially the Azorius, for the murder of Isperia. And especially Izzet. Zarek trusted her, befriended her. He's not likely to forgive her betrayal."

Jace nodded slowly and then turned to Gideon. "Try to Planeswalk," he said.

"What? I'm not going anywhere."

"I'm confident of that. But try anyway."

Gideon shot him a suspicious look. Then he rolled his eyes and vanished with a flash of golden light. He hadn't been gone two seconds when he reappeared, shouting, perhaps in pain, perhaps in frustration. It wasn't clear. A golden circle within a triangle—the crest of Azor—shimmered briefly above his head . . . before fading away.

"What just happened?" Chandra asked.

Recovering quickly, Gideon said, "I was on Kaladesh. At your mother's place. But I couldn't hold the plane. I was pulled back—yanked back. I tried to fight it. Not sure why. I wanted to come back. But it felt unnatural, so I fought the pull with everything I had. Didn't help."

"It's what I assumed would happen." Jace crossed to a bookshelf, pulled off a title and flipped through its pages. "Here," he said, reading to himself. "I think I can show you." He approached a wall of windows that looked out over the city to the east. The rest followed. He held out his hand and rotated it thirty degrees while whispering a single word: "Display."

A few miles away, above the Azorius Guildhall in New Prahv, a gargantuan and intricate version of the circle-within-the-triangle symbol appeared in the sky.

Jace heard multiple gasps but didn't bother trying to decipher who was the most shocked. He said, "It's the Immortal Sun, a powerful talisman created by Azor himself, originally to trap Bolas. Clearly, Baan has activated it *for* the dragon. Its power will keep all of us from planeswalking away, while Zarek's Beacon will draw more and more Planeswalkers here."

"And *that's* Bolas' trap," Ajani said.

"Exactly," Jace said. "There's no escape for any of us now, as long as the Sun is active."

"Which means," Gideon stated simply, "as long as Nicol Bolas lives . . ."

EIGHT

GIDEON JURA

Gideon had stopped pretending he gave a damn about plans.

Strategist? Tactician? That was never me. A general? No. I'm a foot soldier. A sergeant, at best. A fighter. A brawler. And maybe, I suppose, a weapons master.

There was a dragon that needed slaying, an Elder Dragon, and Gideon had acquired a weapon, Blackblade, that had once slain another Elder Dragon.

Get close and stab.

These days, that sounded like Gideon's kind of plan.

On the other hand, his attempt to slay Bolas on Amonkhet—admittedly with the wrong weapon—had proven that *"get close and stab"* was easier said than done. Bolas had quite literally bounced Gideon around like a rubber ball. Gideon's magical invulnerability had protected him, but he never got close enough to any of Bolas' vital organs to make stabbing a viable solution.

So Gideon was fine with the current compromise. A small unit. Jace, Teferi, Lavinia and Gideon. Jace was already using his power of illusion to make all four invisible. He'd initially insisted it was only a scouting mission. But Jace didn't need to be telepathic to know that if Gideon got his shot, he would take it.

So when they got close, Teferi would, at the crucial moment, use his control of time to slow the clock around the dragon, allowing Jace to use his power over Ravnica's magical law, as its Living Guildpact, to literally *arrest* Bolas in place, so that Gideon could bring Blackblade to bear. Lavinia— a fine warrior in her own right and the only native Ravnican in their little group—would have their backs, in case one of Bolas' endless series of minions attempted to rescue his or her master. (Lavinia had announced—in a low voice that almost gave Gideon chills—that she was hoping said minion would be Tezzeret. She seemed to have a score to settle with that one.) Again, a simple plan.

Direct. Clean. No nonsense. Or not much nonsense, anyway.

Chandra had objected: "Come on, Gids! You can't leave me behind!"

Gideon had sympathized, but Jaya Ballard had pointed out to her protégée that neither pyromancer could generate enough heat and flame to harm an Elder Dragon. Fire was the first magic Bolas had learned, probably when he was still an egg. He literally inhaled and exhaled the stuff. Jaya and Chandra wouldn't be helpful, and the fewer people Jace had to mask, the better.

Which was also why Ajani and Karn had stayed behind. Or part of the reason. Deep down, Gideon hadn't needed to catch Beleren's subtle nod to them to know they remained in Jace's sanctum as a fail-safe. Ajani, Karn, Jaya and Chandra could rally whatever Planeswalkers were summoned by this Beacon thing to take Bolas down in the event that Gideon and company fell. Gideon wasn't actually afraid of dying. His invulnerability made that unlikely, and frankly he hadn't feared death since he was a kid on the plane of Theros. Kytheon Iora—the name he'd been born with, before foreign pronunciation had altered it to Gideon Jura—owed the Multiverse a death. If today was the day that debt came due, so be it. But damn if he wasn't going to take the dragon along for the ride.

Tenth District Plaza was nearly empty. Those who hadn't fled when Bolas' Citadel and statue had risen were mostly staying inside. But there were a handful of hardy (or foolish) souls who still scurried about for reasons of their own. The four invisible warriors raced past five or six humans, two goblin children and a blue-skinned vedalken.

They were about halfway across the plaza when they paused for just a moment to look up at the towering obelisk upon which Bolas had set his own image. Gideon had to stifle the urge to attempt to push the thing over. He didn't have the strength for it, and it would have warned Bolas. Still, he'd have almost been willing to risk the latter if the former had been within his power.

Jace, keeping even telepathic communication to an absolute minimum, waved them forward. They started up again, passing three more children—a human, an elf and another goblin.

What's with all the children in the plaza? Don't they have anyone who cares enough to get them out of harm's way?

Of course, Kytheon hadn't had anyone at their age. No adults, anyway. Just his Irregulars, the oldest of whom wasn't much older than he had been, before—

Anyway, from what he knew of his companions, most of them hadn't had anyone to take care of them, either, for much of their childhoods. Maybe it was a Planeswalker thing.

But there had to be responsible parents and guardians on some *damn plane, didn't there?*

Again he had to fight off the temptation to do something noble, heroic and idiotic. To stop, turn around and whisk the kids off the plaza. Instead he kept moving. In the long run, the little ones would be safer if Gideon dispatched the dragon quicker.

So no stopping. No turning around.

And just then, he stopped and turned around.

A loud sonic boom and a rush of dry desert air from behind them nearly knocked Gideon and the others off their feet.

The four turned as one, as the sound of crashing masonry echoed across the plaza.

To their mutual horror, a gigantic portal—fifty yards tall— had opened behind them, instantly decimating the Embassy of the Guildpact, shearing it nearly in half. Soft violet light poured forth from the portal, looking almost serene—in stark contrast with the destruction that the tear in space had caused and was causing.

Gideon watched in horror as an ogre stumbled forward before collapsing, her entire upper right quadrant evaporated by the portal's arrival. Too far away to help, Gideon saw the embassy's crumbling façade fall, crushing two more bystanders beneath its formerly polished stone.

This was the Planar Bridge that Tezzeret had stolen for Bolas from Kaladesh. With it, the two of them could transport inorganic matter from one plane to another. Jace had warned them that this would be part of Bolas' plans, but Gideon hadn't realized the Bridge would be this large, this devastating. And worse . . .

I left Chandra behind! She and the others are still inside the embassy!

NINE

DACK FAYDEN

Amid a puff of purple smoke, Dack Fayden planeswalked to Ravnica, empty-handed and annoyed. And four feet above the ground.

"Gods-be-damned!" he said aloud as he dropped in a heap. This had happened to him more times than he cared to count. He didn't know many other Planeswalkers, but none he had met would admit to materializing in midair and falling like an idiot. Of course, *he* didn't admit to it, either, so maybe it happened to them all.

Yet somehow, I doubt it, he thought as he picked himself up off the cobblestone alleyway, rubbing his now sore ass.

Dack hadn't planned on coming back so soon. Ravnica might currently be the closest thing he had to a home, but he had spent considerable time and energy casing a number of valuable treasures on the plane of Innistrad, and leaving without even one was professionally embarrassing for the man who had once declared himself the Greatest Thief in the Multiverse.

But here he was, back on Ravnica with no Amulet of the Kralmar, no Seelenstone, no Bloodletter, no Praying Gargoyle, no Tome of Eons and no Grimoire of the Dead. Nothing to use his psychometry upon, stealing its spell of creation. And nothing to fence to J'dashe down in the Lower Sixth. Dack had borrowed expense money from the Orzhov pontiff (a.k.a. the self-proclaimed Greatest Fence in the Multiverse) a few weeks before J'dashe had died. The Innistrad score would have squared Dack with J'dashe's ghost, but now interest on the loan would continue to pile up.

I hate owing money to the dead. They are so impatient.

It was no longer about the coin to J'dashe. After all, what use did she have for it now? "It's the principle of the thing," the pontiff's spirit had said, just before Dack left for Innistrad. But Fayden knew J'dashe really meant "the principal" . . . *and* the interest.

So why did I come back?

The truth was he hadn't been able to help himself. A combination of dread and anticipation—not to mention a light show that no one else on the streets of the High City of Thraben seemed to see—had called him to Ravnica.

It made no sense, beyond the obvious cause: *magic.* Magic of some kind. Magic powerful enough to summon a Planeswalker. And powerful enough to spark Dack Fayden's curiosity.

Well, he'd better get to the bottom of it all, and the sooner the better. After all, the treasures of Innistrad weren't going to steal themselves.

Dack adapted a tactile spell he'd once acquired off the Amulet of Tarantual and quickly scaled the wall of the alley. He pulled himself up onto the roof of the nearest building to get his bearings. But he still wasn't high enough to see anything that might provide a clue as to what was going on.

Lithely, he made his way from rooftop to rooftop, running, jumping, climbing when necessary. This part he enjoyed.

This is freedom.

The only thing that would have made it better was if it had been night and not morning. A cool night with only a sliver of moon. That was a thief's time. Simply being out in daylight left him feeling exposed. Last thing he needed was to be picked up by a Boros patrol or an Azorius Arrester. Of course, for once he wasn't carrying any stolen goods. (Frankly, he wasn't carrying much of anything. Not much left of J'dashe's loan even.) Broke and bereft as he currently was, he could actually risk being out in the sun. In fact, when he ultimately *did* see a patrol of Boros Skyknights (and then another and another), Dack Fayden, Master Thief, grinned up at them and waved.

He was heading northeast, toward the center of the city, figuring if there was something to be seen or some bit of intel to be learned, he'd find it there.

He wasn't wrong. Minutes later, Dack leapt across an urban canyon, his hands sticking to the side of a sandstone wall. It was a little slick from a predawn rain, and his tactile spell didn't hold perfectly. But he managed to spider his way up to a high rooftop overlooking Tenth District Plaza.

From this height, he immediately saw three things that shouldn't be there, three things that definitely *were not there* when he left Ravnica a month ago: a huge pyramid-shaped citadel, a looming column with a statue of a dragon atop it . . . and a *gods-be-damned hole into another world*!

TEN

CHANDRA NALAAR

Chandra didn't know what hit her.

With a groan, she raised herself onto her hands and knees, pushing up off the floor of Jace's library. A floor that was now sloping at a forty-five-degree angle. Through clouds of dust and a soft purple haze, she tried to clear her head and comprehend what had happened. The whole room was aslant. No, not the *whole* room. Because a good third of said room was simply gone. Only a foot away from her right shoulder, what had been floor and ceiling and shelf after shelf of books and half of a long wooden conference table around which the Gatewatch once met were now nothing but a curve of violet light.

The Planar Bridge! It's open!

Its activation had wiped out a chunk of the building, collapsing and tipping what remained of the embassy toward the gaping portal. Chandra looked down. Part of an old leather-bound volume rested on the floor against her hand, looking as if a very precise monster had taken a perfectly curved bite out of the tome's corner. She picked up her hand, and the book slid down across the slanting hardwood floor, falling off into an indigo void.

If I had been standing a foot to my right . . . Or if Nissa had been here . . .

"Chandra! Chandra, are you there?" It was Jaya's voice, calling from Jace's office, which moments ago Chandra had left in a snit, because Gideon and Jace hadn't let her go with his squad.

"Yeah," she answered thickly—and too quietly to be heard. She heaved herself up onto her feet, cleared her throat and called out, "I'm here! I'm okay!"

"Then get in here and help!"

She stumbled "uphill" toward the door, managing to grasp the knob and pull herself up the final distance. She turned the handle, and when the door swung open toward her, she nearly lost her balance, nearly let go of the doorknob, which would have resulted in her sliding down across the smooth floor and off its edge into . . . into *what,* she wasn't exactly sure.

But she held on. Even managed to grab hold of the door-jamb and pull herself up into the other room. She pulled and latched the door behind her so nothing else could fall out into whatever oblivion lay beyond the Ravnica side of the Bridge's giant circular portal.

Jace's sanctum was even more dust-filled than the library had been. Calling out, "I'm here!" she squinted and looked about till she spotted Jaya's flame. She leaned in and carefully trudged up to the elder pyromancer, who was using precision flames to burn through a fallen oak beam that had pinned a fallen Ajani Goldmane to the smooth hardwood floor. Ajani was bleeding from a cut above his one good eye, but his own magic was rapidly healing the wound beneath a semi-transparent white glow.

"Should I help?" Chandra asked.

"Can you help," Jaya responded (a little crossly, Chandra thought), "without setting what remains of the place ablaze?"

Chandra bristled slightly but instantly realized this was not the moment to take offense. After silently patting herself on the back over this little bit of maturity, she asked, "Where's Karn?"

"Here," the golem called out through the haze, while pushing Jace's large cedar desk off one silver leg.

From somewhere, Jace's mind reached out urgently to hers: *Chandra? Are you all right?*

Her thoughts raced back to him, spilling out in a loud psychic jumble. *I'm fine. We're fine. What about you? Is Gideon okay? Lavinia? Teferi? Jace, it was the Planar Bridge that Tezzeret stole. It opened up inside your library. Or inside the building. Or through the building. I could only make out a part of its curve, but the portal must be massive. Bigger than the embassy. It could easily have swallowed us whole. We're lucky to—*

Chandra, slow down. Clear your thoughts. I need you to focus. I don't want to leave this psychic link open for too long or let it create too much telepathic noise. We're fine. We were halfway across the plaza when the Bridge opened. But it's a true disaster. There are people dying out here. Do you need help? Can the four of you make your way out on your own?

I think so. I mean, no, we don't need help, and, yes, we can make it out.

Then I'll shut off the link for now. I don't want it to alert Bolas to our presence. He knows we're coming, but he doesn't necessarily know we're here. Not yet anyway. And in any case, I don't want him to be able to pinpoint our locations. Take care.

The link went dead. Jace's mind was silenced within hers. Usually, she disliked his mental intrusions—any mental intrusions—but right now the loss of his "voice" felt like an absence, another void. She instantly missed him. And Chandra wondered whether his precautions weren't pointless. She found it hard to believe the Planar Bridge had opened where it had at random. By now she knew enough of Bolas to know everything he did was done with purpose. Or two purposes. Or twelve.

Still, Jace is right. We don't need to advertise. If there's even a chance the dragon doesn't know where we are, we'll need to exploit it for all it's worth. We'll get him. We'll get Bolas yet.

ELEVEN

NICOL BOLAS

f these ants weren't so insulting, I'd almost find them amusing. Did Nalaar, Beleren and the rest of their little friends actually believe they could hide themselves from Nicol Bolas?

No, the dragon had felt every individual arrival the moment each had landed on Ravnica. How could they not imagine that Bolas was tracking every move the "mighty Gatewatch" made? Truly, these so-called heroes were even more naïve than he had thought.

Beleren, Jura, Teferi and the Azorius woman Lavinia were all in the plaza below him, under the preposterous impression that a little spell of invisibility could hide them from the mind of an Elder Dragon. Even his weak brother Ugin would have noticed their presence. And they thought *Bolas* could be fooled?

And their allies? Goldmane, Nalaar, Ballard and Karn were

inside the embassy. It *was,* Bolas had to admit, a minor miracle that they had all survived the opening of the Bridge's portal. But that would be the last miracle any of them would see today.

Vess, of course, was in position. Ready to do her master's bidding in order to save her own mystically tattooed skin. Another minion, Baan, guarded the Immortal Sun.

Bolas let his mind range wider. What other Planeswalkers were on Ravnica? There was a boy he didn't recognize, newly sparked, with the scent of Gobakhan upon him. He was close by, as was the thief Fayden. The dragon's former stooges, Kaya and Zarek, were en route, after separate attempts to consolidate their power within their two guilds, which each now led by default. (Neither had met with tremendous success, as both owed their ascensions to Bolas. When they abandoned his service, the dragon, in turn, abandoned them. And without his support, they had little hope of consolidating a meat pie, let alone a guild.) Likewise, "Guildmaster" Rade was sitting by a bonfire in the Gruul crater trying to lock in his own feeble power base. Bolas could still help him if he chose, and he considered it. He had arranged for Rade's rise, too. But there was no point. Bolas had no use for Rade now.

No use but one.

At the other end of the city, Tamiyo and Kiora had arrived mere minutes ago and were now seeking to join up with Goldmane. Narset and Samut had each come separately in response to the Beacon.

And just this second another Planeswalker had arrived in Rakdos territory.

Who? Ah, yes. Ob Nixilis. He, at least, is mildly interesting. Well, maybe interesting isn't quite the right word? Slightly less dull, perhaps?

And more were coming. More would come. Bolas knew all their names; he knew all their abilities. Their strengths and weaknesses. The cracks in all their armors. Bolas had made it his business to know.

Before the day was over, a few hundred Planeswalkers would answer the call of Niv-Mizzet's Beacon. The invention had been that infant dragon's fail-safe plan. If all else failed, Zarek would activate the Beacon, summoning the Planeswalkers, who would arrive to save the day. Since all else *did* fail, since Bolas had reduced Mizzet to a pile of bones, the Beacon was indeed activated. And not a single pathetic-excuse-for-a-sentient-being had noticed that Bolas himself had planted the idea for the Beacon in what passed for Niv-Mizzet's "Firemind."

Bolas couldn't help but smile.

The Planeswalkers are coming—oh, maybe not all of them, but enough, enough.

They'd follow the Beacon in and be trapped on Ravnica by the Immortal Sun, leaving them at the mercy of the dragon's machinations. His plans proceeded like clockwork. Tezzeret was on Amonkhet and had already activated the first knell of that doomsday clock by opening the Bridge.

Bolas realized he was gloating and wondered for a moment whether such an emotion was beneath him. But it was difficult to engage in any real self-reproach. So far, his enemies had managed to engender literally no surprises for the Elder Dragon. None. The only thing that even verged on surprise was how little the Gatewatch had prepared for this day. After the way he had brutalized them on Amonkhet, he had assumed they'd have come up with *some* kind of plan to face him now.

Something! It would certainly have been pathetic and hopeless, but at least it would have been a strategy.

But ants don't strategize. They simply follow their instincts, endlessly repeating the same actions, trodding the same course, over and over and over again, no matter the results.

Oh, yes, this time the ants might march a few feet to the left instead of to the right. But they still march, even if they march toward certain doom.

They simply never learn.

Bolas was actually a little embarrassed for them.

The only Ravnican Planeswalker Bolas couldn't locate right at that moment was Vraska. His mind scoured the city-world, leaving him confident she was no longer on the Plane. She must have fled to another. That wasn't a surprise, either, but it was a small disappointment. He had very much wanted to punish her for her stray moments of rebellion. But he'd catch up with her eventually. He'd catch up with every single Planeswalker in the Multiverse eventually, whether they came to Ravnica today or not.

After all, there was time. He was an immortal. Once, he had even been a god. And soon—*very soon*—Nicol Bolas would be a god again . . .

TWELVE

JACE BELEREN

Enough was enough.

Jace was, after all, the Living Guildpact. It's not like he had wanted that power. In fact, he generally resented the responsibilities that came with it. There had been an ancient sphinx, a puzzle, a maze, a bailiff and a gift that generally felt more like a curse. It was all so complicated, but it added up to this: The magics that bound Ravnica through its ten ruling guilds and the leylines of power that ran beneath the city had found their primary locus in the person of Jace Beleren.

The magical muscle that came with being the Living Guildpact was indeed mighty. What Jace declared as law came instantly into being. He had to be careful—or at least selective. He couldn't abuse the process. Like a judge, he had to interpret the actual written Guildpact in making his pronouncements. He couldn't simply wish anything into being—or non-being, for that matter. He'd tested that a couple of times on insignificant matters. Wished for a slice of glazed trdeljic cake and the like. No cake had appeared, of course, because there was nothing in the law that said an individual was entitled to a free dessert simply because he, she or they happened to be in the mood. But on much more weighty matters, Jace had wielded tremendous mystic authority by following either the letter or the spirit of the law, or both.

That's why he had hesitated up to this point. If it had been within his scope, he gladly would have banished Nicol Bolas from this Plane. Or wished him dead. But there was nothing in the Guildpact that made the dragon's appearance on Ravnica illegal. Even the creation of the pyramid and the statue were debatable offenses, as Tenth District Plaza was neutral territory. If Jace had tried to command them away or used them as an excuse to attack Bolas, it might have worked. But given Bolas' own considerable power, it might have failed. And Jace would have shown his hand—and the limits of it.

When the four of them had left the embassy, the plan had been simple enough. Use Jace's own mental powers of illusion and Teferi's control over time to get them close enough to Bolas so that Jace could issue a magical arrest warrant on charges as simple as disturbing the peace. Jace would "interpret" that warrant as a spell of temporary paralysis, and then Gideon would use Blackblade to kill the dragon. Under the law, Gideon would have to be punished for this crime. But Jace could use a mercy clause in the Guildpact to minimize that punishment to nearly nothing. Community service. Picking up trash, maybe. Gideon might even enjoy that.

But the Planar Bridge changed everything. The portal had killed people and demolished the Embassy of the Guildpact. Any attempt to interfere with the Guildpact was punishable in any number of ways—including death—and any demonstrably devastating threat to Ravnica was clearly within Jace Beleren's legal purview. Now he felt certain he could use the Guildpact's power. Close that Bridge and end the threat Bolas presented by ending Bolas once and for all.

Jace, Gideon, Teferi and Lavinia were still invisible to all other eyes. Gideon had started back toward the embassy, but Jace grabbed his shoulder and reached out with his mind. *They're all right,* Jace whispered telepathically over the link. *I checked. They're all alive, unhurt and making their way out.*

That's good. But there are bystanders over there, hurting and still in danger. We need to help, Gideon stated.

And we will. But give me two minutes to act as the Living Guildpact, and I can stop all this. Once the dragon's dead and the portal's closed, "helping" will be considerably easier.

Jace could see that Gideon was still chomping at the bit to jump into action, but even Mr. Great-Big-Hero could see the wisdom of what Jace was saying.

Two minutes, Gideon thought at him.

Or less.

Jace exchanged glances with Lavinia and Teferi. Lavinia nodded once. It might not seem like much to anyone else, but Jace knew that for her, it was the equivalent of a rousing speech, and it heartened him. Truthfully, Lavinia had always (gruffly) believed in Jace's potential as the Living Guildpact more than Jace himself ever had.

Teferi shrugged a little and offered, *Good luck.*

Jace steeled himself, gathering up Ravnica's magic. Something felt different. Something felt disconnected. Something felt wrong. Or maybe that was just his own insecurity, his own doubts. This was no time for that. With one last touch upon Lavinia's mind and its firm resolve, Jace Beleren summoned the full power of the Living Guildpact.

"The dragon Nicol Bolas has murdered Ravnican citizens

and interfered with the Guildpact by destroying its embassy. As Living Guildpact, this is my decree: Close that portal. Execute Bolas."

Nothing happened.

"CLOSE THAT PORTAL."

Nothing.

"EXECUTE THE DRAGON NICOL BOLAS."

Nothing.

Jace searched for the Guildpact's power. He reached down deep into himself. He reached out wide across Ravnica.

Nothing. Nothing.

What's wrong? Gideon asked with a touch of impatience that made Jace want to punch him.

I don't know.

But Jace thought that maybe he did. He realized that maybe he'd spent the last few minutes talking himself into believing something he already knew wouldn't work.

I've lost it. I've lost the power.

Jace—

Damnit, Gideon, I'm no longer the Living Guildpact!

How?

Lavinia thought, *The alliance among the ten guilds has always been tenuous at best. When Vraska killed Isperia and we were all betrayed the result was catastrophic. The allegiances among the guilds were totally shattered. Perhaps the Guildpact itself was extinguished.*

Then reignite the damn thing! Gideon commanded.

If only it were that simple, Jace thought to himself.

And then grimly over the link: *It's not about the guilds. They've never trusted each other, which was the whole point of the Pact. No, it's the leylines. The leylines of Ravnica converged on the Embassy of the Guildpact. That's why it was built there. And that's why Bolas had the Planar Bridge open there. So that the leylines would be disrupted. It did the job. The Guildpact*

*and the magic it commands have dissolved. Perhaps perma-
nently.*

And your word-is-law thing?

Gone. Over. Done. One more weapon in our arsenal lost . . .

Somewhere in the back of his mind, Jace Beleren could
hear the dragon laugh.

THIRTEEN

GIDEON JURA

Gideon growled and took off, racing toward the portal to save whomever he could from the disaster.

Teferi shouted over Jace's telepathic link: *Nine Hells, Gideon, wait! I'm not as young as I used to be, and I can't keep up!*

"We have to save those people!" Gideon shouted out loud over his shoulder.

Jace reminded him: *Will you be quiet? We're trying to keep that sword hidden from Bolas!*

Lavinia was the only one fast enough to grab Gideon's arm. He wheeled around on her, eyes wet.

We have to help. Every second counts.

She grabbed his face between two gauntleted hands and whispered for him alone, "I know. This is my world. These are my people. But you must stay hidden. Blackblade is our last hope."

He nodded once and wiped his eyes.

Jace thought, *Obviously, we're not going after Bolas right now. I'm dropping the invisibility spell around us so I can focus my energies on masking Blackblade and its power.*

They all started moving back toward the Planar Bridge.

And that's when Gideon saw her. She was stepping gingerly up onto some wreckage. She reached the top of a fallen balustrade, stood up straight and paused.

Liliana Vess.

She'd made it to Ravnica after all.

Gideon smiled. He turned to glare at Jace.

I told you so! I told you she'd come!

Jace didn't respond. He simply stared in Liliana's direction.

Gideon told him, *Link her up. We need to bring her up to speed.*

Jace still didn't respond. Gideon realized he wasn't looking at Liliana. Jace was staring past her at the portal.

Gideon turned.

Something was emerging from the portal.

An army. An army was marching through the Planar Bridge.

But that's not possible, Gideon thought. *Nothing organic can travel through the portal.*

And then instantly he knew. This was not an army of organic beings. Not anymore. They were Eternals from the devastated plane of Amonkhet. The plane that Nicol Bolas had all but destroyed.

On Amonkhet, the Gatewatch had uncovered another of Bolas' long-term plans. For decades, the people of Amonkhet had trained themselves to be warriors. Then, when the best of the best had trained to perfection, they were killed and mummified, embalmed in layer after layer of the blue lazotep mineral, until they were fully coated, fully shielded. Little about them remained organic at all. Then they were resurrected, with all their skills and strength—and absolutely no will of their own. Now they served only Bolas.

Gideon had seen them in action on Amonkhet. They had murdered everyone in their path. Brothers killed brothers. Parents killed children. Lovers killed those they loved the most.

This was the fate Bolas had in store for Ravnica. This Dreadhorde was Bolas' invasion force. And once again, the Gatewatch had failed to stop it.

Unless . . .

Gideon turned back to Liliana. She was the most powerful necromancer Gideon had ever seen.

If she could take control of the Eternals . . .

He watched her don the Chain Veil, its burnished-gold links glinting in the sun. Gideon bit his lip. The Veil increased Liliana's power, but that power had come very close to killing her. And he wasn't always sure just how much she controlled it—or it controlled her.

Still, if any scenario calls for taking that risk . . .

The Veil covered most of her face. But even at this distance, he could see—and more so feel—its mystic energy flow through and about her. The etchings on her exposed skin—forehead, chest and fingers—began to glow purple. Her eyes began to glow purple behind the Veil. He could see the power rippling off her. He could hear Liliana Vess scream.

She's doing it . . .

He turned toward the Eternals. Their eyes glowed purple, too. As one, the marching Dreadhorde halted and turned to look at their mistress.

She's taken control of them. She'll use them as a weapon against the dragon . . .

But then, with a clear wave of her arm, the Eternals turned to march toward the citizens of Ravnica, still recovering from the portal's destruction and staring as the approaching Dreadhorde closed in. Gideon wanted to believe Liliana was using the undead to aid the living. He wanted to believe that desperately. Still, he started running again.

Please, please . . .

The Eternal on point reached a young human woman, who was trying to free her husband or boyfriend or brother from under fallen stone. She looked up at the approaching Eternal. Paralyzed with horror, she didn't move a muscle as the Eternal stepped up and snapped her neck. Gideon was still some distance away, but he heard the crack, felt it in his own body.

No . . .

They all ran toward the mounting carnage, Jace, Lavinia and Teferi just behind Gideon. Heartbroken, he glanced back over his shoulders at their grim faces. The link was silent. Gideon had expected an *I told you so* from Jace, who'd been saying for weeks that Liliana couldn't be trusted, that she had been using the Gatewatch to kill her own personal demons, to free herself from the contract that bound her to their will. They had done that. Gideon and Liliana had together used Blackblade to kill the last of these demons. He had personally seen to it that she won her freedom. Had delayed coming to Ravnica to do it. He had believed that freedom would grant her the power to help them defeat Bolas. He had believed her when she said she *wanted* to use that power to help them defeat Bolas. Instead she now used it to serve the dragon.

Leading his army to make this plane his own . . .

Jace offered no *I told you so*. But none was necessary. Gideon had believed in Liliana, and she was lost to them. She had betrayed them.

So now Liliana Vess would have to die . . .

FOURTEEN

LILIANA VESS

She had been on Amonkhet when the Eternals were first released. Even so, Liliana Vess had no idea there were this many. They continued to emerge from the portal, flesh replaced with lazotep, shining metallic blue in the morning light. Phalanxes of eternalized humans and eternalized minotaurs marched onto Ravnica's plane; squadrons of eternalized aven, angels, demons, drakes and even three eternalized dragons flew above the ground troops. No matter the species, each and every individual Eternal was a master warrior of Amonkhet, bred and trained for battle, the best of the best, now bereft of anything resembling free will. All were decorated with a lazotep cartouche, glowing softly blue as they emerged from the Planar Bridge, shifting to purple as they fell under Liliana's spell.

My spell . . .

She told herself she had no choice. Long ago, she had been a Planeswalker when that term still meant something. Back when the Spark that granted the power to traverse worlds wasn't handed to every Beefslab who could wield a sword or child who could summon up a bit of fire. Back then, Planeswalkers were immortal. Back then, Planeswalkers were nothing short of gods.

And Liliana Vess was a—goddess!

Then came the damn Mending. The Multiverse shifted, and Planeswalkers were mortal once again. Instantly she had felt the centuries weigh upon her. She would grow old and die. Most of her great power was lost already; the rest would float away on her ashes or be chewed up by the worms and maggots that fed on her corpse.

She wondered now what would have resulted if she had simply accepted that fate. But even at this juncture, her mind rejected that course. And in any case, it was too late, pointless to speculate on such things. Accepting fate had never been her way.

Desperate to recover her power, her youth, her immortality, she had turned to one who understood what she had lost. She had turned to Nicol Bolas, another Planeswalker, another former god of the Multiverse. And the dragon had come through—or so it seemed. He negotiated a deal for her, a pact, a contract, between Liliana Vess and four demons— Kothophed, Griselbrand, Razaketh and Belzenlok. She became their servant, and in return Liliana was Liliana again. Young and beautiful in her dark way. And powerful.

And the best part was that she had fooled them all. The demons had made her *too* powerful. One by one, she had killed them all. Or manipulated the Gatewatch into doing the killing for her. After Gideon helped her kill Belzenlok with Blackblade, she sincerely thought she was free. She was ready to join them for the rendezvous on Kaladesh. For the battle on

Ravnica against Bolas. Liliana knew she was one kind of monster, but Bolas was another kind altogether. He had to die.

She still thought so. But everything had changed on Dominaria. There he informed her of a quite unfortunate truth. Bolas had brokered her deal with the demons. And with all four dead, her contract had defaulted to him. She was his servant now, as he had always planned her to be. And while the demons had been arrogant and foolish enough to allow her sufficient autonomy to bring about their deaths, Bolas was arrogant but no fool. His control was ironclad. If she defied him, she died. It was just that simple—and just that horrific.

But . . .

But if she played along for now, there was always the chance—*the chance*—she could turn the tables, kill Bolas and free herself forever!

She so wanted to believe that. To believe in herself that much. Before a few hours ago, she had.

Yet even as she attempted to rationalize her actions, deep down she knew that was all she was doing: rationalizing.

At her command—and per the dragon's plan—the Eternals attacked the citizenry. Swords were drawn; axes were raised. They came down, slicing through the morning air. They came back up with bleeding edges.

She had desperately questioned the need for this. Gone so far as to ask the dragon why he would slaughter "his future slaves."

But Bolas had insisted the carnage was necessary: *Your little Gatewatch needs to be drawn out into the open to stop the killing. So killing there must be. And plenty of it. All the Planeswalkers must believe they're thwarting an invasion—so they'll be unprepared for what comes next.*

"I won't do it," she had said.

Then you'll die horribly, he replied simply.

Screams echoed across the plaza. It was a slaughter. Before her, around her, innocents were dying horrible deaths. She was choosing her life over everybody else's. Choosing one precept over every other. Jace had been right about her.

Everyone can die . . . as long as Liliana Vess lives.

FIFTEEN

KAYA

Kaya and Ral were already heading toward the embassy when they heard the sonic boom ahead of them. They exchanged quick anxious glances, then took off at a run.

Immediately Kaya felt winded. Winded and annoyed.

I'm in better shape than this. I shouldn't—

Then she realized. This had nothing to do with her physical conditioning. If she was tired, weak, out of breath, it was because of the magical weight she was carrying.

Kaya wasn't just a Planeswalker. She was also a highly trained ghost-assassin. That wasn't a metaphor. She killed ghosts for a living. Sent those spirits that refused to leave the mortal plane(s) on to their final rest. Or she had done so until very recently, when she naïvely took on a contract from Bolas to kill the entire Obzedat, the Ghost Council of the Orzhov Syndicate. She had been wildly successful, but with each spirit patriarch and spirit matriarch she had dispatched, the mystic contracts they held had fallen upon her soul. And the Obzedat held *thousands* of mystic contracts. They were debt collectors, loan sharks really, who didn't let a little thing like the lack of a pulse stop them from getting their percentages.

Taking out Karlov, the late, unlamented chairman of the Obzedat, had sealed it. A technicality—one the dragon had counted on—made Kaya the guildmaster of the Orzhov, and laid another ton of contractual debt onto the shoulders of her soul. It affected everything she did now, and she was constantly fighting off exhaustion. Bolas had offered to arrange her release, but the price, being his puppet, was too stiff to pay. She had opted to live with the responsibility, at least for the short term.

In the last few days, she had, out of pity, forgiven the debts of poor families outrageously burdened for generations by what had begun as the smallest of loans. This eased a little of her burden—but created difficulties within the guild she now led. The Syndicate, to put it mildly, were greedy bastards. They did not approve of Kaya's charitable inclinations, and Kaya was very aware that rebellion was in the air. The greatest source of which was Karlov's living granddaughter Teysa. Teysa and Kaya had been allies for a time, but clearly that time had passed.

Ral's lover, Tomik Vrona, had been somewhat helpful in guiding her through the maze that was the Orzhov, but Tomik was Teysa's assistant and had spent the last couple of years secretly trying to help Teysa overthrow the Obzedat and become guildmaster herself. Kaya liked Tomik, but she'd be a fool to trust him completely.

Still, they all had a common enemy in Bolas, who had betrayed Kaya, Teysa, Ral and pretty much everyone else on this damn plane. So at this particular moment, Kaya figured that her backstabbing guild was the least of her worries.

She was right.

She and Ral turned a corner and entered the plaza in time to witness the start of the slaughter. Undead creatures covered in some kind of blue mineral were pouring out of a giant portal and relentlessly killing anyone and everyone they could get their hands on.

Ral didn't hesitate. He charged up the Accumulator on his back and immediately began blasting the undead army with bolts of lightning, often taking out two or three at a time. He strode forward, a look of fury on his face, his hair standing on end, his hands white-hot with electricity, and the blue warriors exploded before him.

Kaya had hesitated. Another wave of exhaustion had hit her, but she saw a red-haired mother huddled over her red-haired child and realized that exhaustion would just have to wait. She drew the two long daggers she wore on her hips and launched herself at the undead killer raising his sword over the young woman's head. Kaya's daggers, glowing purple with her magic, sank deep into the creature's back. Kaya's powers and weapons were specifically designed to end spirits, ghosts, zombies, and whatever the hell this walking mineral-covered corpse was. It collapsed in a heap in front of the shrieking mother, who pulled her son closer to her bosom and stared up at Kaya, more frightened than grateful.

Kaya said, "Run."

The woman blinked twice. Then she snapped out of the fear-induced paralysis that had nailed her to the cobblestones and ran toward the nearest building with her child in her arms. Kaya barely had time to see them enter when two more of the monsters rushed her. The closest and largest swung an axe. Like a ghost herself, Kaya activated her greatest mystic gift, the ability to turn herself incorporeal, and the axe swished harmlessly through her. This seemed to confuse her attacker, and Kaya took advantage of the respite to recorporealize and slash the throat of the incoming second creature. The pale-purple light from her daggers seemed to briefly war with the dark-purple light radiating from the warrior's eyes and cartouche. But like a poison, Kaya's powers seeped through the corpse, infecting it. It fell.

She turned back to the axe wielder, who swung at her again. Again she went intangible and again the axe passed through her, leaving her opponent open to take both daggers in the abdomen. He didn't go down right away. Solid once more, she dragged the blades up and gutted him. Her daggers were sharp, but it was more effort than she usually required to dispatch a ghost. And still she felt the Orzhov contracts weighing down her arms, making them heavy. She was already breathing hard.

And more of these things were emerging from the portal every second.

She saw Ral up ahead, making a stand from atop a park bench, defending three more children, one of whom cradled a rubber ball with much the same protectiveness that the mother had used for her son. Ral was smiting the metallic warriors, one after another. But Kaya could see that each successive bolt was slightly less intense than its predecessor. Ral's Accumulator would eventually run out of juice.

They'd soon be overwhelmed.

Kaya ran to join Ral, slashing at the creatures as she went. She dropped one. Somersaulted over another to impale a third. Did a low leg sweep to topple the second. Drove her daggers down into its chest.

She finally reached Ral's side by ghosting through another creature, slashing as she went.

"You running low?" she asked.

"I'm trying to summon a storm, but it's a little hard to focus right now."

"I'll try to buy you some time."

Then once again, she turned to the bystanders and called out, *"Run!"* The three kids instantly obeyed, taking off toward the same safe haven into which the mother had vanished.

Kaya just had time to think, *I wonder how long that particular haven will remain safe.*

Then another was upon her. Again her body lost all substance. The warrior stumbled right through her. It turned. She turned. She solidified and drove her daggers into its eyes, deep into whatever was left of its brain. It dropped like a marionette whose strings had been cut.

She watched it for a second too long. A mineralized minotaur slammed into her and sent her sprawling across the cobbles. She groaned and struggled to regain her feet. Her ribs ached, and she stumbled as she tried to rise; the Orzhov contracts seemed to pull her back down to the stones. The minotaur advanced, and Kaya fought to shake off the drag of her mystic obligations, but she still felt dazed, foggy. She wasn't sure she could even turn incorporeal.

Suddenly a girl ran past, dodging out of the way of the minotaur. The creature ignored her and continued toward Kaya with the clear intent of finishing the Planeswalker off.

And just as suddenly a young man—barely a man, a boy actually—stood over Kaya, erecting a triangular shield of light to protect her and himself from the creature. Its mace smashed into the triangle, which flashed brightly but held its form. The boy grimaced but held his ground, chanting low. Kaya blinked twice as the mother had and found herself staring at a perfect circle of light that the boy wore as a kind of earring on his right earlobe.

The minotaur reared to swing its mace again. The girl, bearing two small daggers of her own, leapt onto its back and drove her blades into the beast's neck. It roared and bucked and threw her off. She went flying, still holding her knives.

Then a bolt of blue-white electricity ignited the creature, which exploded into flaming piles of melting blue.

As Ral approached, the boy exhaled and dropped his shield. The little circle of light at his ear vanished, too, and his shoulders slumped. He helped Kaya to her feet. Her head was starting to clear, and she was looking around for the girl. Ral pulled a pair of goggles down over his eyes. He looked at the boy and stated, "You're a Planeswalker."

"I'm a what?" the boy asked.

"How do you know he's a Planeswalker?" Kaya asked Ral. But before he could answer, she finally spotted the girl. She was weaving among the warriors, who seemed to ignore her unless or until she stabbed them. She cut the hamstrings of one, and when it dropped to its knees she stabbed it in the eyes. Then she scurried over to join Kaya, Ral and the boy, dodging another monster en route.

Impressed, Kaya wryly asked her, "Those things don't seem too interested in you. What's your secret?"

The girl stared at Kaya for a beat.

Ral filled the silence by saying, "They're interested enough."

Ignoring him, Kaya addressed the girl again: "You okay?"

"Oh, yes," she responded. "I just never expected the mighty Orzhov Guildmaster to take any notice of me." Then she muttered under her breath, "Wow, two in one day. That's almost weirder than the big hole in the world."

SIXTEEN

RAL ZAREK

Ral Zarek's goggles, based on a design provided by Niv-Mizzet, could identify Planeswalkers summoned by the Beacon. Well, any Planeswalkers, really, though the Beacon was the key to the goggles' identification. Through the goggles, Ral could see the young man's Spark, manifested as a trail of golden energy that led from the kid up to the Beacon.

Ral turned to Kaya, whose aura appeared as another trail of gold, arcing toward the Beacon. He briefly glanced down at his own hands, which buzzed with their own aura. He looked up. And saw that he, too, was bathed in the Beacon's golden light. Ral suddenly didn't like knowing he was so easy to out as a Planeswalker.

Kaya asked, "How do you know he's a Planeswalker?"

Ral debated what to tell her. Then wondered why he was hesitating with the simple truth.

Perhaps sensing his hesitation and not wanting to push him, she changed the subject: "Those things don't seem too interested in you. What's your secret?"

At first he thought *"those things"* referred to the goggles, then realized she was referring to the blue horde, which—deterred by his lightning—was currently granting their little group a minutely wide berth. Still, it wasn't like he was immune to danger, so slightly annoyed, he said, "They're interested enough."

"You okay?"

"I'm fine," he said. "Sorry. It's the goggles. They're the Firemind's design. I can use them to identify Planeswalkers. It's . . . mildly disconcerting."

"Any others around? Planeswalkers, that is. Not goggles. Cuz we could use the help."

Turning from Kaya and the boy—who was clearly so new to being a Planeswalker, he had never actually heard the word before—Ral scanned the sky and followed the golden arcs from the Beacon down to the ground. He quickly spotted Beleren fifty yards away across the plaza. Lavinia was with him, as were two other Planeswalkers. One, Ral had never seen before. The other he recognized as an associate of the Living Guildpact.

Gideon, I think his name is.

Ral and Gideon had never actually met, but Ral had seen him from a distance once, and he cut a figure that was difficult to forget.

As Jace's quartet fought their way through the creatures, Ral reached out with his mind, calling to Beleren. Ral was no psychic, but he counted on the Guildpact's telepathy to do the heavy lifting. It worked. The mind-mage turned to look for him.

Ral, where are you?

Here, but—Jace! Look out!

One of the creatures leapt at Jace. But of course, it wasn't really Jace. It was an illusion. The monster passed right through the false Beleren and literally landed on its face. Ral couldn't see the real Jace, who had clearly created an illusion of invisibility around himself, but Ral saw the fallen creature telekinetically rupture.

Jace's sardonic thoughts reached Ral: *Oh, Ral, you* do *care. You even called me by my first name.*

Just get over here, Beleren. We need—

To compare notes.

I was going to say, a plan.

That, too.

Ral watched as the Beleren illusion signaled his fellows. Fighting as they went, they made their way toward Ral and Kaya. And the boy, whose name Ral still didn't know.

Beleren's unknown ally was using some kind of time magic to slow down any blue fiend that came within ten yards of their small troop. That made them easy targets for Beleren and Lavinia, who, as always, was a master with her sword. But the revelation was this Gideon, who wasn't just a pretty face attached to a stunning body. With an ordinary broadsword, he made hash of the creatures, whether magically slowed or not.

Ral unleashed a lightning bolt that took out a couple of the monsters in Beleren and Gideon's path. The latter nodded to Ral in acknowledgment. Then Gideon spotted something behind Ral and shouted, "Chandra!"

Ral turned. More Planeswalkers were fighting their way from the direction of the Embassy of the Guildpact—or what used to be the embassy. Again he recognized one, a female pyromancer with flaming—*literally flaming*—red hair, as one of Jace's associates. She fired off tremendous blasts of fire that reduced the enemy to puddles of molten lazotep. She was accompanied by another female pyromancer, this one with long steel-gray hair; a leonin, whom Ral guessed hailed from the Alara plane; and a massive silver automaton, which Ral normally wouldn't have considered to be alive, except that his goggles confirmed it indeed had a Spark.

The two groups converged beside Ral, Kaya and the boy. Through the goggles, Ral saw arcs of glorious golden light rising from all but Lavinia. Ten Planeswalkers, together, all ready and willing to fight for Ravnica. Bad as things already were—and despite his well-earned cynicism—Ral actually took some comfort from their presence.

He wasn't the only one. The one-eyed leonin didn't need goggles to glory in their united front. He raised his arms toward the heavens and roared. It was a sound of triumph, and though perhaps premature it had its desired effect. For the first time all day, Ral felt something akin to hope.

"Form up!" Gideon shouted.

He's even more impressive at close range, thought Ral, who followed Gideon's gaze toward the ruins of the embassy. More of the monsters continued to march and fly out of the portal. Instantly Ral's feeling of hope turned to ashes in his mouth.

Gideon shouted another command: "The Eternals are still coming! We need to save as many people as possible!"

Ral appreciated the sentiment, the desire to rally his fellow Planeswalkers to save his fellow Ravnicans. But as more of these *"Eternals"* charged toward them, Ral wasn't even sure they could save themselves . . .

SEVENTEEN

VRASKA

Far from Ravnica, on the floating city known as High and Dry on the plane of Ixalan, Quartermaster Amelia, Navigator Malcolm and Deckhand Breeches were all drinking merrily at the Boatswain's Rear, a famed alehouse.

Breeches, the gregarious goblin, was already three sheets to the wind, shouting *"Captain, Captain!"* at the top of his lungs every sixteen seconds like clockwork. The near-giantess Amelia and the siren Malcolm, who were both holding steady at two and a half sheets, cheered every time.

The subject of their enthusiasm smiled wanly. It was good to see her crew again, certainly. But Captain Vraska wasn't really in the mood for celebration. She was nursing her wounds (which were minor) and her bitterness (which was mighty). She could feel the call of Ral Zarek's Beacon, summoning her and every other Planeswalker to Ravnica, and a part of her hoped that many a hero would answer that call.

But the gorgon Vraska would not be among their number.

For reasons unknown, Breeches ran all the way around the oaken table three times. He then stopped in front of his beloved captain, tilted his head like a child, and asked at high volume, *"Jace? Jace?"*

Vraska suppressed a groan. Last time she had been on Ixalan, she and Jace had been crewmates—and perhaps something more. But that seemed a lifetime ago. Before she had instructed Jace to remove her memories as part of their brilliant strategy for taking Bolas down.

Best-laid plans and all that . . .

Instead Vraska's memories had been restored by another telepath: Xeddick, one of her insectoid kraul allies and the closest thing on Ravnica she had to a friend—before he was killed in her service.

With her memory restored, she had known what Bolas was—had known he was using her—and still she hadn't been strong enough for that knowledge to matter. Though she had been sincere when she approached Ral and Kaya and Hekara to volunteer her services and her guild in their fight against the dragon, she had ultimately betrayed them . . . and herself.

She couldn't control her need for vengeance and had assassinated the Azorius guildmaster, Isperia, as payback for the sufferings of her youth.

Isperia had once ordered her imprisonment for the crime of being Golgari. That incarceration had been a hellish nightmare of overcrowding, starvation and beatings. She didn't regret Isperia's death. But killing her when and where she did had destroyed Zarek's chance of uniting the guilds against Bolas. She had known it would, known killing Isperia was exactly what Bolas wanted. And she had killed Isperia, anyway.

Vraska also couldn't control her need for power and had allowed Bolas to blackmail her into fighting on his side, in order to retain her title as Queen of the Golgari. She had put her faith in the kraul death priest, Mazirek, master of the Erstwhile, the Golgari undead. The kraul and the Erstwhile had been the two pillars of her ascension to guildmaster. But Mazirek had turned out to be another of the dragon's minions. She could have killed the death priest herself, but she had been too afraid that without Mazirek's backing—without Bolas' backing—she'd lose the support of both the kraul and the Erstwhile and be deposed. She had known letting the situation stand would make her a servant of Bolas once again. And she allowed herself to become the dragon's minion, anyway.

Breeches prompted again: *"Jace? Jace?"*

She snapped back at him, "Jace isn't here! He's never here when you need him!"

That much was true. Jace had promised to return to Ravnica with help. To stand by her side, help her battle Bolas and save her home plane. But he had not come back. Or maybe she had left too soon.

Breeches wasn't getting the message, but Amelia and Malcolm were hearing their captain loud and clear. They pulled the drunken goblin away, with him still calling out alternately, *"Captain, Captain!"* and *"Jace? Jace?"*

Vraska was left alone at the table. Alone in the alehouse, except for a barman, endlessly wiping down his filthy counter with a filthy rag.

In the end, she had done the best she could for the Golgari, freeing her people from Bolas' last hold upon them.

So why did I continue to work for Bolas? Why did I fight Zarek?

It was a question she could not answer to her own satisfaction. Ral had done her no harm, yet she had been prepared to kill him. Perhaps in self-defense, but more likely because he was a living reminder of her treachery. Or maybe she simply needed to prove to herself that she was truly the monster that her world had always told her she was.

And Ral had been so angry, had felt so betrayed. His final lightning blast would certainly have destroyed her if she had not planeswalked away, if she had not left Ravnica behind. For good.

Because I have no place on my homeworld anymore.

She knew she could not return as the Swarm's guildmaster. Her support within the Golgari would have evaporated without the Erstwhile and kraul to back her. And she couldn't expect any help from her former allies after betraying Ral, Kaya and Hekara to Bolas.

Hekara . . .

Hekara—the last true friend she had—had died trying to save Ravnica from Bolas. From Bolas and from his hench-gorgon Vraska.

Xeddick. Hekara. It's dangerous to be a gorgon's friend, isn't it?

Besides, what if the Beacon finally summoned Jace? How could she face him after what she had done?

No. There's no place for a monster like Vraska on Ravnica . . .

EIGHTEEN

LILIANA VESS

So predictable.

Surrounded by Eternal bodyguards, Liliana was crossing the plaza to the Citadel, watching from a distance as Gideon led Jace and the others forward.

They were all stylistically so different. Even the two pyromancers, Chandra and Jaya, had little in common. The former with her massive eruptions of fire, charring two or three Eternals at once; the latter with her precision strikes of flame, taking out one at a time, but with more accuracy and at a faster rate.

Their priority was clearing the plaza, the so-called heroes evacuating the so-called innocents from the path of Bolas' (*of her*) oncoming army.

Swordplay, knife-play and fire-play. Time disruption, shields, telekinesis, illusion and sheer strength. Individual Eternals, despite their years of training on Amonkhet, stood little chance with their limited free will and limited agency against these Planeswalkers. Even against Lavinia. It helped that the Eternals also had limited instruction and supervision from Liliana. But she saw no reason to remedy that. Conquering Ravnica was Bolas' goal, not hers. She had to do just enough to honor their contract. And not a whit more.

She watched this expanded Gatewatch lift urchins into their arms—at one point Gideon was holding three—and ferry them out of harm's way. She watched them run interference for bystanders too frightened to mount any defenses of their own. She watched them destroy Eternal after Eternal. And she shook her head in pity, if not disgust.

The Gatewatch had clearly lost sight of the *big picture*. Gideon probably never comprehended it in the first place, but even Jace was completely distracted by the business of rescuing one foolish straggler at a time. They had literally done *nothing* to contain the overall threat. For the Eternals, as per the command of Bolas (*of Liliana Vess*), were already leaving the plaza and spreading out across the city. Meanwhile, more Eternals emerged from the portal every second. While the Gatewatch succeeded in rescuing individuals, they were most certainly failing at saving the city, at saving Ravnica.

And stopping Bolas?

That didn't even seem to be on the agenda anymore.

No wonder the dragon always wins. Though he's already revealed nine-tenths of his plans, Bolas still runs circles around these completely predictable fools.

How had she ever thought they stood a chance?

She found herself nodding. She had made the right call, counting on her own craft, her own wiles, to bide her time, giving her the chance to bring Nicol Bolas down. If she'd even attempted to maintain her alliance with Jace, Gideon, Chandra and the others, she'd already be dead, and they'd still be busy digging their own graves. There was no denying it. It was simply fact.

So why did she *still* feel like crying?

NINETEEN

TEYO VERADA

Teyo was exhausted. On his heaviest day of acolyte training, even during the worst diamondstorm of last summer, he had never erected so many light shields in such a short period of time.

But here he was, using his geometry over and over and over again to protect men, women, children and . . . other things—and not from forces of nature, diamond and sand, but from undead warriors—these Eternals, as Jace Beleren called them—who attacked with mindless fury. (Yet not quite mindless enough for his tastes.) Acolyte Verada chanted up a three-pointer here, a four-pointer there, using them to block sword strikes and mace blows.

Pressure?

The abbot at his most ornery had never put this much pressure on Teyo. If his shields fell, people would die. Rat would die.

I'd die!

He knew he didn't belong here. It wasn't just the danger or that this wasn't his fight or even his world. It was that he didn't feel worthy to stand among these strangers and champions. Why had he been chosen to make this journey? How many times had Abbot Barrez shaken his head over his poorest student? Once a day, at least. Any one of his fellow acolytes could do better.

By the Storm, why not one of them? Or one of the vested monks? Or the abbot himself?

Out of nowhere, Rat leaned over and said, "Aw, you're doing all right."

Swallowing hard, he nodded to her and put up another shield, a circle that expanded over his outstretched eastern vertex, giving two small elven children the cover they needed to run away from the mineral-covered—or lazotep-covered, as Gideon Jura called it—Eternal that had been chasing them. Teyo's shield held for now, blocking the Eternal from its prey, but a shield couldn't destroy these creatures.

The ghost killer Kaya did that with her glowing blades. The lightning man Ral did it with his bolts of power. Even Rat scurried right up to one Eternal after another and stabbed her little knives through their eyes, deep into whatever was left of their brains. She'd already done it four or five times. The first time, Teyo thought he'd retch, but he was even growing used to *that*.

There had been quick introductions. He had met Ral and Kaya. Jaya and Chandra. (Or was it Ral and *Jaya*, and *Kaya* and Chandra?) Jace and Gideon. Teferi and Lavinia. Ajani and Karn. Plus Teyo and Rat—though everyone seemed to ignore Rat, perhaps because she wasn't one of these Planeswalkers that, preposterous as it seemed, he himself was. Teyo had never seen anyone like either Ajani or Karn before. The former was a kind of minotaur, except with the head of a big one-eyed cat instead of a bull. The latter was a creature of solid, yet malleable, metal. These were wonders to behold, wonders to put Oasis and anything he'd ever heard of on Gobakhan to shame, yet he had barely been given time to register a bit of it. He could hear the abbot shouting: *"By the Western Cloud, child, there are shields to form!"*

There were shields to form. The Eternal smashed at his circle over and over again with a bronze flail. Teyo felt each blow all the way up his arm to the shoulder. And though each attack rocked him, he actually felt a bit relieved. There was a rhythm to the blows and a pause between each. Diamonds of the storm weren't half so polite. They might not hit quite so hard, but they came in multiples and with no interval. Plus the sand kept an acolyte from seeing anything. But now Teyo could see each swing of the flail incoming. He found he could lean into every strike, catching it just *before* the apex of the swing, dulling each blow.

"Teyonraht, push that one this way!" It was Gideon. He and most of the others thought Teyonraht was Teyo's name. (A nervous Teyo had slurred his words when introducing himself and Rat, and they had thought he was only naming himself.)

"It's just Teyo," he squeaked while attempting to obey. Creating a small circle for balance beneath his right ear, he pushed his lore through his eastern vertex to expand his lefthand shield while transforming its geometry from a circle to a four-pointer. It was a complicated move by his standards, but he managed. Succeeded. Buoyed by that victory, he tried another advanced move: Using *both* hands, he added dimension to the diamond shield and walked it forward.

Be the geometry!

The Eternal's flail bounced off the odd angle, throwing the monster off balance. Teyo leaned in and shoved. The Eternal stumbled back, and Gideon cut off its head.

"Good," Gideon barked before turning away to attack another of the creatures.

Teyo found himself smiling.

More praise than I ever got from Abbot Barrez.

Again he heard the abbot's voice in his head: *"This is no time for grinning, acolyte! One success does not a shieldmage make!"* Teyo quickly shook off the smile and turned his shield to protect Jaya's back.

Or is it Kaya?

Jace, their unacknowledged leader, shouted, "We need to summon the guilds! Bring them into the fight!"

Ral blasted another Eternal and shouted back, "I'm not sure that's possible! I can command the Izzet into the field—and maybe Kaya could do the same with the Orzhov." He glanced toward the dark-skinned woman with the halo of curly black hair, finally confirming for Teyo which Planeswalker was which.

Lavinia finished Ral's thought: "The rest of the guilds have retreated to shore up their own territories, more suspicious of one another than of Bolas."

Kaya said, "And that's not even counting the guilds that already serve Bolas. Golgari and Azorius. Maybe Gruul, too."

Teyo saw Lavinia frown at the mention of Azorius. He guessed that was her guild and briefly wondered what each guild represented.

At least with the Carpenters' Guild in Oasis, you knew what was what.

Back-to-back with Kaya as she parried blows with an Eternal, Teyo saw Rat slide in between them. She leaned over and whispered to Kaya, "Call Hekara. She'll bring the whole Cult."

Kaya stabbed her Eternal, then paused to shake her head sorrowfully. "Hekara's dead."

Ral Zarek snapped, *"Don't you think I know that!"*

For the first time since he had met her, Teyo saw Rat lose

her smile. "Hekara was my friend," she said. "She knew me. She saw me."

Teyo didn't know what to do. Pushing his geometry off onto his left hand, he reached out with his right and gave her arm a little reassuring squeeze. Or he tried to make it reassuring, anyway.

Rat responded with a sad but grateful smile.

Ral shouted, "We may have something better than the guilds. Planeswalkers."

Lavinia said, "I told them about the Beacon."

"It should summon every Planeswalker in the Multiverse to Ravnica. More are coming now. Look!"

Teyo looked toward where Ral was pointing. A burst of flames signaled the arrival of a substantial minotaur, wielding a fiery iron chain. The creature was caught off guard by his surroundings and the Eternals, and barely managed to defend himself. But soon his chain was swinging in wide arcs around him, *shattering* any Eternal that came too close.

"I think his name's Angrath," Jace said. "And there's Kiora and Tamiyo, and there's the girl from Amonkhet . . ."

"Samut," Gideon called out. "Her name's Samut."

Again Teyo turned to follow Jace's gaze. He saw four women running toward them.

"Who's the fourth?" Ral said.

"Don't know her," Jace replied.

"She's a Planeswalker."

"How can you be sure?"

"His goggles," Kaya called out from behind Teyo.

Karn said, "Let me see those," and grabbed them right off Ral's head.

"Hey, stop!" For a second it looked as if Ral was going to strike Karn with lightning.

Teyo had just enough time to wonder if that would even hurt the metal man before Karn said, "I see what you've done here." He handed the goggles back to Ral and cast some kind of spell by circling his clublike left hand in the air. Teyo watched as streams of golden light streaked off the golem's silver hand.

One of them struck Teyo right in the eyes. He was temporarily blinded, and his lore faltered, his shield fell.

"By Krokt! Warn us next time, Karn," someone shouted. Teyo wasn't sure who. But when his sight returned, he saw a golden aura surrounding every member of their group except Lavinia and Rat. He saw the same aura around the minotaur Angrath and around the four approaching women.

Karn stated, "Do not worry; it is not permanent. It will only last until sunset. But now we can all recognize the Planeswalkers as they arrive."

Teyo saw Ral frown briefly, as if unhappy his trick had been copied. But the lightning man quickly shook off the frown the way Teyo had shaken off his smile earlier.

The iron-haired Jaya said, "Not every Planeswalker is Gatewatch material, you know. And some are downright nasty."

Teyo wondered what was entailed in being "Gatewatch material"—and only then remembered he wasn't holding his own.

Guess I'm *not Gatewatch material, whatever that means.*

He chanted softly and raised a new four-pointer.

Still, the geometry's coming easier to me now, he thought with not a little surprise.

Gideon said, "You have to assume that nasty or not, most Planeswalkers won't be big fans of Nicol Bolas. We need to split up. Spread out through the city. Save as many people as we can and rally every Planeswalker we find."

Teyo scanned the group. Most nodded and called out things like, "Aye!" and "Agreed!"

All but Jace. Teyo saw his brow furrow. Though the man said nothing.

TWENTY

DACK FAYDEN

Honoring a vague notion that he should continue on to Tenth District Plaza, Dack crossed swiftly from rooftop to rooftop. He was still too far away to see what was happening there in any detail, though it seemed to him that a small army was marching out of the giant portal that had wiped out the Embassy of the Guildpact.

He heard screams below him and stopped short to look over the side of the building. He saw nothing, heard more screams, and crossed to the opposite ledge. He looked down.

A phalanx of metallic-blue warriors, glowing with violet light, was attacking the citizenry on the ground. No, not attacking. Mowing them down. Relentlessly. Mercilessly. With sword and axe and mace and their bare metallic hands. Innocents were dying.

Dack was a thief, not a fighter. But this was too much. It

smacked of the massacre of Drakeston, his home village on the plane of Fiora. Everyone had died there while Dack was offworld. And now everyone was dying directly below him.

He was descending the wall before he'd even reached the conscious decision to do so—and definitely before he had devised any conscious strategy for stopping these creatures.

By the time he dropped lithely to the ground behind the horde, he could see they were undead. That helped. Dack wasn't a necromancer, but he'd once stolen a hellblazer ring from a vampire on Dominaria. He'd long since fenced the ring to J'dashe, but not until after he'd leached and learned its spell, which he immediately turned upon a mineral-coated warrior in the phalanx's rear line. The creature started to smoke, burning from the inside out, finally bursting into flame.

It dropped to the cobblestones as a charred husk. Dack smiled. And then looked a little panicked as the entire back line of the horde turned to face him.

This is a problem.

The spell had come from a ring—which was intended to be placed on the would-be victim's finger, and thus was only designed to kill one undead thing at a time. He immediately turned its power on the closest, and it smoked and stumbled to its knees. But before the job was done, three other creatures were closing in.

Dack leapt up the wall and stuck there, just out of reach. Then an undead aven spread its wings and launched itself toward him. The kneeling warrior had burned to a crisp by that time, allowing Dack to turn the power onto the metallic-blue aven. It started smoking but still careened toward Dack, who instinctively created an illusory double on the wall five feet away. The smoking aven seemed undecided as to which Dack Fayden to attack—and wound up crashing into the stone wall halfway between the illusion and the reality. The aven caught fire as it fell, and as luck would have it, it landed on a couple more of its fellows, who burned beneath its fiery wings.

By this time, Dack had the attention of the entire phalanx. He hadn't had anything like a plan, but what he'd done had served its purpose. The civilians were gathering up the wounded—while leaving the dead where they lay—and making themselves scarce. Now all Dack had to do was make *himself* scarce.

Spears flew his way as he—and a few more of his magical doppelgängers—scurried up the side of the wall. A few spears hit their targets, bursting the illusions into blue sparks. One spear grazed his arm. It didn't break the skin, but it ripped through the expensive leather jacket he had stolen on a whim in Innistrad just the night before.

Fortunately, the phalanx had no other fliers. He dodged another spear and achieved the roof, pausing to look down. The phalanx had already forgotten him. They moved on to find their next innocent victims. Dack wanted to burn them all, but . . .

He glanced back toward the plaza. These creatures were the gods-be-damned army pouring out of the portal.

There must be hundreds of them on the streets of Ravnica already.

Much as it would have satisfied him, he knew he couldn't burn them all at a rate of one at a time. There had to be another solution, and he wasn't going to find that solution here. His original instinct had been to head for the plaza, and over the years the thief had learned to trust his instincts.

He started off across the rooftops again . . .

TWENTY-ONE

GIDEON JURA

Ajani and Gideon tore through yet another crop of Eternals, their third since splitting off from the group and leaving the plaza. It was lancers this time, so Gideon led the way, charging ahead of his companion. Eternal lances were less than eternal, snapping against his bright aura of invulnerability. Before the Eternals could drop their broken weapons and reach for their swords, Gideon and Ajani were atop them, among them. Gideon used Blackblade with abandon, slicing off heads and limbs and anything else that came within reach. Or he'd stab the Eternals through their hearts. In fact, the mystic sword seemed more inclined to the latter method of dispatch. It was a strange sensation, yet Gideon could feel Blackblade's preference along the length of his arms and all the way down his spine. In the back of his mind, he knew feeding the weapon's bloodthirsty predilections was a bad idea. He chose to ignore that voice. He could barely remember how reluctant he had been to use the Soul-Drinker, even on the unholy demon Belzenlok. He had few scruples about it now. It helped that these Eternals were already dead, that they were perversions of the great warriors of Amonkhet, forced to serve Bolas through Liliana. He felt he was doing them a favor by ending their un-lives. Yet still, in the back of his mind, he knew he wasn't releasing their souls. If they still had souls, it was not unlikely he was feeding them to the sword.

And somehow, at this moment, he just didn't care.

Gideon glanced toward Ajani. The big cat took no glory in destroying Eternals, but that didn't mean he wasn't damn good at it. Claws and teeth, backed by sinew and magic, ripped the lazotep warriors limb from limb.

Within minutes the entire crop was in pieces at the two Planeswalkers' feet. They moved on.

They were en route to Sunhome, guildhall of the Boros Legion. Gideon's plan was to engage with the Boros guildmaster, the angel Aurelia, and recruit his old friend to the cause. He knew that Boros Skyknights had been the first to engage the dragon. But suffering an early defeat, they had withdrawn to establish a perimeter.

That wasn't good enough.

Knowing the Legion's strength and righteousness, it was imperative the Boros do more than hold an arbitrary line. The Legion had to engage. It had to attack. Preferably in coordination with the growing numbers of Planeswalkers that were arriving every minute.

Case in point: Another Planeswalker materialized right in front of both of them amid a burst of ghostly green light. Female, dark skin, short hair, heavily muscled and armed with a bow, which she promptly aimed at them both.

Ajani said, "Planeswalker?" Though of course that was obvious, both from her arrival and from the arc of golden light that both could see trailing from her thanks to Karn's spell.

She hesitated, then nodded.

Ajani said, "Ever hear of the dragon Nicol Bolas?"

She said nothing, but the burning fury in her eyes told the tale.

Gideon said, "Yeah, that's how we feel. I'm Gideon. This is Ajani. Bolas is here on this plane. He thinks he's going to conquer it. We plan on killing him first. Wanna help?"

She spoke for the first time, anger rising steadily in her voice: "My name is Vivien Reid. And I don't want to help. I want to kill the dragon myself."

"As long as he ends up dead," Ajani said.

She inhaled, trying to rein in her rage. She succeeded. "As long as he ends up dead," she agreed.

"Then follow us," Gideon stated, moving past her.

Vivien and Ajani flanked him.

"I have questions," she said.

"We probably have answers," Ajani offered.

"Not now we don't!" Gideon shouted.

A squadron of flying Eternals—angels, aven, demons and drakes—had just passed overhead. Gideon took off at a sprint to catch up. His two companions were right behind him.

They turned a corner into Precinct Four's Grand Courtyard. The Eternals were strafing the place, attacking everyone within sight. Gideon tried to engage, but the fliers would swoop in and out, always staying just beyond his reach or Blackblade's.

Ajani wasn't having any better luck, but Vivien's bow was extremely effective. Every time she fired an arrow, it would pierce one airborne Eternal—and simultaneously release some kind of green glowing spirit animal, a great owl or hawk or pterodactyl, which would attack and sometimes kill a second Eternal before fading away.

"That's some bow," Ajani said.

She simply nodded and nocked another arrow.

But even with their new companion's help, the battle wasn't going well. There were just too many, and grounded as he was, Gideon felt powerless. The best he could do was gather civilians around him and use his sword to fend off that lazotep aven or this lazotep demon. But invariably, some poor straggling Ravnican, just out of his reach, would be scooped up, flown high and released to shatter against the stony ground. Gideon felt every death as a personal failure.

He looked north. Sunhome Fortress was in full view, and Gideon cursed himself for not reaching Aurelia before this attack had begun.

He needn't have bothered.

Parhelion II—the Response Garrison, the Floating Citadel, the Flying Fortress—rose above Sunhome, perfectly symmetrical, hovering overhead, a glorious sight to behold. Even the Eternals seemed to pause to soak it in. Then, from *Parhelion II*'s two great stone ramparts, the Boros deployed. Battle Angels took wing. Skyknights riding griffins descended to meet the foe.

Gideon searched the sky for Aurelia, suddenly desperate to see her again. And there she was. White feathered wings spread nearly ten feet across. Sword in one hand, spear in the other, leading the charge, barking out commands, and personally devastating the Eternal line.

It was almost a rout. Almost. Gideon ushered the six humans and two goblins he had been protecting toward the nearest building, the nearest doorway. Ajani was doing much the same with his group. Vivien was still firing off a seemingly endless stream of arrows, creating a nearly endless menagerie of spirit animals and aiding the Boros from below. The air above them rang with the sound of battle, a battle Gideon longed to join.

Careful what you wish for . . .

Just as Gideon shut the door to a café that would, for the moment, protect his eight civilians, he looked up to see a Boros legionnaire ride a pegasus toward a trio of Eternal aven. The legionnaire smote two with his sword, but the third swung its wing and knocked the man clean out of his saddle. He fell. The pegasus dived to catch her master, but he slammed headfirst into the stones. Gideon could hear the man's neck snap. A sound he was fast tiring of.

This isn't what I wanted, he told himself.

And he almost convinced himself—but truly, he wasn't going to miss this chance.

Wasting no time, Gideon ran toward the corpse, arriving simultaneously with the pegasus. He grabbed her reins and swung himself astride, giving the beast a gentle kick to guide her back into the air. He feared she would resist him, out of loyalty to her fallen rider or distaste for a strange hand. But the pegasus took to her new commander instantly, and Gideon was soon soaring upward toward the third Eternal aven. Blackblade sheared one lazotep wing right off. The undead creature fell in tight circles, smashing its thin bones against the pavement no more than a foot or two from the dead legionnaire.

Gideon pulled the pegasus around and joined the aerial battle in earnest. As with the lancers, the Eternals fell before him.

"About time you got here," a voice called out. It was Aurelia, grinning that warrior's grin of hers. The kind she only grinned in battle. She had another smile for gentler occasions, but either would have been a welcome sight to Gideon.

"Fashionably late," Gideon shouted with his own grin. He knew it was no time for smiling or quips, but he couldn't help himself. He remembered Liliana telling him once, *"No one likes a giddy Gideon, Beefslab."*

Well, no point trying to please that one anymore.

Aurelia swooped in alongside him. She nodded toward the pegasus. "You like her?"

"She's a fine mount."

"Should be. I trained her myself."

"She have a name?"

Aurelia grinned again and swooped away, calling out, "She's Gideon's Promise."

Gideon's smile broadened. He whispered, "Go, Promise, go!" The pegasus accelerated toward the dwindling enemy.

Perhaps we can turn this tide yet . . .

TWENTY-TWO

CHANDRA NALAAR

Chandra, Jaya and Lavinia were pursuing a crop (or ten) of Eternals deep into Selesnya territory. The two pyromancers would pick off a few from behind every chance they got, hoping the phalanxes would turn and fight. But the Dreadhorde ignored its losses and maintained its course. They were many and moving fast, and the three women had to run just to keep up.

Chandra was reminded that Ravnica—largely a city of tight streets and corners, of tall, heavy buildings and heavier shadows—showed different faces at every turn. The territories held by the Selesnya Conclave were open and sunny, full of green spaces and gardens, with white stone buildings, open to the air, that were often little more than shells housing yet more gardens. Selesnya was a forest of open-air cathedrals . . . or maybe an open-air cathedral of forests.

And the grandest cathedral of all was the sacred world-tree Vitu-Ghazi, which towered over all the Conclave's holdings. For ten thousand years, it had been their guildhall, with arches and terraces and chambers built into and upon it. Chandra wasn't exactly a child of nature—wasn't anything *like* a child of nature—but it still took her breath away. And the thought of Eternals scampering over its bark and roots and branches made her physically ill.

Fortunately, Vitu-Ghazi wasn't undefended. A line of Ledev Guardians—armored humans and elves, riding wolves the size of bears—met the Eternals dead-on. The clash was epic as wolves launched themselves at the Dreadhorde. But Chandra saw that the Guardians relied too much on their archers. Their arrows struck with accuracy, piercing the Eternals' lazotep coating and slowing them down *not at all.* Many of the undead creatures continued forward with five, ten, twenty arrows sticking from their chests and limbs. But that wasn't enough damage to thwart their advance.

Catching up to the horde, Chandra and Jaya began incinerating Eternals from behind. As before, they took these losses and ignored them, focusing their attack forward, pushing against the Ledev line to reach the world-tree.

Lavinia moved forward to engage, as well. But a deep voice pulled her up short: "Back, Lavinia of Azorius! You are not welcome here!" They all turned to see a powerful armored centaur, a Spearmaster of the Conclave. He was trampling an Eternal under his four hooved feet, but his focus was on Lavinia. "Take your 'friends' and go! We need no Azorius Arresters here!" he shouted at her.

"Boruvo, you fool, we're only here to help!"

Jaya hissed, "I'm not sure calling him a fool is gonna convince him."

Lavinia ignored her. "Besides, Spearmaster, I'm no longer an Arrester, no longer a member of the Senate at all!"

"And you expect me to believe that? Now who's the fool?"

"It's still you!"

"Selesnyans don't trust Azorius, especially your new Guild-master Baan."

"I don't trust Baan, either!"

Just then, a squadron of Eternal warriors riding lazotep drakes flew in, yanking Guardians off their wolves and dashing them against wood and stone. The Ledev line broke and the Dreadhorde rushed forward. Chandra thought she recognized the Eternal leading the charge: a formerly human woman named Makare, whom Chandra had met on Amonkhet. Makare had been deeply in love with a man named Genub, and Chandra briefly wondered what had happened to Genub, wondered whether he was alive or dead, wondered if he would kill the thing his love had become if he could.

Lavinia shouted at Boruvo, "Are you done holding grudges, Spearmaster? Or would you rather see Vitu-Ghazi fall?"

Boruvo grunted something indiscernible as Makare led her crops forward to chop and hack at the sacred tree itself while the drakes spat fire at its leaves and thick branches.

"Enough!" Chandra growled, heating up. "Back away, centaur!" She released a torrent of flame, starting at the back of the Eternal phalanx but rapidly moving toward the front, toward the Eternals attacking the tree.

Jaya grabbed her arm and pulled her back, warning, "We can't save the damn tree by setting fire to it!"

Chandra was about to protest. She wasn't going to burn down the world-tree.

Okay, yeah, maybe a few branches will get singed, but the drakes are doing that anyway—

Something stopped her from speaking. She couldn't put her finger on what exactly, but it felt . . . *familiar*. Instinctively, she looked up, looked around. Standing on a balcony, across a green swath from Vitu-Ghazi, was a tiny figure—a small woman—surrounded by swirling green magic. No, *bursting* with green magic. She was unmistakably Nissa Revane.

Nissa's power manifested as a green cyclone, which swirled away from her, spinning not toward the Eternals, but toward Vitu-Ghazi. The world-tree seemed to suck the cyclone in— and then the world-tree started to move. Roots ripped free of the ground, dislodging the Eternals hacking away at them; the Dreadhorde now seemed like tiny fleas as the tree rose and stood erect. Branches became arms and hands. Trunks and roots became massive and powerful legs as Vitu-Ghazi took its first steps. The sacred tree had become a living, walking and *stomping* elemental, over a hundred feet tall, with buildings and archways still attached, looking and acting like armor for this new gargantuan guardian that had entered the fray and was fast triumphing.

Makare and those around her were crushed underfoot. Drakes were slapped out of the sky into shattered fragments of lazotep by immense hands of ancient wood.

Boruvo *and* Lavinia cheered (even though Lavinia was hardly the cheering type) as Vitu-Ghazi stepped forward to crush every Eternal in her path while effortlessly flicking off any Eternal still clinging to her roots and trunk. And it was soon clear that the great elemental had only just begun its march. It strode forward toward the city center, toward the Eternal army, toward Bolas himself.

But Chandra barely noticed the towering elemental, or the chaos in its wake. Nissa Revane was her entire panorama. Chandra's eyes filled with tears, though she was already burning so hot that the tears instantly turned to steam. She watched rapt as Nissa descended, leaping lithely from balcony to terrace to balcony until she stood among them.

Boruvo and even Jaya Ballard stood in awe of her—or at least of her accomplishment.

Lavinia greeted her.

Nissa didn't reply. She looked at Chandra. Chandra looked at Nissa. Chandra swallowed. Nissa managed an embarrassed smile. Neither spoke a word.

TWENTY-THREE

RAL ZAREK

Ral knew what he *should* be doing. He should be helping Kaya and the new kid Teyo fight Eternals or rally Planeswalkers or some such. Instead, when he had told Kaya what he wanted—*needed*—to do, she had simply nodded and said, "Go."

It soothed his conscience only a little that before taking off, he had at least remembered to order Chamberlain Maree to lead the Izzet League into battle against the Dreadhorde. But the truth was that if anyone should be leading Izzet forces into battle, it should be their new guildmaster. By choosing to run a personal errand instead, he wasn't exactly demonstrating stellar leadership skills.

He didn't care. Tomik filled his every thought.

He ran a hand through his silver hair and checked his Accumulator. It was down to forty-six percent. There hadn't been a chance to recharge. He thought of summoning another lightning storm—but had neither the time nor the mystic stamina to manage it right now.

He spotted another Eternal. A platoon or phalanx or crop or whatever the bloody hell they called themselves, assuming the undead automatons bothered to call themselves anything, had split up and scattered throughout Dogsrun to kill any living soul they could find in the district.

"Hey, you!" he called out.

The Eternal turned and instantly rushed him, two axes held high to strike. He reached out his arms, his hair stood on end, and he blasted her with lightning. It felt immensely satisfying to watch her spasm, sizzle and fry.

But that was stupid. You could've taken her out with half the juice. You need to conserve.

He checked his stores again: Forty-two percent.

Idiot.

He was making his way to the apartment he shared with Tomik Vrona. They had chosen a place in Dogsrun because it was a backwater area just beginning to improve: nice but not so nice as to draw attention, and outside both Izzet and Orzhov territory, where they'd be less likely to be seen together by anyone in their respective guilds. He needn't have worried. Their "secret" apartment was apparently the worst-kept secret in all of Ravnica. Which only increased his fears now. Bolas knew of the place. And the dragon couldn't be happy that Ral had abandoned his service. If Bolas struck at Ral through Tomik . . .

There was another Eternal. This time, Ral controlled himself, using a precision strike to blow off the creature's head. It collapsed, jerking, then stilled.

He checked again: Forty-one percent.

At least I'm losing the battle at a slower pace.

A guildmage of the Izzet had no business falling in love

with the personal assistant to the heir of the Orzhov. And Ral had denied for as long as he could manage that *love* had anything to do with his relationship to Tomik. But he was past that. There was no point in maintaining that convenient fantasy. The truth was simply this: No one in his life had ever mattered to Ral as much as Tomik did now.

A block away from his destination, he turned a corner and found yet another Eternal murdering a young woman, while two male friends cowered and watched and did nothing but whimper her name: "Emmy, Emmy. No, Emmy." He blasted the Eternal and rushed past her friends, growling, "Get off the street, you idiots."

He checked: Thirty-nine percent.

A dozen or so Eternals were coming down the lane in the other direction. *Too many to mess around with.* He spread his arms wide and fired simultaneously at the Eternals on the far left and the far right. He was lucky lazotep was such a good conductor. With a little effort, he created a circuit between himself and the dozen. They squirmed and jerked like butterflies pinned to a wall until he shut the electricity off, and as one they dropped to the cobblestones, smoking.

Thirty-four percent.

He was at the front door, was actually reaching for the handle, when he heard the shriek. He whipped about and spotted an eternalized angel descending toward him from above.

He fired.

He missed.

He barely dodged out of the way. Rolling, he came to a stop, face up.

Thirty-three percent.

He felt like an overturned tortoise. The Accumulator on his back was as light as he could engineer it to be. Which meant it wasn't any heavier than it had to be. Which meant it was still damn heavy. He was used to it, had trained with it, had fought multiple battles with it, but that didn't make it any easier to recover and roll and make ready to fire again.

He managed it.

The angel descended, wearing bronze talons over its knuckles.

Ral fired again.

Missed again.

Dodged again—but not quite quickly enough. The talons of the angel's right hand shredded his leather jacket and sliced shallow gashes into his shoulder. He inhaled with a hiss—and hoped that the talons hadn't been dipped in poison.

Thirty-two percent.

The angel was swooping around for another assault. Ral spread his arms, winced and chanted softly through the pain.

He generated a virtual net of crisscrossing electricity in the air.

The angel barrel-rolled away from it, accelerated straight up and dived down on Ral's side of the net.

Twenty-seven percent.

Ral jerked his fists back toward his chest, and the lightning-net sped toward him—only slightly faster than the dread angel.

It entangled the angel's lazotep-coated wings, and the thing was done for—which didn't exactly stop it from plowing into Ral as it thrashed and died.

It was a damned good thing Ral was immune to his own electricity, as the creature took a good thirty seconds to fry. And as Ral *wasn't* immune to the heat its death was generating, he screamed as the red-hot Eternal burned through his jacket, tunic and a good percentage of his pants.

He pushed its husk off him.

Twenty-one percent.

He got to his feet as quickly as he could manage. What remaned of his clothes were in scorched tatters, and patches of his skin could use a good healing spell. But none of that mattered now.

He looked around for any more lingering Eternals and, seeing none, grabbed the door handle and entered the building.

He rushed upstairs to find Tomik, to take him in his arms.

But when he reached their apartment . . . he found it empty.

TWENTY-FOUR

KAYA

For whatever reason, the Eternals had—as far as Kaya could tell—not yet chosen to enter any buildings. Phalanxes and crops of the Dreadhorde were scouring Ravnican streets, but the citizenry was at least temporarily safe if they remained indoors. It was hardly a scenario that could be counted on to continue. It wasn't exactly a Bolas trait to knock first before creating mayhem. But the Planeswalkers would happily take whatever slight respite they could get for as long as it would last.

Thus Kaya, Teyo and Rat were fighting Eternals as they made their way through the streets, byways and alleys of the city—saving bystanders as they went. But it was easy enough to tell those rescued to find shelter somewhere, anywhere. The trio could then move on without much further concern for those left behind. Moreover, they never had to venture inside themselves, which was a small blessing. Going house-to-house, building-to-building, would have been much more dangerous and time consuming.

They were making their way toward the Orzhova, the Cathedral Opulent, to summon the forces of the Orzhov Syndicate into battle against the enemy. Since there were only three of them—and since Teyo's abilities were largely (well, almost entirely) defensive—they tried to avoid the larger contingents. But their success rate against individual Eternals or small crops was fairly spectacular.

Kaya did most of the heavy lifting when it came to the actual killing of these creatures. They seemed particularly vulnerable to her ghost daggers. And they couldn't touch her when she was incorporeal. She had to pay careful attention, of course; there was always the risk that while she was killing one, another might find its moment, but being careful was nothing new to the ghost-assassin. Neither was slaying the undead. Plus Teyo was there, watching her back.

He claimed to be a novice shieldmage, and the boy was clearly operating at the point of near-exhaustion, but he did his part, protecting their backs, their fronts, their sides. He was quick and smart and if the situation weren't half so desperate, Kaya might have been amused at the way he was constantly surprised by his own rapidly growing skills.

And Rat was no slouch. She was small and quick. *Basically well named.*

And she was talented with her own two daggers. She'd wait for her moment, then duck out from behind one of Teyo's diamond-shaped shields, dodge two or three Eternals and then stab one that hadn't seen her coming, plunging both daggers into the Eternal's eyes, deep into its brain. The creature would fall instantly, and Rat would race away before another of the Eternals even reacted to her presence.

During a brief respite, as they crossed a wide but empty

thoroughfare—empty of everything but a handful of corpses that showed the Eternals had already made their presence known here—Teyo turned to Kaya and asked, "So are we Gatewatch now?"

"I don't know," she replied. "Never heard of 'Gatewatch' before today. Not entirely clear what it is."

Rat said, "The good guys, I think."

Teyo nodded. "Ravnica's equivalent to the Shieldmage Order."

Kaya shook her head. "I don't think they're limited to Ravnica. All the members are Planeswalkers. Perhaps they're the Multiverse's equivalent of your Order."

Rat shrugged. "So . . . the good guys."

"Yes."

"Then I think both of you *are* Gatewatch," Rat said. "Not me, of course. I'm not a 'walker." A thought seemed to strike the young girl, and she laughed, saying, "I'm not Gatewatch; I'm Gateless. That's the Rat. Always Gateless."

"You've killed more Eternals than I have," Teyo said.

"That's such a sweet thing to say, Teyo. You're such a sweet boy. Isn't he a sweet boy, Mistress Kaya?"

"Very sweet," Kaya said while scanning for the next crop or phalanx.

Teyo frowned slightly, saying to Rat, "I'm pretty sure I'm older than you."

She ignored him. "That's why I adopted him first thing."

"I—"

She turned back to cut him off. "How's that cut? I can't even see a scar."

Thrown by her rapid changes of subject, Teyo rubbed his head where the cut used to be. "Fine, I guess. I can't feel it at all."

"It was nice of Mr. Goldmane to heal it for you. It's not like he wasn't busy with other things, what with all the Eternals he was killing left and right. Wasn't it nice of Mr. Goldmane, Mistress Kaya?"

"Very nice," Kaya said while nodding absently, thinking about how exactly she might convince the Orzhov to join the fight. She had already seen Maree lead the Izzet into the field, fighting side by side with bio-warriors of the Simic Combine, under the command of a merfolk hybrid named Vorel. It was a rare moment of unity between guilds. And it was a pleasant surprise to see the Simic step out from behind their walls of isolation to help.

Now if only I can get my own guild to do as much.

She was dubious about her chance of success but realized there was no chance at all if she didn't get to Orzhova.

She could now see the spiky spires and the (literally) flying buttresses of the Cathedral Opulent looming above other closer, shorter structures. Anxious to finally get there, Kaya raced down a side street—practically an alley—that seemed a more direct route, running diagonally between two tall buildings. Rat grabbed Teyo's hand and followed.

A hundred yards in, Rat said, "I don't think we want to go this way."

"We do if it'll get us to the Orzhova faster."

"It's a dead end."

Kaya stopped short. She turned to face Rat and said, "You might have mentioned that sooner."

"You looked so confident. I thought maybe you knew about a secret passage. I mean there are a lot of secret passages through Ravnica. *A lot.* And I pretty much know all of them—or most of them, anyway. But I figured that Guildmaster Kaya might know one or two I don't, right?"

"Rat, I've been guildmaster for a matter of weeks. I've only been on Ravnica for a matter of months. I barely know this city any better than Teyo here."

"I only arrived this morning," Teyo said rather needlessly.

"I know that," Kaya growled.

Rat's head bobbed. "Right, right. So from now on, the native navigates. This way."

Still holding Teyo's hand, she pulled him back the way they came. He let himself be dragged away. Kaya followed, feeling both angry and silly at the same time.

Why was I in the lead?

"Okay," Rat said, "maybe back the other way."

"Why?" Kaya asked a split second before she knew the reason. A crop of Eternals was entering the mouth of the alley twenty feet ahead. Too many for them to fight in this enclosed space. The creatures spotted the trio and instantly charged after them. Kaya, Rat and Teyo turned and ran.

Kaya shouted, "You said this was a dead end!"

"It is!"

"Then where are we running to?"

"There's a door to a speakeasy at the end of the alley. It won't get us to the cathedral, but if we get inside maybe the creepies will forget about us."

It seemed as good a solution as any.

The Eternals were fast, but they weren't running for their lives. Rat, Teyo and Kaya beat them to the end of the alley and the heavy iron door. Finally releasing Teyo's hand, Rat tried the door handle. It was locked. She banged on the portal with both fists. There was no answer. She knelt and said, "It's okay. I can pick the lock."

"So can I," Kaya said, staring at the advancing Eternals, "but I don't think there's time."

"I'll buy the time," Teyo stated. He began chanting and formed a largish diamond shield of white light to separate them from their pursuers mere seconds before the crush of Eternals smashed into it. Teyo grunted painfully but maintained the shield, even expanded it into a rectangle that spanned the width of the alleyway so that none of the creatures could slip around it.

"I didn't know you could do that," Rat said over her shoulder while working the lock.

"Neither did I. Never done it before. But I can use the alley walls to substitute for the geometry. It's like leaning in."

"If you say so."

He didn't respond. Kaya was close enough to see the beads of perspiration forming on the boy's forehead and cheeks. He chanted under his breath, his lips stretched tight and nearly white. The Eternals slammed their weapons against his shield relentlessly, and he seemed to feel every blow. She wondered how long he could hold out under the strain.

Something clicked softly. "Got it," Rat said, standing. She grabbed the door handle. It still wouldn't budge. "It's unlocked! Must be bolted from the inside!"

"Leave it to me," Kaya said. She ghosted through the door.

But on the other side, the news wasn't good. A heavy iron bar had been placed across the door—with large padlocks at either end. Kaya was fairly confident she could pick both locks—but not necessarily fast enough to get the two kids inside before Teyo's shield failed.

I could leave them behind.

She barely knew either of them. She hadn't known they existed before today. Kaya was an assassin and a Planeswalker, constantly on the move, constantly leaving people, even worlds, behind. She wasn't exactly the type to make lasting bonds. Friends, she well knew, were a liability in her line of work.

I should leave them behind.

But I won't.

She ghosted her head back through the door and said, "I'll get it open, but you need to hold out a bit longer."

Teyo, eyes squinched shut, nodded once but said nothing. He was no longer chanting. Just gritting his teeth and leaning toward his shield with both hands, as a lazotep minotaur head-butted it over and over, while the rest of the Eternals smashed maces against it or the butts of their sickle-shaped swords. White light flashed at every impact. It wasn't going to hold.

Recognizing the danger, Kaya ghosted her body back into the alley. She drew her daggers and reached inward, pulling on the many Orzhov contracts she controlled as its guildmaster, pulling against their resistance in order to *summon* the full strength and numbers of her exalted position, the inherent *power* of it, to this location. She knew that many of the highest-ranking members of the Syndicate considered her an interloper (which she was)—one who'd released many a poor soul from crushing debt (which she had)—and would love to delay answering her call just long enough for her to perish (which she just might). She couldn't count on them arriving in time or even releasing the raw power it would take for her to blow out all these Eternals.

Fortunately, help came from another quarter. From behind the crop, Kaya heard shouts and whoops and hoots. She didn't understand, but she saw Rat smile and put a reassuring hand on Teyo's shoulder. "Just a few more seconds," she said to him. "It'll be all right."

Gruul warriors—male and female—attacked the Eternals from behind, axes chopping through lazotep. Tusks piercing. Hammers raining down. One particularly burly human with long dark hair smashed two Eternal heads together with enough force to shatter their skulls into lazotep and bone fragments.

The Eternals instantly forgot the trio and turned toward their new foes. Teyo slumped, dropping his shield. Rat stood over him protectively with her daggers out.

Brandishing her long knives, Kaya began attacking the Eternals from behind.

A young callow grinning Gruul warrior cut off an Eternal's head with a long weighted scythe. She could see a golden trail of energy leaching off him and heading skyward in the general direction of the Beacon. He was a Planeswalker.

He glanced over at her and cackled out, "You must be Guildmaster Kaya, the almighty ghost-assassin. Lucky for you, Domri Rade was here, enjoying the bloody chaos!"

"You're Rade?"

He looked immediately insulted: "'Course I'm Rade! Who else?"

Kaya had heard of Domri Rade, new guildmaster of the Gruul Clans. His predecessor, the cyclops Borborygmos, had lost face with the Clans by agreeing to join Ral's attempt to unite the guilds. When that had blown up in everyone's face— *when Vraska blew it up*—the cyclops was out of a job and Rade was in. But Kaya had never actually seen Domri before.

How had this arrogant little snot—Planeswalker or not— managed to rise up among the brutal Gruul to even be in a position *to take command?*

She suspected him of being another Bolas pawn. Yet here he was killing Eternals and—thankfully—saving her ass.

"I'm grateful," she forced herself to say.

"Damn right you are!" he responded, quite pleased with himself. By this time, most of the Eternals were in pieces on the ground. Domri snorted and shouted to his warriors, "Okay, mates, fun's over here. Let's find us some more!"

They started to head back up the alley, Domri leading the way and the burly dark-haired warrior taking up the rear. Problematically, one of the Eternals wasn't quite dead enough. It was missing an arm, but that didn't seem to trouble it much, and it leapt to its feet with a sword in hand, prepared to stab it into the burly man's back.

Teyo reacted first, reaching out a hand and launching a small but solid sphere of white light at the back of the creature's head. It impacted hard, and the Eternal stumbled briefly, making just enough noise to alert Burly to the danger. The big man turned in time to see Teyo hit the Eternal with another sphere.

Then Kaya was upon the Eternal, stabbing up into its guts with both her knives. The Eternal was dying—but didn't seem to know it yet. It was still swinging its sword at Burly.

Suddenly Rat was riding the Eternal's shoulders. She stabbed her daggers down into its eyes and deep into its skull. It collapsed under her.

Burly frowned. With some reluctance, he grunted thanks to both Kaya and Teyo while ignoring Rat completely. Then he turned and trotted off to catch up to his fellow Gruul.

"Who was that?" Teyo asked.

Rat shrugged. "The big guy? That's Gan Shokta. My father."

TWENTY-FIVE

JACE BELEREN

Only Jace, Karn and Teferi had remained on the plaza to stem the tide of Eternals marching through the Planar Bridge. Per Gideon's command, the rest of the dozen or so Planeswalkers whom they'd already identified had spread out across the city, some—like Zarek and that Kaya woman—to attempt once more to rally the guilds, the rest to identify and recruit new Planeswalkers as they arrived. And *all* to slay as many Eternals as they could find.

And they would slay a lot, Jace knew. But there was considerable distance between *"a lot"* and *"enough"* when more and more of the Dreadhorde continued to emerge from Amonkhet.

The Gatewatch's mission to Amonkhet had been an unmitigated disaster, a devastating horror. Yet Jace had not realized how little of the actual horror he and his companions had witnessed. The number of Eternals they had seen that day was

clearly only a fraction of Bolas' true army. Moreover, the massacre of Amonkhet's populace had resulted in corpses already
repurposed into yet more lazotep warriors. Such was the fate
promised for the peoples of Ravnica.

Still, that can't be all there is to this.

If all Bolas wanted was to conquer Ravnica—even if that in
and of itself was merely a step toward creating an even larger
Dreadhorde to use against Dominaria or Innistrad or . . . the
entire Multiverse—then the dragon's plans were too complicated by far. Why bring and activate the Immortal Sun, thus
forcing your greatest potential enemies to stay here and fight?
Wouldn't he prefer a clear field? And could it really be a coin-
cidence that Niv-Mizzet's Beacon was summoning Planeswalkers for the Sun to trap here?

No.

Jace would lay odds that Niv and Zarek had somehow been
manipulated by Bolas into creating and activating the Beacon. The Beacon and Sun in combination were a huge piece of
this puzzle. This wasn't just a trap for the tattered remnants of
the Gatewatch.

This is a trap for every damn Planeswalker in the Multiverse.

Jace *knew* that with as much certainty as he knew anything.

*But the final piece is still missing. The trap is set. How and
when will it be sprung?*

Teferi strained to slow time around the Planar Bridge, to
slow the advance of the Eternals and to slow their reaction
times. Jace created illusions as close to the portal as possible
to set the Eternals against one another and create a traffic
jam right in front of its gaping maw. Karn was ideally posi-
tioned to crush as many lazotep-covered skulls as he could
manage from among the Eternals that passed through the
spells of Teferi and Jace. Among the three of them, it was an

effective strategy. But it wasn't enough. It was a finger in a dike, with Eternal waters pouring and spurting out around the sides.

Using a version of Lavinia's telescopic spell, Jace glanced over at Nicol Bolas on his throne. Despite the illusions of invisibility that Jace was using to hide himself, Karn and Teferi from the Eternals, he felt certain Bolas knew they were there.

And he just doesn't care. In fact, he may actually be happy about it.

Still using the spell, Jace glanced over at Liliana Vess. He made a cursory attempt to read her mind, but there was too much psychic noise from the Onakke spirits that possessed the Chain Veil she wore. Plus Bolas was probably blocking any attempts to read, reach or influence his pawn.

Jace was incensed at Liliana. And yet he pitied her also. She had given up true friendship by siding with Bolas. And there might be no one in the Multiverse who needed a true friend as much as Liliana Vess.

Gideon had come to trust and rely on her, to *believe* in her. Chandra had loved her as a sister. And Jace . . .

Did I love her?

Once, maybe. Liliana had used and manipulated Jace at every turn. She had treated him like a plaything—or a tool.

In every sense of the word.

But that didn't change the fact that he had once had true feelings for her. Or, if he was being honest, that he *still* had feelings for her. He was no longer *in love* with her, no longer infatuated with the smoky mysteries of that temptress Liliana Vess.

But damnit, I do still care *about her!*

And he couldn't shake the notion that he had failed her, too. That *somehow* there must have been *some way* to reach her, to touch her, to draw this infamous dark necromancer into the light. He knew she had reached out to him, that even while attempting to manipulate him she had tried in her halting, wounded way to make a real connection with Jace Beleren. And he knew with certainty that at one or two key moments, he had rejected that connection.

She deserved it after the crap she pulled.

But she deserved better from him, as well.

Of course, she wasn't the only one he had failed. The list was long and began with the ten guilds of Ravnica.

Hell, not just the guilds.

He could now put every living being on Ravnica on that list. Jace had never truly embraced being the Living Guildpact, but he certainly missed that power now. Ral and Lavinia had explained what went wrong in their attempt to unite the guilds and give Niv-Mizzet the power to destroy Bolas. And Jace had wanted to be furious at their hubris, but there was plenty of blame to go around. If the Living Guildpact had been here, doing his damn job, then Niv and Ral's efforts might never have been necessary.

Worse, if Jace hadn't done what he'd done to Vraska, hadn't wiped her mind of all true knowledge of Bolas' evil, she might not have destroyed any hope for a guild alliance. If he had come to Ravnica when he had promised and restored her memory *as* he had promised, she might still be here, fighting by his side, backed by the might of ten united guilds and the full mystic power of the Living Guildpact.

All that's on me, he thought.

I miss her, he thought.

Through all this *thinking,* Jace maintained his invisibility, Karn's invisibility, Teferi's invisibility and the illusions at the mouth of the portal that made every Eternal think every other Eternal was a living being and potential victim. It was a bit of a strain but not exactly the most difficult spellcasting he'd ever attempted. Not even close.

I should be doing more.

I should be taking charge.

Jace had allowed Gideon, with his natural and uncompromised moral authority (not to mention all his natural and uncompromised charisma), to issue his commands and scatter their troops. A part of Jace—well, really, *all* of Jace—had known it was too slapdash a solution. It was typical Gideon, well meaning and direct and almost entirely without any true attempt at forethought. Gideon Jura fought symptoms with no thought of how to cure the underlying disease. Which hadn't stopped Jace from saying absolutely *nothing* in dissent.

Why? So I could complain about it later like always?

He didn't want to be *that Jace* anymore.

His time with Vraska on Ixalan had changed him, for the better he believed. He didn't want to be a poor man's Liliana, playing games, solving puzzles, and manipulating his friends into taking on the responsibilities he refused to truly shoulder or embrace.

By finally being able to see his true potential through Vraska's golden eyes, he had thought he'd found another way. But outside her influence, he had quickly reverted to old habits.

I don't have to be Gideon's sniping second. I don't have to be Liliana's pouting ex. I can face the challenge of this day and become—

Suddenly a war cry from above roused Jace from his internal monologue and rote illusion-casting.

The voice was familiar, and even before Jace looked skyward he knew it signaled the return of Gideon Jura. He was riding a pegasus, of all things.

Look at him. Gideon was born to ride a damn flying horse!

Gideon wasn't alone. Flanking him were Ajani Goldmane and a female armed with an impressive bow, both riding griffins. Their three golden auras, marking them as Planeswalkers, soared behind them like aether contrails.

Then came the Boros guildmaster, the angel Aurelia, leading a squadron of Boros angels and Skyknights. And moving in slowly behind them all was the Boros Sky Fortress, *Parhelion II.*

Jace sent a quick telepathic message to Gideon *not* to attack right at the mouth of the portal, where his and Teferi's magics were still having their effect. It wouldn't help to have the Boros forces slowed by Teferi's time field or thrown into disarray by Jace's illusions. And there were plenty of Eternals left to fight beyond the Planar Bridge.

Gideon signaled Aurelia with one hand: a few brief military gestures that somehow instantly related all salient knowledge.

A soldier's telepathy, Jace thought ruefully.

Aurelia signaled back to her Skyknights. They swooped in to fight Eternal fliers that Karn could never reach. They descended to strafe lazotep warriors with arrows and spears.

This is actually going very well.

Employing the telescopic spell again, Jace glanced at Liliana Vess, her expression hidden by the Veil. Nothing in her posture had changed, however, which was a little troubling.

Jace glanced at Nicol Bolas. Nothing in his expression or posture had altered in the slightest. And that was *more* than a little troubling.

What am I missing?

He reached out with his mind. But it was his ears that registered something first. He gradually became aware of a slow, deep pounding beat. As it got louder, the ground began to shake in concert.

What now? Is this it? Is this Bolas' endgame?

Jace looked toward the portal, but it wasn't the source of the disturbance. And by this time, he wasn't the only one who had noticed it.

Karn shouted, "It's coming from behind us!"

Yes, it was.

Jace turned just as a mighty green elemental appeared above the buildings, stepping around a marble tower and stepping over a limestone hotel, stomping toward the source of the action.

Is that . . . Vitu-Ghazi?

Jace focused the telescopic spell on the tiny figures riding the elemental's branches and columns.

Is that Chandra? Jaya? Lavinia?

Is that Nissa Revane?

Golden light flowed off his former Gatewatch ally. Despite telling him she wouldn't, Nissa had returned, had allowed the Beacon to summon her to Ravnica, had joined the battle by their side.

He gently touched her mind: *Thank you* was all he said.

She responded with the psychic equivalent of her measured smile. It washed over his mind like a summer rain. Jace felt an immense flood of relief. Then felt the need to test it.

He glanced toward Liliana Vess. Still no change.

Damn.

He glanced toward Nicol Bolas. The dragon was sitting up in his chair, smoke pouring out of his mouth.

It's working!

They had moved the dragon. Surprised him, at least. He might join the fight at any moment, so Jace sent out a warning message to Nissa, Karn, Teferi, Gideon, Ajani, Aurelia and Lavinia. He didn't include the new Planeswalker, the archer. He didn't know her and didn't know how she'd react to the telepathic intrusion.

Aurelia made a wide sweep with her arm. The *Parhelion II* turned toward Bolas, its mystic cannon ready to fire—but waiting for the signal.

Nissa didn't wait. She made no military gestures, issued no

signals. None were necessary. The massive tree elemental turned. Not toward Bolas himself, but toward the obelisk in the center of the plaza and the Bolas statue upon it. It was an eyesore and a symbol of Bolas' contempt for them all.

Vitu-Ghazi reached toward the great column and wrapped its two trunklike hands around it. Mighty wooden sinews pulled. Marble cracked, the pillar shifted on its base, and as Vitu-Ghazi stepped back, obelisk and statue came crashing down. The noise was simply spectacular.

So was the sight of it all.

And so was the reaction. The cheer from the Boros forces rang through the plaza, as if Bolas himself had been toppled. Ravnicans who had been hiding inside the surrounding buildings, peering through windows with fear at the Dreadhorde, threw those windows open and joined the cheering. Some even came outside—though the danger was far from over.

And as if they had come from other worlds to help with the celebration, Jace saw two, three, no, four new Planeswalkers that he did not recognize materialize in the plaza, trailing the telltale golden light of Karn's spell.

Jace watched as Vitu-Ghazi turned back toward the Planar Bridge and began crushing Eternals underfoot. Jace quickly removed the invisibility spells hiding himself, Karn and Teferi.

We don't need to be accidentally squashed.

Jace heard the flapping of wings, and Gideon's pegasus landed beside him. Its master didn't dismount but leaned down over his mount and exchanged a grin with the grinning Jace. "The tide has turned," Gideon said.

Jace nodded. He knew this was a huge moment. Bolas hadn't been defeated, but something like hope was in the air.

Vitu-Ghazi paused briefly to lower Nissa, Chandra, Jaya and Lavinia to the ground beside Jace, Gideon and the pegasus. Gideon slipped down off his saddle to hug Nissa. Jace couldn't help shaking his head. They all knew that Nissa didn't particularly like being hugged. But she seemed to at least appreciate the sentiment.

Hell, even Lavinia's smiling. Maybe. I think that's a smile. Well, at any rate, she's not frowning.

He said to her wryly, "I bet the guilds'll join the fight now."

She replied with a deadpan "Everyone wants to be on the winning side."

Jace kept one eye on Bolas. Smoke huffed from his jaws and nostrils. But he still made no move to join the battle.

Once again, Jace became gradually aware of another deep pounding beat. Smiling, he turned to Nissa.

Gideon said what Jace was thinking: "You woke another one?"

But Nissa was staring at the portal, and she wasn't smiling.

Jace glanced back at Nicol Bolas. He was.

The pounding footsteps were coming from the Planar Bridge. And then she emerged, ducking her head, as she exited the portal: Bontu—Amonkhet's immense God of Ambition, who had been killed by Bolas during an hour of pure devastation, when that plane had fallen. Only now she had been resurrected as a lazotep-covered God-Eternal. And she wasn't alone. Kefnet, God of Knowledge followed. Then Oketra, God of Order. And finally, Rhonas, God of Strength. All dead. All Eternal. All as big as Vitu-Ghazi.

The God-Eternals advanced. The *Parhelion II* fired its cannon, but to little effect, and was forced into retreat.

Vitu-Ghazi strode forward to meet these new opponents— only to be rocked by a blow from Bontu.

On the ground, Nissa seemed to feel the blow as if she herself had been struck. She doubled over as Chandra and Gideon both rushed to her side to support her.

The four dead gods quickly surrounded the elemental. They

beat Vitu-Ghazi. Rhonas tore out one of its arms. Nissa screamed . . . and relinquished her control. The elemental collapsed, inert.

Rather hopelessly, Gideon asked Nissa, *"Do* you have another one?"

Jace watched her shake her head no and collapse into Gideon's arms.

TWENTY-SIX

TEYO VERADA

The three of them still hadn't achieved the cathedral, but they were no longer alone. Teyo, Rat and Kaya were now in the company of an increasing number of Domri Rade's Gruul warriors, including Rat's father Gan Shokta, plus shamans, druids, an ogre and a couple of bipedal lizard-women that Rat called viashino. During a battle against another Eternal phalanx, they had also been joined by what Rat called "terraformers, super-soldiers and merfolk" of the Simic Combine, led by "Biomancer" Vorel; and by Izzet "mech-mages"—human, goblin, and blue-skinned vedalken—led by Chamberlain Maree. A second battle had added two more Planeswalkers to their ranks: a merfolk woman named Kiora from a world called Zendikar, and a young human woman named Samut from Amonkhet, which was apparently the source of the Eternal threat.

Samut fought with a fury and a passion Teyo had never

seen before. She seemed to know the names of every single one of her lazotep foes, grimly saying, "You are free, Eknet. You are free, Temmet. You are free, Neit," as she slew each one.

Teyo had come to realize that Gobakhan—with its diamondstorms and monks, its humans, dwarves and djinn—was a rather tame world relative not just to Ravnica, but to every other plane that every other Planeswalker hailed from. He no longer felt overwhelmed by this. He was so far beyond the concept of being overwhelmed that the remarkable, the astounding, the sensational washed over him like the unending wheel of the sky, leaving him in a permanent state of awed wonder, to which he was simply growing accustomed.

This seemed to amuse Rat to no end: "You've never seen merfolk before?"

"We don't have much water on Gobakhan."

"You've never seen a vedalken?"

"I know people with black skin, brown skin, tawny skin and tan skin, but I've never seen anyone with blue skin before."

"You've never seen a viashino?"

"Maybe some of our lizards grow up to be viashino?"

She laughed at every answer. It was a lovely sound, like precious water, flowing from a miraculous plum faucet. He knew she was teasing him, and he had always hated being teased by the other acolytes—but with Rat, he somehow didn't mind.

"Ever seen a rat before?"

"I've seen many rats on Gobakhan. None like you."

She laughed again and punched him in the arm. (Not gently, either.)

If anything, the one bit of strangeness most curious to Teyo Verada was the schism between father and daughter. Gan Shokta refused to even look at his daughter, let alone speak to her, let alone thank her for saving his life. Araithia Shokta would steal the occasional glance at her father, but she made no attempt to confront him, reach out to him or communicate with him in any way. Teyo, an orphan, longed to ask why, longed to know the history behind their sad divide, but though she seemed to take this snubbing with uncommon composure, he could tell that beneath the surface it caused his new friend substantial pain. Maybe he *would* ask her sometime, if they survived long enough to ever have a private moment.

At *this* moment, they were in the midst of yet another battle against yet another crop of Eternals. The Dreadhorde had the high ground atop a cobblestoned hill, and Vorel shouted a command to take the invaders out.

The Izzet leader Maree was about to object to taking orders from the Simic biomancer, but before she could speak, Rade scornfully told Vorel he could take his orders and shove them someplace Teyo thought was anatomically impossible.

Rade nevertheless led his troops uphill, shouting, "C'mon, mates! We don't need these lab rats teaching us how to knock heads!"

Teyo glanced at Maree, who had clearly decided she'd rather be Vorel's ally than Domri Rade's peer.

So the Gruul, Simic and Izzet stormed the hill, accompanied by Teyo, Rat, Kaya and Kiora. Teyo looked around for Samut and realized she was already up there, killing Eternals: "You are free, Haq. You are free, Kawit."

Just as Teyo reached the summit, two women suddenly materialized within arm's reach of him. Karn's spell instantly identified both as Planeswalkers with golden auras trailing into the sky—in case the materializing hadn't been enough of a clue. Both of these Planeswalkers had warm brown skin. Otherwise, they could hardly have looked less alike. One— whom he later learned was named Huatli—was armored and armed, with a long tightly braided black ponytail emerging from beneath her helm. She was short but powerfully muscled with searching eyes and a determined mouth. The other—later introduced as Saheeli Rai—had on a long swirling dress, decorated with plentiful gold filigree. She was taller and wore her hair in swirls atop her head, which made her seem taller still. She was lithe and graceful with curious eyes and a smiling mouth.

Despite their differences, they were clearly friends. Attempting to size up the situation, they exchanged a quick glance but stood there doing nothing, perhaps unsure which side they should be on. Teyo inadvertently answered their unspoken question by throwing up some small bit of geometry to block an axe thrown by one of the Eternals that might otherwise have split the taller girl's skull.

She thanked him, as did the shorter girl on behalf of her friend.

Glancing the newcomers' way, Rat scurried past them to attack another Eternal. They paid her no mind, and Rat returned the favor.

Teyo increased the size of his four-pointer to protect all three of them.

"Might we ask what's going on?" asked Saheeli.

"Or where we are?" asked Huatli.

"You're on Ravnica. I just arrived here myself. I've been a Planeswalker for all of four hours, so I'm probably not the best person to fill you in, but we're all fighting these undead monsters. They're invaders to this plane, attacking and killing everyone they can. They're called Eternals, and they work for an evil dragon named Bolas. That's the short version. Rat could explain it better."

Saheeli asked, "Invaders? Are they all Planeswalkers?"

"No. They came—well, really, they're still coming—through something called a 'Planar Bridge.' It's a big portal. Like a window to another world."

Saheeli's mouth became a straight line. Her eyes became

slits. She said coldly, "I know what it is." She reached into a small purse at her side and drew something out. It seemed to be a little ball of spun gold. But it quickly spooled open, transforming into a kind of golden clockwork hummingbird, which hovered before her face. She nodded once. The bird nodded back.

Then it shot straight up into the air, flying over Teyo's shield. At high speed it flew right through the forehead of one Eternal, emerging out the back of its skull. The Eternal staggered and dropped. But the bird never slowed. It repeated the process on another Eternal and another.

Huatli had drawn a short curved weapon, the likes of which Teyo had never seen before. She nodded to him. He didn't understand but nodded back. It seemed the polite thing to do.

"Let me out from behind this," she said curtly.

Teyo nodded again, slightly embarrassed. His four-pointer reduced down to three points, covering only Saheeli and himself. Teyo was briefly distracted by the fact that he had achieved that tidy little bit of shieldmagery without chanting anything. He wasn't quite sure when he had stopped chanting, but he'd been creating geometry without words for some time now without noticing it.

He smiled grimly: *The abbot would not approve.*

Huatli, meanwhile, was taking quite well to the killing of Eternals.

The battle was not without casualties. The Gruul ogre had rushed in too far ahead of his fellows. Though he crushed five or six lazotep skulls with his stone hammer, the Eternals eventually swarmed over him, dragged him down and stabbed him about thirty times. A Simic shaman took a moment too long to cast her spell and wound up beheaded. The fallen head did manage to speak the last few necessary words before expiring, and the creature who had killed her exploded in a shower of lazotep and goop.

Despite these horrific setbacks, the battle was over a few minutes later. They had won, and not a single Eternal remained alive or undead. As the small crowd of heroes caught their collective breaths, Teyo heard a remote but earsplitting *CRACK*, like heat lightning in the middle of the Western Cloud. They all turned, and from their vantage atop the hill they could see four immense Eternals towering over the distant Tenth District Plaza.

Rat said, "Whoa. Big."

Samut cursed.

Kaya asked, "What are they?"

"They were our gods," Samut said bitterly. "But Bolas killed them or had them killed. Now they are his. His God-Eternals."

For the first time in hours, Teyo remembered what "overwhelmed" felt like.

The entire group watched in silence as the four God-Eternals tore at an equally large tree elemental and brought it low.

The silence was broken by Domri Rade . . . *who cheered:* "Woohoo! Ya see that! That was Vitu-Ghazi they trashed! Krokt, they taught those Selesnya droops a lesson!"

Two or three of his men nodded or grunted their agreement. The rest of the assembly stared at him in stunned disbelief.

Rade said, "Gruul, we're fighting on the wrong side! This dragon's shaking things up! He'll tear the guilds down! He'll tear Ravnica down! Isn't that what we've always wanted? When the guilds fall, chaos reigns, and when chaos reigns, the Gruul will rule! Ya hear? We're joining the dragon!"

Gan Shokta stared at Domri before speaking in a barely controlled whisper. "Rade, you'd serve that master?"

"Partner, mate, not serve!"

"You don't know the difference, boy. You're no clan leader. You're a follower. I'm going back to Borborygmos."

Rade seemed stunned. The big man scowled down at him, then turned and walked away, departing—once again—without a glance toward Rat.

Teyo looked at her; as usual, she simply shrugged, apparently finding his lack of concern for her to be quite normal.

Domri Rade pouted for a moment then called out, "Forget Gan Shokta. He's an old droop, too! This is our moment, ya see?"

Kaya said, "You're a fool, Rade. Bolas doesn't keep faith with those he *chooses* to bargain with. Do you truly believe you can win his favor unbidden?"

But Domri ignored her, leading his warriors downhill toward the Plaza, calling out to the dragon as he went: "Help's on the way, dragon! We'll knock 'em all down together!"

Kaya looked angry enough to follow and drag him back.

But another crop of Eternals was coming up the other side of the hill. With a collective sigh, they all prepared for another fight.

TWENTY-SEVEN

DACK FAYDEN

Dack Fayden stood on a rooftop that looked down on Tenth District Plaza. But Dack Fayden was currently looking up.

He had achieved his current vantage point in time for a front-row seat to the hope-filled arrival of a walking, living Vitu-Ghazi and had watched with a grim smile as the elemental—which he had previously thought of as an extra-fancy tree house—smashed the lazotep infestation underfoot.

Now his smile had vanished, leaving only grimness behind. Gods of some alien plane had come through the portal and all but taken Vitu-Ghazi apart. In any case, they had most certainly taken the elemental down. Dack himself had once saved the world-tree from a different kind of threat, but now soldiers and heroes and powerful mages, on the ground and in the air, could do nothing against four such titans, not to mention the *immense dragon* enthroned atop the new pyramid Citadel that towered over the rest of the plaza. Even the Boros Legion's Flying Fortress was retreating.

Dack knew he should do the same.

But before he could, he witnessed the noisy arrival of the Gruul. They were led by Domri Rade, which surprised Dack a bit.

Since when does Domri carry any weight among the Clans?

Dack knew Rade, knew Rade was a Planeswalker and knew Rade had a chip on his shoulder about a mile wide. Domri had always wanted to lead but had never had the clout—literal or figurative—to enforce his would-be authority.

Now suddenly this little general seems to be in charge? Everything's upside down. What the hell happened while I was on Innistrad?

Domri and the Gruul were making a beeline toward the Citadel and the dragon. Dack could just barely hear Rade shouting something but couldn't make out what. Using a fairly simple spell cribbed off the Loxodon Horn (also long since fenced with J'dashe), Dack summoned Rade's rantings to his ears.

"Hey, dragon! I am Domri Rade, champion and master of all the Gruul Clans! You and I should be talkin', mate! How 'bout I swear allegiance to you and yours! We'll burn Ravnica to the ground!"

Dack felt the heat rising in his chest and up his face.

Domri's swearing allegiance to the monster who clearly brought this hell to this world?

Dack was almost furious enough to go after Rade himself. The thief might not be up to challenging a dragon, but it would give him a lot of gods-be-damned satisfaction to take out this traitor to Ravnica.

Before he could even admit to himself that he wasn't going to brave the plaza for that dubious goal, something caught the corner of his eye. Some kind of magical flare rose up from the dragon's throne.

A signal, maybe? Or a spell?

Prior to anything else happening, Dack was overcome by a sudden sense of dread that chilled his bones and all but paralyzed his movement. This was worse than the lights that had summoned him back to Ravnica from Innistrad. This was primal, an elder magic, like nothing he had ever encountered before.

He watched as lazotep warriors quickly surrounded Domri Rade and the Gruul. The Gruul were fearsome. Everyone knew that. But their slaughter was swift and merciless. Dack was no longer sure how he'd managed to take down four of these creatures just minutes ago.

Had they been holding back? Or is their new prowess part of the ancient magic just unleashed?

One of the creatures, a tall warrior with an impressive helm, grabbed Rade, apparently by digging his fingers deep into Domri's chest. Rade screamed loud enough to require no Loxodon Horn to hear. And it only got worse from there. Dack watched in horror as the helmed warrior reached not simply into Domri's chest but into his very soul, *harvesting* a bright core of mana that Dack somehow *knew* was Rade's Spark, the part of him that made him a Planeswalker. The part of him that made him Domri Rade. Domri begged for mercy in a whisper that echoed in the thief's ears.

There would be no mercy. Domri was rapidly drained, of Spark, of soul, of life, even of moisture. His Spark gone, what remained was a dead husk of what had once been Domri Rade. The helmed warrior released the husk. It fell to the ground with a sickening thud.

The Eternal drew Domri's Spark inside its lazotep frame. But such a nexus of pure magical energy was too much for the undead thing. Immediately the warrior incinerated from within. And Rade's Spark flew skyward toward . . . the dragon.

Dack's attention had been riveted on Domri and the helmed warrior, but with both now dead, husk and ashes, he began to scan the plaza floor. Lazotep warriors were grabbing hold of other individuals—each a Planeswalker, he belatedly realized—and harvesting their Sparks while reducing them to dry lifeless shells. In turn, the Planeswalkers' Sparks fried their murderers, and the spell drew the energy up into the air as purple light that sought out the dragon. Soon the air was full of Sparks arcing toward the Citadel and the evil enthroned upon it.

This can't be happening. You can't steal a Planeswalker's Spark! You can't!

Except that's exactly what the dragon was doing. Over and over and over. Dack could almost perceive the beast growing in stature with every new acquisition.

Dack swallowed hard.

Well, that's sure not how Dack Fayden wants to die. Maybe fighting undead harvesters and dragons isn't *a job for a thief.*

He tried to Planeswalk away—only to discover he couldn't. This had never happened before. In a panicked fury, he pushed on the walls of space and found himself under Innistrad's moon for perhaps a second—before being ripped back to Ravnica in daylight. No, not ripped.

Stretched.

It felt as if he'd been stretched like a rubber band that had reached the limit of its elasticity and had *snapped* back to its origin. He tried one last time but couldn't even manage to dematerialize. Something had bound him to the Ravnican plane.

No, no, no, no, no, no, no . . .

He was trapped. And he feared that more than the harvesting itself.

He discovered he was crying.

Gods-damnit, Dack, suck it up!

He wiped his eyes. There wasn't much he could do about any of this now. And as the metallic-blue gods led the dragon's horde forward, Dack turned and fled the plaza . . .

ACT TWO

TWENTY-EIGHT

NICOL BOLAS

The entire plan had been flawless. Every contingency addressed. Every potential threat neutralized. Bolas had been doing this kind of thing for millennia, yet even he was impressed. Over his endless lifetime, Nicol Bolas had seen everything. And still, the Elderspell was a sight to behold.

He sat on his throne, watching the sky darken. Watching the Sparks fly up from dead and drained Planeswalkers, from undead and burned-out Eternals. He watched their arcing progress through the air as they approached the Citadel.

The mystic vortex swirled above him as Spark after Spark sailed up to flow down through that vortex and into the Spirit-Gem floating between his horns.

And with each Spark came power. Power rushing into the Gem. Power rushing into Nicol Bolas. Not simply the powers of Planeswalkers, not when they were combined like this. No. This was the power of a god. And not just *any* god.

He had known power like this before. Power that belonged to Bolas before the Great Mending. He was only taking back what was rightfully his.

Let them all die. Once I was immortal. Not simply long-lived like all dragons, but truly, unendingly immortal. With power beyond measure. I was a god. What mended Dominaria and the Multiverse unraveled that power. Stole away my birthright. What was the Mending of Dominaria next to that crime? What was the healing of the Multiverse next to that evil? So let them all die. Their gains had been at my expense, so I will take back what was taken from me—with interest. They deserve everything they get this day. I will be a true, unending immortal again. But I shall not settle for being a mere god again. Now I will be the God. We *will be the Multiverse's sole GOD. Its GOD-EMPEROR. And We will become that . . . today.*

Smoke puffed from His nostrils. He remembered His torturous earliest days on Dominaria, when He and His twin, Ugin, had hatched from a single egg-stone as the so-called *runts* of the Ur-Dragon's litter. He'd shown His dragon siblings and cousins—blunt objects all—what sort of runt they were tormenting, ignoring, underestimating in Nicol Bolas. He'd shown them all. Now He was showing Ravnica. And very soon, He'd show the Multiverse.

At the threshold of His thoughts, Bolas heard that mouse Jace Beleren squeak out a telepathic order to retreat. And BOLAS, the GOD-EMPEROR, chuckled.

TWENTY-NINE

KAYA

Five short sentences. They rang through Kaya's mind, and though she could hardly disagree with their message or import, she found the sensation—the intrusion—*extremely* disagreeable. It smacked too much of Bolas. Distracted—even a little pained—by the mild psychic assault, Kaya was nearly split in two by the axe of an Eternal minotaur.

Rat pulled her out of the way.

"Did you hear that?" a confused Teyo asked.

Rat piped up: "Hear what?" as she jumped on the minotaur's back and—unable to reach around its horns to stab it through the eye sockets—plunged her two daggers into its neck.

Kaya nodded to Teyo.

The telepathic call had found them fighting side by side with four other Planeswalkers—Samut, Kiora, Saheeli,

Huatli—whom Kaya had only just met. Plus Vorel and his Simic warriors, and Maree and her Izzet.

Rat's attack did little damage to the Eternal—but it got the creature's attention. Rat jumped off and scurried away behind one of Teyo's shields.

The confused minotaur looked around for its attacker—long enough for Kaya to use her own spectral daggers to send the Eternal to its eternal rest.

Suddenly a large viashino with lime-green skin materialized right in front of her, surrounded by the distinct gold aura of a Planeswalker.

He had just enough time to hiss, "What izzzz thissss?" before a female Eternal grabbed him from behind. The Eternal used no weapon on the lizard-man. Nevertheless, what followed was pure horror: The Eternal seemed to draw the viashino's Spark right out of his back, absorbing the golden aura until the Spark glowed from within the Eternal, like cracks in her lazotep shell. The viashino fell, a lifeless husk, as the Eternal burst into flames from the inside out. The Planeswalker's Spark rocketed into the air, shooting like a comet toward Tenth District Plaza. The burned-out Eternal collapsed atop the dead lizard, as if they had been lovers, perishing together in a final embrace.

Kaya couldn't move, couldn't breathe.

It was extremely fortunate that Huatli was killing the last Eternal of this particular crop, because in that moment Kaya was incapable of defending herself.

The five sentences repeated. A voice-without-a-voice in their minds that somehow sounded like the echo of Jace Beleren, mind-mage, former Living Guildpact and Gatewatch leader: *Retreat! We need a plan. Contact every Planeswalker and guildmaster you can find. Meet us at the Azorius Senate. Now.*

THIRTY

JACE BELEREN

Jace had been close enough to that fool Rade to see the Eternal draw out Spark, aura, soul and—to add insult to injury—all moisture from the young Planeswalker's body. He had seen the desiccated husk of Domri Rade fall; he had seen the Eternal combust from the inside; and he had seen Rade's Spark soar in a fiery blaze up to the dragon Nicol Bolas.

Immediately Jace understood the danger they were all in. He sent out a telepathic command, stringing it along Karn's spell of identification, telling every Planeswalker to retreat, regroup and reconvene.

But Jace, invisible to the Eternals, lingered to study the horror that followed as Planeswalker after Planeswalker died. He made himself stay. Forced himself to watch, to learn. It was necessary. But it was also his punishment. All the

Planeswalkers who fell owed their deaths to the . . . *tardiness* of one Jace Beleren.

If only I had returned sooner, had used the power of the Living Guildpact before the leylines were disrupted, none of this would be happening.

So Jace Beleren would suffer through, to gain whatever knowledge he could, to stop this as soon as he could.

A few things became clear.

Karn hadn't been the only one to cast a spell of recognition. When Bolas' spell was activated, it granted the Eternals the same ability to distinguish Planeswalkers from the crowd. The Eternals still killed "civilians" (whether actual civilians or Boros warriors) with swords and axes and their bare hands. But they didn't need to work that hard to kill a Planeswalker. All an Eternal needed to do was establish a solid grip, and the Planeswalker's Spark was harvested.

Jace didn't even know the names of the fallen. Hadn't even realized there *were* this many Planeswalkers *to* fall.

Who was that vedalken? Who was that tall elven woman? Who was that four-armed ogre or that very short green-haired man or that ancient crone or that frightened teenager or . . . ?

All Jace knew was that—between Ral's Beacon calling them, and the Immortal Sun preventing them from departing for the safety of another plane—some of the most powerful souls in the Multiverse were being chewed up by Eternals and spit out to feed Nicol Bolas.

Jace could practically see Bolas growing more and more godlike before his eyes. This was the dragon's true goal all along. To lure not just the Gatewatch—but every damned (*very damned*) Planeswalker in the Multiverse to Ravnica for harvesting. Conquering Ravnica was just another lure.

Jace stole a telescopic glance at Liliana. But it revealed nothing. She hadn't moved. If she was even the slightest bit affected by what she was seeing—what she was participating in—she gave no indication behind her Veil. He attempted to reach out to her mind, but Bolas' smirking consciousness blocked his path.

Jace turned to watch Gideon. He was, perhaps, the only Planeswalker in the Multiverse with some level of immunity to the Eternals' harvesting. Many an Eternal tried, but Gideon focused the white aura of his invulnerability toward all oncomers, allowing none to get a grip on his actual person. Those that did try were soon cleaved or stabbed or beheaded by Blackblade.

But the Dreadhorde kept coming. And coming. And coming.

Gideon couldn't share his immunity with others, but he could and did put his own body between them and any of the Eternals that came within range, as he and Ajani and Aurelia and the rest fought their way out of the plaza en route to Jace's designated rendezvous at the Azorius Senate House.

Lavinia did her share, as well. She had very quickly sized up the new reality. Realizing that Planeswalkers were now *more* vulnerable than the planesbound, she became a bodyguard to the people who were supposed to have been Ravnica's saviors.

And Teferi? He threw out waves of time distortion to slow their lazotep pursuers. Probably saved more people than all the rest put together.

And Jace Beleren?

He stood there. Protected by illusion and invisibility. The Eternals still seemed to rely on their sense of sight, even to identify a Planeswalker. One after another, they marched and charged right past him. By masking his Spark's golden light and creating the illusion of a decorative pillar where he stood, he didn't even have to dodge. The Eternals simply parted around him, to either side.

Did I think Gideon was the only Planeswalker with immu-

nity to Bolas' machinations? Well, that wasn't quite true. Jace Beleren's power makes him immune, too.

The saving grace, as he saw it, was that Gideon's power could stand up to anything, whereas Jace's abilities were a drop in the bucket compared with Bolas'. The dragon was the superior mind-mage. For now he was too busy gorging himself on the Sparks of those with no defense. Eventually, however, Nicol Bolas would turn his mind to Jace's. He'd rip apart Jace's fragile sentience, dissolve Jace's illusions and leave him vulnerable to any Eternal's touch.

Good. If I can't stop this, I don't deserve to survive.

Now, finally, Jace understood Gideon's warnings against hubris. Jace's own hubris horrified him even more than the carnage. Every clue had been revealed. He had known about the Planar Bridge, about the Eternals, about the Immortal Sun, about Ravnica. And he had led everyone he knew and loved to their doom.

This blood is on my *hands. I* have *to stop this. I have to.*

Better get to it then.

By this time the plaza had been cleared of everyone except Jace, Bolas, Liliana, the Eternals and a seemingly infinite quantity of corpses. There was nothing more to be done here. Nothing more to be learned here.

Jace forced himself to turn and walk away. He was needed at the Senate House . . .

THIRTY-ONE

RAL ZAREK

R al understood—with the Embassy of the Guildpact in ruins—why Jace had spontaneously chosen the Azorius Senate House as his fallback position, but the mind-mage could hardly have chosen worse.

The stone corpse of Isperia had not been moved from the chamber. Probably *couldn't* be moved without sacrilegiously breaking off a wing or two. So Vraska's victim now stood as an unmistakable reminder of shattered guild alliances.

Ral had sent Izzet representatives to every other guild, summoning their guildmasters to this emergency conference, yet despite the obvious external threat from Bolas and the Eternals, the response was less than encouraging.

He ran through a mental checklist of all ten guilds:

The Izzet League.

Ral, himself, was there, of course, as guildmaster of the Izzet, and although they had never exactly been great fans of each other, Chamberlain Maree was by his side. She, at least, understood that this was no time for petty infighting. Besides, they had one last plan, one last gift, one last wild stab at salvation from the late, great Firemind to pitch to the other guilds.

The Orzhov Syndicate.

Ral was relieved when Guildmaster Kaya arrived safely to represent the Orzhov, though how much loyalty she actually commanded within the Syndicate was debatable.

"Not even debatable," she said. "Teyo and Rat and I finally made it to the Cathedral Opulent. The pontiffs and oligarchs hardly deigned to put up a façade of cooperation. When they said they would stand behind me, their words translated to '*far* behind me.' They could barely stifle their contempt long enough to pay me lip service."

"See, that's where you went wrong," he said ruefully. "You should have known they were stingy about paying *anything*, lip service included."

She ignored the crack. "It didn't help when they learned Jace was no longer the Living Guildpact. It made my cold reception all the chillier. No open defiance, mind you. And an honor guard was sent here along with me. But you'll notice no other nobles from my guild came to Beleren's little party."

"So basically Orzhov's out?"

"Largely. But a giant named Bilagru approached me and seemed more inclined to listen than the old-guard Orzhov. So I made the point that the guild's debts would be difficult to collect if the dragon's Eternals murdered every debtor on Ravnica along with every debtor's offspring—not to mention every member of the Syndicate. He nodded down at me and grumbled that ghosts and spirits have run things inside the Orzhova for so long, everyone forgets that most of the collecting's done by the living. Then he promised to take his enforcers out into the streets to protect Orzhov investments."

"I can't believe appealing to his rationality worked."

"It probably helped that when the pontiffs began to object, I threatened to forgive every single Obzedat debt in one fell swoop. In the Cathedral Opulent, rationality only goes so far, but greed can cover the final distance."

The Simic Combine.

There was Vorel, stating he'd been authorized by Prime Speaker Vannifar to represent the Simic. Ral nodded and expressed his appreciation, not admitting that he hadn't even known Vannifar *was* prime speaker.

When the hell was Zegana ousted?

Ral had heard of Vannifar. She was an elf—or if the rumors were true, a former elf now mutated by Simic biomancers—but he knew precious little else about her. He'd certainly never met her.

Vorel, perhaps noticing Ral's discomfort, reassured the Izzet guildmaster that Vannifar was a fighter, one who had been preparing for war since long before the dragon was known to be a threat. "Under our current circumstances," Vorel stated conclusively, "Vannifar is a much better choice for prime speaker than Zegana."

Ral allowed himself to be reassured and made the conscious decision *not* to ask the obvious question: *Who exactly was Vannifar preparing to war with before Bolas?*

The Boros Legion.

That old reliable angel of order and combat, Guildmaster Aurelia of the Boros, was of course one of the first to arrive. She gazed angrily from Isperia to Ral, as if blaming the storm mage for the sphinx's death. Which was fine, since he pretty much blamed himself.

Well, myself and Vraska, anyway.

But Aurelia was nothing if not pragmatic. And she was the strongest ally they had among the guilds.

House Dimir.

Ral also took it for granted that Dimir's shapeshifting Guildmaster Lazav was present in one form or another. As head of the spy guild, Lazav loved to play his little games. But so far he had been surprisingly cooperative. Not trustworthy, but cooperative.

And like Aurelia, Lazav was a pragmatist. Bolas was bad for business.

Who'll hire an assassin if everyone on your world is already dead?

The Cult of Rakdos. The Golgari Swarm. The Gruul Clans.

After the death of his emissary Hekara, the demon Rakdos and his Cult declined to send a representative. And with Vraska gone and Domri dead, the Golgari and the Gruul had both been left in complete disarray with no guildmasters at all.

The Selesnya Conclave.

More disappointing, the Conclave remained entrenched within its territory, sending no one.

Ral had hoped that the near-complete destruction of Vitu-Ghazi would have made them see the light. But it had the opposite effect. They were digging in their roots and showing no leaves.

The Azorius Senate.

Azorius Guildmaster Dovin Baan—who, like Vraska, had been working as a shill for Bolas—unsurprisingly demurred from attending this meeting, even in his own seat of power. He was, by all accounts, holed up in one of New Prahv's three towers, keeping that damn Immortal Sun safe for Bolas.

Lavinia and a few other old-school Azorius *were* in attendance, having disavowed Baan and his leadership, but truth be told none held any real authority. The bylaws of the Azorius stated that Baan was guildmaster. And the Azorius did love their bylaws.

All told, that meant only Izzet, Simic and Boros had truly committed their forces to the cause. Worse still, fifty percent of the guilds weren't even officially represented at Beleren's conference.

And that's the real problem.

Ral and Maree compared notes. He asked, "Fifty percent won't be enough, no matter how we squeeze this, will it?"

She looked grim. "I'm sorry, Guildmaster. But even *ninety* percent won't be enough. We tried to play percentages last time. When Niv-Mizzet was alive, we might have been able to get by with eight of ten guilds. With him dead . . ."

"With the Firemind dead, the only option is Operation Desperation."

"And for that to succeed, you'll need cooperation from *ten* of ten guilds. There can be no exceptions."

Ral nodded. Her assessment matched his calculations. It was the first time he'd *ever* hoped Maree might have better math.

Ten of ten. There can be no exceptions.

"Bring me options," Ral said, knowing full well there were none.

But Maree nodded curtly and dutifully walked away to find some.

Seeing Ral alone, Kaya approached. The boy Teyo kept a respectable distance but remained in her orbit. He was muttering to himself, looking awkward and unsure of his place. Ral had an uncharacteristic moment of sympathy for the kid.

His first Planeswalk and he walks into this.

Not unkindly, Kaya asked, "Did you and Tomik meet up?"

He shook his head. "I was hoping you'd had some word of him." Tomik was Orzhov, and Ral knew he liked Kaya.

So maybe . . .

She shook her head, too. "He wasn't at the cathedral. Or if he was, he wasn't showing his face. He still works for Teysa Karlov, who very much wants to be guildmaster in my place. She may have him sequestered with her. In fact, given the lack of cooperation I'm receiving, the thought's crossed my mind that Teysa's attempting to strike a new alliance with the dragon behind my back. I don't think Tomik would willingly participate in that, but it might explain his absence."

It was an upsetting thought, but it beat the possible alternative, Ral's greatest fear: that the Eternals had found Tomik before Ral, Kaya *or* Teysa.

Kaya took Ral's hand and squeezed it. She whispered, "I'm sure he's all right." But she sounded more hopeful than convincing . . .

THIRTY-TWO

GIDEON JURA

Gideon and Jace—*two sides,* Gideon thought, *of the same scarred coin*—stood in front of Isperia, former guild-master, champion and lawbringer of the Azorius Senate, current ornamental statue of the Azorius Senate Hall.

"Sphinxes," Jace muttered with no little disgust. "Bigger troublemakers than dragons."

Gideon raised an eyebrow.

Catching Gideon's unspoken question, Jace seemed to actually struggle before belatedly and begrudgingly offering up a slight correction: "Than all dragons but one."

"Didn't know you had such a problem with sphinxes."

"Alhammarret. Azor. Isperia. Never met a sphinx who wasn't an arrogant, aloof pain in my—"

"Whoa, whoa, whoa. Isperia did a lot of good on Ravnica.

In fact, if Vraska hadn't turned her to stone, we might be in much better—"

"Vraska's vengeance was well earned! You don't know her. You don't know her story." Jace's voice was a low, quiet whisper, but his passion on this topic was obvious.

"I suppose I don't."

Who is Vraska to Jace? More than just an assassin, obviously. First Liliana, now Isperia's killer. Jace sure can pick 'em.

Gideon put a calming hand on Jace's shoulder. Jace looked about ready to knock it off.

Instead he took a deep breath and even managed a weak smile.

"We need to get to it," Gideon said. "The longer we're sequestered in here, the more damage Bolas and his army can do out there. So take a minute. Compose your thoughts, and then let's call this meeting to order."

Jace nodded and started to walk away—before pausing to say, "You're a good friend, Gideon. I don't know if I've ever told you that."

Gideon chuckled. "I'm *quite* sure you haven't. But to be fair, I don't think I've ever said it to you, either. I'm a little bit ashamed you beat me to it . . . old friend."

Jace smiled again. He looked simultaneously boyish and old. Gideon was aware Jace often created an illusion of a younger, more vigorous Jace Beleren to present to his audience. He didn't think the mind-mage was using that trick today. Jace was clearly fitter than Gideon had ever seen him before. Certainly fitter than he had been when they last fought together on Amonkhet. He looked leaner, more sinewy, tougher. He even had some color in his cheeks. But the guilt in the telemancer's heart showed his age on his face. And the weight of many worlds clearly rested on Jace Beleren's slightly stooped shoulders. It was a sensation Gideon Jura knew intimately. It was a sensation Gideon Jura was keenly aware of experiencing that very second.

He straightened his back in defiance of that sensation and turned to scan the crowd.

The guilds could be better represented, but the Planeswalker head count is somewhat encouraging.

The entire Gatewatch—himself, Jace, Chandra Nalaar, Ajani Goldmane, Teferi, and, *thank the gods,* Nissa Revane—was present (sans Liliana Vess, obviously). Plus there were Jaya, Karn, Samut, Kiora, Tamiyo, Saheeli Rai, Kaya, Ral Zarek, the archer Vivien Reid and the new kid Teyo Verada. Gideon even saw the demon-man Ob Nixilis, incongruously and contemptuously making his way through a crowd that parted to avoid him. Gideon hated Nixilis' guts, but when your opponent was Bolas, beggars could not be choosers. Of course, that didn't mean Gideon wouldn't be watching his back when the demon was around. It wasn't that long ago that Ob Nixilis had sworn eternal vengeance against the Gatewatch.

Apparently, eternal vengeance can wait as long as Bolas' Eternals are around.

There were new faces, too—or new to him, anyway. Gideon being Gideon, he had already traversed the Senate House, making an effort to introduce himself to and familiarize himself with as many as possible . . .

Dack Fayden was a somewhat nervous type constantly looking over his shoulder.

And not just, Gideon felt certain, *because we're all up against impossible odds.*

His instincts about Dack were confirmed when Aurelia spotted Fayden and started toward him, growling, "That little thief has the gall to show his—"

Gideon put a hand on her shoulder and whispered, "Now's not the time."

Aurelia swallowed her anger and nodded.

Gideon moved on, introducing himself in succession to Narset, a former Oiutai monk; to Huatli, the warrior-poet of Ixalan; to the lithomancer Nahiri, a white-skinned kor of Zendikar, who was scanning the crowd as if looking for someone specific; to Mu Yanling and Jiang Yanggu, who had both planeswalked to Ravnica from a place they called the Plane of Mountains and Seas, bringing Jiang's dog Mowu with them.

"How did you cross the Blind Eternities with a dog?" Gideon asked, perplexed.

"He's a magic dog," Jiang said with a shrug, as if that explained everything.

"He's made of rock," Mu offered, as if that somehow sufficiently filled in the gap.

Gideon met the minotaur Angrath, who was laughing boisterously with a woman of Innistrad named Arlinn Kord, who had a pleasant smile that showed all her white teeth. Angrath surreptitiously sniffed at the woman every time she turned to speak to Gideon. When she moved off, Angrath cocked his head in Arlinn's direction and said knowingly, "Werewolf."

That was all he'd had time to meet before his little conference with Jace in front of the late and somewhat unlamented Isperia. But thanks to Karn's spell, Gideon saw at least thirty or forty more Planeswalkers gathered in the Senate House. Together they amounted to an unprecedented force of stunning magical power, and Gideon was frankly chomping at the bit to get back out there with them all, to fight the Eternals and end Bolas' threat once and for all.

But he was instantly reminded of the first occasion when he'd sought to battle a god. Once upon a time, Gideon Jura had been a young man—or really, a boy—of Theros named Kytheon Iora. In those days, he ran with a tight crew he called his Irregulars: Drasus, Epikos, Olexo and Zenon. When Kytheon had foolishly attacked the god Erebos, that attack was effortlessly turned back on the Irregulars. Kytheon's aura of invulnerability protected him, but his four best friends in the world—the four best friends a man or boy could have on *any* world—had all perished. Kytheon Iora had sworn he would never again risk losing those he cared about to his own arrogance, his own hubris. To be honest, it was an oath Gideon Jura had not always kept, but he silently renewed it now.

Jace returned, nodding to Gideon, who nodded back. It was time. With Gideon at his side, Jace stepped to the front of the dais and spoke, his voice magically enhanced to fill the hall: "Let's bring this to order, please. We need a plan."

Ob Nixilis' rumbling voice, which required no magic to be heard, dripped venomous sarcasm: "And you two strategic geniuses think you can come up with one?"

A low buzz rose up from those assembled in response. No one seemed to like Nixilis, but it was clear that plenty shared his opinion. Jace's tenure as the Living Guildpact had been . . . haphazard, at best, and his leadership wasn't universally recognized, even by his closest allies. Even, from time to time, by Gideon, if truth be told.

But the fastest way back into the breach was through Jace Beleren, so Gideon stepped forward and exercised his own deep, loud voice to good effect. "There'll be time for everyone to have their say. But standing around muttering to each other isn't getting us anywhere. So how about we stow the snide comments for the time being and *listen*?"

There was another, briefer, collective murmur, but that was followed by an uneasy silence that Jace took advantage of: "We face a number of problems. Five to be exact. Some of you are aware of them all, but many have only just arrived and haven't had the time or opportunity to get your heads around the whole picture. So let me offer some clarity now."

Jace looked at Ral Zarek, who shrugged, knowing what Jace was about to say: "One. The Izzet's Beacon is luring more and more unsuspecting Planeswalkers to Ravnica, where they run the risk of becoming more fuel for Bolas' power."

As if to illustrate the point, another Planeswalker materialized in the middle of the crowd amid a flash of turquoise light. He was an older man with turquoise eyes and a carefully trimmed white beard. Gideon whispered to Jace, "Could you have planned *that* any better?"

Jace sighed heavily and went on: "We need to disable the Beacon, which is under Izzet and Azorius guard at the aptly named Beacon Tower. Getting there may be difficult, but the real problem is the machine itself, which was built with safeguards to prevent Bolas from shutting it off."

"Brilliant," Angrath snorted. "How you fools love to play right into the dragon's claws."

From across the room, Huatli countered, "As you did by coming here?"

Angrath snorted again—but said nothing more. Gideon decided he liked Huatli.

Jace jumped back in: "Problem Number Two. The Immortal Sun. Once the Beacon summons the Planeswalkers to Ravnica, the Sun keeps them trapped here. So like the Beacon, we need to shut the Sun down. It's not far from here in one of the New Prahv towers, being guarded by the new Azorius guildmaster, Dovin Baan, whom we've learned is a pawn of Nicol Bolas."

Gideon shot a quick glance at Chandra. Her eyes flared with fire, but she was keeping her temper for the time being.

"Three. The Planar Bridge from Amonkhet allows a seemingly endless army of Eternals to enter Ravnica and slay the Planeswalkers lured by the Beacon and held by the Sun. We have to shut it down, and we can only do that from the Amonkhet side."

Samut called out: "But how? I've tried to planeswalk back to Amonkhet, but the Immortal Sun—"

Jace held up a hand, saying, "I know. And we can't wait for Problem Two to be solved. So we'll utilize the portal itself . . . to travel to Amonkhet."

Jaya scoffed, "*While* the Eternals march out of it? That sounds like a great plan for committing suicide."

Jace actually smiled. "There are steps we could take to make it only a mediocre plan for committing suicide."

"I'm game," Samut said.

Jace thanked her with another smile. But turning to Gideon, that smile quickly faded. When he spoke again, it was as if he was addressing his next point to Gideon alone, as if he half expected Gideon to challenge him on it. "Problem Four. Liliana Vess. She's clearly controlling the Eternals for Bolas. We need to make sure she can't do that anymore. Ever."

Gideon found himself wincing at Liliana's inclusion on Jace's list, though he could hardly deny the necessity for that inclusion. He said nothing.

Jace exhaled and continued: "Finally, Five. Bolas, himself. Though if we can't deal with the first four problems, the fifth is pretty damn hopeless."

Another general murmur echoed that sense of hopelessness.

Gideon stepped forward, "There's a sixth problem. We have a responsibility to protect ordinary Ravnicans, since none would be in danger if not for Bolas' hunger for Planeswalker Sparks."

Jace put a hand on Gideon's shoulder. "That's right. Six problems."

"Seven." It was Zarek. "We need to reconstitute the Guildpact by uniting all ten guilds. Without the Guildpact's combined might, we'll never truly stand a chance against the dragon."

"You tried that already," Vorel shouted, pointing at Isperia's remains. "Look at the result. Isperia's dead, and today you couldn't even assemble representatives from all ten guilds during Ravnica's greatest moment of crisis. What in the world makes you think you can reconstitute the Guildpact now?"

Another wave of murmurs threatened to become a roar, but Ral enhanced his own voice with magic. It buzzed and crackled as he spoke over the crowd: "I'm honestly not sure we can. But we must try. The Firemind left behind one final stratagem. It's a bit desperate—"

"More desperate than his last stratagem?" Vorel asked, incredulously.

"Yes, in fact," Ral acknowledged. "But it might be our only chance."

"All right," Jace said, before the crowd could splinter into argumentative factions. "Seven goals—or six, anyway, if we subtract going after Bolas for the time being. I propose splitting up our collective forces to achieve these goals."

The murmuring began again, and the tenor of it seemed less than enthusiastic. One Planeswalker, an aven Gideon didn't recognize, said, "What if we surrendered? Throw ourselves on the mercy of Bolas."

Dack Fayden turned to the aven and said, "I don't think Bolas is the merciful type. You probably didn't see it, but a Planeswalker named Domri Rade attempted to switch sides and join up with the dragon. He was the first Planeswalker harvested."

Another Planeswalker, a woman with jet-black hair and glowing green eyes, said, "Then let's go into hiding. At some point, Bolas himself will want to planeswalk. He'll have Baan shut off the Immortal Sun, and we'll *all* be able to escape."

Vorel, growing angrier by the minute, shouted: "*That's your solution? Hide and abandon Ravnica to the Eternals* and the dragon? You Planeswalkers are the reason Bolas is here, the reason Ravnica's in danger." He turned to the aven. "But I like your idea. The surrender—an enforced surrender, if necessary—of your type would allow Bolas to eat his fill. Once sated, he'll leave Ravnica alone."

A bitter Vivien Reid said, "Bolas is never sated."

An equally bitter Samut concurred. "That is truth."

"Fine," Vorel said. "But let me make this clear. If you Planeswalkers hide while Ravnica burns, you'll find little help or succor from its citizens and guilds."

By this time, Gideon was lost in thought. Vorel's argument that Planeswalkers were to blame for Ravnica's plight resonated with him. He found himself turning to Jace and saying, "Maybe we *should* surrender."

Jace looked exasperated.

Samut stepped forward. "Gideon Jura, it is noble of you to wish to make such a sacrifice. But do not forget the fate of Amonkhet." She turned to face the crowd. "Bolas left my world completely desolated. Even now, a mere handful of survivors struggle to defeat the monsters that Nicol Bolas left behind to slaughter us. Bolas will not leave Ravnica as he found it."

"Bolas. Is. Never. Sated," Vivien repeated. "There is literally nothing left of my world Skalla thanks to him. The dragon *must* die."

There were shouts of accord at this—followed by shouts of discord. It was all falling apart.

Lavinia spoke up. "One thing is certain. If we fight among ourselves, we stand no chance against Bolas."

Aurelia shouted, "Hear, hear! The fate of Amonkhet and Skalla must not befall Ravnica."

Gideon, who still seemed less than convinced, noticed Ajani studying him from the side. The leonin held out his hand.

Gideon took it and stepped down off the dais. Ajani said, "Remember your Oath. The Oath of the Gatewatch. Surrender is not the answer, my friend. The archer is right, and you know it. One such as Bolas will never be sated, nor will he show mercy. He views such things as weakness, and any attempt at such an appeal would only enhance his appetites."

Gideon took this in and nodded. Then he ventured into the crowd, moving among the Planeswalkers and guilded alike. He spoke, and they listened. "Now that you all know of our existence, you could be forgiven for believing our ability to traverse worlds is an excuse for a Planeswalker to always run from a fight. But we of the Gatewatch took an Oath to always stay. It was a choice we had the luxury to make, and somehow we thought that choice made us superior. Now we stand among you with that choice taken from us. Now the choice is whether or not to fight."

He unsheathed his sword with intentional dramatic effect, raising it high into the air. "This is Blackblade. It has already slain one Elder Dragon, and it can destroy Bolas, as well. With it, I hereby vow to take back this world. Who's with me?"

His speech roused the crowd, which began to gather around him. Ajani put a hand on his shoulder, and that simple gesture acted as a trigger. From every side, Planeswalkers and Ravnicans reached out their hands to touch Gideon or—if farther back—to touch someone touching Gideon, as if to draw strength from the strength of his conviction.

It was a galvanizing moment. Gideon felt Jace Beleren's touch within his mind. He had remained up on the dais and was smiling down at Gideon Jura.

I don't know how you do it, Jace thought to him. *But I'm damn glad you do.*

Just then a small Izzet goblin entered from a balcony door, shouting, "Masters, one a' them God-Eternals approaches, at the head of a small army of those undead creepies! You got about eleven and a half minutes 'fore they's here!"

Gideon chuckled.

"Eleven and a half minutes." One had to admire Izzet precision.

Jace called out, "Six challenges! Six missions! We need volunteers! Now!"

THIRTY-THREE

KAYA

Finding a workaround for recruiting the Azorius Senate and its collaborating guildmaster, Dovin Baan, was assigned to other volunteers. But as guildmaster of the Orzhov Syndicate, Kaya was tasked with bringing the other four wayward guilds—the Golgari Swarm, the Cult of Rakdos, the Gruul Clans and the Selesnya Conclave—to the table for Ral Zarek's Operation Desperation. It was thought that, as an outsider, she'd bring less baggage—and suspicion—to the endeavor than Zarek himself, but that as a guildmaster, she'd still bring enough prestige to be granted the necessary audiences.

Her first stop would be Selesnya, which she hoped would be the easiest of the four. Kaya had three companions, Teyo and Rat (both of whom had somehow become her entourage) and the nearly silent elf, Nissa Revane, whom Jace hoped would get on well with Emmara Tandris, the elven leader and acting guildmaster of Selesnya.

Unfortunately, getting to Tandris was proving difficult. To begin with, they had to avoid the Dreadhorde being led by the God-Eternal Rhonas, which was just minutes shy of overrunning a packed Senate House and taking out all of Bolas' significant opposition in one fell swoop.

Fortunately, Rat was able to lead them down passages, alleyways and shortcuts that the invaders from Amonkhet couldn't know.

Revane seemed impressed enough with the speed of their progress to actually say a few words. "You know the city well," she said to Rat while avoiding all eye contact with the girl, in her somewhat distracted way.

As they approached Selesnya territories, they did run into a single—and unavoidable—crop of Eternals, searching for victims. Teyo put up a shield and from behind it, Revane asked permission of an old birch tree, which promptly grew multiple branches that spiked through the brains of each and every lazotep skull before retracting. The attack was so swift that two or three seconds passed before the Eternals began dropping to the ground, well and truly dead.

They found the Conclave well and truly fortified. And unwelcoming. A long line of Ledev Guardians and Sagittar Archers blocked their path. No one would let them pass, even on their diplomatic mission. Revane, in particular, seemed to be public enemy number one for having awakened Vitu-Ghazi, resulting in the elemental's departure, dismemberment and near-complete destruction. The victories that Vitu-Ghazi had won before encountering the God-Eternals—not to mention the cheers of the Selesnyans until that moment—were well and truly forgotten.

Kaya began to think she'd have to ghost her way in to get an audience with Emmara when Teyo called out, "Where's Araithia?"

Nissa asked, "Who?"

Impatiently rolling her eyes, Kaya was about to explain to the elf that Araithia was Rat, when suddenly Rat's voice called out, "Over here!"

Teyo and Kaya turned to find Rat approaching from *behind* the Ledev line, riding on the back of a centaur. Kaya was frankly stunned. She'd known centaurs on her home plane, and if you even looked like you wanted to ride one, you were as good as dead.

Oh, well. Maybe the centaurs of Ravnica are more accommodating.

Ledev Guardians parted, bowing, to allow the centaur to pass.

Rat said, "Mistress Kaya, Teyo Verada . . . and Miss Revane, allow me to introduce you to my godfather, Spearmaster Boruvo."

The centaur bowed his head to Kaya and Teyo in turn, but seemed to make a point of *not* bowing to the elf, who watched the proceedings in silence, looking extremely uncomfortable the whole time.

Rat continued in her mile-a-minute manner, "Boruvo was Gruul Clan once, before joining Selesnya. He's a good friend of my parents. And they made him my godfather. I mean, he was the obvious choice, the only practical choice, when you think about it. I think my father's always been a little jealous of my relationship with Boruvo. Not that *that's* why Boruvo left the Clan. He had a calling, you see. He thinks I have one, too, and really wants me to leave the Gruul and join Selesnya. And sometimes that does feel like the right path for me. But I guess I'm pretty indecisive when it comes to—"

The centaur cleared his throat and said, "Goddaughter."

"I'm rambling again, aren't I?"

"It's understandable. But I believe we have business to attend to." He turned to Kaya and Teyo, saying, "Anyone with the good taste to take notice of our Araithia deserves a chance to be heard."

Again Revane leaned in to whisper, "Who is this Araithia?"

And again Kaya was going to tell her that Araithia was Rat. But Rat grinned and shook her head, and Kaya turned to study Nissa. She was looking directly at Rat and yet looking right through her, as if Rat weren't there. It suddenly occurred to Kaya that Rat was invisible to Nissa. She thought back to Ral's reaction or *non*-reaction to Rat—and the way *everyone* had combined Teyo and Rat's names when Teyo had introduced them both. Was Rat invisible to everyone except Teyo, Boruvo and Kaya? Invisible, perhaps, even to her own father?

Rat said, "It's not invisibility exactly. I'll explain later."

Invisible . . . and maybe just a little psychic?

Had the girl read Kaya's thoughts . . . or just read into her expressions? Kaya had felt no touch upon her mind, as she had earlier that day with Beleren. Then again, Beleren had been shouting loud commands to a few dozen people simultaneously. Maybe he could be equally as undetectable when he wanted. Kaya knew Jace created illusions, too, rendering himself invisible to the naked eye—or the naked brain.

Is that what Rat's doing?

"Send the elf away," Boruvo said, immediately commanding Kaya's full attention. He was glaring at Revane with intense contempt. "Send her away, and I will escort the rest of you to speak with Emmara Tandris."

Kaya was about to protest. After all, Nissa Revane was supposed to be their secret weapon to win Tandris' favor.

But Revane was already backing away, looking somewhat relieved. She said, "I've never been very good at talking. You two go with the centaur. I'll join Gideon."

THIRTY-FOUR

GIDEON JURA

Gideon flew Promise into battle alongside Aurelia and her Skyknights, while Angrath led a ground force of thirty or forty Planeswalkers and three times as many warriors of Simic, Izzet and Boros.

Huatli, who seemed to have a history with the minotaur, had warned against Angrath's self-interest and rashness.

"Eh, you don't have to worry about me," he huffed with some internal bitterness. "All I want is to defeat the damn dragon so I can get back to my daughters. Honestly, I don't know why I ever leave 'em in the first damn place! I always think, *I'll just take a little break 'n planeswalk away for a couple days,* and then I wind up on some damn plane with that damn Immortal Sun and get stuck there for years at a time. Well, I'll be damned if I'm gonna let that dragon cost me more years away from my family. So put me to work. You won't be sorry."

Gideon thought him sincere, and even Huatli seemed convinced—and she was certainly prepared to admit Angrath would be a dangerous foe to the Eternals.

"Damn straight," he had said. "I can take out five at a time with my chain, I wager."

Still, when Gideon looked down, he saw Huatli at Angrath's side—at least in part to keep an eye on him.

They had all gone out to intercept the God-Eternal Rhonas. The Serpent God was closing in on the Senate House with multiple phalanxes of Eternals marching in his long shadow, while Eternal aven, drakes and angels circled his head like flies.

Or they circled until the Skyknights approached. Then they sheered away from their god to attack.

Fortunately, the air battle was right in Aurelia's wheelhouse. Gideon was the only Planeswalker in the sky, and he was protected by his aura of invulnerability. So there was no need for any special defenses. It was straight-up aerial warfare, and frankly the Eternals, though dangerous, were simply outmatched.

It was a different story on the ground, as Gideon noted, while swooping this way and that atop Promise and slicing off lazotep-coated heads with Blackblade at high speeds.

Below him, he could see that with few exceptions, the Planeswalkers were reluctant to get too close to the Eternals, instead using their magics to destroy the enemy from a distance. This was understandable but not always effective—and was certain to cause even more resentment among the guilded.

Among those exceptions was Angrath, himself. The minotaur ignited his heavy iron chain with his pyromantic power, and sure enough, as he swung it round in wide arcs, he'd destroy four or five Eternals with every rotation.

He had waded deep into the crops. Too deep, to be honest,

given that all an Eternal had to do was get a good solid grip on him. The length of his chain tended to keep them at bay, but on occasion its impact with a lazotep shell would disrupt his swing, leaving him extremely vulnerable.

That's when Huatli would step in—or rather step *out* from within the arc of his chain to have the minotaur's back. She might not like Angrath much, but she wasn't going to let him die.

Inspired by the pair, a few of the Planeswalkers began to engage the enemy directly—and not without success. But also not without danger, a danger once again made obvious when a vedalken Planeswalker was grabbed by two Eternals and harvested before everyone else's eyes. One of the two Eternals combusted, as the vedalken's Spark shot up into the sky, arcing toward the plaza and Bolas. The second Eternal also combusted, thanks to a vengeful Angrath, who whipped his chain around the creature and pulled it taut—while Huatli once again backed the minotaur, driving her blade into the heart of yet another Eternal, who was attempting to ensnare Angrath from behind.

Clearly, the vedalken's fate had a chilling effect on the rest of the Planeswalkers, who again pulled back en masse to settle for ranged attacks.

And even that didn't necessarily work. Rhonas reached out faster than Angrath's chain, grabbing a human Planeswalker with a shaved head and metal-casting powers. She attempted, in the few seconds she had left, to summon her flying shrapnel to attack the God-Eternal's tail to free herself. But it was all too little, too late. The shrapnel did no discernible damage to an Eternal of Rhonas' size, and within seconds her Spark had been harvested. Gideon hoped that if nothing else, the Serpent would combust, as the other Eternals did when delivering their stolen Sparks up to Bolas. But no such luck. The God-Eternal had the power to harvest, deliver and still survive. He moved on, crushing two Simic biomancers without even trying.

Understandably, this put an even bigger chill on the efforts of the other Planeswalkers. And it wasn't doing much for the guild warriors, either. Fear was setting in.

But Gideon had no such delicate constitution.

Rhonas had turned his attention to the aerial combat and was quickly becoming a significant problem. The flying Eternals—bereft of soul, passion and real independent thought—might be overmatched by Aurelia's well-trained, passionate, and freethinking Skyknights, but the Serpent God was not. He swatted them from the sky left and right. Gideon decided it was time—once and for all—to learn just how potent a weapon Blackblade actually was.

"C'mon, girl," he whispered to Promise, and she responded instantly. With only a slight touch on her reins, he was able to direct her between two Eternal drakes (one of which he sliced open to its spine in passing), toward the God-Eternal's left side.

Rhonas had just backslapped a Boros roc and its rider out of the sky, and as the god's hand swung around, completing the arc of its swing, it briefly flattened out, palm up. That was all Gideon needed. He leapt off his pegasus and right onto Rhonas' outstretched hand.

The God-Eternal turned his head. Despite the lazotep plating covering his snaky features and the decided lack of anything resembling a true sense of self, the Serpent actually looked . . . surprised. But only for a moment. He closed his fist around Gideon, and purple light emanated from between his lazotep plates as he attempted to harvest Gideon's Spark.

But Gideon's aura shone white around him. He remained invulnerable, untouchable. Rhonas could make no direct contact with Gideon's skin—or even his garb. Of course, being squeezed (virtually crushed) by a giant cobra wasn't exactly a picnic, but Gideon's hieromancy largely—*largely*—protected him from that, too.

Once again Rhonas' face expressed an actual, if brief, emotion: this time, confusion.

Why did this Planeswalker not die?

The Serpent God lifted Gideon up to study him at eye level.

And once again that was all the opening Gideon Jura needed. He reached back with his sword and stabbed it forward with all his might—piercing the Cobra God's eye.

Blackblade, the Soul-Drinker, drained into itself whatever remained of Rhonas' essence. Gideon could actually feel the weapon getting heavier. Maybe not physically heavier, but morally, magically, psychically heavier, without a doubt.

Rhonas was quickly reduced to a husk, a husk not unlike those of the Planeswalkers he had harvested. And just as quickly that husk began to crumble to dust. Gideon's footing, on Rhonas' hand, disintegrated beneath him, and he began to fall. He was easily a hundred feet up. Aura or no aura, this was going to hurt.

Or it would have. Promise swooped in and caught her rider across her back. The saddle horn drove into Gideon's ribs. His invulnerability protected him.

It still hurt.

But it was worth it.

A cheer erupted from all sides.

That's one down, Gideon thought, and it was a thought shared by a smiling Aurelia, by Angrath, Huatli and every other non-Eternal combatant in range.

Inspired, they all pressed forward. The Eternals—at least these Eternals—were now clearly doomed.

Gideon pulled himself upright onto Promise's back and from that lofty perch looked toward the plaza. He couldn't help it. His thoughts turned to Liliana.

He knew Jace's squad was going after her. A part of him wanted to fly over there to stop them, to save her. A part of him *still* believed she was salvageable. But another part of him couldn't defend her anymore. Liliana Vess had crossed too many lines.

THIRTY-FIVE

LILIANA VESS

Though she was too far away to see the specifics, Liliana could feel Rhonas cease. (Her connection with the Serpent God had moved in and out of the forefront of her consciousness as other Eternals intermittently required more immediate attention.) His destruction came as a relief: one less god to control, one less burden to carry, *that many fewer victims weighing on what passes for my conscience.*

She couldn't be a hundred percent sure, but she'd wager heavily on good old Beefslab being the cause of the God-Eternal's demise, which came as something of a relief, as well. Gideon's invulnerability, in essence, made him immune to the Elderspell. After every other Planeswalker fell, Gideon Jura would still be there with Blackblade, attempting to kill Bolas.

Liliana wouldn't be able to help, of course. Her contract with the dragon made that impossible. But that didn't mean she couldn't root for Gideon. After all, she sure wasn't rooting for Nicol Bolas.

In fact, she was doing her best—within the bounds of her contract—to thwart the dragon as much as possible, to mitigate the damage he was doing to life and limb. She gave Bolas' Eternals very little agency and even less assistance. She was doing everything in her power to prevent them from entering any buildings, from following their prey indoors. Frankly, if more Ravnicans had simply had brains enough to stay off the streets there might have been a *lot* less carnage this day. Now, with the Elderspell giving the Eternals a view of every Planeswalker's Spark, it had become more difficult, but still she tried her best to curtail their actions without drawing the dragon's attention.

I mean, given my circumstances, what more can they expect from me?

So, *of course*, she wanted Gideon to win.

And if Gideon does win? Well, I know I've crossed a line today. A few lines. More than a few.

But she'd always been able to explain those lines away to Beefslab. To manipulate him into seeing things her way.

She could still save herself.

Of course I can . . .

THIRTY-SIX

TEYO VERADA

It wasn't like he'd never seen greenery before. He had, of course. Gobakhan wasn't a complete desert. Oasis had a small park in the town square. And there was a garden at the monastery, too. But once again Teyo Verada was made to feel as if he'd come from a very small world into (*onto?*) a plane of wonders. He had never seen such a quantity and variety of shades of green before in his life—and *inside,* no less. Vines that reached up a hundred feet, two hundred feet, scaling marble walls and balconies. Bushes, shrubs—honestly, he didn't even have the vocabulary to describe what he was seeing—that spilled out across the tiled floors.

Trees growing indoors!

That is, if you could call this "indoors." Every space was open to the air. It'd be useless—even dangerous—as a shelter during a diamondstorm. Or during an Eternal attack, for that matter. But so far, neither had reached these halls.

And the scents, the rich aromas and perfumes of all this green, and all the flowers, and all the . . . the *Selesnya* of the place were intoxicating.

Rat was still riding on Boruvo's back as he led Teyo and Kaya for their audience with Emmara Tandris, the Selesnya Conclave's acting guildmaster. The corridors of almost glowing marble were lined with archers and soldiers, all wearing armor decorated to look like leaves or like blades of grass. Many were elves. All lowered their heads in slight bows to acknowledge Boruvo. All of them eyed Teyo and Kaya with the slightest hint of a threat. None of them seemed to even glance at Rat. They passed through an arch guarded by two immense creatures holding axes. Each had large tusks, bigger than a boar's, and each had a snout that stretched way beyond its face. As usual, Teyo had never seen anything like them. They, too, nodded to Boruvo, glared at Teyo and Kaya, and took no notice of Rat.

Light was just beginning to dawn on Teyo when Kaya spotted the look on his face and leaned over to whisper: "Only the centaur, you and I can see Rat. Somehow, she's invisible to everyone else. Even her father."

It makes no sense, and yet it explains everything.

Teyo must have been staring at Rat, because she grinned back at him and gracefully slipped off the centaur's back to slip in between her new friends and attempt to clarify: "I'm not invisible," she said. "I'm insignificant. A rat. A little rat. You see one, you look away. You try to pretend you didn't notice it. You try to forget about it until you *do* forget about it. Your mind rejects its presence."

"You're not insignificant," Kaya protested.

"You're sweet to say so, Mistress Kaya, but I am."

"It's magic," Teyo said.

"I suppose," Rat replied with a shrug. She was still smiling, though Teyo thought her grin had faded into something bittersweet. "Magic I was born with. Not many people can see me unless they know I'm there and concentrate. My father's good at that, but he has to know I'm around to manage it. Before today, there were only three people who consistently have been able to notice me on their own: my mother, Boruvo and Hekara."

Kaya nodded. "That's why you were so upset when I told you Hekara was dead."

Rat shook her head emphatically. "No. Well, maybe that was part of it. But mostly I was upset because Hekara was wicked cool and wonderful. But yeah, I guess it hurts to know there's one less person who'll take notice. Of course, then I found the two of you."

Teyo and Kaya each took one of Rat's hands and gave her reassuring squeezes.

At which point they all turned a corner and came face-to-face with what could only be Emmara Tandris. She was a tall elf with pointed ears, pale eyes, and hair the color of cornsilk. Or maybe just the color of light. She wore a long white dress with a long white robe or cloak—or maybe cape—draped over her shoulders. She stood before what Teyo at first thought was a tree. No, not a tree. A woman. Or three women. Or one woman with three torsos and three heads. Or one three-torsoed, three-headed woman, who was also a tree, with hair made of autumn leaves.

The center head/torso/woman seemed to be asleep. The other two faced away from each other. The one on the left was crying hot tears. The one on the right crossed her arms angrily. Teyo had given up trying to understand this strange world. Girls who could not be seen by their own fathers. Women who merged with trees and each other and yet could not get along. Teyo decided there and then that all he could do was try to be of some use.

Boruvo bowed low, which was an interesting sight to behold in a centaur. He said, "Milady Tandris, you know Guildmaster Kaya of the Orzhov Syndicate. With her are her associate Teyo Verada and my goddaughter Araithia Shokta, still Gateless."

Teyo tried not to smile when the centaur called him an associate. He wondered briefly how Abbot Barrez would have responded to his new title.

Emmara Tandris was squinting, scanning the room. She said, "Araithia is here?"

Rat waved, the sad smile replaced by the old Rat grin. "Here, milady!"

Tandris blinked twice and said, "One more time, please."

"I'm here, right between Teyo and Mistress Kaya."

Boruvo offered some help, too. "She's between the other two, milady."

"Ah, yes," Emmara said, suddenly beaming with pleasure.

Teyo swallowed hard.

Have I ever seen such a smile?

The elf said, "Oh, child, I wish this wasn't so difficult. It's such a joy to see your face and hear your voice."

"Only because each time is like the first. Trust me, milady, if you saw me every day, you'd grow quite tired of both."

"I sincerely doubt that."

Rat shrugged, still grinning. "I could prove it with five minutes of conversation, milady—but that's not why we're here."

Tandris sighed heavily, grew serious and turned her eyes on Kaya. "I know why you are here."

"Emmara, please," Kaya said. "We need to unite the guilds. Ral has a plan passed down by Niv to save Ravnica, but it won't work without all ten guilds cooperating."

"And it may not work even *if* all ten guilds cooperate, correct?"

Kaya didn't respond, but her silence spoke volumes.

"Guildmaster Kaya, we both know Ral Zarek and Niv-Mizzet loved their plans, their strategies, their blueprints. So far, every one has been an unmitigated disaster for the guilds, for Ravnica, and especially for Selesnya."

"But this time—"

"The Izzet always have names for their projects. Nothing is real to them unless they name it, define it, give it limits. Which is why we have so little in common. What is Ral calling this one?"

Kaya hesitated, looking almost embarrassed. But then she straightened her back and said in a clear voice: "Operation Desperation."

Emmara Tandris almost chuckled. She certainly smiled as she shook her head, the way a mother would shake her head at the antics of a child.

Kaya was ready for that. "I know what it sounds like, but desperate times do call for desperate measures. The Planeswalkers and the guilds must unite to defeat Bolas."

"I don't disagree, Kaya."

"Well, then—"

Tandris interrupted her again. It was strange. She had a way of interrupting that didn't seem rude. She seemed to glide in, her voice growing up between Kaya's words the way blades of grass grew up between paving stones. She said, "I'm sorry, but there's little support for anything resembling unification within Selesnya. Things were bad enough before the loss of Vitu-Ghazi. But now . . ." She trailed off.

Teyo turned to see how Kaya would respond and noticed that Rat was no longer standing between them.

He quickly glanced about and saw the girl whispering something to Boruvo, who was leaning down for just that purpose. Teyo thought the centaur would literally bend over backward for Rat. Teyo then realized that he would, too.

Boruvo cleared his throat and said, "Milady, it was Bolas' creatures that devastated Vitu-Ghazi."

"Yes," Kaya said, "exactly. And this wouldn't be the first world where Bolas has wreaked havoc. Two Planeswalkers—Vivien Reid from Skalla, and Samut from Amonkhet—report that both their worlds were absolutely devastated by Bolas. Skalla is completely dead. And Amonkhet's few survivors are struggling to, well, *survive*, while Bolas' monsters continue to ravage what's left of their home. In fact, I suspect the troubles on *my world* may be Bolas' handiwork, as well. Make no mistake, Emmara. The dragon is turning all of Ravnica—if not the entire Multiverse—into a grave."

Suddenly the center tree/head/torso/woman woke, crying or keening or maybe just humming. Teyo found he could not quite identify the sound.

The other two turned toward her.

As did Emmara Tandris with a gasp, and Boruvo with a low bow.

Teyo must have looked as confused as he felt, because Rat was again at his side, quietly offering up an explanation: "She is the dryad Trostani, the true guildmaster of Selesnya, the voices of its parun . . . um, you know, its founder, Mat'Selesnya. Mistress Cim, in the middle, is the dryad of Harmony. She has been asleep and unresponsive for months. Now she's awake."

"Yeah," Teyo said, "I got that last bit."

"The dryad on the left is Mistress Oba, the dryad of Life. On the right is Mistress Ses, the dryad of Order. Without Mistress Cim, they have been at odds, split and unable to reach a decision for their guild. Milady Tandris has been trying to keep Selesnya together during Trostani's . . . um, absence?"

The keening of Mistress Cim got louder, peaked and fell away. Everyone waited with bated breath. Finally, she spoke—or rather sang or, oh, well, Teyo wasn't quite sure *what* she was doing. Though Mistress Cim's mouth moved, her words were like music in his mind, like a breeze across the sands. Or through trees, he imagined. It was much, much gentler than the telepathy of Jace Beleren, and yet as with Jace, Teyo *felt* the words more than he heard them.

I have heard the song that plays in the wind, sisters. The dryad of Harmony turned to the dryad of Order: *Ses, Bolas' Order is the Order of the Grave. You have fought with your sister, but she is* still *your sister. Is it truly your wish to see her ended? To see all* Life *ended?*

With that encouragement, Mistress Oba appealed to Mistress Ses, as well. *There is a great Order to Life. Is that not enough?*

Mistress Ses was silent for a time. She looked away from her sisters. She looked up at the sky. Frankly, her expression reminded Teyo of nothing more than that of the abbot after one of his most pathetic acolyte's many failings.

Then, with a nod, Mistress Ses acquiesced, saying (*singing*), *Trostani is once again in Harmony. It is the will of Mat'Selesnya that the Conclave join the other guilds to defeat Nicol Bolas.*

THIRTY-SEVEN

RAL ZAREK

Mizzium turbines churned as the small almost-skyship ferried Guildmaster Ral Zarek and Chamberlain Maree toward Beacon Tower, deep in Azorius territory.

Last time Zarek had ridden aboard Golbet Frezzle's *Cloud-Lifter*, it had been raining—and the wind had blown cold and wet through the open-air gondola, chilling him to the bone. This time, the sky was grimmer still, dark with the Elderspell, lightened only by the harvested Sparks arcing through the air toward Bolas atop his Citadel.

Zarek and Maree watched from above, through telescopes of various magnitudes, as one, two, three more Planeswalkers arrived on Ravnica—and as two of those three were almost immediately harvested by Eternals.

A fourth Planeswalker, a tall elf with a long white hooded cloak, was scooped up by the God-Eternal Kefnet, who didn't even have the decency to burn for his crime as he sent the elf's Spark to the dragon.

Zarek felt grateful that *Cloud-Lifter*'s ascending screw engines blotted out any sound of screaming. But it hardly mattered. Through his telescope's highest magnitude lens, Zarek could see every detail as the faces of the perishing Planeswalkers tightened in rictuses of fear, allowing his mind to conjure every sound of horror he was missing—and reminding him of his own culpability in the slaughter. The Beacon had brought these Planeswalkers here to their doom. It had been Niv-Mizzet's brainchild, but Zarek had designed the cursed thing and even supervised its construction from a distance. Amid all his failures, including his ruinous attempt to unite the ten guilds, this—*this*—had been his one success. He'd been quite proud of it, of course. He'd fought to turn it on. He'd *killed* to turn it on.

Such are the successes of Ral Zarek, he thought bitterly.

Minutes later, *Cloud-Lifter* moored alongside the top floor of Beacon Tower. Ral and Maree found it lightly guarded by Azorius and Izzet soldiers. The Izzet quickly made way for their new guildmaster. Ral had thought he might have to fight the Azorius troops. But, no. Perhaps they were unaware that *their* new guildmaster, Dovin Baan, was secretly working for the dragon and thus would disapprove of Ral's intentions at the tower. Or perhaps they let Zarek pass because they were *very* aware of Baan's betrayal of Ravnica. Either way, they provided no opposition.

No. Guards aren't the problem. The problem is my own damn thoroughness.

Chief Chemister Varryvort, an Izzet goblin and the Beacon's primary engineer, rushed forward to greet his guild's two top officials: "Master Zarek! Chamberlain Maree! So good of you to visit while all hell is breaking loose."

Meaning, Ral thought, *Why aren't you out there doing something useful instead of bothering me?*

He said, "We've come to shut the Beacon down."

Varryvort balked. "Creating the Beacon was the last command of the Firemind!"

"I know that, Chief Chemister. But now it's being used to serve Bolas' ends. Bolas, who *killed* the Firemind."

"Yes, all right. I see that. But there's nothing we can do. I can't shut it down. You can't shut it down. Per your own orders, Master, the device was designed with no way to shut it down—in order to prevent *Bolas* from shutting it down."

"I know that, too, but I also know that any chemister worth his salt would still install some kind of backdoor fail-safe."

Varryvort shrugged. "The Beacon still requires power. No power, no beacon. That's the best solution I can offer you."

Maree rolled her eyes. "If only we knew someone with an endless appetite for power."

Ral knew she was talking about him but thought her words also applied to herself, not to mention half the sentients on Ravnica.

Still, at least I know what I have to do.

He turned on his Accumulator, placed his hands on the Beacon's metal control panel and began to suck in raw electricity through his fingers. It was fortunate that he had neglected to recharge the Accumulator since before he had made his failed attempt to find Tomik. It was unfortunate that the Beacon contained a tremendous surplus of raw power. Ral drained and drained and drained power from the Beacon, but he could sense he was barely scratching the surface.

He knew that very soon he would have to release some of this energy or his Accumulator would blow, taking off the roof of the tower and killing everyone inside it—all without damaging the built-to-withstand-an-Elder-Dragon Beacon.

Varryvort started to lean away, a hand shielding his eyes, shouting "Master . . . Master . . ." over the whine of Ral's Accumulator.

Maree watched sternly, but a corner of her mouth twitched once.

The Azorius soldiers were backing away. The Izzet smirked at them—then exchanged nervous looks.

Ral glanced back over his shoulder and saw that Golbet was piloting *Cloud-Lifter* out of range. Nevertheless, Ral kept at it, trying to drain the Beacon dry. He was making progress, but the Accumulator emitted a higher-and-higher-pitched whine. Then it started sparking excess power.

It's no good. I've got to release, or we'll all be fried to a crisp.

He broke contact with the control panel and stumbled toward a balcony, desperately scanning the horizon for a safe angle of release. Spotting Kefnet in the middle distance, Ral unleashed a massive lightning bolt that sheared off Kefnet's right arm. The Ibis God didn't seem to notice.

Ral stumbled back to the Beacon's controls, out of breath and sweating. Maree, with an actual—if perhaps temporary and situational—look of concern for him, attempted to steady him. But the static discharge crackling around him sent her flying back two feet. She landed on her ass, largely unharmed but glaring.

Ral ignored her. Again he placed his hands on the control panel. He instantly felt he had made some progress. Not much, but some. Enough to test and prove the theory that the method had merit.

I can do this.

He continued to drain the Beacon's power source.

This could take some time, but the end result is inevitable.

The Beacon will be silenced. No more unwitting Planeswalkers called to Ravnica like lambs for the slaughter. It won't stop Bolas, but it will set a limitation on his power source, limiting the number of Sparks he can devour. And that, at least, is something.

THIRTY-EIGHT

TEYO VERADA

"Something's changed," Teyo said.

"Yes," said Kaya, "I feel it, too. Ral must have succeeded in shutting down the Beacon."

"Planeswalkers can still come?" Rat asked.

"Yes, but they won't be drawn here. There's no summons to answer anymore."

"And that's a good thing?"

"I think so. We're enough to defeat the dragon. Or enough to die trying, at any rate."

Rat punched Kaya on the shoulder, saying, "Well, aren't you a ray of sunshine?"

"Ow."

Rat scurried ahead, calling out, "This way."

Kaya shushed her.

Rat rolled her eyes. "No one else hears me. No one else

wants to. Besides, we've almost reached Skarrg. Now, when we get there, you guys should let me do the talking."

"I thought they can't hear you," Teyo said—and then regretted it immediately, afraid he might have hurt Rat's feelings.

But apparently she was largely immune to that hard truth. "Most can't. But my mother, Ari Shokta, can. And my father can if he's paying attention. Same with Borborygmos. He thinks I'm adorable, which I am. I'm an adorable Rat!" She laughed, and the laughter echoed off the curving walls of the tunnel, tinkling back on the trio like a kind of music. Teyo thought that the "music" of Emmara Tandris and Trostani had been otherworldly and magnificent. But he believed he preferred the music of Araithia Shokta's laughter over any he'd ever heard in his life.

Her eyes are the color of Solstice plums, he thought.

Then he blushed.

They were moving through sewer tunnels like, well, *like rats*. It was dark and humid and close. Teyo, raised in arid climes, was dripping with sweat. He worried Kaya and Rat would think he was sweating because he was afraid.

I am afraid!

But he didn't need or want them to know that. They were both so fearless, while he still struggled merely to be somewhat useful. Still, for all the horror and confusion, there was something liberating about being on Ravnica.

They don't know me. They don't know what a failure I am.

Their ignorance had gone a long way toward keeping him in the game. The abbot *knew* Teyo Verada couldn't raise a decent shield to save his life. These good people had no idea. And so Teyo had been able to fool them, on occasion save them, and thus save himself.

They came to the end of a long brick tunnel. The stench was starting to get to Teyo. Rat approached an iron door and knelt before it to quickly pick the lock.

Quick enough to impress Kaya, who said, "You *are* good at that. Better than I am, and I'm something of an expert."

Rat rolled her eyes again: "Please, I learned to do that when I was six. When no one knows you exist, they don't unlock *anything* for you." She swung the door open, and instantly the trio could hear angry voices and the sound of weapons clashing.

Rat scurried ahead up yet another tunnel, and Teyo and Kaya struggled to keep up.

The tunnel soon opened up onto an immense underground chamber, the cratered remains of a huge palace. Immediately multiple axes flew toward Teyo and Kaya's heads. Instinctively, Teyo raised a three-pointer, and an axe ricocheted off it. Kaya went incorporeal, and an axe sailed right through her, sticking a good two inches deep into the wall behind her. Both Planeswalkers readied themselves for the next assault—only to realize they weren't being attacked. They were simply standing between two Gruul opponents: Rat's father, Gan Shokta, and a massive cyclops.

"That's Borborygmos," Kaya said. "That's who we've come to see."

Their sudden appearance caused both combatants to pause their conflict. They had been fighting before a giant bonfire that only made Teyo sweat all the more. And they weren't alone. Thirty or forty others—Gruul Clan warriors, Teyo assumed—had gathered to watch the battle. They now glared at Teyo and Kaya, grasping and regrasping their weapons with clear hostile intent.

Teyo looked around for Rat but didn't see her.

Can she make herself invisible to me, as well, or has she abandoned us?

Neither seemed likely.

Borborygmos squinted with his one eye at Kaya. He began grunting elaborately.

"What's he saying?" Teyo asked in a nervous whisper while wishing he didn't sound quite so nervous.

"I can't understand him," Kaya whispered back, not a little nervous herself. "But I'm sure he recognizes me from Ral's earlier attempt to unite the guilds. Agreeing to attend that gathering cost him his supremacy among the Clans."

The cyclops raised a four-foot-long mace and grunting, slammed the handle into his free hand for emphasis. What exactly he was emphasizing was less than clear.

Gan Shokta grumbled out a translation: "Borborygmos is half inclined to kill you right here and now, Ghost-Assassin. He holds you and the storm mage responsible for his fall."

"I understand," Kaya said carefully. And then pointedly: "On the other hand, Teyo and I helped save your life. And besides, we're friends of your—"

Before Kaya could mention Rat, an angry Gan Shokta barked out: "I need no reminders of my . . . *momentary failing.* I owe you. I acknowledge that. But don't think for a moment I'm any happier to see you than the cyclops. Believe me, you couldn't have come at a worse time."

"We don't want to be here any more than you want us here. But there's no choice, Gan Shokta. There's no choice, Borborygmos. We need the Gruul to—"

A female voice interrupted, calling out with a mixture of elation and urgency: "She's here, Gan!"

Gan Shokta turned: *"Here? Where?"*

A woman stepped forward with her arms around Rat. The woman was considerably taller and considerably more muscular. She was also armed to the teeth, with a sword and an axe, two long daggers and an iron chain wrapped around her waist like a belt. Nevertheless, she had the same dark hair and almost the same smile. The resemblance was obvious. Without a doubt, this was Rat's mother, Ari Shokta. She responded to her husband, saying, "Right here!"

All eyes around the bonfire turned toward the big woman. Gan Shokta squinted. He said, "Call out, girl!"

"I'm here, Father," Rat said.

"She's here in my arms, Gan," his wife said.

Then Gan Shokta smiled: "I see her."

Borborygmos grunted his own acknowledgment.

A few others in the crowd nodded, too, though Teyo thought most were just pretending to see the girl to impress their betters.

With a surprisingly formal air, Rat addressed her father and the cyclops: "Great Borborygmos. Legendary Gan Shokta. You must unite the Clans and help the other guilds. Or it will be the end of us all."

Gan Shokta growled his response, pointing at Borborygmos: "That's what I've been telling him. But the stubborn fool won't listen."

Borborygmos lurched toward Rat and held out his huge hand. She slipped out of her mother's arms and into his grip, which closed around her, practically eclipsing her.

Involuntarily, Teyo took a protective step forward, but Kaya put a hand on his shoulder and whispered, "She knows what she's doing."

The cyclops lifted Rat up. She whispered something in his ear.

He shook his head violently.

She cupped her hands and whispered something else. Then she kissed his cheek. *By the Storm*, Teyo thought, *did that monster just blush?*

THIRTY-NINE

DACK FAYDEN

Dack flinched as two of his "compatriots" knelt to flank him on either side. The first, the silver golem Karn, was intimidating enough. The second, the demon Ob Nixilis, was flat-out terrifying, an effect Nixilis seemed to enjoy—if not glory in—producing in Dack. The demon chuckled under his breath and said in a low whisper, "Are you prepared, flea? That Bridge was only designed to transport inorganic matter from plane to plane. The Eternals get away with it thanks to their lazotep coating. But all you've got to pull you through is your fragile Spark. I think you'll most likely burn up the moment you pass the portal's threshold. You seem like a betting flea. Care to wager on your survival?"

"Oh, leave him alone," Karn grumbled.

"What?" Nixilis said, taking mock offense. He patted Dack none too gently on the back with a clawed hand that felt a bit like it was made of hot lava. "I'm doing no harm to the flea. I could swat him, after all. And what difference would it make to the Multiverse? One less flea? One less flea, who—when you think about it—is hardly likely to survive the day?"

Dack glanced over at Karn, who didn't take the bait.

Ob Nixilis actually yawned then and said, "But I won't swat our little flea. I've grown quite fond of him in the last three minutes." Pat, pat, pat. "His palpable fear smells so delicious. And I can always swat him later, chew him up and swallow him, if he begins to annoy. He wouldn't make *much* of a meal, but if I get peckish during the mission . . ." Ob let the semi-implicit, semi-explicit threat hang.

Dack swallowed hard and sucked it up.

I can get through this.

They had a clear task to accomplish: sneak through the Planar Bridge and shut it down from the other side, on some plane called Amonkhet that Dack had never visited before. Fortunately, his third and final compatriot—an extremely intense human warrior named Samut—was a native of that world. She was at the opposite end of the roof, ready and waiting to take a running start.

Frankly, having three scarily dangerous partners in crime should have been reassuring. Dack had, after all, volunteered for this assignment with more than a vague notion of self-interest. The only way off Ravnica and away from the Spark-harvesting Eternals was *through* that portal, so through it he would go. He'd been assured his Spark would indeed protect him during the crossing. That this assurance was belabored with a "probably" from Beleren, and a "most likely" from Saheeli Rai, had perhaps undercut its credibility, but survival on the streets of Ravnica, among Bolas' Planeswalker-hunters, seemed no more certain and considerably less appealing after the horrifying death of Rade. On the other hand, whether Dack would return post-mission to continue the fight was a different matter entirely. After all, if he helped close the portal—thus preventing more Eternals from infesting Ravnica—he'd have more than done his part for his adopted world. He did, after all, feel *some* responsibility toward Ravnica. He had a handful of friends here. Marik and Leona were decent people. And Dack had grown quite fond of Leona's daughter Kella. Not every Ravnican was another J'dashe. But if he pulled off this little caper, he felt just fine with leaving the rest of the work to the real hero-types. Dack was a thief. He was nobody's gods-be-damned hero.

Crouching on a nearby rooftop, "the Planar Bridge Quartet" had gotten as close to the portal as they dared without attracting attention. Now the demon slapped a wing against Dack's shoulder and said, "You're up, flea."

Dack concentrated. Touching an Eternal mind—let alone multiple Eternal minds—was more disconcerting than anything he'd ever tried before. Their thought processes were so remote, so, well . . . *deadened*, it made the hairs on his arms stand on end.

But the spell was simple enough. He focused on a crop of Eternals thirty yards in front of the portal, making them all think they were surrounded by Planeswalkers with harvestable Sparks. Inevitably, they attacked one another. Swinging their weapons. Grabbing hold and attempting to ingest. It was soon a melee.

And the more Eternals that emerged from the portal, the greater the melee.

Karn signaled Samut, who zipped past them at an incredible speed. She literally ran straight down the side of the building and waded into the crowd.

Karn leapt down, shaking the ground as he landed.

Ob Nixilis stood. Dack didn't like the demon but felt obligated to say, "Remember, you can't even let them get a grip on you, or you'll lose your Spark."

Nixilis growled, "I'll never allow anyone or anything to take my Spark again."

Again? Dack thought. *You can lose your Spark more than once? I bet Rade wishes he knew that.*

Ob Nixilis grabbed Dack under his arms, spread his wings and flew them both toward the portal.

Gods-be-damned, it feels like my armpits are on fire!

Ob chuckled again: "Enjoying the ride, flea? Last one you're likely to take!"

Dack tried to ignore him. He looked down. Below them, most of the Eternals were fighting one another. Karn and Samut were making short work of the few that attempted to get in their way as they cleared a ground path for themselves to the Bridge.

But Nixilis didn't seem too interested in whether or not they'd make it. He soared right over them and, without stopping, flew Dack right into the portal to Amonkhet.

As they crossed the threshold, Dack Fayden screamed in agony . . .

FORTY

RAL ZAREK

"Please," Ral said. "Enough." He had caught up to Kaya and Teyo just before they had all entered Korozda together. "I've just spent a full sixty-six minutes draining the Beacon. I'm tired, and I don't have the patience for your games. Or your imaginary friend."

"It's not a game; Rat's not imaginary, and by the way open your bloody mind, Ral. You'd think you'd never encountered an invisibility spell before."

"Well, if she's using an invisibility spell, tell her to stop using it."

"It's not that simple with her. It's . . . innate. She can't turn it on and off."

Kaya turned then; Teyo, as well, as if they were both listening to this "Rat." Ral Zarek rolled his eyes.

"Worth a try," Kaya said, then without warning she ghosted right through him, which was extremely disconcerting.

"Damnit, Kaya, what the Krokt are you—"

From behind, Kaya literally grabbed his face in both her once-again-solidified hands and aimed it at . . . at . . . *there's a girl there, smiling and waving.* "Hi."

Where did she come from?

"I came from the Gruul Clans, initially. But I'm Gateless, in case you were wondering. My name's Araithia Shokta, but you can call me Rat. Everyone does. Well, not everyone. Not my parents or my godfather, but everyone else who knows about me. Hekara called me Rat. I miss her. I bet you miss her, too. I know you pretended not to care about her, but I also know you valued her friendship. She was *such* a loyal friend, right? And *so* funny. She made me laugh and laugh and laugh. Not many people do that with me. Not on purpose, anyway."

He had to focus to see and hear her, though that didn't exactly deter her verbiage.

"Don't be offended. Hekara asked, and I'd have done anything for her. Absolutely anything. She knew you wouldn't notice me. I mean, I think initially she hoped you would, but it was pretty clear pretty quick that you didn't. And Guildmaster Rakdos had told her to stick with you, and you kept ditching her. So she *had* to ask for my help, really. That's kind of your fault. So I tracked you, pretty much everywhere you went."

The girl looked past Ral at Kaya, and it occurred to him that people must look past her—through her—every minute of every day. He remembered that feeling, growing up on Ravnica, destitute and hungry. People looked through the poor boy all the time. He felt a catch in his throat. When he remembered to focus on her and not himself, he looked up, but she was gone. He squinted again, focused on the girl, on

Rat, and her voice faded into his consciousness; her image followed a second later.

"That's why I'm surprised *you* didn't notice me," Rat was saying to Kaya.

Kaya finally released Ral and crossed to the girl. "The first time I saw you today, I thought you seemed vaguely familiar, like I had seen you around town. But I'm a stranger here, so I see a lot of locals that don't fully register, as long as they're not a threat."

"And there was no way you could know you weren't *supposed* to be able to see me, so you never mentioned it. Or even said hello!"

"Yeah, well, I am sorry about that."

"Yeah, well, I do forgive you," Rat said, mimicking Kaya's cadence with a smile and taking Kaya's hands.

Trying to catch up, Ral interjected: "So you've been following me since I met Hekara?"

"On and off. She didn't need my services when *she* was with you. But I tried to stay in the vicinity, so I could pick up your trail and report back if and when you sent her packing. By the way, that guy you're with, Mr. Vrona, is really cute in a bookish sort of way. You guys are just *adorable* together, too."

Kaya smirked; Ral struggled not to blush, and the girl disappeared again. *Damnit!*

Teyo noticed Ral's confusion and offered, "She's still right beside Kaya."

Ral focused, and there she was again. "I guess I'm sorry I couldn't see you," he said.

For more reasons than one.

It seemed she knew a lot more about him than he knew about her. Which wasn't surprising, since he hadn't known she existed until a minute ago.

"I'm used to it. And really, I'm kinda impressed at what

you're doing now. My mother says it took my father three months after I was born to master focusing on me. You've picked it up pretty much instantaneously. You're more open to new things than you think you are."

"I think I'm *very* open to new things."

"No, you don't. You want to be. But you don't believe you are. But you are. Isn't that strange?"

Ral realized his mouth was hanging open, so he closed it.

Kaya was still smirking as she said, "There's no time to dwell. We need to get a move on."

Kaya led the two of them—*no, damnit, the* three *of them*—deeper into Korozda, the Maze of Decay, which meant by definition that they were walking in circles. Concentric circles leading deeper and deeper into Golgari Swarm territory, assuming they didn't get lost along the way, which was a distinct possibility, despite the fact that both Kaya and Ral had solved its puzzle and walked its decaying fungal hedgerows half a dozen times while allied with Vraska.

Before Vraska betrayed us.

They had already been admitted into Korozda by passing beneath the fortress of Pevnar, the Hanging Keep, an upside-down castle with foundations fixed to the ceiling. Ral had been prepared for opposition from the Krunstraz that garrisoned the keep. But the insectlike kraul warriors simply watched the four of them—*well, actually, they probably only saw three of us*—enter the maze.

Now, as they approached the center, Ral realized they had not only met no opposition, they had met no one *at all*. Which meant they were expected. Or perhaps that they were walking into a trap. Or more likely both.

He scanned back and forth for signs of an ambush—and realized he'd lost track of Rat again. He was vaguely aware she must still be there with them, but now he was having trouble even remembering what she looked or sounded like.

Still, there are worse things than having an ally no one else can see or hear.

Ral took a deep breath, checked his Accumulator, which was as full from the Beacon as it could possibly be, and sped up past Kaya to enter the great circular amphitheater, with its many rows of stone seats, all covered by a soft downy moss.

Vraska's Erstwhile lich, an undead Golgari sorcerer, was waiting to welcome them: "Greetings, Guildmaster Zarek. Greetings, Guildmaster Kaya. The Golgari Swarm welcomes you to Svogthos." Her voice sounded like dead leaves being blown across a grave.

Ral had met this lich more than once.

But for the life of me, I can't remember her name!

At the edge of his consciousness, a voice whispered, "Storrev."

Ral smiled a thin smile and thought, *Thank you, Rat.*

"Don't mention it."

"We appreciate the greeting, Storrev," Ral said with some formality. He thought the Erstwhile looked mildly surprised and perhaps a little gratified that Ral knew him by name, and again Ral thought—a little less begrudgingly—*Thank you, Rat.*

He thought he heard a giggle.

"This is a time of crisis," Kaya said. "We've come to meet with Mazirek." Mazirek, leader of the kraul, had been Vraska's right-hand bug—and the most likely candidate to have replaced her as guildmaster of the Golgari.

Storrev sighed, nodded and said, "Follow me."

They crossed the amphitheater and followed the lich into Svogthos, the subterranean guildhall of the Golgari. Once a grand Orzhov cathedral, arched and magnificent, it had fallen through a sinkhole some centuries ago. The Orzhov abandoned it. The Golgari claimed its ruin as their own.

Storrev led them into a cavernous chamber, known as the

Statuary. A raised stone causeway ran through its center, with statues lining either side. Except the statues weren't truly statues. They were victims. Vraska's victims. Like Isperia, each was frozen in stone. But unlike Isperia, whose final expression was one of mild surprise, each of these trophies had been captured in a last look of terror, hands thrown up too late to protect them from the gorgon's deadly mystic stare.

A number of individuals were gathered at the far end of the causeway around Vraska's massive stone throne. It was telling that none of them were actually seated on that throne. Though honestly, it wasn't a seat Ral would have been eager to fill, either. It consisted entirely of more of Vraska's dead enemies, intertwined and posed before being permanently petrified in place, so that the great Vraska could grant them the final indignity of becoming a repository for her ass.

As they got closer, Ral could see that Mazirek was not among the gathered Golgari.

Storrev made a slight bow, and Ral, Kaya and Teyo (but not Rat, of course) were introduced to the kraul Krunstraz warrior Azdomas, the devkarin leader Izoni, the troll Varolz and the elf shaman Cevraya.

"Mazirek?" Ral asked.

Azdomas made a series of clicking noises in his throat before speaking. There was a dark anger in the clicking and in his voice: "Mazirek was another Bolas collaborator, revealed by Queen Vraska before her departure."

"*Vraska* revealed him?"

"Yes," Storrev said, in her voice of leaves, "Vraska freed the Erstwhile and gave us our tormentor Mazirek."

"He has paid the ultimate price for betraying the Swarm," Azdomas added with finality.

Kaya glanced from Azdomas to Storrev to Izoni to Cevraya and then up to meet the eyes of the huge fungal-hided troll Varolz. She seemed to be taking each one's measure—and gauging just what it would take to bring each one down if necessary.

Ral, for his part, felt no need to be quite as precise with the full-to-bursting Accumulator strapped to his back. But he was ready.

Kaya said, "If I might ask . . . who is your new guildmaster? That is who we've come to address."

They all exchanged dangerous glances that revealed the answer even before Storrev said, "Each of these individuals—myself excepted—has a claim to Vraska's throne."

"Vraska comes to claim Vraska's throne."

Ral turned in time to see a figure emerging, fading up—planeswalking in—out of a silhouette.

It was Vraska.

As she came into focus, Ral remembered to throw a hand up before his own eyes. Kaya did the same. As for Teyo—his hand seemed to be pushed up by his invisible friend. Ral activated his Accumulator. Kaya drew her long knives. Both were as ready as they were going to be to face the traitorous gorgon.

Vraska ignored them, saying, "Does anyone challenge my right to that throne?"

Storrev, Azdomas, Varolz and Cevraya all bowed immediately, saying in unison, "No, my Queen." Izoni didn't look overly pleased, but she bowed and uttered the same assurance, only half a second later than her fellows.

Ral risked a glance at Vraska. Her eyes weren't glowing, which meant she hadn't yet summoned the magic to turn anyone to stone. It was a small relief, but he knew she could summon that power rapidly. And she had other skills, other weapons, as well. For example, the cutlass hanging from her belt.

"You look ridiculous," Ral said, trying to replace the bitterness he felt with an air of contempt. "What are you supposed to be, a pirate?"

She continued to ignore him, passing right by him to take a seat on her throne of frozen horror.

"I'm surprised you've returned to Ravnica," Kaya said evenly, "Shocked, really . . ."

"Appalled," Ral corrected.

"Especially *after* the Beacon was turned off?" Vraska asked, as if *trying* to get a rise out of her former friends and allies.

Ral was charged up and ready for the inevitable fight. Static crackled through his spiky hair. "So which was it?" he growled. "Did you assume Bolas had already been *defeated*—or that he had already *triumphed*?"

FORTY-ONE

DACK FAYDEN

Dack might have passed out for a couple seconds. He opened his eyes—regaining consciousness—just as Ob Nixilis landed. The pain and the memory of it was barely beginning to fade. Nixilis released him, and Dack fell to his hands and knees, gasping for air.

"You're a good screamer, flea. I'll remember that."

Samut raced up to join them. From the ground, Dack glanced up at her. She was breathing hard, and her eyes watered, but she remained standing. Feeling embarrassed, Dack struggled to his feet, managing that heroic effort just as Karn lumbered forth from the portal to steady him.

Dack looked around. At the Senate House, Samut had warned that Amonkhet was a plane devastated by Bolas. She wasn't kidding. Dack could tell that not long ago this had been a teeming and gleaming city. Now the place reeked of death.

There was sand everywhere. The buildings were gutted, some half destroyed as if giants—or gods—had used the plane as a sandbox, kicking great chunks out of all the pretty sandcastles. And of course, there were the Eternals, Amonkhet's warrior dead, coated with lazotep and still marching in troops through the portal.

Ob Nixilis had flown Dack off to the side of their march, and Samut and Karn had joined them there. But the quartet was still within a stone's throw of the advancing Dreadhorde. With four Sparks ripe for the taking, Dack didn't understand why they were being ignored.

Not that I'm complaining, mind you.

Karn must have had a similar thought; he ruminated, "The Elderspell isn't in play on this side of the Bridge. Here their instructions have been kept simple: '*Cross.*'"

"She got it back up," Samut said, emotion filling her voice.

Dack turned toward her. "Who got what back up?"

Samut was staring at an energy field, a semi-transparent wall of pure aether that separated the ruined city from the desert wastes beyond. She said, "Hazoret, God-Survivor of Amonkhet, has raised the Hekma, the shield that protects my people from the horrors of the desert. She was working on doing just that when I departed for Ravnica. She succeeded."

"Then where is she now? Cuz we could use a god's help."

"Careful what you wish for, flea. Gods aren't always careful around mortals. And you're easily stepped upon."

Dack struggled to ignore Ob, but he thought Samut probably saw his lip twitch.

"I imagine Hazoret's still with the survivors in our encampment on the far edge of Naktamun—this once glorious city. We lured the Scarab God and the Locust God outside its confines before doubling back. By that time, the Eternals were focused on their mission and ignored us if we stayed out of their way. So we've been staying out of their way. I've sent my prayers to Hazoret. She'll come to help."

"Because she's done such a glorious job of protecting you so far?" Ob Nixilis said with a dismissive wave.

Samut tensed, intrinsically offended, but Karn put a hand on her shoulder and said, "We can't afford to wait. Let's get to it. Execute the plan."

Nixilis flexed his wings and took flight, attacking the Eternals from above, raining fire down upon them. Once he'd cleared a fiery circle, he landed, grabbed an Eternal and ripped off its limbs. He proceeded to tear apart and/or burn Eternals with his flaming hands, and Dack watched as the demon seemed to grow fiercer, more powerful—and *larger*—with every victory.

Karn and Samut waded in, also. Karn was mechanical and merciless. Samut was full of fury, tears streaming down her face. She seemed to know each and every Eternal by their former names, calling out as she slew them, "You are free, Basetha. You are free, Asenue."

Dack Fayden did not fight, but then again he wasn't there to be the muscle. Using the same spell as before, he turned a crop of Eternals against one another, causing more chaos. Then he moved forward, back up the line, searching for the source of the Planar Bridge.

He kept to the sidelines, but now and then an Eternal would spot him and veer off course to attack. A simple hex of confusion kept him safe.

Safe enough, anyway.

Five hundred yards from the portal, he spotted its obvious source. A man with a metal arm stood on a flattop pyramid with a small portal of his own centered within his own chest. This, Dack knew from his briefing, must be Tezzeret, Planeswalker and Bolas flunky.

The small portal in Tezzeret's chest seemed to be projecting the bigger Bridge through which the Dreadhorde marched. Such a thing would be worth a few zinos, enough to pay off J'dashe twice over—

Come on, Fayden, that's not *why we're here!*

Dack sent up a magical flare. It caught Tezzeret's attention, but Dack used a chameleon spell to blend in with the wall. He saw Tezzeret's gaze pass right over him, his eyes drawn to Samut and Ob Nixilis, who were speeding and flying, respectively, up the line of Eternals, destroying as many as possible along the way.

Tezzeret took the bait, raising his metallic arm and firing off blasts of metal from his fingers.

No, wait. Those are *his fingers! The guy's firing off his actual fingers! And . . . they're coming back to him!*

Fortunately, Samut dodged each projectile easily, and Nixilis, now *clearly* larger than when they'd all started, shrugged off any that connected.

Karn, who could move rather stealthily and smoothly when the situation required it, slid up beside Dack. They nodded to each other. Dack unlaced a pouch on his belt, releasing a small mechanical silver hummingbird, a gift from Saheeli Rai. Karn took mystic control of the elegant device and flew it toward Tezzeret. It hovered before the Planeswalker's face, easily getting Tezzeret's full attention. But as he reached out with his metal hand to crush it, Dack attempted to take mystic control of Tezzeret's entire arm.

Tezzeret reacted with more shock as he fought to regain full control. Both feelings quickly gave way to fury. As Dack attempted to punch the rogue Planeswalker with his own fist, Tezzeret's organic arm grabbed his metal wrist and struggled to hold it at bay while his magics struggled to regain control.

Dack was quite aware his sway over the thing couldn't last. It didn't have to.

Tezzeret roared as he finally regained full command of his limb, but by that time Karn had flown the little hummingbird right into the portal inside Tezzeret's chest—where it *exploded*!

Tezzeret was sent flying backward.

Dack turned to look over his shoulder. The larger portal—the Planar Bridge—instantly collapsed in upon itself. Its energy imploded in a flash of light and mana that briefly blinded Dack.

He squeezed his watering eyes shut, and when he opened them again, the Bridge was simply gone. Half an Eternal—that is, what remained of one that had been crossing right at the moment of implosion—stumbled forward half a step before collapsing to the sand.

Gods-be-damned, it worked!

With the Bridge now closed, the rest of the Eternals all halted their march. They froze in place, unsure what to do. Nixilis, by this time, was huge—he had easily doubled in size since Dack had first encountered him. The demon flew up and down the Eternal line, methodically incinerating each and every remaining Eternal.

Tezzeret, meanwhile, rose to his feet. His chest seemed to be shorting out, throwing magical sparks into the air before him. He groaned and stuck his metal arm into the gaping hole, performing a mystic gesture that sealed it. But he was clearly in considerable pain. As Karn and Samut moved in, Dack felt sure he'd fall to them.

Instead Tezzeret *congratulated* them. "Good work, Planeswalkers. This will be quite a setback for the dragon."

Karn scowled: "Don't pretend you're happy; you face defeat."

"Believe me, I'm quite pleased. I couldn't risk crossing Bolas. Power knows power, and I'd have to be a fool not to recognize the threat he represents. But I legitimately hope you lot can reduce the dragon to dust."

"Why?"

"Because with him out of the way, there'll be no one left with the power to thwart me. As I said, power knows power. And I just don't recognize anything of the kind here."

He laughed and before even Samut the Swift could react, he planeswalked away, vanishing in a buzz saw of blue-silver sparks to some other plane.

Dack silently wished that other plane luck.

Samut seemed to break then. With Tezzeret gone, and the Eternals all in the process of being destroyed, whatever strength had been keeping her on her feet dissolved, and Karn had to literally catch her to keep her from falling.

Dack approached.

Tears streamed down her face. "It's over," she whispered. "Amonkhet is free."

Indeed, it is, child.

Dack felt the voice resonate inside his mind. It was telepathy, he supposed, but it was nothing like the telepathy of Jace Beleren. These words filled him, warmed him, satisfied him, as if he'd been waiting his entire life just to hear them.

Samut whispered, "Hazoret," and raised her head.

Dack followed her gaze and watched, enthralled, as Hazoret approached. She towered above the ruined city, a benign smile on her jackal-like face. Dack had never seen anyone or anything more beautiful.

Ob Nixilis landed beside him and scoffed: "Look, the flea is in love."

Do not mock, demon. We all worship in Our own way.

Nixilis shook his head with a look of disgust on his face.

Dack squeezed his eyes shut.

No. For once, Ob is right. I can't worship this gods-be-damned god who shows up after *the fight is over.*

He opened his eyes again. Hazoret was still extremely impressive, but the natural "spell" of her presence had been broken. She still towered above them, but her height had seemed practically infinite before. Now she didn't even look to be as big as the God-Eternals they had left behind on Ravnica. She carried a long two-pronged spear, but it seemed to weigh heavy in her hand.

It is well, Dack Fayden. You see Us now for what We are. A failed god, struggling to help Her people. But know, at least, that We did not wait for the battle to end. We came as quickly as We might after Samut's prayer reached Us.

The voice was still enthralling—perhaps even more so in its sincerity. Dack wasn't exactly immune, but he was able to place it in perspective, in a box of sorts. One that required no worship.

Samut, who was on her knees, said, "You raised the Hekma."

And the Scarab and Locust Gods are trapped outside it, too weak now without the false God-Pharaoh to augment their strength. But We could not raise it alone. We had help.

Karn was looking past Hazoret, and Dack saw a human— a Planeswalker—approach. He was tall and muscular with pale skin and long dark hair. Karn nodded curtly and said, "Sarkhan Vol." The golem didn't sound particularly pleased to see this Vol again.

Sarkhan Vol's attitude toward Karn seemed no more welcoming. "Karn." Then he turned to the demon and with even less warmth said, "Nixilis."

Ob Nixilis eyed the newcomer with suspicion, "What brought you here?"

"I had word—from . . . Goldmane—that Bolas was headed for Ravnica. I came to Amonkhet with the hope of finding something on this plane that could defeat its former God-Pharaoh."

Unfortunately, We know of nothing here that can defeat Nicol Bolas.

"He's destroying another world," Samut whispered, staring up at her god with imploring eyes.

Sarkhan said, "Perhaps your spear?"

Hazoret raised it, as if in appraisal.

Perhaps. Though it seems unlikely, as it was his creation. Still . . . We see in your heart, brave Samut, that you mean to return to this endangered world. Thus if this weapon might be of some service, it is yours to take with you.

Dack stared at the thing in Hazoret's hand. The spear was *immense.* "Uh, *can* we take it with us?"

Samut considered this and said, "Maybe if all four of us take hold of it?"

Ob Nixilis laughed: "Did you seriously believe I'd return to Ravnica? Like Tezzeret, I have plans of my own—and no intention of voluntarily returning to Bolas' mousetrap, where any stray Eternal might grab my tail and harvest my Spark." And right then and there, the demon vanished in flame.

Dack wanted to kill Ob. In part, because the demon had just stolen a page from the thief's own book. *Not* returning to Ravnica had been Dack's plan. Perhaps for just that reason, Dack decided then and there that he *would* return. He was far from perfect—by his own lights, he was a thief and *no hero.* But compared with Bolas, Tezzeret and Ob Nixilis, Dack Fayden was *Gideon-freaking-Jura!* He would not abandon his adopted world now.

You are a better man than you believe, Dack Fayden.

I doubt that, he thought back at the god.

Doubt it not and go to your destiny with the blessing and thanks of Hazoret and all of Amonkhet.

Dack wished she had said, *go to your victory* instead of *destiny,* but beggars could not be choosers.

Samut said, "I'm not sure three of us are enough to take this spear."

Vol stepped forward. "I will take the demon's place."

Karn shook his head. "This is not about numbers. We are not required to literally *carry* the spear. With my mass and control, I should be able to planeswalk the weapon myself."

Vol said, "I'll still come with you."

Thanks to you, Sarkhan Vol. And to you, Karn.

Each made a curt bow.

And, Samut, most wondrous of all Our children . . . fight well and come back to Us. Amonkhet needs you.

"I will do my best, God-Survivor."

Your best has always been more than enough.

And with that, Hazoret knelt and laid the spear on the ground at Karn's feet. The golem made no attempt to lift the thing. Instead he gently reached down and touched his hand to it. He winced slightly, then vanished with a thunderclap that all but blew out Dack's eardrums.

Vol left next. Samut followed. Dack hesitated briefly.

Buddy, you can still walk away . . .

But he shook off the impulse. Against his better judgment, he would go back to Ravnica. In a puff of purple smoke, a determined Dack Fayden left Hazoret and Amonkhet behind . . .

FORTY-TWO

VRASKA

The monstrous gorgon in the ridiculous pirate costume led the others through the Golgari tunnels—*her tunnels*—painfully aware that her former friends Ral and Kaya were right behind her, one charged and ready to fry her, the other drawn and ready to skewer her.

Ral hissed at her back: "Turn to look at me, and I won't hesitate."

But Kaya said, "I don't know. I'll ask."

"Ask what?" Vraska growled over her shoulder.

"My friend Rat wants to know why you came back. She's inclined to trust you because Hekara considered you a friend. Then again, I was inclined to trust you once, too . . ."

Vraska ignored the question and their judgments. Or at least she tried to.

Why did *I come back?*

She had felt the Beacon shut off. Was it as simple as wondering what that meant? No. She had returned to fight for her people, for the Golgari.

If that results in my death at the hands of either Bolas or my "friends," so be it.

But in the meantime, she was determined to help.

It had hit her hard when she first arrived and found Kaya and Ral standing before her subjects and her throne. She had tried to play it off as if she was unaffected by their presence. Ignoring their outrage and even their questions, the Queen of the Golgari had demanded an immediate briefing.

The kraul Azdomas, leader of her (miraculously) still-loyal Krunstraz Honor Guard, had reported that Golgari, Gateless and other guild civilians were trapped in various pockets of the city, at the mercy of the dragon's Eternals. "Allies of the former Living Guildpact are trying to lead these innocents to safety, my Queen."

"Former?"

"Yes, my Queen. Beleren is in the city but without the power of the Guildpact."

Only then had Vraska learned Jace was on Ravnica.

Well, of course he is. Now. Too late to save my soul. Assuming there was ever a soul within me worth saving. Assuming there was ever a soul within me at all.

When Azdomas finished, Vraska had stated she knew a way to help. She had made the offer. Ral had rejected it. Kaya had started to reject it—before arguing insensibly with herself in front of everyone. Finally, Kaya accepted Vraska's help and forced Ral to begrudgingly accept it, as well.

So now Ral, Kaya, the boy Teyo, Azdomas and Storrev were trudging through the subterranean waterways and sewers of Ravnica on their rescue mission.

Vraska stopped beneath a massive iron grate. She gestured with one hand, careful not to look backward, since even her most harmless glance might trigger a preemptive strike from Zarek.

Azdomas approached and pulled off the grate. The scraping of iron against stone echoed through the tunnels.

From above, a voice roared, "Who's there?"

Ral, forgetting Vraska for a moment—or at least forgetting his hatred of her—stepped forward. "Is that Goldmane?" he said in a fairly loud whisper.

A creature with the head of a lion stuck his head down. "Zarek?" But he spotted Ral before receiving his answer and spoke with some urgency: "I've been leading some of the other Planeswalkers to help evacuate civilians. But the Eternals got the drop on us. Six or seven crops. We've been pinned down inside this old chapel for over an hour. The building's completely surrounded. They're attracted to our Sparks and won't leave. We've kept the Dreadhorde at bay, but it's a losing battle. Khazi was harvested when an Eternal punched its hand right through the wall and grabbed her by the wrist."

Vraska came up alongside Ral and said, "This is the way out."

The lion-headed man squinted at her with his one good eye and said, "You must be Vraska. Jace was hoping you'd show up. He believes in you."

Vraska frowned but said, "Bring everyone down. The Golgari will keep them safe. You have my word."

Ral scoffed loudly but somehow managed to resist the temptation to say what Vraska was thinking: *For all* that's *worth.*

Without a sound, Lion-Head's face vanished from the opening. A minute passed. Then two. Vraska and Ral exchanged confused glances. She noticed Ral had forgotten to shield his eyes. The thought crossed her mind that she could have killed him then. Belatedly, the thought seemed to cross his mind, too. There was no power building behind her eyes, but his suddenly lit up with electricity.

This could be it. He could throw one of his damn lightning bolts at me, and this time I won't be able to Planeswalk. This time, Ral Zarek will get to kill the monster who betrayed him to Nicol Bolas.

But before Ral could act—assuming he was about to— Lion-Head dropped down between them.

He approached the gorgon without fear and said, "We haven't been introduced. I am Ajani Goldmane of the Gate-watch." He reached out his hand.

She tried not to flinch away. Not that she was afraid of this Ajani; it was his unrestricted trust that made her want to run. She neither needed nor wanted another friend to fail. But she grasped his thick furry forearm, and he grasped her smooth one. "Welcome to Golgari territory, Ajani Goldmane. You are safe here."

He nodded, smiling. Then he turned back up toward the tunnel's ceiling and said, "Start lowering them."

One by one, Ravnicans—children, mostly—were lowered into the arms of Goldmane, of Azdomas, of Kaya, Teyo and Vraska. Only Ral stood back, wary. Vraska was handed a young elven girl—five or six years old—that she recognized as the daughter of a devkarin elf that Vraska had turned to stone when she made herself guildmaster during a Bolas-assisted coup. The girl's father's statue, permanently frozen in a look of pure terror, was the third one down from her throne on the left. If the girl knew who Vraska was—or the role the gorgon had played in the current sorry state of her life—she gave no indication. Rather, she buried herself in the monster's breast, heaving great sobs of fear and sorrow.

Wonderful. Afraid I couldn't feel any worse. Good to know there's no bottom to this guilt.

There was noise from above. A voice yelled down, "They've breached the doors!" Vraska thought the voice sounded vaguely familiar, but she couldn't place it.

The last of the Ravnicans descended, and they were followed by two Planeswalkers whom Ajani quickly introduced as Mu Yanling and Jiang Yanggu. The latter called back up, "Mowu, come!"

A small dog leapt down into Jiang's arms. He put the canine down on the tunnel floor, and it proceeded to grow, expanding into a *three-tailed* dog as tall as its master.

Ajani said, "Where's Huatli?"

Huatli. That's an Ixalan name.

"Here!" a Sun Empire warrior called out as she dropped down. "I'm the last, but they're right behind me!" As if to prove her right, a lazotep-covered hand and arm reached down from above, sweeping the air and just missing this Huatli.

The hand vanished into the darkness above and was replaced by the heads of three of these undead Eternals. They started to climb down, delayed only because none of them waited for either of the other two.

That delay gave Vraska the time she needed. She summoned the power; it built up behind her eyes, which she kept focused on the ceiling so as not to trigger Ral's (perfectly legitimate) fears. The gorgon pulled the crying elf child closer to her bosom and covered the girl's eyes with one hand. Then, as the three Eternals filled the opening, Vraska locked eyes with each of them in turn, transforming them all to stone. The sound of them calcifying was quite satisfying and the result was that she had not only stopped Huatli's pursuers from attacking, but had also effectively sealed the hole and their only way down from the chapel above.

Storrev approached her from behind and whispered in her ear. The lich's magics kept her in constant contact with the Erstwhile, and she had news.

Vraska listened and turned to Ral, who took a step back but did not try to electrocute her. Maybe it was because her eyes were no longer glowing, and thus she wasn't an immediate threat. Maybe it was because she was still holding the small softly crying elf child in her arms. Maybe—just maybe—it was because she had finally earned back a little of the lost trust they had once shared.

No. Not that. It's the girl. Unfortunately, I can't go around carrying an innocent child everywhere I go. It's simply not practical.

Her thoughts circled around endlessly. She wouldn't survive this war of the Spark. In that moment, she was as certain of that as she was of anything. She had betrayed too many, including Bolas. The dragon or his allies or her own former friends would kill her. Eventually. They'd have to. Inevitably.

And that's just fine.

But she meant to do some good before her death. She owed the Golgari that much. The monster could not redeem herself. But she could redeem her people.

She said, "All across the city, the Golgari are opening up pathways to safety for every Ravnican they can find. We are fighting Bolas' army and preserving life." And then—more for show than anything—she added with bitter sarcasm, "You're welcome."

Ral said nothing.

But Kaya said, "Good. Now, there's one more thing we need you to do . . ."

FORTY-THREE

GIDEON JURA

It's actually working, thought Gideon.

With fewer civilians in harm's way, Planeswalker and guild forces were converging on the Dreadhorde from all sides, with additional guild forces joining in by the minute, indicating that Kaya must have been successful in her negotiations with the Gruul, Orzhov, Selesnya and Golgari.

From the north, Nissa had joined Angrath and the werewolf Arlinn Kord at the head of a small but enthusiastic army of the Gruul and Golgari. From the east, Tamiyo and Narset fought alongside Vorel and his Simic forcemages. From the south, Tibalt and the diabolist Davriel Cane led a handful of his demons alongside Izzet weaponsmiths and Orzhov knights, giants and gargoyles into battle. From the west, a Planeswalker known only as The Wanderer launched an impressive and destructive attack, her sword cutting a wide swath through the

Eternal ranks, while Boruvo and the Ledev Guardians of Selesnya backed her play. And from above, Gideon himself, riding Promise, fought side by side with Aurelia, her Boros Skyknights, and other guild fliers to rain devastation down on the crops and phalanxes of the enemy.

In fact, Gideon recognized fighters from every guild, save Rakdos and Dovin Baan's Azorius. Even Dimir assassins were stepping out into the open to take the Eternals down.

There were more Planeswalkers, too. Many that he couldn't name. Some of these unknown Planeswalkers fell, their Sparks harvested and stolen, their bodies reduced to grim husks, sinking to the ground in a final embrace with the Eternals that had destroyed them.

And for some bizarre reason, while the rest of them valiantly battled the forces of Bolas, the lithomancer Nahiri could be seen some distance away, atop a building, locked in combat against the vampire Planeswalker Sorin Markov.

Hadn't somebody told him Markov was stuck in a wall?

Gideon felt like flying over to those two idiots and demanding to know what the hell they thought they were doing—but he couldn't afford the time and wouldn't waste the effort. Glancing down, he saw that both The Wanderer (in her unmistakable white garb) and Cane (in his unmistakable black) had battled their way to the center of the conflict, where of course the fighting was the most intense. Too far ahead of their guild support, the two Planeswalkers were soon surrounded by Eternals. Vulnerable, they were ripe for harvesting.

Gideon guided Promise down fast. Her hooves crushed the skull of one Eternal as Gideon leapt off his mount to join these two Planeswalkers whom he barely knew. His own aura flared, blocking the grasp of an Eternal who was reaching for The Wanderer. "Pull back," he shouted over the din of battle. "There are too many!"

The Wanderer was keeping the enemy at bay with expansive swings of her broadsword. But the pure white mana trail that the weapon left in its wake was fading. She turned to Gideon and from beneath her broad-brimmed hat yelled out, *"Hit me!"*

"What?"

"Hit me! Hard as you can! Do it! Now!"

So Gideon Jura hauled off with a roundhouse punch that would have floored half a dozen Planeswalkers and—aura flaring—cracked it across the jaw of The Wanderer. Her head snapped back only an inch or two—as the rest of the blow's kinetic energy was absorbed and transformed into mana that flowed down her arm and into her sword. A second later her repowered weapon was again effortlessly slicing Eternals in two.

Cane, meanwhile, whispered an incantation that summoned a molten demon, which cackled as it burned any Eternal that came near him.

The trio of Planeswalkers and Cane's pet monster fought their way toward Nissa Revane, Angrath and Arlinn Kord. Gideon—too far away to intercept—spotted an Eternal reaching for Nissa from behind. He shouted a warning, but it was Davriel Cane who emerged from obfuscating shadow to grab the Eternal just before it latched onto Nissa. Screaming in pain, Davriel sucked the black Elderspell from the creature, rendering its grip on Nissa harmless. She turned and spiked her staff through the Eternal's head. It dropped.

Cane was doubled over in pain, but Angrath grabbed the collar of Cane's black cape and yanked him right off his feet, dropping him safely behind the minotaur's bulk as he swung his fiery chain in a steep arc to crush and burn their opponents.

Kord, meanwhile, was in a berserker fury, tearing through the lazotep warriors with tooth and claw.

Gideon allowed himself a grim smile.

The good guys are winning.

And so the battle continued. And continued. And continued. Eternal reinforcements continued to emerge from the Planar Bridge, and their numbers seemed limitless. Nevertheless, guild and Planeswalker air and land forces were driving the bulk of the enemy back toward the Citadel of Bolas.

Gideon whistled; Promise descended, and he swung himself back into her saddle. He flew up to join Aurelia.

"It's working," they both said in near-perfect unison. They exchanged dark grins.

Still, when Gideon glanced over at Bolas upon his throne, the dragon hardly seemed to be paying any mind to the battle at all. Instead Bolas simply appeared to glory in the harvested Sparks being absorbed into his Spirit-Gem. This infuriated Gideon, and perhaps the intensity of his emotion briefly attracted Bolas' attention. He turned to look in Gideon Jura's direction. Gideon was too far away to be certain . . . but could have sworn the damn dragon was actually *smiling.*

But then, *just then,* the portal finally irised shut! The endless tide of Eternals crashing in waves from Amonkhet to the "shores" of Ravnica had at last been stemmed. Karn, Samut and the others had succeeded.

By the Gods, has Ob Nixilis actually proven useful *in a good cause?*

Gideon couldn't help but laugh.

Still, the battle was far from over. Gideon spotted an Eternal minotaur he recognized from Amonkhet: Nassor had been an honorable soul; his death, a tragedy. But a second death now would be a mercy and a release. Gideon descended, determined to see it done.

FORTY-FOUR

CHANDRA NALAAR

Nissa had said it just before they'd all divided into squads in service of the many prongs of Jace's plan: "You face Dovin Baan. His magic is the magic of weakness. He sees the flaws in every strategy, in every individual. He knows you, Chandra. He knows your flaws and weaknesses."

Chandra had shaken her head: "After what he did to us on Kaladesh, if you think for one minute I'm not going after that—"

But Nissa clearly had no illusions about Chandra's determination or intent. She reiterated: "Baan knows Chandra Nalaar's weaknesses, so for this mission you must not be Chandra Nalaar."

After this exchange, it had taken some time for Chandra's squad to journey from the Senate House to the center of New

Prahv—not because of the distance, obviously, but because they needed and wanted to avoid being spotted by Baan's automated spy-thopters. The less time a planner like Dovin Baan had to prepare for his opposition, the better. But there was no avoiding observation now.

Chandra, Saheeli Rai and Lavinia stepped into the light of the Immortal Sun, revealed by the simplest of spells. It shone straight up from the ground, into the sky, amid three New Prahv towers, past and through a disk-shaped, gravity-defying stabilizer platform, all based on designs from Dovin Baan's homeworld of Kaladesh. From Chandra's homeworld of Kaladesh. From Saheeli's homeworld of Kaladesh. Baan had done much damage while in authority on that plane. And he was doing worse now on Ravnica, in the name of the Azorius, the guild to which Lavinia had dedicated most of her life. All three thus had good reason to want Dovin's head on a platter. But the priority must be to shut down the Sun that was trapping Planeswalkers on Ravnica, where the Eternals could harvest their Sparks to feed the power of the dragon Nicol Bolas.

They entered the complex. Almost in unison, Saheeli and Lavinia exhaled in response to the tremendous heat the active Sun was generating—a heat only partially alleviated by the cooling waterfalls that spilled down from the top of each of the three towers. (Unsurprisingly, the pyromancer Chandra hardly seemed to notice.) The trio could see the Sun; it was only twenty, twenty-five yards ahead of them on a dais that stood about six feet off the floor, dead center among the three towering structures. A quick sprint could take them there and only a little push of the thing off the dais—in concert with a fairly simple spell dug up by Jace from the mind of its creator Azor (founder of the Azorius Senate)—would disable the Immortal Sun and put an end to its death grip on the Planeswalkers.

If only it were that easy . . .

Like three hundred hives under threat, sliding portals opened up at every level of all three towers, and the bee-like thopters emptied out to strike at Baan and Bolas' enemies. Some of these thopters *were* the size of bees, others the size of horses, most somewhere in between, but *all* dive-bombed toward the threesome, their buzzing wings practically loud enough in unison to blot out the sounds of the waterfalls and the Sun's blaze.

Fortunately, Saheeli was ready with her own small and gorgeous mechanical creations. Shaped like six winged bandar, each no bigger than Saheeli's petite fist, they soared up gracefully to meet the incoming swarm. Three of the six diverged to the sides, each quickly taking position between two towers and rapidly activating a triangular aether field that immediately wreaked havoc on the thopters' targeting systems. Many of the things crashed into the towers or the ground or one another. Some spun in circles. Some flew straight up, up and out of view. But the momentum of more than a few of the thopters took them past the field, and once beyond it their systems righted. Those that attacked were easy enough for Chandra to pick off with a few precision bursts of flame. But many did not bother attacking. Instead they hovered menacingly around the Immortal Sun's dais, a floating, buzzing circular wall of mobile metal. Suddenly a little push and a simple spell had become much more difficult to achieve.

Over the din of aether and wings, Lavinia shouted, "We'll never disable the Sun as long as those things protect it. To complete our mission, we must locate and bring down their master, Dovin Baan."

"There!" shouted Chandra, pointing up to the stabilizer disk that hovered amid the three towers, exactly ninety-nine yards above the New Prahv floor. The blue-skinned vedalken, Dovin Baan, stood atop the platform, hands behind his back, leaning judiciously over the side—not far enough to risk falling, but just far enough to study all three of his opponents, while noting, Chandra was sure, all their strengths and weaknesses.

Lavinia nodded to Saheeli, who nodded back and then pulled out a small silver whistle. She puckered her lips and blew; the whistle emitted no audible sound. But the three remaining flying bandar heard its call and sprang into action, each latching onto a horse-sized thopter to take full control of its clockwork mechanisms.

Saheeli smiled. "Baan's not the only one who has prepared for his opponents."

The three large thopters descended and hovered before Saheeli, Lavinia and Chandra, who quickly mounted and rose, up to the stabilizer disk, up to Dovin Baan.

Baan watched their rise calmly. He stood there, hands still behind his back. Three more thopters emerged from somewhere and targeted the three bandar with metal projectiles that shattered their skulls. Immediately the trio's three mounts were back under Baan's control. They bucked and swerved to dislodge their riders, and it was all Lavinia, Saheeli and Chandra could do to leap off. Lavinia and Saheeli hit the platform rolling. Chandra barely managed to grab its edge and haul herself up onto it in time to raise her arms and fire off three carefully aimed gouts of flame that brought the large thopters down.

The women turned toward Baan, who stood a safe distance away, shaking his head almost sadly. With a sigh, he spoke, just loud enough to be heard over the racket and not a decibel louder: "The decision to send the Azorius apostate and the two Kaladeshi—that is, to send those who hold a *personal* grudge against me—could not have been more predictable. I assume you all volunteered for—or rather *insisted* upon—this assignment?"

They didn't bother answering, since of course it was true.

"Then I suppose," he went on, "it will come as no surprise that I'm thoroughly prepared for each of you, with thopters designed specifically to neutralize your skills while exploiting your weaknesses."

He tilted his head a few degrees, and three hundred more thopters emerged from behind New Prahv's waterfalls to hover around the three women. Lavinia swiftly drew her sword, slashing the closest one in half. Saheeli pulled three more bandar from her pouch and set them loose, taking control of three more thopters, which in turn smashed into and disabled three others. Chandra fired off one apple-sized fireball after another, taking down six more thopters in quick succession. But for each thopter that fell, another took its place.

"I'm not a killer," Baan said. "You may all hate me, but I do not feel such an emotion toward any of you. So please trust me when I say that the Azorius have—under my watch—been both enthusiastic and efficient in the manufacture and production of my thopters. I therefore have more than enough to keep the three of you busy and, well, *useless* to any other endeavor save self-defense, rather indefinitely."

He took a step toward Chandra and studied her closely. "I do admit to some surprise with regard to you, Nalaar. Never in my experience have you demonstrated such restraint and precision in your pyromantic attacks. I hypothesize that you may actually be maturing. It seems most unlikely, but I can come to no other conclusion at this time."

Chandra scowled but said nothing. Instead she took aim at Baan, who exhibited a slight smile, as if to say, *Yes, that's the*

Chandra Nalaar that I remember. Thirty thopters flew into position between her and him—fast enough that Chandra didn't even bother to unleash her fire.

And Dovin Baan was rocked by an explosion nevertheless.

Knocked off balance, he stumbled, an expression of surprise appearing on a face unaccustomed to such emotions. Unnerved, he quickly realized the blast had detonated from below. He looked down off the side of the disk.

Another Chandra Nalaar—the *real* Chandra Nalaar—was unleashing a massive torrent of flame just beneath the wall of hovering thopters. It was melting the base of the dais holding up the Immortal Sun, knocking it out of alignment and shaking the entire complex.

Too late, Baan realized his mistake. He looked up but the Chandra he had been so evenly mocking was gone, replaced by Dimir guildmaster and shapeshifter Lazav, using an Izzet flamethrower to complete the illusion. Before he could recalculate, Lazav unleashed—not more flames, which Baan had been prepared for, but two small throwing stars of a peculiar metal that sliced through Dovin Baan's spells of protection and struck the vedalken right in his eyes, throwing a serious crimp into his ability to detect weakness in others.

Blinded and bleeding, Dovin Baan screamed.

Hearing this from below, Chandra smiled a grim smile of satisfaction while silently thanking Nissa Revane for her sage advice. She then used her fire to blow a wide path for herself through the wall of thopters. She rushed in and with every ounce of her strength strained to shove the Immortal Sun off its deformed dais. Azor's cursed artifact crashed onto the floor of the complex. She had hoped it would shatter but no such luck. So following Jace's instructions, she moved in and stood upon it. Instantly, a power flowed through her. It galvanized Chandra, who briefly knew what it felt like to be a god. It took every ounce of will she had not to release a torrent of flame that would have incinerated all three towers—not to mention her friends. For a moment, she considered *not* turning off the Sun.

There's no reason to give this up. We can use this power. We can use it to defeat Bolas Ourselves! And once the dragon is destroyed, We can take his place atop—

NO!

Forcing her mind back into the moment, she spoke aloud the nine words of Azor that Jace had taught her. The nine words that would disable the Sun. When practicing them earlier, they had sounded odd and unnatural in her mouth, but now they felt like her birthright. It frightened her.

Fortunately, the words quickly worked their magic. Chandra felt her new untold power rapidly recede.

As for the Immortal Sun, she could feel it lose its hold immediately. The lock had been sprung. She could planeswalk again. All the Planeswalkers could planeswalk again. She wondered briefly just how many would.

But Dovin wasn't quite done. He managed to clap his blood-soaked hands. The sound was both pathetic and *sufficient*, unleashing each and every one of his thopters in full attack mode. Yet all this really accomplished was to give the real Chandra the excuse to cut loose. And after what she'd just experienced, cutting loose seemed an almost necessary release.

Two intertwining bolts of fire emerged from her hands. Beneath her flaming hair and glowing eyes, she smiled as her twisting dual infernos sought out each and every one of Baan's thopters—and blew each and every one to kingdom come in a mighty conflagration that had Baan, Saheeli, Lazav and Lavinia covering their faces.

Faced with a defeat, one which he could not calculate even a percentage point's possibility of turning into a victory, Baan instead took advantage of the Immortal Sun being disabled and planeswalked away.

When she saw him disappear in a sideways movement, Chandra lost her bright smile. Blind or not, Baan was still a threat that needed putting down. Still, her mission had been to snuff out the Immortal Sun. Mission accomplished.

FORTY-FIVE

DACK FAYDEN

Returning from Amonkhet, Dack, Samut, Sarkhan and Karn had joined Gideon's assault on the Eternals. A minotaur named Angrath had lit up Hazoret's Spear with flame, and together he and Karn were using it to incinerate more of Bolas' Dreadhorde, three or four at a time.

Samut spotted another minotaur, an eternalized minotaur, and hissed under her breath: "How many times do I have to set you free, brother?"

They went at it. Dack moved to help, but the entire battle was over before he had figured out how he might assist. The minotaur was brutally strong, ripping up an entire paving stone to throw at Samut. But she was just too fast. In the blink of an eye, she was literally riding his back. Dack saw the minotaur reach back and knew that all it would take was a good grip on Samut for her Spark to be lost. She crossed her two khopeshes in front of his neck—and took his head, shouting, "Once and for all, you are free, Neheb!"

Dack was so distracted by Samut's victory, he nearly got "gripped" himself. But Sarkhan Vol transformed his own hands into mystic dragons, which breathed dragonfire, incinerating the two Eternals reaching for the thief. As the creatures burned, a Planeswalker in white sliced off both their heads.

She looked at Sarkhan and said, "Vol."

He said, "Wanderer."

Then they both looked disapprovingly at Dack before rejoining the battle.

Dack looked down and shook his head muttering, "Pay attention, idiot."

He had once possessed a supremely powerful mystic gauntlet that had even helped him fight off a kraken. He'd had to trade the artifact to cure a sleeping curse and hadn't even gotten a zino out of the deal. As he took up the fight again, he wished nothing more than to have that gauntlet back on his hand.

Yet despite his reservations, Dack had to admit that Gideon's strategy was working. The Eternals—even the God-Eternals—were being driven back toward the Citadel of Bolas.

And that's when it happened.

As soon as he had returned to Ravnica, Dack had sensed the oppressive magic that prevented him from planeswalking away. Part of him was glad. He wanted to be brave. Wanted to be the kind of man who stayed and fought. And thanks to the Immortal Sun, there had been no choice in the matter. But suddenly he felt it. The pyromancer's mission to shut the Sun down had clearly succeeded. Dack knew he could leave at any time. And all around him, he saw other Planeswalkers doing just that.

In fact, *so many* did just that, the assault began to falter.

The Eternals pushed back. The God-Eternals advanced again, and from above, Gideon—riding a Boros pegasus—ordered a retreat.

Dack was sorely tempted to depart this world right then.

I mean, I'm just a thief. Who am I to stay when others flee? And we're not just talking about evil bastards like Ob Nixilis now. Plenty of others are going while the going is good. Why not Dack Fayden?

Just then he spotted The Wanderer trapped between two Eternals. She did the smart thing and planeswalked away—only to planeswalk right back behind her opponents and quickly dispatch both with one swing of her sword. Dack was pretty impressed. Planeswalking was draining on a good day, but on a day like today planeswalking twice—back and forth—within a matter of seconds was a feat he flat-out couldn't accomplish no matter how gods-be-damned rested he was.

Still, Dack took heart at this. What The Wanderer had done suited him.

If I get in a jam, I can bug out—and then bug back in soon after. Maybe not two-seconds-later-after, but eventually. Or not. If I get in a jam, I can bug out—and decide then whether I'm coming back. But right now, I stay and fight.

Because ultimately, Dack Fayden refused to be one of *those* Planeswalkers, the kind that runs when things get tough. Maybe he was just a thief and not any kind of hero. Nevertheless, he'd be the kind of thief who *chooses* to stay . . .

FORTY-SIX

KAYA

The first juggler, wearing studded red leathers and ribbons that ended in sharp metal fishhooks, impressively juggled six flaming torches. The second juggler juggled eight human skulls. The third juggled twelve flaming skulls. The fourth juggler was an undead skeleton, bones reinforced with wrought iron, including four wrought-iron horns mimicking those of its master, Rakdos the Defiler. It juggled flaming cat skulls pulled from a small furnace smoldering within its own rib cage.

Without warning, the skeleton flung one of these small burning skulls at Teyo, who barely managed to throw up a circular shield of white light to block it from hitting him in the eye. The skull ricocheted off his shield and struck the skeleton in the face. It laughed a hoarse airless laugh, and Teyo shivered.

Kaya tried to reassure him. "They're just trying to intimidate you."

Teyo looked at the ground and grumbled, "It's working."

The skeleton whispered, "You've got us all wrong, mistress. We're just trying to *entertain* you."

Teyo glared at the skeleton and grumbled, "It's not working."

The skeleton laughed again and said, "Well, at least you're entertaining me."

They were descending the five hundred steep steps of the Demon's Vestibule toward Rix Maadi, guildhall of the Cult of Rakdos. Veins of lava running down the wurm-carved walls shed a dull-red light across all they could see. Another performer was perched on every fourth or fifth step. After the jugglers came the puppeteers, each with a marionette designed to bring nightmares. The last of these made Rat gasp aloud. At first Kaya thought the young girl was afraid—she had been uncharacteristically silent throughout their descent—but upon seeing that the marionette was a brutally accurate caricature of the razorwitch Hekara, complete with actual razors, Kaya quickly realized that Rat's reticence didn't come from fear but from grief. Rat smiled sadly at Kaya and whispered, "It won't be the same here without her."

Hekara's passing was exactly why Kaya had *strongly suggested* that the gorgon accompany herself, Ral, Teyo and Rat to Rix Maadi—and why Kaya had insisted Vraska come without her kraul or Erstwhile defenders. If the Cultists wanted an explanation (or demanded vengeance) for the death of Emissary Hekara, Ral and Kaya wanted Vraska there to explicate (or to pay the price).

Surprisingly, the gorgon had not objected.

Seemingly of its own volition, the Hekara puppet threw very real razors at Ral Zarek and Vraska. The small blades weren't thrown with quite enough force to cause any serious damage to either the Izzet or Golgari guildmasters, though Ral was left with a small cut on his arm and Vraska's face had been nicked and was slowly dripping a line of blood down her cheek. Kaya briefly worried whether or not those razors had been coated with poison. But Rat read her concern and shook her head. "They're clean. But they might not be on the way back *up* the stairs," she said, "depending on how this goes."

Puppeteers gave way to caged horrors with masked devils seated atop the cages, ready and willing to set the little monsters free. These particular horrors, spidery things that huffed and puffed and screeched and wailed, were only the size of raccoons, but then again on this tight, claustrophobic staircase, a raccoon-sized horror would be quite sufficient to do significant damage to any or all of their party. The devils giggled wildly and constantly motioned toward the latches, threatening to open their cages. Teyo flinched every time, which only encouraged the behavior.

The walls were lined, smeared, with hundreds of torn and overlapping banners, some advertising centuries-old performances, most incorporating some insult to one of the other guilds, with Orzhov, Azorius and Boros being the most common or popular targets. Kaya stopped to stare at one banner that appeared as ancient as any but depicted herself, Ral, Vraska and Lavinia hanging like marionettes, each from a single string wrapped tightly around their throats. Their heads lolled, their tongues stuck out, their limbs were slack, their faces bloated and blue. The puppeteer holding their four nooselike strings was a painted image of the Hekara marionette, and the puppeteer working *Hekara's* strings was the Defiler, himself. It didn't bode well for their reception below. Kaya inhaled, exhaled and moved on, glancing back over her shoulder to see Teyo stop for a look, too. Kaya thought he was developing a tic in his left cheek. Rat took some notice and ushered him forward, saying, "At least they don't have a banner of you."

"Yet," he amended nervously.

Past the devils and their horrors were the fire-breathers. Teyo motioned to create a shield, but Rat arrested his hand and shook her head. "You'll only encourage them. Just pay attention, and when they inhale, pass them by."

Throughout their descent, Ral and Vraska remained wary but stoic, each brooding deeply on his or her own dark thoughts, most of which likely revolved around Hekara. Except for Teyo, who hadn't known her, they were *all* mourning the razorwitch to some degree. She had been the unlikely glue that had held this group of unlikely friends together. When Vraska betrayed them, and Hekara died as an almost direct result, the friendship had disintegrated. Even Kaya and Ral, who had done nothing to each other and had no reason for mutual mistrust, felt Hekara's loss looming between them. In part, this was because Ral had held himself aloof from Hekara—taking advantage of her without ever truly acknowledging her as someone he cared about, though of course after it was too late, he realized he cared about her deeply. Kaya knew he felt guilty over this failing, and she surmised that a part (an *irrational* part) of Zarek was angry with *her* for having openly treated Hekara with warmth and fellowship. Mostly, however, he was simply angry with himself.

"And worried about Tomik," Rat added.

Rat is definitely a little bit psychic. And yes, of course, Ral's worried for Tomik. He's been missing ever since Bolas arrived. Ral must be going crazy.

Kaya tried to offer Ral a look of sympathy. But his eyes never quite focused on her enough to see it.

The deeper they went, the hotter and closer the air became, and not just because of the fire-breathers. The red veins in the curving walls were wider down here and more liquid, the searing lava dripped down onto the steps and needed to be carefully avoided if one wanted to keep one's boots intact—or one's feet.

The fire-breathers now gave way to unicyclists, who balanced impressively in place, rolling back and forth within the span of a few inches, on devices that appeared designed for a torture chamber: spokes of barbed wire, clawed wheels, seats made from axe blades. More than one of the riders bled. Every rider came close to slicing gashes in their party of five. One cyclist, who clearly couldn't even see Rat, nearly chopped off her foot. But this sort of near catastrophe seemed to be a common occurrence for Araithia Shokta; the girl had trained herself to be preternaturally aware of her surroundings at all times and easily skipped past the threat.

Finally, they reached the bottom step, and the Vestibule terminated at the Festival Grounds, which were guarded by two immense ogres wearing masks made from actual ogre skulls. Kaya hesitated but the ogres ignored them all—as if all five of them were Rats—so she ignored them back and continued forward across the large courtyard. In its center was a cracked and graffitied fountain featuring a statue of a centaur. From a certain angle, the statue was surprisingly elegant, but as Kaya approached she saw that chunks of marble had been broken off the man-horse as if by a sledgehammer. Water dribbled from broken lips, and that water in turn dribbled out of the cracked fountain and down through a crack in the floor, where it rose again as steam.

Above them, unoccupied trapeze swings hung from rusty hooks, while a single young pigtailed tightrope walker, in a black-and-red harlequin leotard, glided heedlessly across a threadbare strand. Her movements were full of grace, drawing the eye. She glanced down at her new audience, and Teyo gasped. Her lips and eyelids had been stitched shut.

There were empty cages large enough to hold human horrors. And everything, absolutely everything, was haphazardly painted with splatters of what Kaya had to assume was actual blood.

At the far end of the Festival Grounds, two more skull-masked ogres stood guard before the ornate stone façade of Rix Maadi. Like the first pair, these ogres seemed to take no notice of Kaya and the others. Still, their little group hesitated before the entrance's ominous red glow—until Vraska muttered, "Screw it," and marched through the arched gothic doorway. Ral and Kaya exchanged a glance and followed, with Rat and Teyo close behind.

Rix Maadi's façade was literally that. Within was no architecture—just a massive natural volcanic cavern. Steam rose from a huge central lava pit—as big as Lake Keru on Kaya's homeworld—and was vented above by natural chimneys that presumably ran all the way up to Ravnica's surface.

They were all sweating profusely now. Even Teyo, the desert dweller. He shrugged and said, "It's not the heat; it's the humidity."

Stone causeways crisscrossed the lava pit. Steel cables crisscrossed the ceiling, supporting more rusty cages and hooks. Blood-filled basins dotted the landscape. So did dozing hellhounds. The walls were pockmarked with dozens of doors to dozens of chambers. Laughter emanated from some. Screams from others. Both from many. To their left, at ground level, a large aperture in the wall was shrouded by a supernatural mist of pure shadow. A foul breeze wafted forth from within. Something about it gave even the ghost-assassin the shivers.

Rat slid up to Kaya and whispered, "Where is everybody? Rix Maadi is usually packed with performers. I've never seen it so empty."

Kaya looked through the red-tinged gloom. Except for the

hellhounds, and the occasional scurrying rat, there wasn't a soul around, living or dead, except the five members of their party. Then, as if on cue, a startling figure appeared in a burst of red smoke.

"Dame Exava," Rat whispered. "Blood witch. She's the Defiler's current number two."

As the smoke slowly cleared, Exava came into focus. She was tall, muscular and apparently human. She wore an immense and elaborate mask decorated with two sets of what were probably genuine demon horns. A tight bodice accentuated a large chest and a bare midriff. She wore thigh-high boots and a wide belt from which hung numerous iron spikes, all red-stained, again presumably with blood. She stood upon a small stage and, unaware of Rat, stared down at the other four with imperious contempt.

Kaya, Ral and Vraska looked at one another and then bowed their heads in unison. Ral spoke the formalities: "We honor you, Exava, as a blood witch of rare talent, and we beg an audience with your master, the Defiler."

Exava studied them in silence. Then she looked toward the pit. Lava bubbled, but nothing else appeared, including the demon.

"Apparently," Exava said in a rich contralto, "the Defiler begs no audience from you."

But in that moment, Rakdos' booming voice echoed throughout the entire cavern: *"WHERE IS OUR EMISSARY?"*

Ral glared at Vraska, who stepped forward, ready to take whatever was coming to her. But before she could speak, a voice called out, "She is here!"

They all turned toward the main entrance. It was Tomik Vrona, leading a single Orzhov thrull, which carried a covered corpse. Tomik signaled the thrull, which stopped. He uncovered the corpse's face. "I have brought Hekara back to her people."

They all saw Ral rush over to Tomik, but only Kaya and Teyo saw Rat scurry over to Hekara's side. She stood on tiptoe to see her friend and kissed Hekara on her pale cheek.

Ral stopped short of kissing Tomik, though Kaya knew he clearly wanted to.

At which point, Exava cleared her throat impatiently. All eyes turned to face her. She said, "Have your creature place the razorwitch on the stage at my feet."

Tomik gestured, and the thrull complied.

Exava knelt beside Hekara's corpse and jerked the shroud that covered her away. She flung it into the air, and it burst into flames dramatically—*overdramatically.* Its ashes rained down on the thrull, Tomik and the rest.

The blood witch ran a hand from the top of Hekara's head all the way down to the tips of her painted toes in a disturbingly erotic caress. She said, "You should have brought her back sooner."

"Apologies," Tomik said with a bow. "Things have been a bit chaotic up on the surface."

"That is *not* the Cult's concern."

"But it should be," Ral stated.

Exava rose, snapping her fingers dismissively. Or so it seemed at first. But within seconds six more blood witches appeared in six more puffs of red smoke. They came prepared and quickly stripped Hekara's body naked—much to Teyo's obvious embarrassment—and then adorned it in rags and bells. When the process was completed, Exava said, "Have your thrull take Hekara into the Jester's Crypt." She pointed a long elegant finger toward the noxious aperture.

Tomik made two more hand gestures, and the thrull took up the corpse. With Hekara in his arms the creature trod dully through the aperture, flanked by a procession of the six witches.

Rat said, "I hope Mr. Vrona didn't like that thrull. He won't see him again."

And again on cue, they all froze at the sound of the thrull's bloodcurdling death-scream. Tomik looked absolutely horrified. Rat shrugged.

Exava said, "I will return shortly. Stay here." She then burst into flame, much as Hekara's shroud had. Ashes rained down, but not one of their number actually thought Exava had burned.

Ral then grabbed Tomik by the shoulders and growled, "I've been looking all over for you!"

Tomik smiled at his partner and gently leaned his forehead against Ral's. They both just stood there breathing for a few moments. Then Tomik leaned away, shrugged and said, "You have had your duties; I have had my own."

Ral took a step back. "Which are what, exactly?"

Tomik answered Ral but looked past him at Kaya: "I am the executive assistant to the *true* guildmaster of the Orzhov. For years, I believed that to be Teysa Karlov. Now I know it is Kaya. And so I have been about the business of serving my mistress."

Kaya smiled at Tomik and thanked him. Then the epiphany hit: "Tomik, *you're* the one who actually rallied the Orzhov troops into battle."

"That was mostly the giant Bilagru. You made a good impression on him."

"After you sent him to me and primed the pump."

Tomik tilted his left hand as if to say, *Such is my duty.*

Just then, Exava emerged from the Jester's Crypt. She was dressed the same, except now she wore bright-red gloves.

Kaya swallowed.

No, those aren't gloves. Gloves don't drip.

Vraska stepped forward again. "Great and talented Exava,

Ravnica requires your aid. If Hekara were alive, she'd urge you to help us convince your master—"

Exava interrupted, "*Emissary* Hekara died because she placed her trust in you three." She pointed from Vraska to Ral to Kaya. "One of you betrayed her, one of you denied her, and one of you simply failed her."

"All true," Ral said with evident remorse—but no little determination. "And there are no guarantees now, save this: If the ten guilds do not unite, Ravnica is surely doomed."

"Then the Cult of Rakdos will dance on Ravnica's grave. We're quite good at grave dancing. It's a specialty."

"I'm sure you are, and I'm sure it is," Ral said. "But the dead can't dance."

"You'd be surprised."

"Please, listen. Niv-Mizzet left us one last plan to defeat Nicol Bolas. If you allow me to explain—"

"*WE ALREADY KNOW EVERY DETAIL OF THE LATE FIREMIND'S LATEST GRASP AT POWER,*" echoed Rakdos' voice. "*WE'LL HAVE NONE OF IT!*"

Exava smiled dangerously. "I think you should go," she said.

"But—"

"Before you *really* piss him off."

Ral, Tomik, Vraska and Kaya all looked inward, studying to see if there was anything they could do or say that might make a difference. But in the end, their shoulders all collectively sank, and they turned to go.

Kaya saw Teyo turn to Rat and say, "That's it? We're giving up?"

But Rat wasn't listening. She was focused on the opening of the Jester's Crypt. Kaya followed her look and gasped.

"What's your hurry, partners?" Hekara said, emerging from the shadowy space.

Ral, Vraska and Tomik were halfway to the exit; they stopped in their tracks and turned.

"Hekara?" Ral said stupidly.

"Well, yeah," she said with a shrug.

"Weren't you dead?" Vraska said, just as stupidly.

"Well, sure. Miss me?"

"More than you can know . . . my friend," Ral said. The admission seemed to cause him some discomfort, but he got through it.

"Stop it," Hekara said. "You'll embarrass me. *Just kidding!* I never get embarrassed. Be as mushy as you want. It's horrible theater but we all have our guilty pleasures, right?"

Vraska, even more pained than Ral, said, "I owe you an apology, Hekara. I never should have betrayed your trust."

"It was a pretty crappy thing to do. And dying sucked. But hey, it all worked out. After all, you can't be resurrected as a blood witch if you don't die first, right?"

"You're a blood witch now?" Rat asked in some awe.

But Ral couldn't hear Rat and spoke over her, asking, "Can you convince Rakdos to join Operation Desperation?"

"Ooo, good title," the new blood witch said. "Anyway, don't sweat it. I'll represent the Cult in whatever you got planned, mate."

"No, you will not," Exava boomed. "The Defiler has made his wishes clear."

"Really? Cuz he hasn't said word one to me."

"At the time, you were dead and thus a somewhat inattentive audience."

"He could set me straight now."

"There's no need. *I'm* doing that."

"But you're not the Boss. Not the boss of me, anyway. You're just a blood witch. And since I'm a blood witch now, too, I'm thinking I don't need to follow your orders. You don't outrank me anymore, Exava. You just kinda side-rank me."

"Witch, I'll kill you all over again!" Exava leapt, her bloody hands reaching for Hekara's throat.

Hekara cartwheeled away. The cartwheel morphed into a somersault, which morphed into a backflip. Hekara landed on the stage. Once she had the high ground, she materialized multiple razors in both hands and threw them all simultaneously. "Once a razorwitch, always a razorwitch!"

Exava was caught unprepared. She parried most of the blades with a wave of her hand, but more than one pierced her skin. It hardly slowed her down, but Hekara wasn't exactly in this fight alone. Ral fired up his Accumulator and fired off a relatively small bolt that caught Exava from behind. She screamed and dropped to her knees.

One of the hellhounds reacted, springing up to defend its mistress. But Hekara intercepted the brute, saying, "Stop it, Whipsaw. Sit!"

The hellhound stopped but did not sit. It growled menacingly, its mouth dripping an acidic saliva that sizzled when it hit the ground. Ral recharged, ready to fry the beast. Hekara waved him off but didn't even bother to look his way. She just kept speaking soothingly to the hellhound: "Don't mind Ral. He's okay. And Exava will be her old diva self in no time. Now sit!"

The beast sat.

Hekara called out to the still-absent Rakdos, "I'm going to help my mates now. You don't mind, do you, Boss?"

The Defiler remained silent.

"Okay, then," Hekara said with a laugh. "Let's get on with it!" She led the way out, and Tomik, Vraska and Ral followed. But Kaya and Teyo saw Hekara walk right by an expectant Rat—without noticing her at all. Rat's face fell; she looked away. All three of them knew instantly: Whatever process had brought Hekara back to life had changed her enough so that she could no longer see Rat . . . and that broke the young girl's heart.

FORTY-SEVEN

JACE BELEREN

J ace *told* himself she'd left them all with no choice.

He *reminded* himself, as if to prove the point, that even Chandra—*even Gideon*—had not tried to stop him, no matter how unhappy the notion made them. That Jaya Ballard and Teferi, who both knew and liked the necromancer well enough, had agreed to help.

He *insisted* to himself that this was not about his own history with the woman—not the bad or the good of it. That it had nothing to do with his supposed bias against her, his weeks and weeks of telling everyone how untrustworthy she was. No, the decision came down to two simple facts: one, the Eternals were murdering everyone they could get their hands on, Planeswalkers and innocent civilians alike, and two, she controlled the Eternals.

It was for those two reasons, and those two reasons alone,

that Jace Beleren had *forced* himself to plan the assassination of Liliana Vess.

And it was killing him.

His time on Ixalan with Vraska had taught Jace many things. Vraska was a pirate, an assassin and a collaborator with Bolas, and yet their burgeoning relationship had demonstrated in stark terms how unhealthy his liaison with Liliana had been. She had used him every chance she had. Used him for his powers, for his connections, for sex. She had twisted him around her little finger. He was too old to be her puppy dog but looking back on those days and nights, he knew that's exactly how he had behaved—because that's exactly how she wanted it.

She had toyed with him. Leading him on. Pushing him off. Drawing him close. Cutting him to the quick. Playing to his vanity. Making him feel like crap. Even, once or twice, making him feel like a god. Maybe at the beginning, he could have walked away with no problem, but by the time she was done with all that elastic rigmarole, he was as hooked on her as any addict. It had taken a severe—if temporary—case of amnesia and the consistent warmth of a gorgon to get Jace to kick the habit.

And still, and still . . .

Yes, damnit, there is more to Liliana than that.

He *had* to believe there was.

Of course, she's attractive (ridiculously, seductively, entrancingly, mysteriously attractive), but he hadn't been that *desperate, had he?*

Somewhere, buried deep inside her—okay, *entombed* might be the better word—Liliana Vess must have cared for him. At least a little.

Right? RIGHT?

And he must have—*must have*—seen, beneath her impressive defensive shields of selfishness, self-interest and sex appeal, that she had the potential for good at her core.

Just because she hadn't lived up to that potential—had, in fact, betrayed it and him and the Gatewatch entirely—didn't mean that potential hadn't been there.

And if it *was* there, it might still be there. And if it was *still* there, how could he kill her and rob her of any chance at redemption?

Well, the fact that she was trying to harvest every single Planeswalker (with no obvious exemptions being granted to Jace or Chandra or Gideon or any of her "friends") helped justify it, of course. But it wasn't just about his life or even the lives of *his* friends. She was committing genocide on Ravnica. Genocide on the Planeswalkers. She had promised to help them defeat Bolas, and instead she was using the powers and freedom that the Gatewatch had helped grant her in order to murder a world and its people and the Planeswalkers for the dragon, though she knew what the dragon was and what he would do with the power she was helping him acquire.

If I thought I could risk trying to talk to her, trying to reason with her . . .

But they were past that point. She had seen what Bolas had done on Amonkhet—the devastation and loss of life—and had sided with him nevertheless. She had made her choice. She must be beyond anything resembling "reason."

Thus she had to die.

Vivien Reid was the only member of their little squad to object to the plan—and only because she hated Bolas, who had destroyed her homeworld. She would have much preferred an attempt on *his* life instead. The rest agreed, however, that they didn't have the necessary power to kill the dragon from a distance. No, ending Nicol Bolas would ultimately be up to Gideon and Blackblade at close range. But Gideon's path would have to be cleared first, and that meant taking out Liliana Vess.

Jace's plan called for the four of them—Jace, Teferi, Jaya, Vivien—to perch on the roofs of four separate buildings, equidistant on four sides from the Citadel where Liliana stood, serving Nicol Bolas and controlling his deadly army. The timing of the thing had to be precisely coordinated, which was Jace's job. He had linked all four psychically while simultaneously making sure that psychic noise—specifically, the psychic screams of the dying—drowned out their communication, preventing the dragon from reading them.

Next came Teferi, who, on Jace's signal, cast a spell to slow down time for Liliana, who would now move and more importantly *react* in slow motion to their attacks.

Jaya fired first, a precision pyromantic strike. A thin blade of flame to burn a hole in Liliana's chest. Jace doubted whether or not Liliana ever saw it coming. She didn't have to. Faces, indistinct and semi-transparent but with mouths open wide in silent screams, emerged from the Chain Veil and just barely managed to deflect Jaya's strike. The fire ricocheted off their lightless mana and splashed against the pyramid's stones.

These ghostly emanations, Jace knew, were the Onakke spirits that possessed the Veil and had designs on the necromancer, as well. But these spirits had never operated this way before. Liliana had never allowed it. Jace scowled, concluding that Bolas' hold over Liliana had somehow freed her to release the true power of the Veil.

From behind Vess, Vivien fired a single arrow from her Arkbow. Jace found himself hoping the arrow itself might take Liliana's life, quickly and (perhaps) painlessly. Another of the Onakke, however, deflected the arrow from its host. Yet the arrow was never the true threat. Striking the Citadel, the arrow unleashed a spirit of its own: a Skalla wolf that leapt past and through the Onakke and ripped into Liliana's left arm, mauling her badly.

The Onakke regathered and attempted to hold the wolf spirit at bay—giving both Jaya and Vivien the opportunity to try again. The Onakke blocked most of these attacks, but thanks to Teferi the assaults seemed to be coming faster and faster, with more than a few getting by the spirits and doing significant, though not yet mortal, damage.

Liliana was burned. Liliana was pierced. Liliana was torn. Liliana was failing. Jace stifled the urge to save her. With a slight wave of her good right arm, she sacrificed multiple flying Eternals, throwing their bodies into the paths of flame, arrow and spirit beasts. By using the Veil, she drained other Eternals, applying the energies of their unholy resurrections toward healing her wounds almost as she was receiving them.

But Jaya and Vivien were relentless, and the slowed-down thoughts and defenses of Vess and the Onakke couldn't keep pace with the offensive.

Liliana was vulnerable, and Jace knew they'd never have a better shot. And though a voice in his head was practically begging him to stop the others and terminate her torment, he knew the torments of Ravnica outweighed whatever Liliana was suffering. Best to end it.

So far, Jace hadn't participated directly.

Am I trying to avoid guilt by being only a passive participant? No. This is my plan. I'm responsible for it. So stop pretending otherwise.

He fired off his own shot—a psychic attack that grabbed Liliana's attention and held it, as Ballard and Reid took two more shots each.

He heard her moment of recognition from within her mind: *Jace? Jace, please . . .*

Jaya's flames burned the skin off Liliana's chest—though the Onakke circumvented any damage that was anything worse than skin-deep.

Vivien's next arrow sank deep into Liliana's shoulder. A Skalla spider emerged from it and sank its fangs into her neck.

Through it all, her mental screams echoed inside Jace's head. But he held her fast, kept her from calling either the Eternals or Bolas himself to her aid.

She was trying to tell Jace something through the pain, but he would hear no more of her manipulations.

It's working . . . Damnit.

She dropped to one knee. They almost had her . . . until Bolas' perhaps inevitable intervention. The dragon had been distracted by the flying Sparks that were soaring toward him and arcing into his Spirit-Gem. He was looking skyward—not down at his minion Vess. But fire enough arrows and flame streams in the vicinity of Nicol Bolas—even at his most self-involved—and he was bound to notice eventually.

And it seemed he still had a use for Liliana Vess.

The near-godlike dragon fired off four of his own magical blasts. Each collapsed one of the four buildings upon which the four assassins were standing. Jace felt the roof crumble beneath his feet. Thankfully, with great effort, Teferi was able, one after the other, to make each building collapse in slow motion. Jace leapt from one piece of slow-falling masonry to another, as if using stepping-stones to carefully cross a river. He touched down on the ground and ran clear, reaching out with his mind. The other three had also made it out alive and unscathed.

But when Jace looked up, he saw that Vess lived, too. He could see the Onakke drive away the last of the dissipating Arkbow spirit animals. He could see Vess absorb the energy of more Eternals to heal herself. He could see Bolas smile his mirthless smile and turn away, spectacularly untroubled by the efforts of Jace and his allies.

Now that the dragon was alerted, there would be no second opportunity. All they could do was retreat. They had failed.

And a substantial part of Jace Beleren was glad.

FORTY-EIGHT

LILIANA VESS

It hurt.

She had been singed by Jaya's flames, the blackened skin peeling away from muscle and fat tissue. There was an arrow sticking out of her right shoulder blade. And those damn beasts had badly mauled her left arm and right leg—and taken a substantial chunk out of her neck, just barely missing any major veins or arteries.

She was on her knees, breathing in ragged gasps. She glanced up at Bolas, who had saved her life. He paid her no mind now. Though Liliana was certain the dragon had the power, healing his minion was clearly beneath him—or in any case, something with which he simply could not be bothered.

The Onakke called to her in unsubtle whispers, *Release yourself, Vessel. Release yourself to us.*

She ignored them, reaching past their offer to summon

the power of the Veil directly. With it, she drained the animus from two nearby Eternals. They practically melted before her. Lazotep coatings clinked against Citadel stone, but the bodies contained within were soon rigid with morbidity, splayed in rag-doll poses. She used their energy as a healing force, repairing her neck first, since it seemed to pose the biggest threat, and her chest second, since the burn caused the most pain—though of course the moment that skin healed over, the pain from her leg and arm became almost as excruciating.

She was forced to summon two more Eternals and forced to wait as they made their excruciatingly slow progress up the Citadel steps to come within range. Then she drained them, too, to heal her mauled limbs.

Pulling the arrow out of her shoulder was almost an afterthought. She screamed as she tore the barbed point free and collapsed onto her side in a puddle of her own blood. She began shivering uncontrollably. She couldn't focus her vision—let alone her power—to find—let alone summon—another Eternal. But blood was blood. She managed to extend her hand and lick a few drops off her fingers. It was. Humiliating. But it was sufficient. Her necromantic power coalesced within the coagulating blood. Defying gravity, it poured upward, running up her arm to her shoulder. Soon the stones were clean and her wound was healing. She allowed herself to remain prone for a few more seconds, then slowly, tenderly, cautiously began to rise.

Still breathing hard, she made an attempt to regain her dignity. A simple spell cleaned her face. Another repaired and cleaned her black dress. She removed the Chain Veil to silence its whispers—at least temporarily. She was exhausted, but she was herself again, Liliana Vess again.

But it still hurt.

Every inch of her felt tender and sore. Every nerve felt exposed and raw. But what hurt even more than her physical injuries was the echo of Jace Beleren within her mind.

He tried to kill me. Not to reach me. Not to stop me. Not to convince me *to stop. Not even to render me unconscious. He just wanted me dead.*

Of course, a part of her was hardly surprised.

Why should I expect mercy or understanding from my so-called friends? And for just that reason, why should I *have any mercy on them?*

And yet another part of her had to admit that Jace and the others had little choice if they wanted to stop the carnage.

Bolas left me with no choice, and I in turn left them with none.

A third part, buried deep, believed she deserved death.

What kind of life will be left to me when all this is over? And will it ever be over, or will I spend eternity as Bolas' pawn and plaything? Maybe I should have let them kill me.

And a last part—buried deeper still—shed a tear for the loss of a man she knew had once loved her, and whom maybe, just maybe, she had once loved, too . . .

FORTY-NINE

TEYO VERADA

Teyo had no role in the ceremony. He was just a fly on the wall (or what was left of the walls, since they were holding the rite in the ruins of the former Embassy of the Guildpact). Rat stood beside him providing the play-by-play, like the caller at a game of sand-devil, which is to say that much of what she related was either already known to him or dead obvious, but she helped to make the event more entertaining.

"Operation Desperation, the Firemind's final plan," she said, "requires all ten guilds, the leylines of Ravnica, the charred bones of Niv-Mizzet, and that thing."

She was pointing to a brass model of a dragon head—Niv-Mizzet's head, to be specific—being carried forward by the Izzet goblin Varryvort. "It's called the Firemind's Vessel and will contain his spirit when summoned from wherever it's currently residing—assuming this works, that is, and given the name of the plan that could easily be too much to assume, you know?"

Varryvort gently placed the Vessel atop Niv's blackened bones.

"See, Plan A had been to give Master Niv-Mizzet the power to fight Bolas. That didn't work out, and you can see the end result. Plan B—as in Beacon—failed, too. This is Plan C, I think. Unless I've lost count.

"So over there, Master Zarek's consulting with Miss Revane. Mr. Beleren says she's some kind of expert on leylines. Has a magical connection to them. So Master Zarek's explaining what they need to accomplish."

Ral and Nissa Revane were speaking too quietly for either Teyo or Rat to make out the words. But when Ral fell silent, Rat did, as well. Nissa then proceeded to study the problem for six long minutes, during which she remained completely motionless, resembling a painted statue more than a living being. During this interval, Varryvort came over to stand beside Teyo. Not seeing Rat, he would've bumped right into her, but the girl adeptly sidestepped over to Teyo's other side. Finally, Nissa nodded, saying, "It might be possible. The leylines were disrupted by the Planar Bridge, but with the Bridge gone, I believe I can repair them and help Ravnica reassert herself."

"Well, that's promising, at least," Rat said with a grin. "Now all we have to do is wait for the rest of the guild representatives to gather."

Ral, Kaya and Vraska were already present, though each of the three had been guildmaster for less than a month. Lavinia arrived next. Since Dovin Baan had fled, she was now acting guildmaster of the Azorius Senate, a position she'd held for about fifty-two minutes.

Hekara, recently resurrected blood witch and Emissary of the Cult of Rakdos, literally cartwheeled around the deci-

mated chamber, bells tinkling from her costume's leather ribbons. Rat's violet eyes went wide: "She's so cool!" Then her
violet eyes saddened, as Hekara cartwheeled right past her
once again.

Still, Teyo noted (and not for the first time), *Rat's nothing if
not resilient.* When Borborygmos, leader of the Gruul Clans,
arrived with Rat's parents, Ari and Gan Shokta, Rat's mother
smiled at her daughter, pointing Rat out to Gan Shokta and
the cyclops. Both squinted at the space next to Teyo until they
could see the girl. Araithia Shokta's violet eyes lit up like two
stars. "My mom's pretty cool, too," she said.

Emmara Tandris, champion of the Selesnya Conclave, arrived with Boruvo, who exchanged a few dangerous-sounding
growls with his former Gruul clanmates, who seemed to regard him as a traitor for having switched guilds. Teyo braced
himself, ready to create a shield to prevent a fight. But a stern
look from Rat chastened the centaur, the cyclops and her parents. "Can't we all just get along?" she said. They nodded without too much reluctance.

Next came Vannifar, prime speaker of the Simic Combine,
accompanied by Vorel.

Then Aurelia, guildmaster of the Boros Legion, flew in, still
hot from battle.

Only when all the others had shown their faces did Guildmaster Lazav of House Dimir reveal that he had been there all
along—right beside Teyo and Rat—by morphing out of the
form of the goblin Varryvort.

"Damnit, Lazav!" Ral said in a clipped and dangerous voice.
"What the hell have you done with the real Varryvort?"

Lazav "reassured" Ral in a lazy drawl, "Your accomplished
chief chemister is sleeping one off. He'll be just fine come
morning—assuming this succeeds, and *any* of us are just fine
come morning."

Nissa looked uncomfortable, and Rat nudged Teyo with her elbow. He stared at her, unsure of what she wanted. "Help the elf," she whispered.

He nodded and stepped forward, saying, "If everyone would just gather around Miss Revane."

Kaya approached, and Nissa silently indicated where she needed the Orzhov guildmaster to stand. This process was repeated in turn with Hekara, Ral, Lavinia, Lazav, Aurelia, Borborygmos, Vannifar, Vraska and Emmara. There was some grousing—and considerable mistrust among the various guild representatives, with Lavinia and Vraska very nearly coming to blows when Nissa placed them next to each other. But Nissa finally opened her mouth and declared, "Let me make this clear: Without a perfect act of unity from every single guild in concert, the plan has no hope of succeeding. You must put all grievances—petty or otherwise—behind you." The act of saying that many words in sequence seemed to visibly exhaust the elf, but they did the trick. Soon enough, the ten guild representatives were standing in a slightly warped circle around Nissa and the bones and Vessel of the Firemind. The remaining few in attendance—Teyo, Rat, Boruvo, Vorel, Ari and Gan Shokta—stood in something of a clump just outside the circle. Ari seemed to be looking Teyo up and down. She frowned a little in a look reminiscent of those granted to the acolyte by Abbot Barrez. Apparently, Teyo Verada had not quite passed muster as a dependable friend to Ari Shokta's daughter.

"You stand upon the ancient leylines of the Guildpact," Nissa said, pulling Teyo's attention back to the matter at hand.

"Which has exactly what to do with dragon bones?" Aurelia asked in a decidedly suspicious tone.

The elf again looked uncomfortable, and Ral took a step forward before quickly stepping back when Nissa glared at him in frustration for leaving his designated spot. He said,

"We are here to resurrect the Firemind as the new Living Guildpact."

Apparently, this was news to approximately half the guild leaders.

Vorel shouted, "What?" and Aurelia growled, "That's what this is?" more or less in concert. Borborygmos roared along with them both.

Lavinia grumbled, "Didn't we try this already, when he was alive? What makes you think—"

Hekara said, "It's not called Operation Desperation for nothing, you know."

Ral held up his hands and said, "We did try, and we failed. But the same terms apply. Jace Beleren has lost the power of the Living Guildpact. We need that power to defeat Nicol Bolas. If we succeed here, Niv-Mizzet will rise again to that power and use it against the Elder Dragon. Then the Firemind will step down as guildmaster of the Izzet and, as one of Ravnica's most ancient, wise and venerable paruns, take up this new role as impartial arbiter to all ten guilds and Gateless, alike. The gods know he can hardly do a worse job than Beleren."

Lavinia, Vraska and Emmara frowned at that last comment, but the rest seemed to begrudgingly acknowledge the truth of it and settled down.

Rat whispered in Teyo's ear, "I'm glad he acknowledged the Gateless. We're always forgotten when the big mucky-mucks gather to talk guild business."

Hekara was practically bouncing up and down, saying, "I've never been part of an all-guild casting. Now I'm kind of glad the Boss didn't want to come himself."

Aurelia shook her head and scoffed, "The demon can't be bothered to save Ravnica, so Rakdos sends one of his minions."

Rat again whispered in Teyo's ear, "The Boros Legion has always been intolerant of Rakdos."

I can't imagine why, Teyo thought, recalling the caged horrors, skull jugglers and the blood. Especially the blood.

Hekara wagged her finger at Aurelia. "It's not like that at all. The Boss didn't send me in his place. I totally came without his permission."

Vraska smirked. "Hekara, if we're being honest, you came in open defiance of his wishes."

"Exactly!"

This started off another round of grousing and recriminations. Emmara and Vannifar turned on Ral, demanding to know how he expected any kind of success when the Cult's eponymous guildmaster and parun wasn't on board.

Aurelia said, "Even attempting this is virtually pointless."

Hekara, reacting like a child who'd been caught stealing sweets, attempted to backpedal away from her previous blithe rebelliousness. "Don't get me wrong. The Boss is fully behind this effort."

Aurelia eyed her like a mother who'd caught her child stealing sweets. "Is he now?"

"Oh, yeah, completely. Entirely. Probably."

Ral stepped in (verbally—he wasn't about to move from his assigned spot and risk another glare from Nissa): "We might as well give it a shot. The ceremony will only take . . ." He trailed off with a questioning look at Nissa Revane.

"Five minutes at the most," she responded. "Assuming it works at all."

Kaya said, "Five minutes? Time is precious, but at five minutes we can't afford *not* to make the effort."

Nissa looked around the circle. One by one, each of the ten nodded in agreement, some with enthusiasm, some with determination, some with considerable reluctance. But they all nodded nonetheless.

Far from looking enthusiastic, determined or reluctant, a

seemingly emotionless Nissa said, "Everyone, take a deep breath."

Teyo inhaled and exhaled deeply.

Rat giggled. "I think she was only talking to the people in the circle."

He blushed deeply.

"Oh, look. You're so cute when you're embarrassed."

He blushed deeply-er.

"Yeah, like that!"

As Teyo struggled to recover his composure, Nissa began chanting—too low for Teyo to hear. From where she stood, beside bones and Vessel, lines began to alight beneath her feet. Black lines. Blue lines. Green lines. Red lines. White lines. Then, of a sudden, the lines shot out in multiple directions, forming concentric circles beneath the feet of the ten representatives. Teyo was instantly fascinated with the geometry and sought to keep track of which lines connected which representatives. He noted that all of the representatives had two colored circles beneath them, and as far as he could tell no two combinations were the same. Kaya, for example, was surrounded by a circle of white and a circle of black. Black lines connected Kaya's black circle to identical circles around Vraska, Lazav and Hekara. Hekara's second circle was red, which connected her to Borborygmos, Aurelia and Ral. Ral's second circle was blue, connecting him to Lavinia, Lazav and Vannifar. Vannifar's second circle was green, connecting her to Borborygmos, Vraska and Emmara. Emmara's second circle was white, connecting her to Lavinia, Aurelia and back to Kaya. It was so intricate and perfect.

The abbot, Teyo thought, *would approve.*

By the time the acolyte had noted all the connections, the ceremony's eleven participants had fallen into some kind of trance, sporting eleven blank stares. Suddenly golden light

poured out of twenty-one sightless eyes. Operation Desperation had been activated. A colorless portal—like clear water—
opened up above the Firemind Vessel, and wispy smoke of
blue and red emerged and descended, as if sucked down from
portal to Vessel. The bones ignited, bright-yellow and orange
flames rising high—and giving off enough light to blind Teyo,
Rat, Vorel, Boruvo and the Shoktas. Teyo raised a hand to
shield his eyes and, squinting, saw that Nissa was engulfed in
the fire. Engulfed but not aflame. Impossibly, the elf neither
screamed nor writhed nor burned. The blaze expanded from
bones, Vessel and Nissa to encompass the ten guild leaders, as
well. And like Nissa, they showed no signs of being burned by
the fire. Still entranced, they didn't even seem to notice it.

Unfortunately, something else did.

Rat spotted him first, pointing up and shouting over the
roar of the fire: "We've got company!"

As the light from the fire had gleamed brighter and brighter,
it had attracted the attention of Kefnet, the one-armed God-
Eternal, who crossed the plaza in tremendous booming strides
and was soon looming over the ruins of the former embassy,
looking down on Operation Desperation, still in progress.

Teyo didn't even think. He didn't even chant. As Kefnet's
single massive fist swung down toward them, the young
shieldmage reached up with both hands and manifested a
half sphere of light over all seventeen of them. But the acolyte
had never created a shield anywhere near this big before, and
when Kefnet's fist smashed against it, the shield barely held—
and Teyo was rocked, stunned. He sank to his knees, and Rat
prevented him from falling to his face.

"You did it," she whispered. "Keep doing it."

He nodded numbly and raised his arms again.

Another blow came down. The light shield shattered on
impact—but prevented Kefnet's fist from making contact with
any of them. Teyo groaned and tried to clear his head. Dazed

as he was, however, he couldn't summon the geometry to— *literally*—save his life. The next blow would crush them all.

But Teyo had bought Nissa and the guild leaders the time they needed. The ritual had been completed under his shield. Enough mana had been filtered through the participants to flow through and around the bones and Vessel of the Firemind. The yellow and orange flames had turned to gold and ignited the blue and red smoke within the Vessel. The smoke had burned briefly purple before the golden flames overwhelmed all other colors. The blaze seemed to take shape and solidify around the dragon bones, filling them out, turning them from skeleton to living creature.

And then Niv-Mizzet was reborn, with scales of shiny gold to match the golden glow emanating from his eyes. A decagon was etched—seared, really—into his chest, and magical spheres of black, blue, green, red and white swirled around him, like five planets orbiting the sun.

Rat, who was still supporting Teyo's weight, said, "That's different."

Teyo still couldn't speak. His eyes rolled upward in his head, just in time to see Kefnet's fist barreling down toward them.

But just in time to catch that fist was the new and supposedly improved Firemind. Niv-Mizzet spread his wings and launched himself up toward the God-Eternal. His golden wings glowed with a golden light, and his upward arc sheared Kefnet's fist off at the wrist. It landed like a boulder ten feet behind Teyo, Rat and the others, shaking the ground but doing no further damage.

The ibis-headed Kefnet swung his single truncated limb toward Niv-Mizzet, but the dragon easily dodged the blow, flapping his wings once to rise above the God-Eternal. Then Teyo saw the Firemind open his maw wide; his upper and lower incisors scraped against each other, generating a spark, which ignited Niv's breath. An unending torrent of flame engulfed Kefnet, incinerating what remained of its flesh and melting the God-Eternal's lazotep coating into a molten rain that dropped ten feet in front of Teyo, Rat and the others, sizzling against the ground but again doing no further damage.

Ari and Gan Shokta cheered. Vorel growled with obvious satisfaction. Boruvo grunted with the same. Rat smiled, and Teyo struggled not to pass out. Ari knelt beside her daughter and, putting a rough warm hand on Teyo's shoulder, said, "Your boy did well, Araithia."

Now it was Araithia's turn to blush. "He's not my boy," she said. "He's my friend."

"He can see you, and he can protect you."

"I don't need protecting."

"We all need protecting sometimes. Just don't need it too often."

"No, Mother."

The eleven were just beginning to come out of their trances. Ral shook his head to clear it and then looked up . . . *just in time to see Niv-Mizzet fall.*

The dragon crashed down ten feet to the left of Teyo, Rat and the others, shaking the ground—and shattering all their hopes. Niv lay there, breathing heavily and barely moving. One wing seemed bent beneath his body at an angle so awkward it was almost painful to see.

Gan Shokta said, "That's it? Is the great power of the new Living Guildpact already spent from dealing with a single one-armed Eternal?"

Ral looked stunned, and everyone else looked stricken, angry or both. Suddenly, the notion that Niv would somehow have the power to defeat Nicol Bolas himself now seemed foolish and, well, *desperate.*

ACT THREE

FIFTY

RAL ZAREK

Everything I've tried has failed. Everything.

Ral had been forced to leave the catatonic Firemind Mark Two right where he lay—on the ground amid the ruins of the Embassy of the Living Guildpact. With all the resurrected dragon's mystic energies expended on the killing of one over-large zombie henchman, he was something of a disappointment. Niv might recover. He might not. But his current condition only seemed to demonstrate the curse Ral was beginning to feel he lived under. Maybe it was his prior service to Bolas—long but decidedly over—that had compromised his soul and placed all his efforts under a dark cloud of, *well, say it: DOOM.* Maybe he just didn't deserve—had never deserved—all he had worked for, fought for. Who could say why? But the end results were indisputable. Failure. Failure. Failure. One thing after another.

Even the bright spots seemed veined with something dark. Vraska's return, for example. She was fighting on their side now, but she had fought on their side before, only to betray them in the end to the dragon. What made him think she was any more trustworthy now? Nothing. Nothing but the desire to believe in her because he needed to believe in her. And Hekara? It was wonderful she was back. Alive. And she seemed to be her same old wacky self. And yet, and yet . . . something *had* changed in her. He didn't want to see it. And he couldn't exactly put his finger on it, either. She had more authority now, certainly, as a blood witch. More power. But it wasn't just that. There were moments when her eyes shot off to the side, as if she could see something just out of view of the rest of them. He wanted to call it paranoia, a natural reaction to every being's fear of death and the undead. But a part of him knew he'd need to keep a watchful eye on his friend.

Someone was speaking. Ral realized he'd been staring at the floor of the Azorius Senate House, where the leaders of the combined anti-Bolas forces had gathered once more, perhaps for the last time. He looked up. Gideon, the preposterously handsome Planeswalker from Theros, was saying something. Ral tried to focus, to listen.

Gideon: "It was always going to come down to battle. Trying to resurrect Niv-Mizzet was a worthwhile endeavor, but even with his help, it would still have come down to a fight. So, all right, we don't have the Firemind's help. But things are far from hopeless here. We've thinned the Eternal herd. Destroyed half the dragon's God-Eternals. Now we need to finish this by using Blackblade on Bolas."

Ral found himself nodding. Jura spoke with such confidence, such authority. The very tenor of his voice—*baritone, actually*—was reassuring.

"The plan, this time, is simple enough. For the moment, Bolas has pulled back the bulk of his forces to his Citadel. So we'll respond by launching a massive two-pronged attack. On the ground, every guildmember, every Planeswalker—hell, every Ravnican who can hold a weapon—will launch a full frontal assault. Everything we've got. All at once. Everyone. Unless you can fly or can hitch a ride on something that does. Next, while the ground assault keeps the Eternals busy, Aurelia, myself and the rest of our combined air forces will engage from above. I'll make use of my invulnerability to get in close. Then I'll stab Bolas with Blackblade. And it will all be over."

Ral was no longer nodding. In fact, despite Gideon's impressive charisma, Ral Zarek was appalled at the warrior's naïveté.

"It will all be over." Right. Just like that.

He was about to speak out, to inject some (frankly pessimistic) reality into the situation, when he heard Tomik ask Lavinia for a sword.

Ral pushed through the crowd and pulled Tomik aside. "You're not a fighter."

Tomik said, "We're all fighters today."

Ral shook his head vehemently. "You don't need to do this. I'll do this. But I can't concentrate if you're out there."

Tomik stared at him for a long moment . . . then said, "You're a Planeswalker. The Eternals can sense your Spark. You present a much more appealing target than I. Beyond that . . . get over yourself."

Ral did not "get over himself." He was terrified for Tomik. Terrified that the curse Ral lived under dictated that his participation doomed Gideon's plan to failure. Only this time, that failure would include the death of Tomik Vrona.

Tomik read Ral's face and shook his head, as if to say, *There's no curse on you; stop worrying.*

Then he grasped Ral's hand in his own, and they turned to listen as one by one, the Gatewatch renewed their Oaths . . .

Gideon Jura began, raising Blackblade high once more:

"Never again. Not on any world. This I swear: for Sea Gate, for Zendikar, for Ravnica and all its people, for justice and peace, *I will keep watch*. And after Bolas falls, when any new danger arises to threaten the Multiverse, I will be there with the Gatewatch beside me."

Jace Beleren was briefer: "Never again. For the sake of the Multiverse, *I will keep watch*."

Then Chandra Nalaar spoke: "Every world has its tyrants, following their own desires with no concern for the people they step on. So I say never again. If it means folks can live in freedom, *I will keep watch*. With all of you."

Teferi intoned: "From time out of mind, the strong have plagued the weak. Never again. For the lost and forgotten, *I will keep watch*."

Then, smiling at the others, Ajani Goldmane growled out his: "I have seen tyrants whose ambitions knew no limits. Creatures who styled themselves gods or praetors or consuls but thought only of their own desires, not of those they ruled. Whole populations deceived. Civilizations plunged into war. People who were simply trying to live made to suffer. To die. Never again. Until all have found their place, *I will keep watch*."

Finally, these five turned to look at Nissa Revane. She seemed reluctant to speak. Then she glanced at Chandra, who was biting her lip and looking back at Nissa with trepidation.

Did the elf smile then?

If so, it came and went in an instant. She took a step forward and spoke in a soft clear voice, like a bell: "I have seen a world laid waste, the land reduced to dust and ash. Left unchecked, evil will consume everything in its path. Never again. For Zendikar and the life it nurtures, for Ravnica and the life of every plane, *I will keep watch*."

Chandra looked like a giddy schoolgirl, ready to jump up and down in place. But truth be told, as cynical and defeatist as Ral currently felt, the six Oaths were more than a little inspiring.

Gideon looked across the crowd and asked, "Anyone else?"

People sneaked glances at one another or looked at the ground. Jaya smirked a little. Karn crossed his massive silver arms. For a second it looked like Kaya was about to speak—before losing her nerve. No one stepped forward. No one spoke.

Ral looked at Tomik and could see the determination in Tomik's eyes. Ral knew he wasn't going to be able to talk the man he loved out of fighting. So there was a moment when Ral was almost tempted to take an oath of his own, a much more personal, singular oath.

Then Lavinia handed Tomik a sword, and the moment passed.

FIFTY-ONE

CHANDRA NALAAR

Gids and Jace sought Chandra out. Taking her arm, they guided her away from the crowd to the only place where they could get a little privacy: behind the stony corpse of Isperia.

"What?" she demanded, a little too loudly.

Jace gestured with his hands for her to bring down the volume.

She took a breath and asked "What is it?" in a considerably lower tone.

Gideon said, "We have a special job for you. We want you to return to New Prahv and turn the Immortal Sun back on."

"What?" she yelled again. "Do you know how hard it was to turn the damn thing off?"

They exchanged a glance that stopped her outrage in its tracks.

She leaned in and whispered: "You don't trust the other Planeswalkers not to run away."

Jace shook his head. "That isn't it. We need the Sun to do the job it was created for. To prevent Bolas from bolting."

Gids agreed: "One way or another, this ends today."

"Well, then send someone else," she said. "Because you're crazy if you think I'm going to miss this fight."

Gideon actually chuckled then. "Neither of us thought that for a moment."

Jace said, "Take whomever you need. Get the Sun up and running, and leave a strong guard. Then we'll welcome you to the battle."

"I don't know," Chandra groused. "Bolas wants the Sun turned on. I'm not even sure this is a good idea."

"Sounds like a good idea to me." All three of them turned and looked up. A smiling Dack Fayden was sitting on Isperia's back. "Sorry. Didn't mean to eavesdrop."

Chandra scoffed. "Look where you're sitting. Of course you meant to eavesdrop."

"Well, yeah. I see the mighty Gatewatch sequester themselves behind the dead sphinx, and I get a little curious."

"Just a little?" Jace asked, raising an eyebrow.

"Just a little," Dack confirmed. "Look, I know I'm not part of this strategy session, but I'm gonna throw in my two zinos all the same. No one wants to go through this again. And if Bolas gets away, you know we'll all have to. I'm with the big guy," Dack nodded toward Gideon. "One way or another, this ends today."

Gideon and Jace turned to Chandra. Her shoulders sank. "Fine," she said.

Minutes later Chandra had Saheeli Rai by her side and a

small squadron of the toughest rank-and-file guildmembers she could find at their backs. Then, taking a deep breath, she approached Nissa.

"Will you—" she began.

"Anything," Nissa replied.

Chandra smiled, and together they set off once again for New Prahv.

FIFTY-TWO

VRASKA

As they marched toward the plaza, Vraska approached him from behind. They hadn't had an opportunity to speak yet. She wasn't sure what he might know—wasn't sure how he'd react—but she wanted, needed, to get the confrontation over with.

"Jace," she said, choking it out.

He turned, stopped and smiled. He gently wrapped a hand around the back of her neck and leaned his forehead against hers. "Hello, Captain," he whispered.

His trust in her was liable to break her heart.

Get it over with! she shouted internally, then whispered, "You don't know what I've done."

He said, "I do, actually. But it's not your fault. You didn't have your full memories, and I arrived too late."

She leaned her head away from his and whispered again:

"You definitely arrived too late. But the truth is I *did* have all my memories. And it changed nothing."

He shrugged. "Look," he said, "I already tried to kill one ex today. Can we table the angst until Bolas is dead or we are?"

She smiled ruefully. "Oh, am I an ex now?"

"I hope not," he said, looking panicked.

"Don't we have to be an item before we can be exes?"

"I hope so," he said. "Um, the first part, not the second."

He looked so vulnerable. She remembered that expression from their time on Ixalan. Jace at his most insecure—and most adorable. It was hard to let it go, frankly. But she didn't want to play games, didn't want to be another Liliana Vess in his life. She said, "So tomorrow we give it a try . . . after Bolas is dead or we are?"

"Either way?"

"Either way."

He nodded. "Agreed. But again, I'm hoping for the first option, not the second."

"Agreed."

She took his hand. She saw Ral Zarek glaring at them both. She knew Jace's relationship—or whatever it was—with the infamous gorgon who assassinated Isperia wouldn't do much to burnish the former Living Guildpact's already damaged reputation, that was certain. But if it didn't bother him—and it seemed that it didn't, as she saw a grinning Jace offer Ral a little mocking wave—then she wasn't going to let it bother her, either.

Tomorrow, if we live, we give it a try.

Suddenly Vraska very much wanted to live.

FIFTY-THREE

CHANDRA NALAAR

Chandra's squad was incredibly efficient. Two ogres and a giant helped Saheeli align the Immortal Sun. They filled in the melted section of the dais by pouring and pounding the melted remains of fallen thopters into the gap. Saheeli confirmed that the dais was once again level, and her three oversized helpers hefted the Sun into place.

Yet it didn't immediately activate. Chandra knew she could still planeswalk if she wanted to. And if she could, Bolas could.

Why did Jace send me? He's the one who would know if Azor had a spell to get the thing working again.

Chandra racked her brain, trying to figure out what to do. The answer came fairly quickly—but she resisted it. Not because she didn't want to do it but because she wanted to just a little too much.

But there was no getting around it.

She asked Nissa for a boost and once again climbed up on to the Immortal Sun.

Immediately, she felt the rush.

But this time I won't let it take me over. Not even for a second.

She focused. Dug deep. Tried to remember everything Jaya Ballard had taught her. She felt the Sun's stone under her feet. Tried to make herself one with it. Azor had sacrificed his Spark to activate his creation on Ixalan, and Chandra had no intention of doing *that*. But she felt sure it wasn't called a Sun for nothing.

"STAND BACK, EVERYONE." Her voice boomed in her own ears, like a god.

A little stunned, they all complied, taking a few steps back.

Chandra took a deep breath . . . and ignited her entire body from the inside out. She wouldn't sacrifice her Spark, but she'd sure as hell *use it* to fuel her flames. She burned so brightly, the others all had to cover their eyes and take a few *more* steps back. She brought the core of her heat down from her chest to her stomach to her womb. She lowered it down both her legs to her feet and then, with one last push, drove her fire down into the stone.

Instantly it ignited. Once again, its light beamed up into the sky and with it the temptation of its power.

Climbing down off the Sun, Chandra felt sure it had worked, but to test it she attempted to planeswalk to Kaladesh. For just a second she saw her mother's new apartment. But she was yanked back like a slingshot and once again found herself in New Prahv, with Azor's crest glowing above her head.

Success.

Success?

She didn't much like being trapped again on Ravnica. But she knew why she had done it. Bolas had to die. Today. And if he could escape, if he could 'walk, they'd never catch and kill him.

Gids had said it: *"One way or another, this ends today."*

Minutes later, Nissa had surrounded the dais with a veritable forest of oaks, including two massive walking tree elementals, whom she placed on guard. In fact, Chandra and Nissa left their entire entourage—Saheeli, ogres and giant included—on guard and beat a quick path toward the battle.

As they left New Prahv behind, Chandra smiled at Nissa. And Nissa smiled back. Everything seemed so right, Chandra just *knew* they were going to win.

FIFTY-FOUR

DACK FAYDEN

The battle was joined. Dack Fayden was scared out of his mind. There they were, *there he was*, rushing toward the Citadel, most of their forces shouting battle cries (or whatever that racket was supposed to be) at the top of their collective lungs. The dragon loomed atop the pyramid, his wings spread, that gods-be-damned egg floating between his horns, still collecting stolen Sparks flying in from fallen Planeswalkers.

Those Planeswalkers not fallen were side by side with guild warriors, engaging the silent Dreadhorde.

It was chaos. True chaos. Like the nightmares he had suffered through before Ravos and the dead of Theros had put an end to Ashiok's Sleep Curse.

What was I thinking? This is no place for a respectable thief!

Still, Dack was relieved to observe that the two sides were more evenly matched than he could have hoped. There were, without a doubt, fewer Eternals than there had been and—thanks to him and Karn and Samut and Sarkhan and, yes, Ob Nixilis—no more reinforcements arriving.

Dack had raced onto the plaza beneath the shadow of the massive Borborygmos, who was sweeping the area ahead of them both with two huge maces, literally shattering Eternals left and right. The cyclops provided Dack with some protection and allowed him to take on Eternals that were already damaged. Too many allies nearby to risk using the spell that made the Dreadhorde see Sparks everywhere. A mystified Eternal was just as likely to grab someone who actually *did* have a Spark as one of their own. But Dack had found that their metallic lazotep coating responded to a specific kind of artificer's hex that he had long ago mastered. It magnetized the lazotep, causing any two Eternals to crash into each other and, well, *stick*. In their attempts to free themselves, they usually tripped and fell, causing considerable damage to one another—and in any event, they left themselves open to attack. Dack could then move in and finish both Eternals off with a borrowed sword. It was gruesome work but effective.

Occasionally, he'd glance up and spot another warrior at her or his or their own work. Samut raced at high speed through the Eternal ranks, shearing off heads with her curved blades. Dack was too far away to hear her speak, but he knew with certainty that with each head removed, another Eternal had, by her lights, been "set free."

Dack stabbed one of his magnetized Eternals through the forehead, turning the blade until the creature ceased to squirm. Straightening up, he saw Vorel cross the battlefield at a steady and determined pace. Dack had heard that the Simic biomancer had once been a Gruul Clan leader, and now, fighting at close quarters, his barbaric origins were fiercely on display as he used a biomantic mace to seize the Eternals by whatever remained of their flesh, turning them inside out.

The resulting explosion of guts and lazotep was both horrific to behold and—given the circumstances—practically heart-warming.

Dack moved on. He'd allowed Borborygmos to get too far ahead of him. He felt exposed but spotted Karn not too far away, crushing an Eternal's head between his two metal hands. He made his way toward the silver golem, knowing Karn would watch his back. He spotted an Eternal limping toward him, one that the cyclops' mace had already damaged. Its chest was partially caved in, and one arm hung off its shoulder by a strand of flesh. Still, the creature would do the trick. Spotting an able-bodied Eternal, he used his hex to magnetize them both. The wounded Eternal tripped the whole one up, and both crashed to the ground virtually at Dack's feet. He brought his sword down with enough force to cut off the undamaged Eternal's head.

"Nice work," Ajani shouted as he passed without slowing.

Dack shouted his thanks, but Ajani was already too far away to hear him over the din of battle. The leonin Planes-walker carried a double-headed axe and wasn't shy about using it on Eternal after Eternal.

Dack spent a moment too long admiring Goldmane's effi-ciency. When he turned back, he found the damaged Eternal reaching for his foot with its one good hand, seconds from getting a grip on Dack's Spark and his life. As Dack consid-ered whether to use his sword or to Planeswalk—that moment of indecision nearly spelled his end.

Fortunately, a strong hand took hold of his shoulder from behind and yanked him back out of harm's way. It was Karn, of course, who rapidly crushed the offending Eternal's out-stretched hand under his foot and then brought a silver fist down like a hammer to shatter the Eternal's skull against the ground.

There was—experience now told Dack—no time for a thank-you. They exchanged wry smiles for a brief moment, and then it was back to the fighting.

Determined now to maintain his focus, Dack picked out two Eternals—two that were still a safe distance away—and cast his hex. They smashed into each other and tumbled over in time for Kaya to plunge her two long ghost daggers into each of their brains. She continued forward, flanked by two Orzhov giants.

Dack then chose two more Eternals and repeated the process. This time they continued to drag themselves forward together by gripping the pavement with their dead fingers. Dack moved in and cut off all four of their hands, lest they reach out and grab him while he was finishing them off. Then he swung his sword to cut off one of their heads. The sword lodged in the creature's spine, failing to quite do the job. A nervous Dack spent a precious few seconds wrenching it free and making a second, more successful attempt.

By the time he was done, another Eternal was already upon him. But he kept his head and hexed the lazotep adorning the creature so that it was yanked back, anchoring it to the two Eternals on the ground.

That was so amazingly effective, he tried it again. And again. And again. Soon there was a huge mass of tangled Eternals in a pile before him. It was quick, elegant, perfect and repeatable.

Almost like stealing.

He allowed himself a moment to get his bearings. Karn was still at his back. A troop of Izzet mages were using flame-throwers on the Eternals—and came close to singeing Jace Beleren in the process. Jace shouted out a psychic warning that rang loudly in Dack's brain. Another crop of Eternals attacked—and were intercepted by Azorius Arresters.

Never thought I'd be glad to see them.

The Azorius had finally taken the field at the insistence of their new acting guildmaster, Lavinia, who led them forward.

As he magnetized another Eternal to the pile and spotted Dimir assassins and Rakdos Cultists shredding an entire Eternal phalanx, Dack realized he was witnessing a battle like none he'd ever seen before—like none he'd ever even *heard of* before in history *or* legend. And he was there, holding his own. He didn't particularly see himself as a man who'd ever settle down and have kids, but as he stabbed a pile-trapped Eternal through the eye, he thought he'd someday like to have a couple grandkids on his old arthritic knees to tell them this epic tale—and their granddad's part in it.

He looked up to find his next victim—but he had daydreamed a second too long. Again he found himself face-to-face with an Eternal, reaching for his arm, trying to get a grip on his Spark. And again a strong hand on his shoulder yanked him back, so that the Eternal grasped only Dack's sleeve, which it tore away: a sacrifice Dack was more than willing to make—though his expensive jacket was now a totally lost cause. He turned to smile at his savior, assuming it was Karn.

But his savior wasn't Karn. His savior wasn't a savior at all. He'd been grabbed by a gods-be-damned Eternal. Horrified, he hexed its lazotep and its magnetized skull wrenched abruptly backward, snapping its neck, leaving its head hanging limply behind its shoulders. But the thing did not relax its grip. Dack could feel it. It was harvesting his Spark. It was time to planeswalk.

Get out before it's too late!

But it was already too late. He could *feel* it. The Immortal Sun had been reactivated. He was trapped on Ravnica with an Eternal's fingers digging into his arm. He tried to raise his sword to cut off the Eternal's hand but found he had no strength to even hold the sword. His fingers loosened, and he vaguely heard the weapon clatter on the pavement stones.

And then came the pain. Excruciating pain. He thought he must be screaming but by now he could hear nothing; even the great din of the battle had faded away to silence while his vision likewise faded to black. He couldn't hear, couldn't see, couldn't even smell. But he could still *feel*. Past the horrific pain, he could *feel* the Eternal reaching into whatever made Dack who he was and taking it. It felt like his guts were being pulled inside out. Like his body was being drained of all fluids, of all soft tissue, leaving him as nothing but skin and bones. In fact, what the creature was doing was much, much worse. His essence, his soul. His Spark. It was being pulled out and ripped away. For a moment Dack's darkness was illuminated by a bright purple light.

He mouthed the word, "Please . . ."

He thought of Domri Rade. He thought of Atha. And of Sifa Grent. And of Marsh.

He thought of Mariel. He thought maybe he could feel a tear rolling down his cheek and briefly wondered whom exactly he cried for. He hoped it was for her. It was the last thing he hoped. The last question he'd wonder about. That tear was the last thing he felt.

The pain was mercifully gone.

FIFTY-FIVE

LILIANA VESS

Liliana Vess was having a *little* trouble deciding whom to root for. Sure, she *hated* Bolas with a red, white and black passion and wanted him dead for more reasons than she could even count at the moment. But she was past thinking the *"good guys"* could ever forgive her.

Yes, she considered herself a master manipulator.

But there are limits.

And the attempt on her life had exposed her own. If Bolas fell, her *"friends"* might not give her time to work her *"magic"* on them. And with the Immortal Sun reactivated—for, indeed, she could feel the weight of its binding mystery from the moment it turned back on—she wouldn't be able to planeswalk away.

No, to survive a Gatewatch victory, she'd have to do something spectacularly redemptive *beforehand,* something that would truly make them think twice about killing her.

And that's the problem, isn't it?

There was nothing she could do to betray Bolas that would make any difference. Not without dying. And dying pretty much defeated the purpose.

So who do I root for?

She watched the Sparks of the dead and harvested Planeswalkers spiral into the Spirit-Gem between the dragon's horns. Then her eyes focused on something just beyond them. The *Parhelion II* was advancing.

With a mystic gesture, she shifted her vision. Through the eyes of the God-Eternal Oketra, Liliana thought she could see Beefslab himself standing on the airship's deck—next to a pegasus. He practically launched himself onto the winged animal's back and unsheathed Blackblade.

Look at that. Damn me if Beefslab wasn't born to ride a winged horse.

Liliana watched him nod to an angel; the angel nodded back. A horn sounded. Angels descended from *Parhelion II*'s decks. And they were not alone: Boros Skyknights and elven Selesnyan Equenauts rode more pegasi, griffins and eagles. Izzet mages riding flight spheres of mizzium rocketed toward the fray alongside Izzet goblins on sky-scooters and Izzet faeries riding blazekites down. A single small hypersonic dragon flew in side by side with a drakewing, a steam drake, a sapphire drake, a wind drake and a Simic skyswimmer, who'd normally be trying to eat the others. But not today.

Together they were routing what little remained of the Eternal sky cover. Liliana knew she should throw more Eternals at the air assault, but most were busy dealing with the ground assault. (And why did *that* thought thrill her just a little?) Of course, she could use Oketra and Bontu; the God-

Eternals could certainly do considerable damage to Gideon's sky battalion. But she hesitated, using the excuse that the best way to stop a winged serpent was to cut off its head. She'd lost sight of Beefslab among the onrush of oncoming fliers—but Bolas had not.

His now godlike voice cut through her mind, causing her no little pain. *DO YOUR DUTY,* he commanded. *USE OKE-TRA AGAINST JURA. NOW! BEFORE HE BRINGS THAT DAMN BLADE ANY CLOSER.*

Again she looked through Oketra's dead eyes, spotting Gideon in a matter of seconds. Liliana raised an imaginary bow, and Oketra followed suit with her oh-too-real one. They took synchronized aim at Gideon. Together, they loosed a javelin-sized arrow. But at the last second, did Liliana . . . flinch?

Even *she* wasn't quite sure. But Oketra's arrow didn't quite find a target in Gideon. Instead its six-foot length impaled his mount. The pierced pegasus died without a whimper and tumbled out of the sky; Gideon, still clutching Blackblade, plummeted out of view along with it.

Bolas was angry: *HOW COULD YOU MISS?*

Liliana winced: His anger felt like an iron spike driving through her brain.

I didn't miss, she thought back at him. *Gideon's invulnerable. Shooting at him would have little effect. Killing his mount, on the other hand . . .*

Bolas seemed to buy her explanation. At least, he spiked her with no further reprimands.

Liliana wondered if she, too, bought her explanation. And Liliana wondered if even the mighty and invulnerable Gideon Jura could survive a fall from such a height . . .

FIFTY-SIX

KAYA

*T*omik, thought Kaya, *is an idiot with a sword. Worse, he's a* bureaucrat *with a sword.*

But she couldn't help admiring him and his efforts. Or the way Ral blasted every Eternal that came within five feet of him.

She had friends, trusted friends, here and now. But she hadn't had anyone to care about that way—to love that way—since Janah. She didn't miss Janah, but she missed that feeling.

But now wasn't the time to think of Janah or of love. Now wasn't the time to lose focus. There were Eternals to kill. Eternals who could kill her.

Kaya was spending way more time in her ghost form than she ever had before. More time, frankly, than was quite safe for her beating heart. She'd ghost through an Eternal, materialize her hand and stab her ghost blade through its skull. Then she'd ghost her hand while materializing her feet in order to keep her heart beating as she moved in on another of the creatures. But the urgency and the threat and the myriad distractions inherent to the battle made her way more reck-less than usual. She was, after all, trained as an assassin, not a commando. Her job was taking out individuals, not taking on armies. Occasionally, she'd get her rhythm wrong and ghost completely for more than a few seconds; she could feel her heart skip a beat or two before she'd manage to material-ize enough of herself to get her pump started again. It was a bit like having multiple minuscule heart attacks, and she felt the resulting strain and fatigue getting to her. Plus there were still those damn Orzhov contracts weighing her down. Tomik—bless his bureaucratic skills—must have done *some-thing* to reduce their drag, but the drag remained; it just felt slightly less oppressive.

Fortunately, her here-and-now friends had her back. It was almost frightening how this battalion of disparate Planeswalk-ers and Ravnicans had become such a well-oiled Eternal-slaying machine.

Rat, having borrowed an axe from her mother, walked right up to Eternal after Eternal and ended them without ever being noticed.

"Well," Rat shouted over the din, "growing up among the Gruul oughta count for something! And growing up with my particular condition occasionally counts for a lot more!"

Rat expended a good deal of effort protecting Kaya—but a good deal more protecting Hekara. In fact, Kaya watched the young girl shadow the blood witch, who held her own quite nicely for a dead woman and yet never realized how many times her second life was being saved by the friend she could no longer see.

Kaya snuck a glance at Teyo, who had quite come into his

own. He might have little offensive ability—beyond tossing an occasional mini-sphere of solid light at an opponent—but he was alert and quick and ready with his shields to defend all among their ranks who found themselves in trouble.

And then suddenly the boy with little offensive ability discovered he could use his shields as a battering ram, smashing the Eternals back, setting them up for Borborygmos or Kord or Vorel.

Vraska, meanwhile, fought like a demon—a demon with something to lose, or with a newfound reason to live. She used her cutlass like a surgical blade and used the gorgon magic behind her gaze to turn the Eternals she didn't slice apart into stone statues. Sometimes, in the heat of things, she did both.

Jace created multiple illusions of himself to lure Eternals into position for Ajani and Jaya and Karn to slaughter, while occasionally using his telekinesis to do the job himself.

Teferi created bubbles of slowed time around the Eternals, turning them off only when Lavinia or Boruvo or Ari or Gan Shokta was in position to destroy them.

Whatever the conflict was between Sorin Markov and Nahiri had seemingly—and thankfully—been tabled for the time being. While Sorin tore the heads off Eternals with fearsome strength, Nahiri shaped spikes out of stone to impale three or four at a time.

Yet despite their force's obvious success, the fight was neither simple nor easy. And people were dying. Kaya saw a Planeswalker named Dack harvested, and he was not the only Planeswalker to fall.

Still, if this battle had *only* been about the Eternals, she'd have felt pretty confident about a coming victory. But of course, the Eternals were only the symptom.

The big bad disease Bolas still sat on his throne, absorbing Spark after Spark.

No, the Eternals were merely Bolas' cannon fodder. And

everyone fighting knew it. So when Gideon and Aurelia led their sky forces into battle, she cheered alongside everyone else. Gideon wielded the sword that could bring an end to all this—by bringing an end to Nicol Bolas. Kaya could almost taste the palpable hope radiating off her companions on the ground when they saw him.

And she could feel the palpable despair when Gideon's pegasus was shot, and he tumbled—Blackblade and all—behind the Citadel and out of view . . .

FIFTY-SEVEN

JACE BELEREN

There was a pause in the battle when Gideon fell. A hiatus that affected not only Jura's allies on the ground but the enemy, as well. For a moment the Eternals seemed to hesitate, which Jace attributed to the complicated brain of one Liliana Vess. The moment didn't last, of course. The battle was rejoined on both sides. Jace spotted one of his illusory decoys being attacked by an Eternal and responded with a fury that surprised even himself—as he telekinetically ripped the offending creature in twain.

Yes, Jace was angry. Desperate, even. It wasn't the fall of Gideon in and of itself. Jace had known Gideon far too long to believe that falling off a horse—even a horse with wings a hundred feet up in the air—could possibly have killed him. But that horse had been Gideon's best shot at reaching Bolas . . .

Until it wasn't.

Jace saw the smoke first. Then the flames. Then the massive winged demon with the crown of fire.

The blood witch Hekara clapped her hands, jingled her bells, and cheered loudly for her unholy guildmaster: "Go get 'im, Boss!" She turned toward Ral, Kaya and Vraska and shouted, "Toldja he was on board. He *loves* this plan!"

Rakdos. Defiler. Demon. Guildmaster. Parun. Lord of Riots. Big as a dragon, with arms and legs muscled and proportioned like some kind of gigantic Therosian wrestler. Two sets of horns, one set arcing upward, outward and backward like a steer's, the other arcing down and curving up like those of a humongous ram. Burning yellow eyes. Razor teeth, locked together in a rictus grin. A beard of bone spurs emerging from a wide jaw. Bat wings. Cloven hooves. Blood-red hide clothed in chains and skulls. And his brow, a wreath of flame. Here was an evil to match many another.

But could he match Nicol Bolas?

And then, *of course*, Jace spotted Gideon, riding atop the demon's head. *Rising up* within the very flames of Rakdos' crown, Gideon's white aura of invulnerability must have been protecting him from the hellfire, but from where Jace stood, Gideon Jura seemed only to be at the white-hot center of the hellish blaze.

Gideon still had Blackblade drawn and at the ready, and like a child Jace thrilled for the hero and the demon, as the latter soared up high and then dived down precipitously toward the Citadel and its master, his roar echoing across the plaza.

The roaring was a mistake.

It got Bolas' attention. The dragon turned in time and cast a crippling spell that blasted Rakdos back.

But Gideon leapt over the blast, using Rakdos' momentum to plunge toward Bolas with Blackblade poised to strike.

Jace held his breath as Gideon, two hands on the hilt, drove the sword down toward the crease between Bolas' eyes.

That sword had already been known to kill a major demon, a God-Eternal, and even an Elder Dragon like Nicol Bolas.

This is it. This will end it. Even Liliana won't continue this fight once Bolas is dead.

And the blow descended, Gideon thrusting the weapon down with all his not inconsiderable might . . .

And Blackblade simply *shattered* against the God-Emperor's invincible brow.

And shattering with Blackblade: the hopes of every living soul on Ravnica.

FIFTY-EIGHT

GIDEON JURA

Gideon saw it.

Just before he drove the sword down.

That hint of a smile on the dragon's face, that sense of triumph in the monster's eyes.

So Gideon Jura wasn't as surprised as one might expect when Blackblade shattered.

As the pain ripped through both his arms—shrapnel from the ancient, mystic blade tearing through his aura of invulnerability as if it hardly existed—Gideon fell amid the shards of his broken, useless weapon, landing hard on the roof of the Citadel.

The last thing he heard before losing consciousness was the laughter of the dragon Nicol Bolas.

He's laughing at us . . . laughing . . .

And then . . .

Only darkness.

FIFTY-NINE

NICOL BOLAS

*I*T WAS ALMOST TOO EASY, thought **BOLAS**.

SPREAD THE WORD THAT BLACKBLADE KILLED AN ELDER DRAGON.

MAKE IT JUST DIFFICULT ENOUGH TO FIND THE THING, SO THAT THEY APPRECIATE ITS WORTH.

GIVE THEM ONE OF LILIANA'S DEMONS TO KILL WITH IT, SO THAT THEY BELIEVE IN THE UNCONQUERABLE STRENGTH OF THEIR ULTIMATE WEAPON.

BELIEVE IN IT ENOUGH SO THAT THEY NEVER BOTHER TO SEARCH FOR ANYTHING ELSE.

AND WATCH AS THEY COMMIT EVERYTHING THEY HAVE FOR AN ATTACK THAT ABSOLUTELY DEPENDS . . .

ON THE ONE *WEAPON WE ARE THOROUGHLY PRE-PARED TO REPEL.*

The DRAGON laughed with every fiber of his mental, spiritual and physical being.

YES, THE BLACKBLADE ONCE KILLED AN ELDER DRAGON.

AND BECAUSE OF THAT ONE FACT, WE MADE DAMN SURE MILLENNIA AGO THAT IT COULD NEVER. KILL. US.

With a satisfied smile, BOLAS gazed down at Jura, pathetically fighting for consciousness, his arms now shredded bloody messes of skin and black shrapnel.

It made BOLAS laugh again. Laugh loudly enough for the chilling sound to pass into his empowered Spirit-Gem and echo across the entire Multiverse, giving night terrors to children and waking nightmares to adults, the vast majority of whom knew absolutely nothing of this battle, nothing of Ravnica, nothing even of their soon-to-be GOD-EMPEROR and MASTER, NICOL BOLAS.

HE instructed Vess to send Bontu and Oketra out to finish things.

LET BOTH STOMP THE GROUND UNTIL NOTHING MOVES BENEATH THEIR UNDEAD FEET.

WE'VE HAD OUR FUN, the GOD-BOLAS stated. *NOW WE GROW WEARY OF THE IMPERTINENCE OF ANTS.*

SIXTY

LILIANA VESS

And that's that, thought Liliana, trying desperately to ignore her own unresolved feelings toward Beefslab and the rest of the Gatewatch, who would shortly be dying all around her. Easier to focus on herself than on Gideon and what his friendship and trust might have meant to her, might *mean* to her, even now.

So, fine. Focus on yourself, Liliana. Blackblade has shattered. Gideon's fallen—again—though he'll probably survive. With his invulnerability, he's probably the only Planeswalker— other than yourself—who'll survive Bolas' greedy purge. But there's no stopping the dragon now. Which means I'll be his slave ad infinitum.

For over a hundred years, Liliana's sole focus had been on increasing both her life span and her power—with zero cost to herself. So now she had power, tremendous power, and because the dragon had a use for her (and complete control over her) a solid chance at living forever.

And that was when Liliana had a moment of clarity.

This is not a life worth living. Serving Nicol Bolas for eternity is even less appealing than . . . than . . . It was hard for her to even complete the thought, but: *. . . than dying.*

She glanced down at an unconscious Gideon, his arms two bleeding masses. The shards of Blackblade scattered about him. Her eye twitched at the sight. Her mouth went dry. She actually felt . . . *itchy.* Flush. A bead of sweat ran down her cheek.

No, that can't be right. Liliana Vess does not sweat like a common kitchen wench.

So maybe, finally, it was an actual tear. But if so, who exactly was she crying for?

Seriously? Am I really going to do this?

She really was. Dark mana swirled around her despite the *certain* knowledge that breaching her contract meant *certain* death.

Bolas, distracted by his triumph over Gideon and the rest of his dupes, didn't instantly notice her change of heart. He ordered her to send Bontu and Oketra to finish off his opposition.

"Impertinent ants," he called them. *He hasn't seen impertinence yet.*

The two remaining God-Eternals didn't attack the Ravnicans and Planeswalkers. They didn't crush these ants underfoot. Instead they stood at attention. In fact, *every* Eternal on Ravnica stopped fighting and stood at attention.

Now Bolas took notice. *VESS,* he thought at her, and the single syllable of her own name hit her brain like a boulder, rocking her back a step or two. *DO WE REALLY NEED TO WARN YOU OF WHAT WILL COME OF THIS FUTILE ACT?*

She ignored him. Even smiled, as Oketra, Bontu and every damn other Eternal turned to march toward Nicol Bolas.

She wondered what Jace was making of this. She wondered how long it would take him to realize what was going on.

He better appreciate this.

But she told herself she wasn't doing this for him. Not for him or Chandra or Gideon. If killing them all would have set her free, there was no telling how low she might have sunk in Bolas' service. But there could be no freedom for her; she knew that now. So she might as well enjoy what little time she had left . . .

"Bolas," she shouted, though she knew he was reading her every thought, "has anyone ever told you, you have a remarkably flat head? I mean it's lucky you have those horns and that Spirit-Gem to distract people, because I've never seen a flatter head in all my life! I've been wanting to tell you this for decades: Your head is very, very, *very* flat!"

For the briefest of moments she could feel his stunned confusion over the silly insult to his vanity as it wafted across her consciousness. It was short-lived and followed by his immense contempt for her petty and pointless rudeness. But for just a second . . .

Damn, that was fun! Almost makes it all worthwhile. Almost . . .

The Eternals marched toward the dragon. And the repercussions were practically instantaneous. Not to him, of course. But to her. Her eyes and hands blazed forth purple and black magic that exercised her control over Bolas' undead army. But with the sundering of her contract, volcanic heat began burning up through her tattoos, which rapidly became cracks in her skin that revealed the fiery power fast consuming her from the inside out. And from the outside in. Liliana began to literally flake apart. She could feel it, see it, smell it. Her clothing. Her skin. She was now a witness to her own disintegration.

Bolas shook his head, almost sadly, though she knew he wasn't sad for her. He simply thought *she* was sad, which was to say, pathetic.

His voice sounded in her head one last time: *WHAT A WASTE.*

His power radiated as pure unadulterated magical energy that kept Oketra and Bontu at bay.

Liliana struggled to maintain control. If she could just hold out for a little longer, she could push the God-Eternals through the dragon's barrage.

All it takes is a touch . . . just one touch . . . a handhold . . . and they can harvest him like he's harvested so many others this day . . .

But time was running out. Liliana Vess was *dying,* by her own hand, for a cause she couldn't quite see through, to help people—*friends*—who would probably die cursing her name . . .

Then she felt a hand on her shoulder. Half thinking it was a stray Eternal that Bolas had sent to harvest her Spark, she turned.

It was Gideon, bleeding from both arms, but tall and handsome and smiling at her.

She watched as he extended his invulnerability to her, over her.

No, he's not extending it . . . he's gifting it.

She found herself thinking, *Stop. You do this, and you'll take on my burden—without protection. This will kill you. And you don't have to die. You're the one person who doesn't have to die.*

He just smiled again and shook his head. One would've thought he was Jace, his thoughts seemed so clear: *Many have died to stop Bolas. Let me be the last.*

Gideon, please . . .

He whispered, "I can't be the hero this time, Liliana, but you can."

Liliana glowed with Gideon's invulnerability—pure white light, which held her together, bound her back together, replenished her and made her whole.

In exchange, the black death magic of her breached contract crept up Gideon's hand, transferring from her to him. *Her* tattoos glowed across the shredded skin of his arms. He ignited, flaking apart, as she had been doing mere seconds ago.

Make it count, she heard him say or think or something.

Looking back over her shoulder, tears now definitely rolling down her cheeks, she nodded to him—or meant to.

Behind her, Gideon was dying. Though hardly the empathetic type, Liliana could feel his agony. . . . He raised his head, closed his eyes and *HOWLED . . .*

SIXTY-ONE

KYTHEON IORA

Gideon raised his head, closed his eyes and *HOWLED* . . . and then stopped.

The pain was suddenly gone. There was silence around him. No, not quite silence. The sound of battle, of magic, of death and destruction had faded from his ears. But he could hear the sound of birds chirping. A cricket. A brook. It was all like music.

Cautiously, he opened his eyes. He looked down at his hands, at his arms. He was whole. Not flaking apart as he had been just a few seconds ago. Not even bleeding. The shrapnel from Blackblade was gone. Liliana's tattoos were gone.

He looked down at his clothes. His armor was gone. His clothes were now of Theros, his homeworld.

He looked around. He wasn't on Ravnica at all.

I am on Theros!

A field in Theros, with the city of Akros peeking over the next hill. A soft breeze cooled his brow, even as the sunlight warmed his heart.

Did I planeswalk here? No. The Immortal Sun would have prevented that.

Is this a memory?

But he didn't feel young again. He felt older than he'd ever felt before, bone-weary—yet free of pain. And the scars on his arms? There were some from Theros. But there was a big one he'd received on Amonkhet, and there were a few new ones from the shrapnel.

No, this isn't a memory. This is my now. What's left of my now.

He sensed them before he saw them. They seemed to emerge right out of the sunlight, right out of the sound of the brook, right out of the breeze. His Irregulars.

There was Drasus. He had been three years older than Gideon, and now—frozen in time and unchanged—looked so damn young.

There was Epikos. Shaved head. Bare chest. Earring in his right ear. All muscle and a grin.

There was Little Olexo. The youngest of the Irregulars. Never to grow any bigger or any older. The weary (and ancient) Gideon Jura watched the boy approach, wondering how he had ever allowed this child to fight instead of simply grow up. Then again, in those days, Gideon had been a child, too.

And there was Zenon. Tall and straight. With his shaggy, unkempt hair and that Setessan green cloak he was always so damn proud of. Like the others, he smiled at his long-absent friend.

Drasus, Epikos, Olexo, Zenon. His Irregulars. Kytheon's Irregulars. Because he was not Gideon Jura now, here, at the end. He was Kytheon Iora once again. He hadn't gone back in time. Physically, he was still the same scarred, graying warrior. Yet despite that, he was himself before his name had been garbled by foreign tongues on foreign worlds. Before his sense of self had been garbled by his own vain actions. He had denied his true name for too long. It was time to claim it again.

I am Kytheon Iora. And I am with my friends.

He opened his mouth to apologize, to say he was sorry for his hubris, for being the cause of their deaths so many years ago. But Drasus wryly shook his head and silently stilled Kytheon's tongue before a word could escape his lips. All four smiled at him and placed their hands on his broad shoulders. For a brief moment, he felt sorry for more recent friends, for Chandra and Nissa and Jace and Ajani and Aurelia and, yes, Liliana, and so many others. He was here and found. They were back there and still so lost. But just being in this present gave him hope for them.

They'd survive. Liliana would save them. Or Jace would. Or they'd do it all together.

Or they wouldn't.

But if this was the end, then the end, perhaps, was not so bad.

Not so bad for me, certainly. So I can hope not so bad for them.

There was sunlight and a cool breeze. The brook babbled on. There was serenity. Kytheon was at peace. At peace and, finally, *redeemed* . . .

SIXTY-TWO

LILIANA VESS

From an inch away (or maybe a world away), Liliana saw Gideon smile beatifically—before his smile, his teeth, his skin, his eyes, his entire handsome, kind, muscular face began to glow with the hellish light of *her* tattoos, of *her* broken contract.

No, she pleaded, as the blaze expanded, as if attempting to burn her arm—her arm, which could not be burned thanks to Gideon's gift.

Take it back . . . Please . . .

The smile was still there. Right up to the moment that he burst into black flame and disintegrated before her eyes.

His empty armor clattered at her feet. His ashes blew away on the wind. She looked up at Bolas. The dragon looked smug. She cried out in fury and pushed the God-Eternals forward . . .

SIXTY-THREE

CHANDRA NALAAR

Chandra and Nissa arrived at the plaza in time to witness Gideon's complete obliteration—simply, it seemed, from touching Liliana's shoulder.

Enraged, Chandra burst into red-orange flame that quickly roiled into an inferno of blue and white.

Nissa was forced to back away. "Chandra," she said, as if in warning.

But for once, Chandra had no interest in Nissa's words. The pyromancer was ready to kill the necromancer—to burn the woman Liliana Vess, whom she had once thought of as a sister, into ashes.

Ashes would be a fitting end. Ashes such as those that were all that remained of Gideon, of her Gids, of a man her silly younger self had once been foolishly attracted to and infatuated with, of a man she had come to deeply love as more than a brother.

Once and for all, Liliana Vess would pay for her crimes, for all the death and manipulation and betrayal she had brought to Chandra's life, to Ravnica, to the Multiverse.

But Jace's thoughts slammed into hers: *STOP, CHANDRA! It's not what it looks like! Gideon saved Liliana! He chose to save her! And by saving her, he may just have saved us all!*

Chandra, her mind reeling, didn't yet understand, but she obeyed, absorbing her fire inward. It felt, atypically, as if the flames were burning her: her heart, her mind, her soul. Tears streamed down her face, turning almost instantly to steam.

Yet Chandra felt cold. So very cold.

Nissa tentatively placed a hand on her shoulder. A heartbroken Chandra turned to look in the elf's greenish-golden eyes.

"Gids is gone," Chandra murmured.

Nissa nodded sadly.

From somewhere, they heard Ajani call out, *"Look!"*

SIXTY-FOUR

NICOL BOLAS

The remaining God-Eternals, Oketra and Bontu, approached BOLAS from two sides, obeying Vess' command while struggling against the rush of power the DRAGON-GOD held from the Elderspell. Each took a step toward BOLAS' throne—before that power pushed both back two steps.

BOLAS shook his head.

VESS, YOU ARE A FOOL. THESE GODS COULD NOT STOP US BACK WHEN THEY WERE ALIVE AND WE WERE WEAK. HOW CAN YOU POSSIBLY BELIEVE THEY CAN DEFEAT US NOW? NOW THAT THEY ARE DEAD? NOW THAT WE ARE, ONCE AGAIN, A GOD?

Then, out of nowhere, BOLAS experienced pain as intense as any HE'd felt in a millennium. Time slowed for BOLAS. HE looked down. The two-pronged Spear of Hazoret was sticking out through HIS chest, blood and viscera dripping from each tine. *HIS* blood and viscera. It was not enough to kill HIM. Not as HE was now. Even the pain, even the wound itself, could be eliminated with a few simple spells. But how had HE been stolen upon?

WHO WOULD EVEN DARE?

The GOD-EMPEROR looked back. Hovering behind HIM and holding the spear was that infant dragon Niv-Mizzet.

BOLAS' brain snarled, *DIDN'T WE KILL YOU ALREADY?*

In response, Niv thrust the spear farther into BOLAS' back. An audible groan escaped NICOL's mouth.

Niv smiled grimly and thought back at BOLAS, *You above all should know we dragons don't die easy.*

With a flick of a wing, the DRAGON-GOD sent the resurrected Niv-Mizzet flying and watched him crash to the ground three miles away.

HE then attempted to dissolve the spear. (HE could hardly end the pain or seal the wound while the weapon protruded from HIS chest.) Strangely, despite HIS OMNIPOTENCE, the GOD-EMPEROR found HE could not simply make it disappear. This surprised HIM for a moment, until HE remembered that HE HIMSELF had forged the thing for Hazoret. His own newfound GODHOOD was keeping her spear intact, as if by an act of HIS OWN WILL. This was but a minor setback, of course. Having realized HIS error, it would take less than a minute to unweave the spells, disperse its magic and unforge the weapon. Still, it might be faster to simply pull the spear out. That would hurt, but HE could exact his revenge for every instant of pain he suffered upon Mizzet a thousandfold. A millionfold.

But during that split second, while the DRAGON-GOD deliberated between a magical and a physical solution to the problem of removing the spear, everything changed. BOLAS realized too late that HE had forgotten Vess, had given her an opportunity to strike with her own two-pronged weapon.

Liliana's God-Eternals moved in for the kill and were suddenly right on top of HIM. BOLAS barely managed to *OBLITERATE* Oketra.

But weakened by the effort—and by the still-undealt-with spear—HE was too slow to stop Bontu, who bit her former GOD-PHARAOH on the wrist.

The pain was insignificant—certainly relative to the spear wound—but the damage had been done.

NO! NO! NO!

At once and automatically, Bontu began harvesting. All the Sparks the Elderspell had granted Him. All of them, all at once. Bontu absorbed these Sparks but could not contain them. She ruptured into shards, exploding in a light so bright, even Bolas was forced to shield his eyes.

NO. I CANNOT BE HARMED BY MERE LIGHT. NOT NOW. Not now.

A suddenly desperate Bolas tried to reabsorb the godlike power he had only so recently gained. He tried to pull the Sparks back in. In fact, he expected them to return to his Spirit-Gem—only to realize his Elderspell had been disrupted.

But there was still time.

I am still Nicol Bolas, Elder Dragon.

And the Sparks were still there, swirling just above his horns in a vortex of pure power . . .

My Power!

Through a haze of pain and his still-bleeding wounds, he glanced down and saw an army of Eternals marching up the steps of the Citadel toward him. And right behind them a second army of Ravnicans and Planeswalkers.

But that's just fine. In a matter of moments, the ants will once again realize they all march forward to their doom.

And once again, his hesitation would be his undoing. He attempted to recast the Elderspell, but he was too late. The vortex of Sparks above him evaporated, each and every Spark dissipating into nothingness. And with them, all his decades of planning, of scheming, of manipulating and murdering. All of it was fading away, amounting to nothing more than a void where his power had once been.

The void . . . THE VOID!

And then the truth hit him. Bontu hadn't simply harvested the Sparks stolen from dead Planeswalkers; she had also absorbed Nicol Bolas' own Spark.

When the vortex had scattered and the Sparks had dispersed, his own great Spark had disappeared along with them. Bolas was alive, but he was weak—worse, he was surprised, stunned.

I'm no longer a god. I'm not even a Planeswalker.

He had been reduced to being the thing he hated most: a mere mortal.

An ant . . .

SIXTY-FIVE

LILIANA VESS

Liliana watched as Bolas began to dissolve, much as Gideon had dissolved moments ago.

The dragon's telepathic voice—sounding shriller than it ever had before—echoed in her mind one last time: *No. NO! This is incomprehensible! I am Nicol Bolas! This does not happen to me!*

Then, also like Gideon, Bolas HOWLED as he disintegrated, atom by atom, the particles blowing away with the wind. Of course, unlike Gideon, there was nothing at all beatific or beautiful about the Elder Dragon's final moments.

Bolas was simply gone. It was over. Only his Spirit-Gem remained, and it fell to the roof of the Citadel, bounced a couple of times, and rolled to a stop not far from Liliana's feet. It lay there, inert, beside Gideon's empty smoking armor.

The unnatural storm clouds parted and dispersed, giving way to late-afternoon sunlight.

Liliana stood alone atop the Citadel. She could feel Gideon's invulnerability slipping away. Nevertheless, she now had everything she'd ever wanted: her youth, her power, her *freedom.*

But at what cost?

Jace reached out to her with his mind. *Liliana?*

Expecting—*deserving*—his enmity, Liliana braced for an attack, even a fatal one. Braced for it, she nevertheless made no attempt to parry or thwart it.

Liliana, are you . . . are you all right . . . ?

Stunned at his tentative concern for her, she looked down. A veritable wall of unmoving, deactivated Eternals separated the Citadel from the Ravnicans and Planeswalkers—most of whom, she thought, would quite reasonably like to see her dead. She searched the crowd for Jace. She spotted two or three of him, illusions all, which he quickly eliminated now that the crisis had passed. But she couldn't see him, the real Jace. Couldn't spot him anywhere.

Perhaps he's still invisible.

No, I'm here, Liliana, look to your left. You'll see me.

But she didn't look to her left. She stared at the ground instead. At Gideon's empty armor.

Jace felt her pain, her conflict, her lack of understanding of her own feelings. *It's all right,* he told her. *Gideon made his choice. He knew you could save us and chose to help you do just that.*

Jace's fury, she could have dealt with. His sympathy was more than she could bear.

Get out of my head, damnit . . .

She tried to scream it to make him break contact, but it barely came off as a mental whisper.

Listen, he thought. *I've mentally contacted Saheeli. Told her to turn off the Immortal Sun. She's working on doing that now. As soon as she does . . . well, you'll want to leave this plane, Liliana. As soon as you can. I know you saved us, but—but you really aren't safe here right now.*

Get out of my head, damnit . . .

Liliana . . .

Please, stop, stop . . .

She could feel him accede to her entreaty. She could feel him leave her mind. She resisted the impulse to call him back, to look to her left, to find him.

A moment later she felt the Sun's influence vanish. She could planeswalk if she wanted. The crowd below had snapped out of their shocked stupor and was already busy cutting down the Dreadhorde from behind. Hacking them to pieces. Little pieces. It wouldn't be long before more than a few of that crowd would be coming up the stairs to do the same to her.

Kneeling, she reached out, and her hand caressed Gideon Jura's charred chest plate. The metal was still warm. She tried to picture his last smile. She recalled that it had made him beautiful—horribly beautiful—in her eyes. But she couldn't even summon up a specific memory of his face. She *could* remember that face dissolving before her. But the features—and the humanity—were indistinct. Like the wisp of someone she had once dreamt of. Not like a real man at all. He was already legend.

Gideon would live on in Ravnica. But not the man. Few would remember the man. Only the hero.

It was a loss, she knew.

Yes, he was a hero. Yes, he deserves the mythic status he's certain to achieve. But he was so much more than that. And the part that was more . . . was exactly the part I allowed to die for me.

"Kill me now," she heard herself whisper. But she shook that notion off.

That wasn't you, she told herself. *That's self-pity. And self-pity is not your style.*

She found her own pep talk fairly unconvincing. But for now, it would suffice. She wiped the back of her hand across her face, wiping away tears that a part of her was grateful she had been capable of shedding. She pushed that part of herself down.

Down deep.

She reached over and picked up Bolas' Spirit-Gem, gripping it tightly. It felt ice-cold in her fist.

Then she stood, closed her eyes and planeswalked away.

SIXTY-SIX

CHANDRA NALAAR

Upon the disintegration of the dragon Nicol Bolas, a massive cheer went up from the combatants in the Plaza. But Chandra didn't feel much like cheering. She sat—practically collapsed—on the ground. Jace and Nissa sat down on either side of her as spiraling streamers of celebratory green magic flew into the air. People—grown men and women—were climbing up onto the ruins of the Bolas statue, as if it were a playground for children. Children, appearing from out of nowhere, were climbing upon the fallen and dormant Vitu-Ghazi (despite Boruvo's attempts to wave them away). Warriors attacked the dormant Eternals, who stood stock-still, looking up toward a throne that no longer held its emperor. The remains of the Dreadhorde made no attempt to defend themselves as Ravnicans and Planeswalkers, led by

Borborygmos and Angrath, began smashing and chopping the Eternals to bits. It didn't seem to Chandra as if this violence was a result of anger or malice or even revenge. It was a stolid, determined effort. Something that simply needed to be done.

Chandra could feel the hold of the Immortal Sun slip away. She watched from a distance as the tiny figure of Liliana planeswalked off-world. And she was but the first. With the Immortal Sun again disabled and the threat of Bolas and the Eternals past, the three old friends watched from the pavement as Planeswalker after Planeswalker departed Ravnica, as if afraid this nightmare could start up all over again. The Wanderer was the first to go, almost simultaneous with Liliana. Mu Yanling, Jiang Yanggu and their dog went next. Others, too, whose names she didn't know.

"Gids is gone," Chandra repeated.

Nissa hesitantly put a hand on her shoulder.

Staring straight ahead, Chandra said, "You know, I was a little bit in love with him once. I never told him."

Jace said, "I think he knew. He loved you, too."

"Not the way I meant."

"No. But he loved you just the same. Like a little sister. But that's love just the same."

She didn't need to say *I came to love him like a brother,* or even *I love you like a brother, too, Jace.* She could tell from his expression that he knew—no psychic communication required.

Chandra looked at the ground and started to weep softly. This time her tears did not turn to steam. They ran freely down her face, and Nissa surprised her by reaching out and wiping them away with her thumbs. Chandra leaned against the elf.

Nissa stiffened for a moment. Then she eased her body and

allowed Chandra to rest against her. She put an arm around the younger woman's shoulder and even began to slowly, gently rock the softly sobbing Chandra back and forth.

Without looking at her, Chandra whispered, "I love you, too, you know."

Nissa whispered back, "I love you, as well, Chandra."

Chandra finally turned to look at Nissa Revane. Then suddenly someone was pulling her to her feet.

It was Jaya. "Come on," she said. "We have work to do."

Chandra didn't know what Jaya meant and was too tired for whatever *"work"* her mentor had in mind, but Jaya wasn't waiting for a response. With a firm grip on her protégée's biceps, she tugged Chandra along behind her. Chandra barely had time to call out to Nissa, "We'll talk later!" before Jaya had pulled her into the crowd.

They made their way up to the line of (mostly) decapitated and maimed Eternals. Samut was standing there looking five shades of furious. "This is not the way," she growled. "These are my people. They must be destroyed, I know. But not like this. Grant them some dignity."

"That is why we're here," Jaya said with a nod toward Chandra, who only now understood the gruesome job ahead for the two pyromancers.

Angrath and Borborygmos had stopped their work and even waved their followers back. They kept watch. One way or another the threat from these creatures would end here and now, but they respected Samut's feelings enough—or at least respected her battle skills enough—to let it be done in a way that assuaged her pride in these former denizens of Amonkhet.

So under the watchful eyes of the minotaur, the cyclops and the child of Amonkhet, the pyromancers moved through what was left of the inert Dreadhorde and meticulously burned every last one—every last fragment—down to ashes.

SIXTY-SEVEN

TEYO VERADA

This plane's single sun was sinking behind Ravnica's diverse and strange towers, the ones that were still standing, anyway. Twilight was falling. And not the artificial twilight of the Elderspell, but the real thing. Twilight. Dusk. With night to follow. Teyo thought of the Promenade at dawn where Rat had found him. And then, suddenly, it hit him like a diamondstorm that it had been less than a day since he'd left Gobakhan.

By the Storm, it feels like a million years ago.

He was exhausted. Bone tired. Every one of his vertices felt as if it had been burned to a crisp. And if he never saw another geometric shape, it would be too soon. Plus he was hungry. He realized his last meal had been over a day ago and a world away. Moreover, he had another impulse that left him wondering whether or not Ravnica had indoor plumbing.

Kaya seemed to believe she could read his thoughts, or at least his expression. "It's all right," she said. "It's over. You can go back home now."

"Maybe," he replied. "I'm not sure home is where I belong. I was a pretty poor acolyte."

"Well, you're a damn fine Planeswalker," she told him with a smile and a kind stroke across his smooth cheek.

He blushed, and she chuckled under her breath, looking away so as not to embarrass him further.

Teyo sighed and looked around.

Ral Zarek and his lover Tomik Vrona were embracing, kissing. It was nice to see. Reassuring after all the tragedy Teyo had witnessed today. They stopped—and Ral turned his body defensively—as Vraska approached. Ral scowled at her, then, prodded by an elbow from Tomik, seemed to relent (at least a little) and nodded; she nodded back.

Stepping up behind her, Jace Beleren tapped Vraska on the shoulder. She turned to face him. He looked old and a little broken. She melted a little bit, wrapped her arms around him, and gave him a hug. He hugged her back. For a long time they stood stock-still in that embrace. They didn't speak. Then they kissed.

Ral shook his head slightly and looked back into Tomik's eyes.

All around them, people celebrated. Teyo wasn't sure this victory merited much celebration—especially as those not celebrating were carrying away the wounded and the dying. And the corpses. So many, many corpses. "All those poor people died," Teyo murmured mournfully.

"Boy, I don't give a damn about the dead." It was a soot-covered Angrath, fresh from the Eternal funeral pyre. He put a rough but not unfriendly hand on Teyo's shoulder and went on: "I can—on rare occasions—muster up some pity for the dying. But I reserve the bulk of my sympathy for their mourners. The trials of the dead are over, their sufferings at an end. If I shed any tears, they are for those left behind, for those who carry the overwhelming guilt and loss and despair that comes with surviving when their loved ones did not."

Teyo thought he felt some of that guilt—and had only been spared the loss and despair because he barely knew any of the people he had met today. He had admired Gideon but hadn't known him. There had been that other man—Dack, he thought his name was. They had exchanged a few words, trying to reassure each other before the last battle. And yes, Teyo felt guilty that he had been unable to reach Dack with a shield before an Eternal had harvested his Spark. But it was a guilt unconnected to any deeper emotion, any deeper loss or despair, as Angrath had put it. And fortunately, the two people he truly did feel close to, Rat and Kaya, had both survived, largely unharmed.

"It is only the living who deserve your concern, little monk," Angrath said. "At least, they're the only ones who deserve mine. The dead feel it not."

Teyo nodded dumbly.

It's the living that deserve our concern.

I need to find Rat.

He went looking and found her staring wistfully at Hekara, who was occupied in the solitary pursuit of celebrating the momentous victory with two grotesquely and uncannily realistic hand puppets (versions of herself and Ral) that would have forever given him nightmares if he had seen them as a child. She provided the voices for both her hands.

"We beat the evil dragon, didn't we, Hekara?" the Ral puppet said. (It was a fairly successful, if slightly high-pitched, impression of the Izzet guildmaster.)

"'Course we did," replied the Hekara puppet. (Ironically, Hekara's affected baritone for herself sounded nothing whatsoever like Hekara.)

"And all it took was for you to die horribly."

"Sure. But only once. I don't mind dying once. Not every once in a while. You know, for a good cause. Or for the entertainment value."

Teyo saw that Hekara still hadn't noticed—still couldn't see her former friend. And Rat was so fascinated by Hekara and the show, she hadn't noticed Teyo.

Hoping to help, he stepped up to Hekara and said, "Emissary, do you remember your friend Rat? Araithia?"

Hekara said, "Of course, I remember Rat! I love Rat! Where is she?"

Rat beamed, and Teyo pointed toward her. But Hekara merely looked confused. So with a little reluctance, Teyo took Hekara's Hekara-puppeted hand in his, and attempted to guide, lead, Hekara over to the hopeful Rat.

But Hekara hesitated, resisted. For the first time since Teyo had seen her resurrected, the fearless blood witch seemed nervous, uncomfortable, saying, "You know, I can't quite remember what Rat looks like. That's sorta strange, isn't it?"

Teyo wasn't sure what to say. Then he lost the opportunity to say anything at all as the leathery sound of wings and the stench of sulfur caused them both to look up. The demon Rakdos himself was descending to find his Emissary.

"COME, WOMAN," he said in his booming sepulchral voice, "RAVNICA IS OURS AGAIN. THE LONG BATTLE HAS BROUGHT THE PEOPLE LOW, AND THE CIRCUS MACABRE MUST PLAY TO THE CROWD AND LIGHTEN ALL HEARTS. WE HAVE PERFORMERS TO GATHER, ACTS TO PREPARE, AND A READY-MADE AUDIENCE YEARNING TO FORGET THE DAY'S HORRORS—BY BURNING, BLEEDING AND BURNING."

"Oh, goody," Hekara said, seemingly forgetting Rat entirely as she allowed herself to be taken up in the demon's hand like a life-sized Hekara puppet ready to mouth her master's words.

They flew off together, with Hekara squealing, "Burn! Bleed! Burn!"

Teyo had sought to help Rat but realized he'd just broken the young girl's heart all over again by briefly offering her an unfulfilled hope.

Trying to put on a good face, Rat smiled, shrugged and said, "I've lost her." But she couldn't maintain the smile. Her shoulders fell. Her head sank. "I've never lost anyone before. Plenty of people I never had. But she's the first who could see me who I've lost."

As if to add insult to injury, Saheeli Rai chose that moment to walk by. Not seeing Rat, she nearly walked right into her, forcing the girl to sidestep out of the Planeswalker's way.

Teyo felt helpless. More helpless than he had felt since early that morning. He spotted Kaya approaching them and said, "Don't forget, you still have the two of us."

Araithia Shokta nodded sadly and said, "Except you're both Planeswalkers. You'll leave Ravnica eventually."

Teyo, still helpless, looked to Kaya, who was considering Rat's words silently, mulling something over in her mind.

Together, the threesome meandered over to join Saheeli and the other Planeswalkers.

A debate was going on about what to do with the Immortal Sun.

"Destroy the damn thing," Angrath was saying.

Saheeli Rai protested. "But it's an amazing piece of—"

"It's an amazing mousetrap for Planeswalkers. One I've been trapped by twice. And let me make this clear, I've no intention of ever being trapped by it again."

Vraska, her right hand entwined in Jace Beleren's left, said, "Destroying it may be easier said than done. It's made of extremely powerful magics, reinforced by Azor's own Spark."

Jace rubbed his stubbly chin. "Besides, the thing might come in handy someday—for hunting down and trapping Tezzeret."

"Or Dovin Baan," Chandra Nalaar added.

"Or Ob Nixilis," Karn volunteered.

"Or," said Vivien Reid, "Liliana Vess."

Teyo noticed that both Jace and Chandra flinched when Liliana's name was mentioned in this context. Vraska looked at Jace with concern. Jaya Ballard and Teferi exchanged glances. The young shieldmage barely knew any of these Planeswalkers but could see there was a complicated history between them and the necromancer.

Nothing had been decided by the time the rest of the Gatewatch—Nissa Revane and Ajani Goldmane—arrived, on the heels of the angel Aurelia, who was carrying Gideon Jura's scorched breastplate in her arms like it was a holy relic.

Eager to change the subject, Chandra said, "We should bury that on Theros. I think Gids'd like that."

"What he'd like," Ajani said, "is to know that it's not over."

"It's not over?" Teyo asked, horrified.

Ajani chuckled and put a reassuring—if dangerous-looking—paw on Teyo's shoulder. "I do believe the threat of Nicol Bolas has passed." Then he turned to address all assembled. "But we cannot pretend Bolas will be the last threat to face the Multiverse. If we truly wish to honor our friend Gideon, we need to confirm that the next time a threat rises, the Gatewatch will be there."

Chandra looked over at the demolished Chamber of the Guildpact and said, "We lost our clubhouse."

"We don't need a clubhouse," Ajani said. "We just need to renew our Oaths."

"Ajani, we all renewed them earlier today." Jace sighed, sounding a little exhausted—or perhaps exasperated. "Don't you think once a day is plenty?"

Ajani scowled. The paw on Teyo's shoulder involuntarily tightened its grip. The leonin Planeswalker didn't actually draw any blood, but Teyo winced.

Kaya noticed and delicately removed the paw, allowing Teyo to breathe a small sigh of relief.

Rat giggled, and even though she was laughing at his expense, Teyo was glad to see a real smile on her face again—and in those plum-colored eyes.

"Perhaps . . ." Kaya said, "perhaps *I* could take the Oath."

Chandra looked at her hopefully and said, "Really?"

Ral looked at her dubiously and echoed, "Really?"

"I'm not a perfect person . . ." Kaya began.

"Trust me, none of us are," Jace interjected ruefully.

Vraska snorted teasingly.

Kaya basically ignored them both. "I've been an assassin and a thief. I've had my own moral code, but the first tenet of it was always, 'Watch your own ass.' I have the ability to ghost my way through life, to allow nothing to touch me. That's the literal truth of my powers, but it somehow became my emotional truth, as well. But my time on Ravnica as assassin, thief, reluctant guildmaster and perhaps even more reluctant warrior hasn't left me unaffected. Fighting beside you people has been an honor. The scariest and yet the *best* thing I've ever done with my somewhat bizarre life. What the Gatewatch has done here today—" She glanced down at the armor in Aurelia's hands. "—what you *sacrificed* here today . . . well . . . this'll sound corny, but it has been truly inspirational. If you'll have me, I'd like to be a part of this. I'd like you all to know that if there's trouble, you can summon me, and I will stand beside you."

"We'd like that," Chandra said.

"Aye, girl," said Ajani, grinning his leonin grin, which Teyo had to work hard not to regard as more hungry-looking than pleased.

Nissa, Teferi and Jace all smiled and nodded their assent.

Kaya took a deep breath and raised her right hand. Perhaps as a symbol of what she had to offer, she turned that hand spectral, so that it became transparent, glowing with a soft violet light. She said: "I have crossed the Multiverse, helping the dead, um . . . move on, in service of the living. But what I've witnessed here on Ravnica these last few months—these last few hours—has changed everything I thought I knew. Never again. For the living and the dead, *I will keep watch.*" She turned and smiled at Teyo and Rat.

Teyo wondered if he should take the Oath—or if anyone would want him to. But again he was distracted by the sound of wings and the smell of sulfur. He looked up, expecting to see Rakdos the Defiler. But silhouetted by the rising moon, he saw a dragon instead. For a horrifying second, Teyo thought it might be Bolas returned.

Instead it was Niv-Mizzet, who landed in a somewhat showy manner and grinned at Jace. "You're out of a job, Beleren," the dragon boomed. "The Firemind is the new Living Guildpact. As it was always meant to be."

Jace chuckled, "And yet somehow I don't seem sorry to be giving up that particular responsibility."

Teyo glanced around the crowd. No one seemed upset about Jace being replaced by Niv—except maybe Lavinia. She looked briefly wistful, nostalgic perhaps, but her expression soon hardened to its usual stern demeanor.

Ignoring the dragon completely, Nissa leaned her head over one of the many cracks in the plaza's pavement. She closed her eyes and breathed deeply. From between the battle-broken cobbles, a seed sprouted and rapidly grew into a plant with large green leaves.

Nissa nodded to Chandra, who somehow instinctively knew what the elf wanted her to do. The pyromancer carefully plucked three of the bigger leaves from the plant.

Then Teyo, Rat, Kaya, Vivien, Angrath, Saheeli, Niv-Mizzet, Teferi, Vraska, Jaya, Karn, Ral, Tomik, Lavinia, Ajani and

Jace watched, as Aurelia, Chandra and Nissa lovingly wrapped Gideon's armor in the leaves.

Aurelia handed the armor to Chandra, who—flanked by Jace and Nissa—led a solemn procession toward the celebrating (and mourning) crowd. A forlorn Aurelia watched them go but did not follow—though most of the other Planeswalkers did.

Ral touched Kaya on the shoulder and gestured with his eyes for her to wait. Tomik did the same to Vraska, who nodded and called out to Jace that she would catch up.

A confused Teyo and a curious Rat waited alongside them, as did Lavinia, Aurelia, Saheeli and the dragon. They were soon joined by Vorel, Exava, Gan Shokta and Boruvo. (The latter smiled at his goddaughter Araithia, though, as usual, her own father was unaware of her presence.) Once they all were gathered—and as soon as the procession of the Gatewatch had safely gotten far enough away—Saheeli morphed into Lazav, causing Teyo to briefly wonder where the true Saheeli Rai was at that moment.

But other concerns soon forced that concern from his head.

The Firemind spoke first: "As the new Living Guildpact, I have consulted with representatives of every guild."

Kaya raised an eyebrow at Tomik, who nodded.

Niv continued, "We have agreed that certain individuals, those who collaborated with Nicol Bolas, must be punished."

Vraska bristled, her eyes brightening with magic: "I won't be judged by the likes of you."

"You *have* been judged," Lavinia said, sternly but without threat. "And your actions on this day have mitigated that judgment."

Ral, making an effort *not* to raise a hand to cover his eyes, said, "You are not the only one Bolas misled and used. Kaya and I share that particular guilt. We may have realized our error sooner than you did, but we have no desire to quibble with an ally. Not with an ally willing to prove her allegiance to Ravnica and her own guild."

Vraska looked no less suspicious—no less on guard—but her eyes ceased to glow. "I'm listening."

Aurelia said, "Hundreds, maybe thousands of sentient beings died on Ravnica today."

"With untold property damage," Tomik added.

Ignoring him, Aurelia went on, "Such acts of terror must not go unpunished. There are three who did everything in their power to aid and abet the dragon: Tezzeret, Dovin Baan and Liliana Vess."

Without thinking, Teyo said, "But didn't Liliana—"

Vorel interrupted: "Vess changed sides too late. Only after being the direct cause of most of the carnage."

"What exactly are you asking?" Kaya said, unhappily.

"All three are Planeswalkers," Lazav stated. "They are out of our reach. But not out of yours."

The Firemind finished, "Ral Zarek has already agreed to hunt Tezzeret. Vraska, as penance for past sins, we assign you Dovin Baan. And Kaya, the ten guilds wish to hire you to assassinate Liliana Vess."

SIXTY-EIGHT

JACE BELEREN

Jace Beleren walked alongside Chandra and did everything save casting an illusion to hide the truth he felt sure must be obvious on his face.

Nicol Bolas is not dead.

Within moments of Bontu biting Bolas and harvesting all his Sparks, a telepathic voice had echoed in Jace's mind, saying, *Nicol Bolas must not die here.*

It took Jace a second, but he soon recognized the voice as belonging to Ugin, the Spirit Dragon. An incredulous Jace balked at Ugin's command. *You must be joking. Bolas* will *die. Here and now. And don't believe for a second you can protect him.*

I will protect him, and so will you.

You're very wrong.

Think, Jace Beleren. Bolas has died before and was resur-

rected more dangerous than ever. I died, too, and you have seen the result. Do you not think it possible that a dead Nicol might become a Spirit Dragon like his twin? And would that entity be a version of Bolas you'd care to face?

Your twin?! But we can't let him—

Do not misunderstand. I know what my brother is. Help me now, and I will place a living Bolas in an eternal prison with myself as his eternal jailer. You'll be rid of us both. Forever. It isn't simply the safer course, it is the only course that guarantees the safety of the Multiverse.

If you're so determined, what do you need me for?

You and yours have beaten him, weakened him. But he remains an Elder Dragon and will not willingly come with me. It will take all my strength and concentration to take him from this place. I need you to hide our conflict from your fellow Planeswalkers, from your fellow mortals. Even from Niv-Mizzet. I need you to hide the fact that Bolas lives.

If this is the right course, why hide anything?

Any Planeswalker who sought vengeance and came to find him in his prison would risk releasing him. The Multiverse must think Bolas is dead, even though you and I both know we cannot risk killing him.

I don't know that.

You do. Bolas planned contingencies for everything. Death did not stop him before; it will not stop him now. But imprisonment? Bolas could never conceive of such a fate and will not have planned against it.

So Jace followed Ugin's instructions. He used an invisibility spell to hide Ugin's arrival and his attack upon his brother—while simultaneously creating an illusion of Bolas disintegrating before the eyes of all of Ravnica.

Fearing that Liliana might see through the façade, he made his best attempt to mimic Bolas' psychic voice and shouted the dragon's death cry into her mind. In doing so, he *touched* her mind and realized just how desperate and broken Gideon's sacrifice had left her, even in her victory over the dragon. Jace tried to reach out to her as himself, but she begged him to desist.

By this time the invisible Ugin had rendered the invisible and weakened Bolas unconscious. The Spirit Dragon was ready, so Jace had reached out telepathically to Saheeli Rai, instructing her to shut down the Immortal Sun. She did not question the order.

Physically, mentally and morally exhausted, Jace had sat himself down on the broken ground of the plaza next to a crying Chandra and Nissa—as first the two dragons and then Liliana had planeswalked away.

Now Jace walked beside Chandra and Nissa as they bore the armor of Gideon Jura, mourning the man who had sacrificed everything to bring Bolas down. And every step Jace Beleren took felt like a lie.

CODA

SIXTY-NINE

TWO DRAGONS

The Spirit Dragon and his dragon brother stared at each other in silence.

The latter had been brought low. Despite being wrapped in his twin brother's wings, the journey from Ravnica across the Blind Eternities had literally blinded the Sparkless dragon, had scorched the scales off his hide. It had taken weeks for him to regain consciousness, months for him to heal. Even now, his vision was still blurry and myopic. Slumped upon the ground, he looked . . . yes, *vanquished*. He felt like something was missing, too. His Spark, of course, but something else, as well. Glaring at his opponent, he pushed that concern aside. "I thought I killed you," he grumbled.

The Spirit Dragon shrugged. "Times change. Especially on the plane of Tarkir, where I died. You should get used to the idea."

"*You* should get used to the idea that I'm simply going to kill you again in a few minutes."

"Once you catch your breath?"

"Exactly."

"I don't think so, brother. Look at yourself, weighed down by mortality. You don't have the power to kill me in a few minutes or a few millennia. And you no longer have the life span to hold out beyond that. You no longer have your Spark."

"Then I'll take yours."

"Not by force. Not even by guile. Not in a million lifetimes, especially when the quantity of lifetimes you have left is now limited to exactly one."

"You think you can hold me. I AM—"

"I know who you are, brother. And I'm not ever going to forget it."

"You arrogant fool . . ."

The Spirit Dragon chuckled. "*I'm* an arrogant fool? Really? Look into that Pool of Becoming."

Reflexively, the mortal dragon did.

The Spirit Dragon said, "Pot, meet kettle."

His dragon brother burned. He said, "This is my Meditation Realm. *My* place of power."

"Not anymore. You forget it was my realm first. It still *likes* me better. Prefers me. Take a good look around; you'll see."

Though wishing to appear defiant, the mortal dragon, despite himself, raised his eyes to the horizon. The first thing he noticed, even *with* his blurred vision, was that the entire color scheme of the place had been altered since his last visit. Now it sported a distinctive blue tint, the signature color of his twin. Worse, the great horns on the far horizon curved inward—as his did—but then flared outward like his brother's. The realm was marked, branded as belonging to the Spirit Dragon. Yet another loss.

Somewhat abashed, the mortal dragon shook his head. "This is not possible."

"*'This'* is only the beginning."

"No. How? I *demand* to know!"

"You're not in any position to be issuing demands. Still—"

"My plan was perfect!"

The Spirit Dragon sighed. He shook his head slowly from side to side and said, "I know what you're doing, brother. Playing for time. Gathering information. Looking for a way to turn both to your advantage. But there's no need to strategize or wheedle. It won't help you. You have plenty of time. Not eternity, of course. Not anymore. But time enough to learn hopelessness. And as for information, I'll grant you that freely, as well. Ask your questions."

Swallowing his anger—as he still refused to believe the Spirit Dragon's words, and thus was searching for his moment, his opening, his opportunity to reverse his (admittedly) sagging current fortunes—the mortal dragon said, "How did you get past the wards I placed on this plane?"

"Sarkhan Vol helped me achieve this realm. He's actually been quite helpful. You must have *really* ticked him off."

Ignoring the other's attitude, the mortal dragon asked, "And what role did *you* play in my . . ." He almost choked on the word. ". . . . defeat?"

"A very small role, actually. Mostly, I observed."

"How? I know you weren't on Ravnica while I still had my Spark. I'd have sensed you."

"You never realized that the Spirit-Gem you *once* so proudly floated between your horns was made from a piece of *my* own essence.

At the word "once," the mortal dragon immediately reached above his head and searched for the egg-shaped gem. Unable to find it, he again looked down into the pool. His reflection revealed that it was gone. Gone, like his Spark.

The Spirit Dragon ignored both his mortal brother's panic and his despair. "Come now, brother, think! Use that mythic brain of yours to reason this out. You found the Gem here, did you not? Admired it so much, you never once thought about its provenance? But again, this was my realm first, and the Spirit-Gem quite literally came from me. You *used* it without ever realizing you had never *mastered* it. Once I had returned here I was able to use my connection to the Gem to witness every one of your missteps."

"I made no missteps!" the mortal dragon sputtered. In his outrage, he straightened to his full height, inadvertently pulling a muscle in his left wing-shoulder. He automatically summoned a healing spell to correct this minor annoyance. No magic came. The shoulder continued to ache, but his lack of power was the greater injury. He struggled to suppress a tantrum.

"All right, fine, what missteps?"

"Well, to begin with, you had so much contempt for Niv-Mizzet—because the Firemind was neither an Elder Dragon nor a Planeswalker—that you didn't track his spirit after killing him. Relative to you, he seemed insignificant. But Niv was still a powerful ancient dragon, who had done his own share of preparations." The Spirit Dragon pointed down at a little silver box, open and lying on its side. All its delicate filigree, clockwork gears and crystals were charred and useless now. But they had served their purpose. "Niv's ghost was stored in that. And Vol brought it here to me, where I could help preserve it until his resurrection.

"Second, you may have protected yourself from Blackblade, but it never even occurred to you to protect yourself from Hazoret's Spear. Whereas *that* was a weapon you had forged yourself, using—without giving it a moment's thought—the tiniest bit of your own essence. After all, you had power to spare. Why not reinforce the weapon with your own limitless potency when you were gifting it to your proxy and thrall? And so you handed a piece of yourself to Hazoret once you had subdued that god to your will and remade Amonkhet. Of course, the bit of you that existed in the spear is exactly what made you vulnerable to it. So I told Sarkhan to find a way to secure it for the Firemind.

"Then there's your biggest misstep: The way you underestimated the Planeswalkers, their power, their resolve, their capacity for sacrifice, their willingness to do anything to defy you. I know you'd prefer to believe that I'm the one who crossed all your plans, but I never could have managed that alone. The real hero was Liliana Vess. You thought you knew her, thought you could control her through her weaknesses. But I'd been watching her and saw her real strength: a desire for redemption that even she could not see or admit to. I knew all she needed was a chance, an opening. Vol, Niv, the spear and all my planning—they were merely links in a chain that tugged at your attention. They amounted to nothing more or less than a distraction to allow Liliana Vess—and the sacrifice of Gideon Jura—to bring you to your knees.

"Once her work was done, all that remained for me was to bring you here to the Meditation Realm—or, as I now call it, the Prison Realm."

Still in denial, the mortal dragon roared, "No prison can hold the mighty . . ." He trailed off, confused. He knew his names. The one he had hatched with and the one he had given himself. It wasn't that he couldn't say them—

It's that your names no longer belong to you, thought the Spirit Dragon to his dragon brother. *Neither of them. You've forfeited any right to your true name and lost the power inherent in your chosen one. You are nameless. Nothing.*

"*No!*"

YES.

To make his ultimate point, the Spirit Dragon straightened

to his full height and beyond. He seemed to fill the realm and his brother's consciousness all at once. The mortal dragon winced and found himself . . . cowering.

Know this, brother. I am your jailer for what remains of your mortality and will make quite sure you never escape. Your schemes, your machinations . . . all your little dramas are at an end. The curtain has fallen.

ACKNOWLEDGMENTS

So many people helped me complete this story. More than I could possibly list. But this, at least, is a start . . .

At Del Rey, I'd like to thank my editor Tom Hoeler, who's just been a fantastic champion for this book and my involvement. I'd also like to thank Elizabeth Schaefer, who recommended me for the gig (after we had ourselves a good time at a prior party). Thanks also to Scott Biel, Keith Clayton, Alex Davis, Ashleigh Heaton, Julie Leung, David Moench, Tricia Narwani, Eric Schoeneweiss, Scott Shannon and the rest of the Del Rey team. Thank you as well to Elizabeth Eno and Nancy Delia. And special thanks to Magali Villeneuve for creating our amazing cover art.

At Wizards of the Coast, my thanks go out to the invaluable Nic Kelman, who with Tom and myself formed the triumvirate that enabled me to pull this off. Thanks also to Jay Annelli, Doug Beyer, Jenna Helland, T. C. Hoffman, Daniel Ketchum and Ari Levitch, who all provided invaluable assistance and created or helped facilitate the creation of much of what you've read in these pages. Similar props to storytellers Doug Beyer, Nik Davidson, Kelly Digges, Nicky Drayden, Kate Elliott, Cassandra Khaw, Kimberly J. Kreines, Chris L'Etoile, Adam Lee, Ari Levitch, Mel Li, Alison Luhrs, Shawn Main, Leah Potyondy, Mark Price, Mark Rosewater, Ken Troop, Martha Wells, James Wyatt, Michael Yichao and *especially* Django Wexler, who really went above and beyond the call. Plus all the other Magic writers, who laid the foundations I've built upon.

At the Gotham Group: Ellen Goldsmith-Vein, Julie Kane-Ritsch, Gavin Laing, Peter McHugh, Julie Nelson and Joey Villareal.

For putting up with my semi-split focus, I'd like to thank the folks at *Young Justice*, especially my post-production skeleton crewmates: Brent Anthony, Jay Bastian, Phil Bourassa, Marlene Corpuz, Greg Emerson, Jose Grano Gonzalez, Tiffany Grant, Darren Griffiths, Brett Harden, Brian E. S. Jones, Bruce King, Leanne Moreau, Rebecca Underwood and my partner in crime (or, um, justice), Brandon Vietti.

Last but not least, I'd like to thank my entire family for their support. My in-laws, Zelda & Jordan Goodman and Danielle & Brad Strong. My nieces and nephews, Julia, Jacob, Lilah, Casey and Dash. My siblings, Robyn Weisman and Jon & Dana Weisman. My cousin Brindell Gottlieb. My parents, Sheila & Wally Weisman. My wife, Beth, and my amazing (and very grown-up) kids, Erin and Benny. I love you all.

ABOUT THE AUTHOR

GREG WEISMAN's career in television and comic books spans decades. After starting as an editor for DC Comics, where he also wrote *Captain Atom*, he created and developed Disney's original series *Gargoyles*, later writing the *Gargoyles* and *Gargoyles: Bad Guys* comic books for SLG Publishing. He has worked as a writer, producer, story editor, and voice actor on Sony's *The Spectacular Spider-Man* and Warner Bros.'s *Young Justice*, and as a writer and executive producer on the first season of *Star Wars Rebels*. His comic book writing credits include DC's *Young Justice* and *Star Wars: Kanan*, and Marvel's *Starbrand and Nightmask*. Weisman also wrote the original novels *Rain of the Ghosts* and *Spirits of Ash and Foam*, as well as the World of Warcraft novels *World of Warcraft: Traveler* and *World of Warcraft: Traveler: The Spiral Path*. He is blessed to have an amazing wife and two fantastic (grownup) kids.

ABOUT THE TYPE

This book was set in Aster, a typeface designed in 1958 by Francesco Simoncini (d. 1967). Aster is a round, legible face of even weight and was planned by the designer for the text setting of newspapers and books.